MEANT TO BE

Gib took hold of the porch post and leaned close. "Julia." His voice was whisper-soft with a hint of tease. "I could guess your name just by looking at you. You know why?"

Julia stared at him. His nearness made breathing impossible.

"Because your eyes are like jewels. As clear and pretty as jewels."

He watched her for a moment, then leaned down and kissed her, a warm, gentle kiss without haste or passion, and then again, more firmly, a kiss so sweet that Julia felt an odd sinking in her belly, and her knees went weak.

Meant to Be

Elizabeth DeLancey

DIAMOND BOOKS, NEW YORK

This book is a Diamond original edition, and has never been previously published.

MEANT TO BE

A Diamond Book / published by arrangement with the author

PRINTING HISTORY
Diamond edition / June 1994

ISBN: 0-7865-0010-7

Diamond Books are published by The Berkley Publishing Group, 200 Madison Avenue, New York, NY 10016.
DIAMOND and the "D" design are trademarks belonging to Charter Communications, Inc.

PRINTED IN THE UNITED STATES OF AMERICA

10 9 8 7 6 5 4 3 2 1

For
Eythan and Ariella
and their dear old dad

CHAPTER

1

GIB BOOTH SLAPPED the dust off his worn black Stetson. He settled the hat on his head, put his hands on his hips, and took a long look at Stiles, Montana.

The place had sure changed in eleven years. When Gib had last seen it, Stiles was a slapdash, mud-splattered, whiskey-soaked boomtown. Now frame buildings stood tall in the May sunshine, and some were even painted—reds and blues among somber slate grays. There were railings on the sidewalk steps and a bench or two for sitting. Main Street was puddled with mud, but it was clear of tree stumps and boulders, and there weren't any dead-drunk miners wallowing in the muck, as in the old days.

"Hard to believe," Gib said. "It looks downright civilized."

The stage driver pulled Gib's war bag, saddlebags, and bedroll from the boot of the coach. "Civilized or dying, take your pick. The place sure ain't what it used to be."

Gib had ridden up top from the depot at Dillon, taking nips from the driver's flask and catching up on the state of things in the territory. The driver seemed to know the population and prospects of every town from the Idaho border to the Missouri Breaks. The big news was the discovery of copper in Butte. The town had boomed into a city, and everybody was heading there to get rich. Stiles wasn't faring so well. The Continental Mining Company had stopped paying dividends and was laying off men. It was rumored that the big pay streak was pinching out.

Gib had listened to the driver's tales with only passing interest. He'd come to Stiles for one purpose — to take care of business and get out fast. The town had never had much affection for him. Gib doubted that opinions had changed.

"See you next trip, mister." Gib stuck out his hand.

"Good luck to you, fella." The driver gave a firm shake and tramped off to the express office.

Gib dug in his pocket for his pouch of tobacco. He shook a line onto a paper, rolled and licked, then scratched the tip of a match with his thumbnail. Cupping his hands, he fired up, squinting as smoke filled his eyes. His throat was raw from the driver's cheap whiskey, and the rest of him was stiff after nearly a week of rail travel from San Francisco. He wasn't improved by the Continental's stamp mill, crushing ore with a pounding that thumped his head with every stroke.

Gib ran a hand over his stubble of beard and thought of a hot-water bath, a shave, and a good long sleep.

A few doors down, a man stepped out of the Bon Ton saloon and gave a mighty stretch. A melon-sized paunch hung over his sagging brown trousers and strained at his vest buttons. Gib took a look at the man's whiskery face, then picked up his gear and headed down the boardwalk toward him.

"Dellwood Petty, you old cuss."

The man's hound-dog eyes rested on Gib for a minute,

then lit up. "Why, bust my buttons, it's Gib Booth." He shifted his mouthful of tobacco. "I heard you was coming back." Dellwood clapped Gib on the shoulder and surveyed him from head to foot. "Will you look at this, now? The sapling grew into some mighty fine timber."

"Drilling rock and hauling ore builds up a man," Gib said. He poked at the saloonkeeper's belly. "A man sits around, he just gets fat."

Dellwood squirted a stream of juice into the street. "Nothing wrong with sitting or getting fat, neither. I make my living at it." He waved toward a couple of rickety chairs. "Take a seat, boy. We'll have a drink, for old times."

Gib nudged a chair with his boot. "You still roosting on these hunks of splinters?" He thought of the times he'd sneaked up on Dellwood snoring through his afternoon nap. He'd set off firecrackers under Dell's chair just to hear him shout and swear.

"No law against it," Dellwood said, sitting down. "About the only thing that ain't illegal these days. Ladies got up an ordinance to keep liquor off the street. Guns, too. There's more ordinances in this town than toads after a rain. Next thing you know, they'll be closing down the saloons." He pulled a bottle from beneath his chair, splashed some whiskey into a glass, and handed it to Gib. "May as well try to keep the sun from rising."

"May as well." Gib tilted his chair back against the saloon's weathered wall, took a final pull on his smoke, and tossed the butt into the street.

There was plenty of horse traffic, buggies and buckboards and loaded freight wagons. On the sidewalk, men in miner's boots and denim pants passed by, along with wiry cowboys, bustle-strutting ladies, and odds and ends of children. Gib didn't recognize a soul. The only familiar commercial establishments were the *Sentinel* newspaper office, Blum's Groceries & Produce, and, down a ways, the three-story red brick Regal Hotel.

"The town looks good." He swallowed some whiskey.

"Ladies banned spitting on the sidewalk." Dellwood

leaned over and squirted another stream of tobacco juice, just to show what he thought of the idea.

Gib balanced his whiskey glass between his legs and took out paper and pouch. With a few expert twists of his fingers, he rolled a fresh cigarette. As he lit up, he watched two ladies enter Williver & Co. General Merchandise, a brick structure new since his time. The ladies were fixed up in hats and shawls and ruffles on their skirts, as if they were shopping in St. Louis or New York.

"Never could stand ladies trying to improve things," Dellwood continued through his chaw. "It's in their nature, damn 'em."

Gib tipped up his hat and drew in a lungful of smoke. "You've got that right."

The spring sun hinted at summer. Gib liked summer in Montana mountain country. He liked the deep blue of the sky, the green hills decorated with wildflowers, the smell of pine and ripe berries. He liked the way the landscape jutted up and folded in on itself, as if hiding its gold from men's greedy eyes.

He took another pull on his smoke and began to feel nostalgic for the years he'd spent in Stiles, even though he'd done nothing the whole time but raise hell. Come to think of it, that about summed up what he'd been doing since he left. Thirty-four years old, Gib thought, and he'd yet to accomplish one thing worth bragging about.

Doc Metcalf used to get after him to do something worthwhile. Gib had occasionally considered it, but he never seemed able to aim himself in a worthwhile direction. Now he planned to go back east, build a house like a bonanza king's, put his feet up, and take it easy. Doc would probably think taking it easy wasn't much of an ambition, but it sure sounded good to Gib.

"So whatcha up to, boy?" Dellwood asked. "Running or resting or just passing through?"

Gib looked at Dell's doggy old face. "You sure are nosy. Time was, a man could come to town and keep his intentions to himself."

"Well, pardon my pantaloons." Dellwood loosened the top button on his trousers and gave a long, juicy belch.

"Truth is, I've come to see Doc Metcalf about some business."

Dellwood's expression changed. "Why, Doc's dead. Been dead near seven months."

The front legs of Gib's chair hit the sidewalk.

"Happened last October. An accident out Ruby Valley way. Found him laying by the road, buggy turned over, his neck broke."

A vision of a tall, dignified man in a shiny black buggy passed through Gib's mind. His cigarette hand began to shake, and a lump rose in his throat. He washed it away with a gulp of whiskey.

"Had a fine Masonic burial," Dellwood said. "Mighty fine. Brass band and all. Folks as far away as Deer Lodge come to pay their respects."

Gib took off his hat and ran a hand through his hair. "If that don't beat all."

"Turns out old Doc done all right for himself," Dellwood went on. "Mining investments, they say. California, I heard. Left his widow near a hundred and fifty thousand dollars."

"Widow?" Gib almost jumped out of his chair.

"Chicago girl."

A hundred and fifty thousand! Gib's mind exploded with curses. He opened his mouth, then had the sense to shut it. He rubbed his prickly chin and tried to look thoughtful. "Didn't know he had a wife."

Dellwood's droopy eyes narrowed. "A decent woman, in case you got any ideas. When it comes to women, it's a wonder you wasn't shot ten times over."

Gib drew in another breath of smoke while he absorbed the shock of Dellwood's news. A widow. Doc left her everything. Good God Almighty, he thought, wasn't that the limit?

"She's taken over some of Doc's business since he passed on."

"A woman? Doctoring?"

"Yep. Ain't nobody else, except the doc comes over from Dillon, and he mainly looks after livestock."

A female doctor. Gib had seen one in California. She'd worn miner's boots and a mustache, but she'd had a soft spot for good-looking men.

"Doc's wife mostly tends women and young 'uns," Dellwood said. "But she ain't shy of taking care of a man. She pulled a piece of gun cap out of Jim Ferry's eye, and she sews up her share of cowboys celebrating on Saturday night." Dellwood nudged Gib and waggled the toothpick in his teeth. "How'd you like a lady doctor poking around your pecker?" He frowned. "Hope you ain't planning to cause her trouble."

Dellwood's observations were beginning to irritate Gib. "I sure would appreciate it if you'd stop insulting my character, Dell."

"Hell, boy, I didn't know you had one. Say, that reminds me. A couple of mean-looking fellers passed through a while back. Seemed pretty impatient to get their hands on you. One had an ear that looked to be near chewed off."

Gib swore aloud this time, a long streak of profanity that exhausted his cursing vocabulary. He might have known Wylie and Trask would still be on his trail. If those two buzzards caught up with him, he had a good chance of ending up as dead as Doc. Folks wouldn't come down from Deer Lodge to pay their respects, either; he'd be lucky if they buried him in the church graveyard.

Gib drank off his whiskey and told himself that if he had half the brains of a Missouri mule he'd catch the next stage back to Dillon and get the hell out of the territory.

Dellwood nudged him and nodded across the street. "Look yonder."

They were coming out of Williver & Co. General Merchandise, the two ladies Gib had seen going in—a tall thin one and a short plump one.

"Tall one's her," Dellwood said. "The other's George Williver's wife. Mrs. Williver's the queen, runs everything in town. Mrs. Doc Metcalf's the princess, the second-in-command."

The ladies headed across the street. Mrs. Williver was talking; Doc's wife listened. She was dressed all in black, a tall, trim silhouette. No miner's boots. No mustache. The ladies climbed the sidewalk steps.

Gib pushed his whiskey glass under his chair and got to his feet, holding his cigarette behind his back. "Get up, Dell."

Dellwood struggled to his feet. The queen and her princess sailed closer.

Gib touched his hat brim. "Ladies."

"Ladies," Dellwood echoed, not bothering to hide his whiskey.

"Good afternoon, Mr. Petty," the ladies answered in chorus.

Gib stared at Doc's wife. Her face was thin and high-boned, her skin like cream. Shiny hair the color of walnut shells was swept up under a small curl-brimmed hat. Beneath her black wool cape Gib saw the bodice of a high collared dress done in perfect little pleats.

She looked right at him, and Gib's heart started pumping. She had eyes like jewels, aquamarines he'd seen in Mexico.

She appeared startled for an instant, as if she might have guessed who he was. Gib put on the smile he reserved for well-bred ladies, the smile that came mostly from his eyes. Honest and friendly, without a trace of disrespect.

It seemed to do the trick. Her expression softened, thick lashes swept down. Then she was past, leaving behind the faint scent of something clean. Gib stared after her. From the back she was as graceful as a swan, a black swan skimming along the boardwalk, head high, bustle twitching.

"Sit down," Dellwood said. "In case you don't know it, you're standing there with your yap open, every thought in your head plain as day."

Gib sat. He'd expected Doc's wife to be older, plumper, more substantial. The princess might pull gun caps out of men's eyes and sew up their hides, but she had the soft, trusting look of a girl.

"She's young for Doc," he said.

"She's old enough to know to stay away from your kind."

Gib thought of her slender proportions, her ladylike air. "She's not my sort of woman, Dell."

Dellwood gave a snort. "A rich, good-looking woman is any man's sort of woman."

Gib felt the heat of his cigarette burning his fingers. He tossed it away, wondering what Doc's widow might know about him. Doc had probably told her some, though surely he'd spared her the details.

His thoughts took on a purposeful shape that began to turn into a plan. He would clean himself up and get a good night's sleep. Tomorrow he'd take himself out to Doc's place. Pay the widow a condolence call, work his way into her good graces.

One way or another he'd get what he came to town for.

Julia Metcalf rested her elbows on the sturdy mahogany desk, wriggled her backside deeper into Edward's leather armchair, and stared at the paper before her. In the space of an hour she had managed to write only ten lines on the topic of proper ventilation. The piece wasn't due at the *Sentinel* office until next Tuesday, but Julia found that writing several drafts of her semiweekly health articles ensured a high standard of content and style.

She chewed the end of the pen, trying to focus on the benefits of open windows and the dangers of gas stoves. But her mind kept wandering.

Gib Booth, she thought, then said it aloud. "Gib Booth."

Julia pulled herself back to the subject at hand. Pen scratched across paper. "In the practice of domestic sanitary science, no effort can be of greater benefit to the family's health than infusing the home with fresh air," she wrote. "Along with tainted water, corrupted air is the major cause of the spread of disease."

Pure air, pure water, efficient drainage, cleanliness, and light—without them no house would be healthy. Julia thought of her own house, dirty with the accumulated dust and soot of a long winter. As much as she hated the thought, she would have to get to her spring cleaning; it was embarrassing not to practice what she preached.

"A small current of cold outside air will suffice to push the warm air up the chimney, thereby preventing smoke from lingering in the room."

Julia's thoughts wandered again, back to the tall, broad-shouldered man she'd seen yesterday morning in front of the Bon Ton. His boots and trousers had been spattered with mud, and he'd worn several days' growth of beard. Like his reputation, his appearance was disgraceful, even dangerous. Yet he'd looked at her in a disarming way that no woman would have found offensive. Quite the contrary.

Mercy's sake, Julia thought. Gib Booth had been run out of town for murder, and if Louise Williver was to be believed, he'd compromised half the town's female population before he left. Mrs. Julia Frye Metcalf was a respectable woman, not yet widowed a year. She had no business being curious.

Her pen moved on: "The more fresh air admitted into the sleeping room, the better for the occupant's health."

"Settle accounts," the wire had said.

Julia put down her pen and took a yellow paper from one of the desk's pigeonholes. She smoothed out the creases as she'd done innumerable times and read the message: "Heading east. Arrive Stiles soon. Settle accounts. Gib Booth."

Had he come to get money? Revenge? Despite the circumstances of his departure, Julia couldn't imagine he meant Edward any harm.

The pendulum-case clock bonged. Julia looked up. Ten-thirty. She was letting this business occupy her mind this morning, as if she didn't have enough to keep her busy.

She dipped her pen to write her conclusion, but no thoughts came. Skipping to the bottom of the page, she wrote, "In her next column, the author will consider proper lighting in the home, its influence on the eyes, and the economy of its use."

Julia blotted the paper, then read the paragraphs she'd written. The ideas were hardly original, taken as they were from books and journals, but her readers were sure to find them worthy of attention.

The front door knocker banged, making her jump. Goodness, she'd been so absorbed in her thoughts, she hadn't heard footsteps on the porch.

Julia got up from the desk and secured the hairpins in her loose topknot. As she stepped into the hallway, the knocker banged again, rattling the door's decorative frosted-glass panes.

"I'm coming," she called.

She brushed at the cat hairs clinging to the bodice of her black bombazine dress. Edward had often said that black flattered her. With her pale complexion, light brown hair, and blue-green eyes, he had thought she looked lovely in anything. "But black," he'd said with a smile, "gives you an air of mystery."

Now she wore black every day, in mourning for him.

Julia checked her appearance in the mirrored hall stand, then reached for the doorknob.

He stood on the porch, his handsome straight-featured face expectant, a well-brushed black Stetson in his hand. Little furrows in his damp brown hair attested to careful combing, and a razor had scraped every last whisker from his cheeks.

"Ma'am, I'm Gilbert Booth, a friend of Doc's."

Julia felt a flutter beneath her heart. Nerves, she thought. Ridiculous. "Yes, Mr. Booth. I thought you might come by."

He looked like a new man. His white shirt was freshly laundered, and his string tie drooped in a perfect bow. Beneath his coat he wore a fancy black vest brocaded with silver threads. There was a well-worn look around his eyes, but his expression made him appear harmless and more than a little attractive.

"I'm Julia Metcalf." To her own ears, she sounded remarkably composed. "Please come in."

"Ma'am." He stepped into the hallway.

He had the heavy shoulders and arms of a miner, and the hands, too, hard and square and as big as bear traps.

"I'm sorry about Doc." His clear gray eyes took on a soulful look. "He was the best man I ever knew."

"He is greatly missed by everyone," Julia replied in her best widow's manner. She allowed herself a quick glance down the rest of him. A healthy man, she thought. Admirably strong and healthy.

"I suppose he told you about me."

The touch of anxiety in his voice almost made Julia smile. "Edward told me a good deal about you. As have other people in town."

A look of resignation crossed his face. He stared at the floor. "Ma'am, I don't know all you've heard, but I'm sure the stories are exaggerated."

Julia was impressed that he would address the question of his character so directly. "Mr. Booth, I am not a lady who makes judgments based on gossip," she said. "No doubt you have your faults, as we all do, but I daresay yours have gotten more attention than they deserve."

She'd meant to put him at ease, as she would have done with any guest, but her words seemed to transform him. His cautious eyes turned lively, and his face broke into a most appealing smile.

"I'm pleased to hear that, ma'am. Mighty pleased."

He looked as if she'd pinned a medal on him, which made Julia wonder if she might have given him too great a benefit of the doubt. "Come and sit down," she said in a cooler tone.

"I'm obliged."

They proceeded to the front room, quiet except for the ticking of the little gold clock on the mantel. The pounding of the Continental's stamp mill could be heard in the distance, but it was so constant, day and night, that it seemed no more noticeable than the breeze rattling the windows.

"I have tea water heating," Julia said, motioning Gib to the black horsehair sofa.

He remained standing until she was settled in her blue plush armchair. When he sat down and placed his hat on his knee, it occurred to Julia that she should have taken it at the door, a task that Mary Hurley usually performed. "I don't have a maid at the moment," she said in explanation. "The girls are all moving to Butte. I lost my girl last month."

Gib draped an arm along the back of the sofa in the

manner of a man accustomed to making himself at home. "I heard a lot of maids were heading up that way."

Julia was surprised. "Did Mr. Petty tell you?"

"Yes, ma'am."

She thought of Gib Booth and Dellwood Petty drinking and smoking in front of the Bon Ton, all the while discussing the shortage of housemaids in Stiles. "We may be forced to raise wages, with the supply of girls so short."

"Is that so?"

His interest encouraged Julia to continue. "During spring and fall cleaning, the girls have us over a barrel, so to speak." She wondered momentarily if that remark might suggest something improper. "All the ladies become rather desperate."

"I guess they might."

Gib fiddled with his hat brim and gave her a smile that seemed to come from his eyes. They were intelligent eyes, Julia thought. It had grieved Edward that a young man as clever as Gib had been so determined to waste himself.

"I received your wire, but I didn't know where to send a reply," Julia said. "I'm terribly sorry you had to come all this way only to find Edward gone. Is there something I might help you with?"

"No, ma'am. I'm on my way back east. I just wanted to stop by to say hello."

Gracious, Julia thought. A four-hundred-mile detour from Salt Lake City just to say hello was remarkable. "How thoughtful of you, Mr. Booth," she said. "What is your destination?"

"Massachusetts, ma'am."

"Of course. That is your home, isn't it?" During the war, Edward had been regimental surgeon to the Fifty-seventh Massachusetts Volunteers. He'd forged a bond with many of the soldiers, including Gib.

"Yes, ma'am."

Silence descended, then lengthened. Gib was certainly not a great one for talk, Julia thought, as she discreetly plucked a few more cat hairs from her sleeve. But it was pleasant to sit with a man who wasn't trying to sell himself.

Harlan Hughes, the superintendent of the Continental Mining Company, seemed poised to snap her up as soon as her mourning period ended. Every conversation with him seemed to include in one way or another his suitability as a husband.

"In your wire you mentioned something about settling accounts."

Gib sat forward on the sofa and began examining the silver studs that decorated his hatband. "It's just a figure of speech, ma'am. You see, I caused Doc so much trouble in my younger years, I wanted to apologize. Settle accounts, in other words."

His consideration touched Julia. She thought how pleased Edward would have been to find Gib Booth's character so much improved. "There is no need to apologize, Mr. Booth," she said. "Edward may have been bothered by your behavior from time to time, but he never lost his affection for you."

Gib gave her a grateful look. "I appreciate those kind words, ma'am. I really do."

The kettle started rattling in the kitchen. Julia got to her feet. "The tea water," she said. "I'll only be a moment."

Gib stood up. "Yes, ma'am."

She swept out, slim as a willow, that little twitch to her bustle. When she disappeared, Gib let out a soft whistle and tossed his hat to the ceiling. Things couldn't have gone better. She wasn't in the least suspicious; far from it, she downright admired him.

He clasped his hands behind his back and wandered around the room. It was pleasant enough, with the cozy grouping of sofa and armchairs and a decoratively carved upright piano, but not very fancy for a woman who'd inherited a fortune. Most likely the princess planned to build herself a mansion, the same sort of bonanza king's house he had in mind.

Gib stopped at the piano. The candle bracketed to the music rack was burned nearly to the quick. The songbook was open to "In Tears I Pine for Thee." Gib's eyes moved to a picture of Doc on top of the piano, a recent photograph, from the look of his thinning hair. His full mustache swept down to his strong square jaw, and his kindly expression was just as Gib remembered.

Doc was a fine man, Gib thought, the most honorable man he'd ever known, the sort of man who should have lived to be a hundred. It was hard to think of him dead. Julia probably missed him every day.

Gib went over to the bay window where a calico cat dozed on a cushion. The window faced southeast and let in the morning sun, along with a nice view of the hills and mountains. There was nothing like Montana light, Gib thought. If this were his house, he would pull down the heavy velvet drapes to let in that light. Take up the carpet, too. And he'd give the place a good scouring. Gib looked at the gray walls, the dust on the whatnot, the lamps' cloudy chimneys. He ran his fingers along the windowsill and frowned at the resulting streak.

"I must apologize for the grime, Mr. Booth." Julia came in, carrying a silver tray. "I should have started cleaning weeks ago, but I'm rather busy these days. I'm looking after patients until a new doctor arrives, and I'm in charge of the public health activities of the Civic Betterment Committee. It's hard to find time to keep up with the dirt."

"You don't have to explain, ma'am." The thought of cleaning suddenly gave Gib an idea. A surefire idea that would win her trust and her gratitude along with it. He wiped his dusty hand on his pant leg and cleared a place on the tea table, which was covered with stacks of medical journals.

Julia set down the tray. "Now that Mary Hurley's gone, I have no one to help me, other than the hired man. You know Morris Swain, don't you, Mr. Booth?"

Gib thought of Mossy with his melancholy nature and his lame back. Mossy wasn't exactly lazy, but Gib couldn't imagine him moving living room furniture. "Yes, ma'am. Mossy and I were in the same regiment. We both followed Doc to Stiles after the war."

"That's one thing we never discuss with Mossy," Julia said, settling herself before the tea tray. "The war."

"He had a bad time of it."

Julia sighed. "Didn't everyone?"

She began arranging cups and saucers while waiting for the tea to steep. Gib looked on from the sofa, not saying a word. Julia found it hard to tell what he was thinking, but she sensed that he noticed a lot more than he let on.

"I'd like to offer my services, ma'am."

Julia glanced at him questioningly. "In what capacity, Mr. Booth?"

"Spring cleaning."

She stopped her arranging, unsure of his meaning. "You know of a girl I might engage?"

"Not a girl, ma'am. I was thinking of myself."

He didn't appear to be joking. In fact, he looked so sincere—not to mention strong enough to move the piano by himself—that Julia couldn't imagine a more gallant man in the whole world.

"Surely you don't know about . . . well, polishing grates and scrubbing walls and beating dusty old carpets?" Julia stumbled over her words, trying to keep the hopeful tone from her voice.

His smile was so engaging that any lingering doubts about his character faded away. "As a matter of fact, I know a lot about spring cleaning. When I was a boy, my mother took in washing and hired out as a scrubwoman. I went along to help her with the cleaning."

Julia tried to imagine him as a boy, helping his mother with her humble chores.

"Chances are," he went on, "your barn and the sheds could use some work, and there's a few boards on your porch that need fixing."

"Why, Mr. Booth," Julia said, clasping her hands in a gesture of gratitude, "I don't know what to say."

"No need to say anything, ma'am, other than tell me when to begin."

CHAPTER

2

"LADIES? LADIES!" LOUISE Williver pounded her gavel. "Come to order, please. We mustn't gossip all day long."

Julia turned her attention to Louise, who put down the gavel, patted her frilly peach bodice, and began arranging her papers on the lectern. Louise insisted on using a lectern at meetings; she said it made the proceedings more businesslike.

"The business at hand is the Independence Day fair." Louise's ringing voice silenced the last giggle and whisper. "The committees are all in place, I believe." She looked at Dorothy Cady, who was charged with assigning committees.

"All except for the prettiest-girl-at-the-fair committee," Dottie said.

There was a ripple of laughter. Dottie caught Julia's eyes and winked.

Louise continued as if Dottie hadn't spoken. "Mrs. Renate Blum is in charge of the auction; Mrs. Emma

Redfern, the booth games; and Mrs. Harriet Tabor, the picnic. We are especially fortunate that Stiles's own Marshal McQuigg will organize the band concert.''

Julia struggled to hide a smile. Dottie and Louise were an odd pair, as close as sisters, yet as different as chalk from cheese. Louise worried about propriety, fussed with her hair, and wore the most up-to-date fashions. Dottie looked on the light side of things, her brown curls were salted with gray, and she dressed for comfort, which meant her corset got little wear. Both ladies had grown children and were old enough to be Julia's mother, but they were her very best friends. When she first came to Montana as Edward's bride, Dottie and Louise had turned heaven and earth to make her feel welcome.

"I believe I have made my feelings quite clear, Dottie," Louise was saying in response to another of Dottie's protests. "I don't approve of rewarding the vanity of girls or encouraging men to dwell on women's physical features. But I shall open the floor for discussion.''

Dottie glanced around the room in search of support. The faces of the ladies reflected expressions that ranged from amused to evasive, but no one spoke.

"There doesn't appear to be any more discussion on the matter." Louise banged her gavel, sounding the death knell for the prettiest-girl contest.

Louise proceeded to the next item on her agenda, and Julia cast Dottie an apologetic glance. She would gladly have supported Dottie, but she was already in trouble with Louise for not behaving like a proper widow.

"I can't understand why you insist on driving around the country, calling on all manner of people, pretending you're a doctor," Louise had said. "You have enough money to last three lifetimes, and you should be redecorating your house.''

Louise believed that appearances counted for everything when it came to a lady's reputation, and of course she was right. But Julia was not about to abandon pregnant women and ailing babies to a horse doctor from Dillon. As for the house, it was comfortable and more than adequate for her needs—although since Edward died and Mary Hurley left, it did seem rather gloomy. A good cleaning would improve things, Julia thought, which reminded her of Gib Booth and brought on an unexpected rush of anticipation.

"Mr. Harlan Hughes has kindly agreed to supervise the boys' wrestling matches," Louise said. "Mr. Barnet Cady will organize the baseball contest, Mr. Abner Ames will arrange for the rock-drilling competition, and Mrs. Julia Metcalf is in charge of the magic-lantern presentation." Louise lowered her list and looked at Julia. "The program, Julia?"

"Pictures of the Holy Land. Edward sent away for them. They've only just arrived."

The ladies gave a collective sigh. They had all adored Edward. Any mention of him still inspired sympathetic murmurs.

"We all look forward to it, I'm sure," Louise said.

She next recognized Harriet Tabor, who insisted that a new committee be formed to clean the picnic area before the baseball contest. Since no one ever paid much attention to Harriet, a buzz of whispers started up. Dottie leaned over to Julia. "Barnet and I will drive you to Louise's dinner party tonight. Unless Harlan is taking you."

"Harlan said he would take me," Julia whispered back.

Dottie patted Julia's hand approvingly, a gesture she found unsettling. Dottie and Louise had apparently embraced the notion that once her mourning period was over, she would marry Harlan Hughes. The ladies hadn't said anything directly, but they saw to it that she was seated next to him at dinner parties, and they made her his partner at whist and croquet. And at every opportunity, Louise reminded her that Harlan was the most marvelous catch in the territory.

Louise banged her gavel. "We shall adjourn to the living room for refreshments and meetings of individual committees."

Voices rose, chairs scraped the floor, fabric rustled. Stiles's leading ladies made their way out of Louise's dining room, which on the second Friday of each month was transformed into a meeting room complete with potted palms flanking the lectern.

Dottie took Julia's arm. "Barnet says Harlan is thinking of running for delegate to the constitutional convention in Helena." She gave Julia a meaningful look. "The election is in November, soon after your mourning period comes to an end. The convention is in January."

Julia looked at Dottie in alarm. "For heaven's sake, what are you saying?"

"Only that come November you'll need to make some decisions about your future, dearie. That's all I'm saying."

"I don't see why I have to make any decisions at all," Julia said, but Dottie was yoo-hooing after someone and didn't seem to hear.

In the living room, Emma Redfern and Harriet Tabor took up their posts at the tea and coffee pots. The rest of the ladies gathered around the marble-topped table, admiring bowls of primroses and exclaiming over how well the flowers matched Louise's new fireplace screen, painted in various shades of pink.

The spacious Williver home was beautifully decorated and filled with the finest furnishings, as befitted the home of Stiles's leading merchant, but most enviable from Julia's point of view were the two Irish girls George Williver had brought home from his business travels to be live-in maids. The girls kept the house spotless. Even in winter the carpets were beaten and the windows shone as clear as ice. Louise's spring cleaning was always finished well before anyone else's.

"I think we'd better talk about that handsome devil who called on you yesterday," Dottie said, slipping an arm through Julia's.

Julia's heart sped up. "What handsome devil?"

"Don't play innocent with me, dearie. Everybody's heard."

"If you're talking about Gib Booth, he merely stopped by to make a condolence call."

Dottie eyed her up and down. "He's a troublemaker. You'd better watch out."

"He's perfectly harmless," Julia said, feeling a sudden dampness under her arms.

"That's what you think. You weren't here years ago when he was raising Cain all over town."

"He's a grown man, for heaven's sake."

"Worse yet."

Julia glanced at Harriet Tabor, seated behind Louise's sterling silver coffee service from Wanamaker's in Philadelphia. Harriet's pince-nez swung from the massive slope of her black silk bosom, but even without the spectacles fixed on her nose, her eyes were as sharp as hornets' stings. With the news of Gib Booth's return apparently on everyone's lips, Julia decided it would be best to stay out of Harriet's line of vision. She stepped back from the table, prepared to forgo the pink-iced tea cakes, but too late.

"Gilbert Booth is back in town," Harriet announced.

Julia gazed around the room, pretending the remark hadn't been directed at her.

"He called on you, Julia. I can't believe you received him."

A hush fell over the company. Julia moistened her lips. It was ridiculous to feel embarrassed when she'd done nothing wrong. "He was a friend of Edward's," she said. "From the war."

"You don't have to tell me about Gib Booth." Harriet's voice was laden with judgment. "He's a murderer and a fornicator. He robbed my husband and set fire to my house. Twice."

The atmosphere in the room had turned decidedly unpleasant. Julia gave Dottie a desperate glance.

"Harriet, for gracious' sakes," Dottie said. "This is a social occasion, not an inquisition."

Harriet ignored the admonition. "What did he want, Julia?"

"He . . . offered his condolences. He behaved perfectly well."

"He's after your money," Harriet snapped. Her hair, pulled back tight, added to the severity of her expression. "He heard Dr. Metcalf was gone, and he came back to take advantage of you. The man hasn't a decent bone in his body."

Julia thought of Gib's good manners, his detour all the way from Salt Lake to apologize to Edward. She remembered Mossy's face when he'd seen Gib yesterday, how his eyes had filled with tears. Gib had flung an arm around Mossy's shoulders and had taken him out back, where they'd stood by the barn, talking.

"Mr. Booth was very kind," she said curtly. "I'll have you know he offered to help with my spring cleaning."

She hadn't meant to say it, but there it was, laid out for the ladies to consider. They stared at her as if struck dumb.

"As I live and breathe," Dottie murmured.

"Mary Hurley's gone to Butte, and Mossy's back is lame," Julia said. "When Mr. Booth offered, I accepted with thanks."

"Good *heavens*!" Harriet's eyes bulged.

"Oh, Julia!" Louise cried. Her face was crimson to the roots of her flawlessly dressed and hennaed hair. "You can borrow Birdie for your cleaning. If you need Theresa, you can have her, too."

Julia saw the looks being exchanged, heard the murmurs all around. She thought of Gib's kindness, his soft gray eyes. "Thank you, Louise, but I have accepted Mr. Booth's offer."

"I am absolutely appalled!" Harriet exclaimed.

"You're always appalled," Dottie said.

Louise clapped her hands, silencing the hum of voices. "Ladies, if you will kindly take your tea and gather in your committees, we can conclude our business in good time." She cast Julia an anxious look.

Dottie took Julia firmly by the arm. "Let's have a talk."

Julia allowed herself to be steered to the cushioned window seat, where Dottie sat her down well apart from the other ladies.

"How much do you know about Gib?"

Julia made an impatient face. She was twenty-eight years old, ten years married, seven months widowed, a medical practitioner acquainted with every aspect of human nature, and yet she was being treated as if she were incapable of judging a man's character.

"He's changed, Dot. And even if he hasn't, he's not going to do me any harm."

"Do you know about the trouble he caused?"

Julia sighed. "I know he shot a man in broad daylight on Main Street, and he misbehaved with girls, and he and Lee Tabor tried to launch a hot-air balloon and in the process started some fires. But things were different then. The town was wild. Everybody knows that."

Dottie didn't look convinced. "We don't know what he's been up to or what he's doing back in town. Remember, Julia, Edward took very good care of you."

"For heaven's sake, I'm a grown woman."

"A wealthy woman. An attractive, young, wealthy woman. With no husband." Dottie enunciated each word to emphasize her meaning. "I'm not saying that Harriet is right about Gib's intentions, but keep in mind that he can be very charming when it suits his purpose."

"Oh, Dot—"

"Just promise me you'll take a little care."

Julia was surprised that lighthearted Dottie should be so concerned. "You mustn't worry," she said. "Really, I'll be just fine."

The stable smelled like any barn filled with hay and warm horseflesh, but to Gib, Tabor's Livery smelled of memories. It brought back winter nights, hitching up the four-seater sleigh after old Levi was asleep and sneaking girls into the hayloft when there was no other warm place to go. One time he and Lee had hidden a cache of rifles for some road agents who'd scared the bejesus out of them, then paid them with a five-dollar gold piece. When Levi found out, he'd turned the boys over to the marshal and they'd slept in the jail for two nights, enjoying every minute of it.

Gib shook off the memories and said, "Lee, I need a horse."

"Sure, Gib. Take your pick."

Lee had changed. He'd gotten husky, his yellow hair had

darkened, and he wore a mustache. But more than that, the boy who'd been game for anything had disappeared. Lee looked glum, as if he'd forgotten how to smile.

"I'm a little short, Lee."

Lee waved his hand. "Forget it. Pay me when you can."

"Appreciate it."

Gib didn't like asking Lee for credit, but he was down to seventy dollars and change. He was paying Dellwood seven a week for a room over the Bon Ton, and he had to eat. He'd also need a hot water bath every couple of days, and a few new duds if he wanted to keep up appearances.

"You heading out right now?" Lee asked.

"That depends on what you've got in mind."

"Thought you might like to sit a spell. Chew the fat."

Gib hesitated. He'd planned to go down to Williver's mercantile store and buy some equipment so he could do a little placering. It was a sad day when a hard-rock miner like him was reduced to shifting through played-out gravel, but he would need a pouch or two of gold dust to tide him over, and placering was the fastest way to get it.

"Sure, Lee. My pleasure." It was good of Lee to treat him like a friend. After talking to Dellwood, Gib thought the whole town hated him.

They headed through the barn's dusty light toward the room Lee's father used as an office. "How're your folks?" Gib asked.

"Ma's all right. Pa passed on five, six years back."

"Sorry to hear it." Poor old Levi, Gib thought. Harriet Tabor was enough to send any man hurrying to his grave. "So the livery's yours?"

"I run it. Belongs to Ma."

Good God, no wonder Lee was glum. "No wife?"

"Nah. Yourself?"

Gib laughed. "Who'd want me?"

Lee closed the door to the office and motioned Gib to an old chair with one arm missing. He opened the bottom drawer of his desk and pulled out a bottle and a couple of glasses.

Gib declined the offer.

"Nothing for old times?" Lee asked.

"Let's just say I've joined the temperance movement."

Lee cracked a smile. "Ma might have to change her opinion of you."

"Jesus, I'd sure hate to see that happen."

Lee's smile widened a little as he filled his glass to the rim. "It's good to see you, Gib. Real good."

Gib longed for a smoke. There was a hungry ache in his chest, and his nerves felt jumpy, but Julia had made it clear yesterday that she didn't like smoking, so he'd temporarily given it up. He couldn't take a drink without wanting a smoke, so he'd temporarily given that up, too. He'd also decided not to play around with ladies, lest she hear about it. Which left him without a whole lot to do except play billiards and a hand or two of cards at the Bon Ton.

He consoled himself with the thought that giving up the good things in life would save money, and maybe he'd get so desperate he'd think faster when it came to figuring out a plan for getting his hands on Julia's money.

Gib's eyes fell on the old safe, the same one he and Lee had gotten into more than once. They'd never taken more than a few dollars, and only one time had they spent the money on whores.

"Did your pa ever miss the money we took out of that safe?"

Lee shook his head. "Ma's the one that counts the money. I think she had her suspicions."

"That's the only safe I ever busted into," Gib said, admiring the dusty old hunk of steel. "Had a real talent for it. Could be a rich man today, if I'd kept it up."

Lee chuckled. "I don't call it safecracking when the thing's unlocked."

Gib feigned surprise. "The hell it was."

Lee was grinning real wide now. "We had some good times, didn't we, Gib?"

"We sure did."

Lee was talking like a man who figured he didn't have any more good times left in him. He was young, too, Gib thought. Probably not a day over thirty.

"Looks like you need some cheering up, Lee," Gib said. "How about you and me heading over to the Bon Ton tonight? A few hands of cards, a look at the girls."

Lee glanced away. "Don't think so, Gib. Thanks just the same."

It was his ma, Gib figured. Now that she didn't have old Levi to yank around, she kept Lee on a short lead.

"I better be going," Gib said, getting up. "Thanks for the horse. I'll be heading up Doubletree Gulch one of these days to see Rawlie Brown. I hear he's still guarding that snake pit of a mine he and Digger found."

Lee tossed down the last of his drink. "You heard Digger's dead?"

"So Dellwood said. Tangled with a bunch of rattlers. It's a shame those two old coots never let a gang go up there for a good old rattlesnake hunt. They were so scared of claim-jumpers they shot just about anybody who came in sight. You and I nearly got winged a few times, remember?"

Lee smiled weakly. "Yeah, I remember."

"Digger's little girl is all grown. Works at the Bon Ton, I see. She sure turned into a fine-looking woman."

Lee swallowed hard. "Yeah."

Something in Lee's face gave Gib pause. He wondered if Lee's trouble had to do with Sarabeth Brown. Years back, Lee had been real partial to Digger's half-breed daughter. Gib scratched his head and considered mentioning it, then thought what the hell. He hadn't come back to Stiles to get mixed up in anybody's business.

He clapped Lee on the shoulder. "What do you say to supper at the Pickax tonight? I heard the food doesn't kill a man."

Lee brightened a little. "The biscuits are hot at six o'clock."

"Sounds good."

"How about it's on me?"

"Sounds better," Gib said.

After leaving the livery, Gib went down to Williver's General Merchandise to price mining equipment. He looked around for a while, then wondered if there was any use placering. The Chinese had probably sifted through the dregs of Cottonwood Creek. They were damned patient, following abandoned claims and working them clean. They even dug in sandbars and dumps.

Thinking of the Celestials reminded Gib of the times he and Lee used to prowl the alley that was Stiles's Chinatown, hoping to glimpse the inside of an opium den or a China girl hobbling around on little feet. They'd go into Charlie Soon's store and listen to him talk about the benefits of snake oil. They got a kick out of Charlie's fast way of talking, especially when he spoke English.

Gib's mind paused; something pricked his imagination. Snake oil, he thought. Charlie Soon. Julia's money. A plan began to form in his mind, a plan so elaborate and interesting that he stood in front of a display case of cutlery and glassware thinking it through. He didn't even notice the clerk until the man cleared his throat.

Gib brushed off the clerk and headed for the door. Outside, a look at the sky told him it was too late in the day to get to Doubletree Gulch and back again in time for supper with Lee. Just as well, he thought. He'd let the plan cook awhile, make sure he had everything square in his own mind before he took things too far.

He headed up Main Street, enjoying the chilly late afternoon air. Folks were coming and going at the express office, Blum's grocery, and the First National Bank of Stiles. Buckboards and spring wagons rattled down the street, freight wagon drivers hoorawed and swore and cracked their whips, while loafers lounged in doorways, watching the passing scene.

The town had a purposeful feel to it, Gib thought, a far cry from the days when there were two dozen saloons instead of three, and every living soul was in a hurry to get rich, drunk, or killed and hang the consequences. Gunfights, fistfights, brawls—they'd been daily events, going hand in hand with round-the-clock drinking. The activity had kept Doc busy digging out lead and sewing up hides. Now his widow was doing it—a lady. It sure was hard to believe.

Thinking of Julia quickened Gib's steps. He decided to go out to her place and polish her apple some more. He'd made a good start, but he had a long way to go before he got what he'd come for.

Doc's house was up Cottonwood Gulch about a mile from town, just off the stage road to McAllister. As he walked along, Gib admired the hills dotted with stands of spruce and nut pine and splashed with color where wildflowers bloomed. The vigorous air made his head feel clear and his vision sharp. He fingered the pouch of tobacco in his pocket. Things seemed to smell better when he didn't have a nose full of smoke.

At the house, Mossy trotted out of the barn like a big friendly dog. "Say, Gib. What d'ya say?"

Mossy was the sorriest-looking man in the world, square-set and bowlegged with arms too long for the rest of him and a back bent with rheumatism. Yesterday he'd taken one look at Gib and started to cry. Mossy couldn't seem to get the war out of his mind, couldn't stop thinking about the Wilderness back in '64 and all the boys who'd died there, burned up in the wildfire.

"Thought I'd take a look around," Gib said, nodding toward the house. "This place could use some work."

Mossy's face fell into its mournful expression. "I don't keep it up like I should."

"Hell, Mossy, it's not that bad, just a loose board here and there. Mrs. Metcalf around?"

"She's gone out to the valley on medical calls."

Gib was disappointed. He'd looked forward to getting to work at winning her over.

He walked around the house, Mossy trailing behind. It was a well-made two-story clapboard affair with green shutters and first- and second-floor verandas. The bay window was handsome and well fitted. Out front stood two gnarled apple trees. Shrubs sprouting buds snuggled close to the house. A neat white fence around the yard seemed more for decoration than anything else.

"What's that lead to?" Gib asked, nodding toward a side door with a big bell hanging off it.

"Doc's surgery," Mossy said. "Folks ring the night bell when they need help." His eyes grew moist. "Mrs. Metcalf helped Doc a lot. He always said he couldn't get along without her."

"She doesn't go in much for housekeeping," Gib said, leaning down to pick up a shingle lying on the ground.

"She can cook real good."

"No matter one way or the other. Housekeeping's our job now, Moss. Better get a good night's rest. It's spring cleaning tomorrow."

Just then Doc's buggy turned into the yard, drawn by a high-stepping buckskin. Julia was at the reins, wearing a wide-brimmed hat to keep the sun off.

Gib put on his polite face and ambled over. "Afternoon, ma'am."

"Why, Mr. Booth. What a pleasure." Gib saw that she indeed seemed pleased. Her cheeks turned a little pink, and her jewel-colored eyes shone.

"The pleasure is mine, ma'am." He meant it, too. The way she looked at him boosted his spirits.

Mossy took the bridle, and Gib handed Julia down. Her black outfit looked pretty with her pale skin and shining nut brown hair. Gib bet she would look even prettier in something colorful.

"I'd hoped to see you before you began work," Julia said. "We should discuss what needs to be done."

Gib cleared his throat. "If you don't mind, ma'am, you tell me what you want me to do, then go about your business. I don't work so well being watched over."

The breeze blew the ribbons on her hat and the ruffle of black at her throat. "You sound like Mary Hurley. Mary always said she would do her own work the way she thought best, thank you very much."

"Us maids think alike."

She laughed, which pleased Gib. He enjoyed making women laugh, especially pretty women like her.

"Is that shingle from my roof?" She was staring at his hand.

"Yes, ma'am, it is. I'll get up there and look around. I'll

check the chimney, too. Any work needs to be done, I'll take care of it."

Julia cocked her head at him, as if sizing him up and liking what she saw. "You're a man of many talents, Mr. Booth."

Gib felt himself flush. "Yes, ma'am."

She glanced at the small gold lady's watch that hung from a fob at her waist. "I'm going out this evening, but I have a little time now. When you're finished looking around, come inside for a cup of coffee. You, too, Mossy."

She was still smiling when she set off for the house. Gib watched her go. The heavy black fabric of her skirt swayed as she walked. She wasn't wearing a bustle, and he saw that she didn't have much in the way of hips. Didn't have much on top, either.

"She's a fine lady, Gib," Mossy said.

"She seems to be, Moss. Just the right lady for Doc."

Mossy led the horse and buggy around back. Gib stood in the front yard, thinking. Julia sure seemed to like him. It made him wonder if he could get more out of her than money.

Then he remembered Doc and felt embarrassed. She was Doc's wife, for God's sake, a decent woman. Besides, he was there for a purpose; he damned well better not get sidetracked.

CHAPTER

3

A THICK SLICE of moon spilled light across the landscape, outlining peaks and draws and a few nearby trees. The night air, spiced with juniper and sage, had a frosty bite. As the buggy bumped down the hill from Louise's house toward Stiles, Julia was grateful for her lined gloves and for the blanket that Harlan had tucked around her knees. She was equally grateful that Louise's dinner party was over. She'd had a hard time paying attention to the conversation, which focused on territorial politics and taxes, neither of which she found to be of much interest.

"Louise said she's trying to talk you into a shopping trip to Denver," Harlan said. The moonlight shone on his profile, handsome and clean-cut except for the little roll under his chin. He hadn't yet developed a paunch, but he carried an excess of flesh that would most likely increase with the years.

"She has been ever since the snow melted," Julia said. "But I can't think of anything I need to buy."

Harlan glanced at her, a humorous crease at the corner of his full-lipped mouth. "My dear Julia, it doesn't matter what you need, only what you want. You don't need to pinch pennies these days."

"I don't need to spend money foolishly, either."

Julia was embarrassed by any mention of her wealth. Barnet Cady, Dottie's husband and Edward's attorney, and Mr. Coolidge, president of the First National Bank, had assembled an investment portfolio of railroad and mining stocks, municipal bonds, and parcels of real estate. But Julia didn't take much interest in any of it, since to her way of thinking, she'd done nothing to earn it.

"Frugality is an admirable trait in a woman," Harlan said. "However, I would suggest that you risk a portion of your assets on Continental stock."

Julia looked at him in surprise. She'd heard this was a terrible time to invest in the Continental. The mine was shipping low-grade ore, the company had stopped paying dividends, and Harlan was laying men off. If it hadn't been for the small mines like the High Top and the Empire and the ranchers in the valley, Stiles might have turned into a ghost town by now.

"I shouldn't think Continental stock would be an especially wise investment just now," Julia said.

"On the contrary," Harlan said. "The best time to buy is when the price is down. If we strike big at number four level, the stockholders who bought low will do themselves proud."

Speculating in a failing mine didn't make sense to Julia, but Harlan certainly had more expertise in such matters than she. When he'd first come to Stiles six years ago, the Continental's ore yields had been all but worthless. As superintendent, Harlan had built a modern mill, cut new drifts, brought in more men and better equipment. He'd struck bonanza ore, which realized tremendous profits for the company's stockholders.

"I'll speak to Barnet about it," Julia said.

"There's no need to involve Barnet. I can arrange the purchase. All I need from you is a bank draft."

"I'll consider it."

Julia was anxious to let the subject drop; the last thing she needed was more Continental stock. Shortly before his death, Edward had bought two hundred shares, which were now probably worth a fraction of their purchase price.

Julia settled back in the buggy seat, content to enjoy the fresh air and listen to the whirs and chirps of the night, which provided a pleasing counterpoint to the team's thudding hooves and the cheerful jingle of bridles.

"Dottie and Louise are concerned about you," Harlan said after a moment. "We all are."

"You needn't be. I'm doing wonderfully well these days. I'm too busy to mope around, although I do miss Edward terribly."

"I'm talking about that fellow Booth."

"Oh, good heavens." Julia felt a prick of annoyance. She'd had quite enough of people's interference. There had been Harriet Tabor's embarrassing outburst that morning in front of all the ladies, followed by Dottie's dire warnings. Probably Dottie and Louise had rounded up Harlan to add his voice to the Cassandra chorus.

"I know you think of him as Edward's friend," Harlan said. "That's exactly what he wants you to think."

"But he *was* Edward's friend. Edward didn't speak of him often, but he was fond of Mr. Booth. Just ask Mossy."

"I wouldn't call Mossy the most reliable person to attest to a man's character," Harlan said. "At the very least, Booth is an opportunist. He could be dangerous."

Dangerous! Julia made a face at the passing trees. "Edward would have wanted me to welcome him. I'm certain of it."

Harlan made no response. He let the silence drag on, as if he was giving her the opportunity to consider her foolishness. When he spoke again, he took up where he'd left off. "I'm not acquainted with the man, but I have heard plenty. And from what I hear, your friend Mr. Booth is not the sort of person a respectable lady would allow inside her home."

"I'd rather not discuss him," Julia said, but Harlan went on as if she hadn't spoken.

"Look at it from his point of view. An old acquaintance dies, leaving an attractive widow, a lady with a generous heart and a large inheritance. Perhaps she is a bit lonely, in need of a man's companionship. Adding up all those factors, Booth would conclude that he'd found a tempting mark in the person of Mrs. Julia Metcalf."

Julia dismissed his words with the wave of her gloved hand. "Mr. Booth was on his way back east. He only stopped in Stiles for a visit. Until he got to town, he didn't even know of Edward's passing or that I existed."

"So he said, and so you believe. He's a confidence man, Julia. He intends to win your trust, then strip you of your money and your reputation."

Julia's patience was wearing thin. "I've never heard such nonsense," she said. "This afternoon he came in for coffee and didn't utter one word that could have been taken as the least bit insulting. Quite the contrary, he was extraordinarily considerate."

She recalled the poignant moment when she related the circumstances of Edward's death. There had been a damp shine in Gib's eyes, and she'd wept a little herself, just enough to blow her nose. Mossy had choked up, too. They'd all sat there staring at their coffee cups, feeling sad.

"You'll have to meet him yourself," she said. "Then you'll see that your suspicions are groundless."

They turned north from Hill Road onto Main Street and drove on up the gulch, past moon-silvered scrub and boulders and dark stands of cottonwoods.

Harlan maintained a grim silence until they pulled into her dooryard. "I don't want to see you humiliated and deceived, Julia. I could never forgive myself if anything happened to you."

"Nothing will happen to me, for heaven's sake." She folded up the buggy blanket and placed it on the seat beside her. "I am quite capable of looking after myself."

There was banging at the front door, a muffled shout. "Mrs. Metcalf!"

Julia woke with a start, blinking at the sunlight that

poured through the window. Good heavens, where was she—fallen asleep in the chair! Then she remembered. After Harlan brought her home last night, she'd felt a bit lonely and uncertain. After tossing in bed for a while, she'd gotten into her robe and slippers and had come down to the comfort of Edward's study, as she often did when she couldn't sleep.

The pounding on the door came again. "Ma'am? Are you home?"

Julia got to her feet and stumbled across the carpeted floor of the study. "I'm coming!"

She hurried down the hallway and opened the front door. There on the porch stood Gib Booth. He wore a half smile beneath his black Stetson, which he hastily removed.

"Reporting for duty, ma'am."

"Oh, Mr. Booth," Julia said, clutching her robe close about her. "I forgot all about you . . . not *you*, but today. Spring cleaning." She swiped at her hair and realized that her braid had come apart, leaving strands falling about her shoulders and face. "Do come in. My, isn't it chilly? More like October than May."

Gib rubbed his big hands together and stepped inside. "Yes, ma'am, it's a mite sharp all right." He looked handsome and manly in his worn denim trousers and big sheepskin coat.

"Come get warm by the stove," Julia said, leading the way down the hall. She was about to offer him coffee when she realized that there was no coffee, nor was there a fire in the stove.

"I'm way behind myself this morning," she said as they entered the kitchen. "I haven't built a fire or started the coffee."

She opened the firebox and began raking ashes that were not quite dead. "I was out visiting last evening. Then I fell asleep in the chair in Edward's study." She wondered if her explanation made any sense.

She saw Gib glance around the room, taking in Mary Hurley's neatly labeled tins and drawers, the woodbox, the oilcloth-covered floor. He had a way of looking at things as if he was absorbing every detail.

"Hello, cat," he said to Bee, who sat on the worktable washing a front paw.

Bee cast him a lofty glance and continued her bath.

"That's Bee," Julia said. "She's ten years old. She was just a kitten when Edward gave her to me as a wedding gift."

Bee stood up and stretched and allowed Gib to scratch between her ears.

"You go along and get dressed, ma'am," he said. "I'll take care of the fire and the coffee."

Julia straightened up from the firebox. "You needn't trouble yourself."

"It would be my pleasure."

Gray eyes met hers. They lingered, perhaps a moment too long. Julia felt an embarrassing rush of warmth to her cheeks.

"The coffee and mill are there," she said hastily, nodding at the sideboard where tins stood in a soldierly line. "And the coffee pot is on the stove. There's milk in the shed icebox, and the pump's out back."

"I'll figure it out, ma'am." He stood easily, hands shoved in hip pockets, looking right at home.

Julia backed out of the kitchen. "Thank you, Mr. Booth."

She hurried down the hallway and up the stairs. In her room, she sat on the edge of the bed and tried to collect herself. It had been unnerving, not to mention improper, to converse with him so early in the morning while dressed in her nightclothes, her bed not even made. He was freshly shaved and combed and polite as pie, but there had been a look in his eye that was just a bit too knowing, or maybe she'd imagined it.

Dottie's warning flashed in her mind: "You'd better watch out." And Harlan's: "Confidence man."

Julia jumped to her feet and began smoothing bedclothes. She tucked sheets and plumped pillows and arranged the colorful quilted coverlet. She'd forgotten to take a jug from the stove's reservoir, so she washed in cold water. Just as well, she thought with a rueful shiver. A cold-water bath was healthier for both body and mind.

When she'd fastened herself into a simple black skirt and warm shirtwaist, she stood before the marble-topped dresser and brushed her thick, straight hair. She twisted it into a topknot and stuck in a score of hairpins. No matter how tightly she pinned it, long strands would soon be slipping down. Louise advised a dollop of pomade to hold things fast, but pomade made Julia's scalp itch, and she didn't care for its smell.

She opened her jar of lemon-scented face cream. Gently she dabbed and stroked. As she replaced the top on the jar, she glanced at the small portrait that stood on the dresser. A woman smiled from the jeweled and gilded frame, her eyes lively beneath a strong brow and a mass of fair curls. In her mind, Julia heard familiar words offered in a voice gay with laughter: "Men are wonderful creatures, darling. If you treat them well, they will do anything for you."

Julia laid her palms flat on the dresser and stared at her reflection. It seemed like two lifetimes ago that she'd sat beside her mother at her mirrored table laden with colored bottles and jars and cloudlike puffs of powder. Mama had promised her beauty and passion and a host of wonderful young men, all for herself.

"They will adore you," she'd said.

Julia thought of Gib's easy manner, his smiling eyes, his handsome mouth. "Oh, Mama," she whispered.

She turned away from the mirror and sat down on her small upholstered stool. Each morning and night she asked God to give her strength, to guide her along the proper path. Today she prayed just a little bit harder.

Downstairs in the kitchen the fire was going, coffee steamed in the pot, and Bee was rubbing herself against Gib's denim-clad legs. He labored over a mixing bowl with a manly sort of clumsiness, the sleeves of his black shirt rolled up to the elbow, his muscular forearms bare.

He glanced up, looking sheepish. "I used to make pretty good biscuits."

Julia saw a trail of white on the floor leading from the flour bin to the worktable, and a few gobs of lard as well. The mixture in the bowl looked like wallpaper paste.

"I don't think we'll get too far with those biscuits," she said.

He looked so embarrassed that Julia was tempted to give him a comforting pat, but she kept her hands firmly clasped. "I'll take over, Mr. Booth. If you would be so kind, go out back and see about Mossy. Perhaps you could give him a hand with the chores."

Gib seemed relieved. He brushed his hands on his faded denims and reached for his Stetson and coat.

"Mr. Booth?"

"Ma'am?"

"Do you know about Mossy in the morning?"

Gib's face relaxed into an expression of understanding. "If I remember correctly, it takes some coaxing to get him going, some days more than others."

He went out the kitchen door; an instant later the shed door banged shut behind him.

Julia cleaned the flour and lard from the floor and threw out Gib's biscuit dough. She was glad to have someone else to deal with Mossy. He tried hard to cooperate, but when he drank too much, he woke up surly and stubborn.

As she mixed a new batch of dough, Julia debated whether to serve breakfast in the dining room or the kitchen. Gib had refused to accept money for spring cleaning, but he'd readily agreed to her offer of home-cooked meals. Since he was more hired man than guest, Julia decided on the kitchen.

The table leaves were open, the biscuits were hot from the oven, and a pan of potatoes and eggs sizzled on the fire when the shed door creaked. Julia heard stamping feet and the sound of men's voices. She patted her topknot to make sure it was secure.

Gib and Mossy had washed at the pump; their hair was damp and their cheeks ruddy from a cold-water dousing.

"Good morning, Mossy," she said.

"Morning, ma'am. Sure smells good."

Mossy's eyes were red-rimmed and his nose had that telltale glow, but he seemed cheerful enough.

"The eggs are ready," Julia said. "Sit down, both of you."

They sat with a scraping of chairs and considerable ma'aming. Julia put plates of eggs and potatoes on the table and poured the coffee. When she took off her apron, preparing to sit down, Gib jumped to his feet and held her chair.

"Thank you, Mr. Booth."

"My pleasure, ma'am."

The men hung their heads respectfully while she said grace; then Julia started passing around plates of food.

Gib broke open a steaming biscuit. "I couldn't have done better myself," he said, giving Julia a look that seemed to include a wink. He spooned on some raspberry preserves. "A good breakfast can sure improve a man's state of mind."

"It sure can," Mossy agreed with uncharacteristic enthusiasm.

Gib's manners were exemplary. He chewed with his mouth closed, and he knew how to use a napkin, a skill that many men had not yet mastered. He also kept his elbows close in. Mossy shoved food into his mouth with arms pumping, as if he were sawing wood.

"Speaking of breakfast," Gib said. "I've got a pretty good breakfast story. Want to hear it?"

"Sure," said Mossy.

"Of course," Julia agreed. She was accustomed to dead-quiet breakfasts. She and Edward had read in the morning, conversing only at dinner.

Gib put down his fork and settled back in his chair. "It was on the trip out to Salt Lake from San Francisco on the Union Pacific. I was riding the plush for a change instead of the rods—"

"The rods?" Julia asked.

"That's the bars that hold up the underside of freight cars," Mossy explained. "You ride that way when you can't pay your fare."

"I see," Julia said, taken aback.

"So anyway," Gib continued, "up in the mountains the trains cross wooden trestles that wiggle over about a thousand feet of nothing. Nice view, if you don't care much about living."

"I've seen pictures," Julia said. "It looks rather dangerous."

"It sure does, ma'am. Well, this one evening, I joined some gents in a private car for a friendly game of cards, which didn't turn out so friendly." He gave Julia a glance as if to gauge her opinion of gambling. "Fellow that owned the car was scared of the train falling off a trestle. The only thing that kept him going was a case of the best bonded scotch whiskey I ever tasted." He gave Julia another quick, assessing glance. "This gent was so drunk he couldn't keep his wig on straight, and he was losing bad. He was what you might call a touchy drunk—got mad at the drop of a hat. Between drinking and losing, he wasn't exactly pleasant company."

Gib looked suddenly uncomfortable. "Maybe you don't want to hear about drinking and card-playing, ma'am."

Julia hid a smile behind her coffee cup. "I am a Methodist, but I'm sure I'll manage."

Gib took a few more forkfuls of eggs and potatoes. He wiped his mouth with the napkin and leaned his elbows on the table—his first lapse in etiquette.

"So this gent, name of Leland, wanted to fight. The whiskey'd made him brave enough to cross the trestles. Now it was making him brave enough to cuss us one side to Sunday. Cheating bast . . ." He stopped. "Excuse me, ma'am."

"Of course, Mr. Booth."

"About that time I suggested it was time to put on the feed bag. It was near ten o'clock in the morning, and we'd been at it all night with nothing in us but whiskey and cigars.

"Leland had his own cook, who stirred up some eggs and ham and boiled some coffee. Leland had calmed down, and we all settled in to eat. I'd just said how there was nothing like a good breakfast to improve a man's state of mind, when *bam!*" Gib smacked his fist into his palm. "The train stopped like it hit a wall. The table started to slide, and the curtains were swaying, and the trestle was wiggling. Reminded me of this earthquake down in Mexico—that's another story. Well, we hung on to our plates and looked at each other. Couldn't see land, just air down below. I thought, Mother, here I come."

"God Almighty," said Mossy.

Gib chose that moment to open another biscuit and drizzle some honey on it.

"Then what happened?" Julia asked.

Gib chewed his biscuit and drank more coffee, all the while looking from her to Mossy, drawing out the suspense. Then he put down his cup and wiped his mouth. "Leland starts yelling, and next thing you know, another *bam!*" Gib jumped halfway out of his chair. "This time we all went flying, plates and cups and eggs all over. 'Holy Christ! Sweet Jesus!' Leland yells—excuse me, ma'am—and he dives through the air and cracks his skull on the doorknob. Out cold as a flounder. I'm waiting to hit bottom, thinking this train is taking its own good time falling into the ravine. But nothing happens. I crawl up off the floor to look out the window and"—his voice changed to a tone of wonderment— "we're on land."

"Heavens!" Julia exclaimed. "So you didn't fall off after all."

"No, ma'am, we didn't. Turns out some cars came uncoupled just as most of the train was off the trestle. The engineer pulled the brakes to wait for the rest to catch up—that was the first jolt—and when those last cars caught up, they slammed into us, and the shock of it went all the way to the engine. Just about every plate and glass in the diner car was smashed to smithereens. Lucky no one got killed."

Gib returned to his breakfast.

"Is that the end?"

"Yes, ma'am, it is. Except it turns out the engineer was

asleep and the fireman was running the train. He should have gotten all the way off the trestle before stopping for those loose cars."

"And Mr. Leland?"

"When Leland came to, he didn't know where he was. The rest of us had a good laugh once we'd calmed down, but Leland . . ." Gib shook his head. "We never saw him again. He holed up with his case of whiskey, and we had to find a new place for our card game."

Julia sat back in her chair. "Well," she said. "That's quite a story, isn't it, Mossy?"

"Sure is." Mossy was looking from her to Gib, a big grin on his face.

"It's a good thing you weren't riding the rods that time, Mr. Booth."

Gib laughed out loud. "It sure is. I'd have been a goner for sure." He looked at her in an admiring way that made Julia flush.

"Perhaps we should get started on our chores," she said, pushing back her chair.

Gib was on his feet. "I'll wash the dishes."

"No, I'll take care of the dishes. But first I'll show you the house so you can see what needs to be done. Mossy, I'd appreciate your filling the woodbox in the meantime. Come with me, Mr. Booth."

Gib followed her up the stairs. The second floor had a good-sized central hallway and four doors leading off it. Julia headed into one of the front rooms.

"This is my room."

Gib liked it right off. The morning light streamed in through two big windows that looked out over a second-floor porch. There was a bright sunburst quilt on the bed, blue cushions in the chairs, and a shine on the dresser and armoire. Gib detected a faint lemony smell, the same clean scent that Julia wore. It reminded him of lemon pie and expensive soap and the way sunlight looked on her hair.

Julia was going on about curtains and walls and bedding and all the things that needed to be done. Gib wore his attentive expression, all the while thinking about the way she'd looked when she opened the front door—soft-cheeked and sleepy-eyed, snuggled in a big brown woolen robe that had probably belonged to Doc, her silky tumble of hair falling down around her shoulders. There was something about a woman just out of bed that sure got his attention.

"Now I'll show you Edward's room. I've cleaned out some of his things, but there are still clothes in the wardrobe."

Gib was surprised to hear that Doc had had his own room. As he followed Julia down the hallway, he wondered if sleeping alone had been her idea. It was none of his business, but Doc must have been crazy not to bed down with her every night.

"Mr. Booth."

"Huh?" They were in Doc's room. It was darker than Julia's, with a solid walnut bed, white doilies all around, and pictures on the wall of places that looked like Europe.

"I was saying that the bedding should be put out to air first thing."

"Yes, ma'am. I'd say put it out early to get the dew. It'll get a good soaking, and the sun will dry it during the day."

Julia looked skeptical. "What if it rains?"

"We'll bring it in."

She seemed about to pose another question, then apparently thought better of it. "I'll leave things up to you."

"That's what I like to hear."

She smiled. "I'll show you where Mary Hurley kept the buckets and brushes. Then I'll leave you and Mossy to your work. By the way, I've never seen Mossy so cheerful as he's been since you arrived."

Gib accepted her words as a compliment. "You need to use just the right touch with Mossy."

The smile abruptly slid from her face. "You mean getting him to do things he might not want to do?"

The wariness in her eyes put Gib on guard. He could almost see her imagining the things he might get her to do against her will. "Mossy needs encouraging, that's all," he said. "As Doc used to say, 'Put a man in a situation where something's expected of him and he'll rise to the occasion.'"

It was a theory that had never made much sense to Gib, but it seemed to satisfy Julia. As he followed her down the back stairs, he decided that the princess was probably a fair judge of character. He'd better not take anything for granted.

CHAPTER

4

THE NEXT DAY was Sunday, a day off from cleaning. Gib rode out of town, heading west. When the road veered south about a half mile from Cottonwood Creek, he left it and followed a diagonal track up the slope of the gulch to a grassy benchland. The wind was raw, and last night's rain had left the trail muddy. Gib pulled his Stetson low and was grateful for his sheepskin coat.

As he urged Lucky up the slope, Gib glanced back at the low hills and gullies of Cottonwood Gulch. All around Stiles, the hills were pocked with abandoned mines and old shacks, reminders of the boom years of the sixties and seventies when saloon music wafted down Main Street day and night, men paid in gold for their flapjacks and whores, and the population was close to ten thousand souls. At the head of the gulch, Gib could see the sloping roofs of the Continental Mining Company. Beyond, distant mountains were still crowned with snow.

The town itself was spread across the flank of a hill—

Main Street laid out in a neat line along Cottonwood Creek, the rest of the town straggling off in all directions. Gib picked out Julia's house, north of town. He remembered that some slats in the shutters were broken; he added them to his mental list of things to fix.

He'd spent yesterday at her place scrubbing walls and ceilings with soap and water and a long-handled brush. Julia had worked at the desk in Doc's study and later had gone out to see patients. Still, she'd found time to cook a fine dinner and had even baked a chocolate cake. Mossy had said it must be a special occasion, since she didn't go in much for baking cakes.

Lucky climbed the muddy track past gray-green sage-brush and scattered wildflowers. Ahead were the rocky heights of Doubletree Gulch. Gib could have followed the road around the hills and into the gulch from the other side, but it would have taken twice as long and he didn't care to climb the heights in full view of Rawlie Brown's cabin. Claim-jumping was a thing of the past in these parts, but Rawlie and his twelve-gauge hadn't heard the news.

Gib reached an outcropping of rocks that marked the site of the Rattling Rock mine. The headframe was overgrown with scrub, its timbers sagging. He rode past the tailing dump, a pile of gravel and rock extracted from the diggings. According to Lee, no gold had come down the trail since well before Digger died. In the sixties, Digger and Rawlie had dug down nearly twenty feet, finding close to thirty thousand dollars in gold before the rich vein went off into the wall. After that, the brothers hadn't done much of anything other than peck at worthless rock and shoot at imagined claim-jumpers. The abandoned shaft had eventually attracted a nest of rattlesnakes, which had given Rawlie and Digger an excuse to lie around and smoke their pipes.

Gib dismounted above the clearing where two ram-shackle cabins and a tumbledown shed perched on the hillside, overlooking ridges and hills that rolled off toward distant white-capped peaks. He tethered Lucky well out of shotgun range and headed down the hill, staying close to the edge of the clearing and the trees that provided cover.

The cabin ahead was a sorry-looking place. The boards were weather-beaten and the roof sagged around the chimney where smoke curled out. Twenty yards or so beyond Rawlie's place, Digger's abandoned shack looked to be near collapse.

Gib stood behind a thick-trunked tree. "Hey, Rawlie!" he hollered.

There was no answer. Gib considered stepping out into the clearing, then thought better of it. He didn't want to be in the line of fire if Rawlie decided to unlimber his artillery.

"It's Gib Booth, Rawlie," he shouted. "I'm coming down. Don't shoot, now—"

Boom! Boom! The reports of Rawlie's shotgun thundered across the hillside.

"Jesus Christ!" Instinctively Gib reached for his Colt and pressed back against the tree, his heart hammering. Lee had said that Rawlie was half blind; he must be deaf, too. "It's Gib Booth, you old buzzard bait!"

After a few minutes he heard the squeak of hinges as the cabin door opened. "Whatchersaying?"

"Goddammit, Rawlie, it's Gib. Gib Booth. Any chance of me coming out from behind this tree without you filling me with lead?"

Rawlie stood in the doorway, his twelve-gauge in hand, his shaggy beard blowing in the breeze. He wore the same gray soldier's overcoat and forage cap he'd worn since he was mustered out of the sesech army.

"By gum, it sounds like Gib," Rawlie announced. "Why, more'n likely it *is* Gib! Where are you, boy?"

Gib holstered the Colt and walked down to the cabin. "You near killed me, you son of a gun." He grabbed Rawlie by his thin shoulders and gave him a friendly shake.

"Eyesight ain't what it use to be," Rawlie said. He peered at Gib's face through a hazy film. "Why, I do declare. All growed into a man." A toothless grin parted his beard. "Where you been all these years?"

"It's a long story, partner." Gib sniffed coffee. "How about a cup? I could use a warm-up."

It was dark as dusk in the cabin. There were newspapers

all over—nailed to the wall, stacked on the dirt floor, stuffed into broken windowpanes. Food-caked tin plates littered the table, along with more newspapers and grub sacks of dried apples and jerked beef. A coffee pot sat on the stove, along with a blackened kettle and a fry pan crusted with what once might have been corned beef hash.

"When was the last time you cleaned this place?" Gib asked.

Rawlie pawed his whiskers. "Come to think of it, Sarabeth was here cleaning. About five years back, I reckon."

Gib looked over Rawlie's skinny frame. Beneath his overcoat he wore a red flannel undershirt, a moth-eaten sweater, and a pair of blue military trousers. Gib wasn't surprised to see the Union pants with the Confederate overcoat. Rawlie had fought for the South, but without much enthusiasm. "Are you eating, old man?"

"Digger's gone, y'know. He done the cooking."

Gib went to the stove and poured himself a cup of muddy coffee. He couldn't imagine Rawlie taking care of himself. It was a wonder he hadn't burned down the shack and himself along with it.

"Why don't you move to town? Let Sarabeth look after you."

Rawlie sat down in his old rocking chair, his twelve-gauge across his knees. "Can't leave. Mountain's crawling with jumpers."

The old man sure was a crank when it came to claim-jumpers, Gib thought. "When's the last time you made representation on this claim?"

Rawlie looked thoughtful. "Can't rightly recall. 'Twas before Digger went in after them rattlers. Got bit to death."

"Did you ever buy the patent?"

"No, sir. Recorded it, though. Right down at the county seat."

Gib tipped back his hat and scratched his head. "If you don't put in a hundred dollars of digging a year on an unpatented claim, any prospector passing through can stake it himself, right on this spot. You know it as well as I do."

The rhythmic squeak of Rawlie's rocking chair stopped. "I'll shoot the hide off any sumbitch come up here."

"Doesn't matter. He's still within his rights."

Rawlie sat still, twining his gnarled fingers in his beard. Gib watched him, feeling sad. Rawlie had once been quick-witted and strong. Generous, too. He and Digger had never minded Gib using their place as a hideout when he got into trouble in town.

"I'd hate to see the day when they hang you for shooting somebody," Gib said.

"Hanging don't bother me none. Nobody's getting this claim."

"I'll stake it, Rawlie."

"Huh?"

"I'll take over the claim. We'll throw in together. I reckon there's some rich pockets in there just waiting for us."

Rawlie worked his jaw for a while, his mouth collapsing around toothless gums. "Don't know about that. Place is full of rattlers. Whole nest of 'em. Digger got bit to death in there."

"I've got an idea how to clean 'em out."

"Don't want no hunters. No, sir. You get up a rattlesnake hunt and next thing you know there's fellers crawling all over my claim. Any feller tries to jump my claim will be eating lead for breakfast."

Gib sat down on the bunk. "You know Charlie Soon?"

"Chinaman. Runs the store with the red chickens hanging in the window."

"That's the one. He sells herbs and potions, too. Big on snake oil, claims it'll cure everything from rheumatism to female complaints. The venom sells in San Francisco for near four hundred dollars a pint." Gib paused, watching Rawlie closely. "Rattler poison doesn't bother Charlie, did you know that?"

Rawlie looked impressed. "That so?"

"That's so. He let himself get bit by baby rattlers. A man does that, he gets so the venom doesn't hurt him."

"Must be peculiar to Chinamen."

Rawlie seemed so interested that Gib plunged ahead. "I

bet Charlie'd like to come up here and clean the rattlers out of the mine."

Rawlie's face closed. His fingers fondled the twelve-gauge. "Don't want no Chinamen up here, neither."

"Now look, Rawlie, all Charlie'd do is go in there and get the rattlers and boil them for oil. He won't want your claim; he wants snake oil."

"No Chinamen."

Gib expelled a long, impatient breath. "When was the last time you heard of a Chinaman jumping a white man's claim?"

Rawlie thought. "Shoot, Gib, I guess never."

"That's right. Never."

Gib didn't say anything more. He'd give Rawlie a chance to paw his beard and think things through. Gib took another drink of coffee, but it had gone stone cold.

"Dang it, Gib, I guess you're right," Rawlie said after a spell of thinking. "No point in a good mine laying idle on account of a bunch of rattlers that some Chinaman wants to boil."

"Glad you see it that way, partner." Gib got to his feet. "I'll tell Charlie you're agreeable. He'll sure be pleased."

"Say, Gib," Rawlie said, looking wary again. "I don't want no digging around here. Around Digger's cabin, neither."

So that's where his money is, Gib thought, buried in the ground right outside. Thirty, forty thousand dollars, enough to hold a man for a good long time.

"You've got my word on it, old-timer."

Before he left, Gib stoked the fire in the stove, tidied up a bit, and hiked to the spring for water. As he rode back to Stiles, he congratulated himself on how well things were progressing. He would need some more time to win over the princess before he got her to invest in his mining enterprise. Once she loosened the purse strings, he'd rake in the pot and skedaddle. He wouldn't take all of her money. Fifty, sixty thousand, maybe seventy-five—an even split. Not enough to live like a bonanza king, but enough to get along.

The only thing that nagged at him was using Rawlie to

further his scheme—the old man would get all excited about opening up the Rattling Rock—but Gib eased his mind by telling himself that Rawlie needed someone to look after him more than he needed a paying mine. Once Gib moved into Digger's cabin, he'd fix Rawlie decent meals and clean up his shack. He'd poke around till he found the money, then go out some night and dig it up. He'd put it in the bank and move Rawlie to Stiles where Sarabeth could keep an eye on him.

Dusk was falling when Gib rode into town. Streetlamps and lighted windows gave off a welcoming glow. The rollicking saloon sounds of pianos and banjos made Gib yearn for a good smoke and a few shots of whiskey. But more, he wanted to stop by Julia's place. He imagined her flushed from the stove, the house warm with dinnertime cooking. After supper they would sit on the front room sofa. He would tell stories, make her laugh, watch those pretty eyes of hers admire him.

The idea was tempting, but Gib decided against it. Women had a weakness for him, which he made the most of when he had the time and the inclination. Trouble was, they always cried like a rainstorm when he decided to move on. Sure as the Lord made Moses, unless he was real careful, the same thing would happen with Julia.

Taking her money was one thing, Gib told himself, but he sure didn't want to break her heart.

It rained hard that night and into the morning, mixed with a few flakes of snow. When Gib appeared at the house at seven o'clock, he stuck his head in the kitchen door to say hello, then headed out to the barn to get Mossy.

He returned alone. "Rheumatism's acting up," he said. "I took care of the chores."

From the look on his face, Julia knew that Mossy had been drinking again.

She piled a stack of pancakes on a plate. "I thought he was improving. He seemed so pleased to have you back."

"A man's demons come and go, ma'am. There's not much anybody can do about it."

Julia filled her own plate and sat down. Gib kept his attention on his pancakes. He was subdued this morning, no breakfast stories, no showing off. Julia felt a little disappointed; she'd looked forward to his lively banter.

"The war ended nearly twenty years ago," she said, breaking the silence. "I would think he'd get over it."

Gib glanced up. "The war tends to stick with you, ma'am."

"Did it stick with you?"

He shrugged. "I was crazy for a while, forgot how to act civilized."

He didn't have anything more to say on the subject. Julia, curious though she was, didn't pursue it. After a few moments, she got up to get more coffee.

"Mossy had a family, you know," Gib said, holding out his cup.

"No, I didn't know."

"Doc never said?"

Julia shook her head. Mossy had been in Stiles before she arrived. She'd never thought of him having an earlier life, except for the war.

"I guess he figured it was Mossy's business," Gib said. "Doc never got into a man's business unless he was invited."

Julia sat down and pushed a forkful of pancakes through a pool of syrup.

"But that doesn't mean he didn't care," Gib went on. "During the war, Doc was about the best friend a soldier could have. He had more than one run-in with Colonel Hayes—that was the regimental commander—over how he drove us. And the cooks knew better than to pass off bad food when Doc was around." Gib took a mouthful of pancakes and washed it down with coffee. "And that's not counting the lives he saved. We all thought the world of him."

The expression on his face reminded Julia of Edward's on those few occasions he'd talked about the war, a weary sort of tenderness.

"Mossy was real homesick for a while," Gib continued.

"He didn't eat, didn't sleep. When he got letters from home, he'd burn them. Didn't even read them. He just set them on fire and watched them burn, tears running down his face. For a while there was talk of sending him to the hospital for the insane up in Washington."

Julia put down her fork. Edward had never told her that story. "How dreadful."

"Ma'am?" Gib looked at her as if he'd just remembered she was there. Julia realized he'd been reminiscing to himself more than talking to her.

"Nostalgia can make a person insane," she said.

"Homesick is all it was. Doc helped him out." There was an edge to Gib's voice, as if he was annoyed. He returned to his pancakes. "Mossy's life is his business, none of ours."

Julia made no reply. She had lived in the West long enough to know plenty of men who'd chosen to forget their past. Women, too.

After breakfast Gib headed upstairs to scrub walls and mop floors. Julia worked in the kitchen, then went into the study to finish her article for the *Sentinel*.

An hour later she took a cup of coffee upstairs to Edward's room where Gib was working. He accepted it gratefully. "Maid work takes a lot out of a man," he said, flexing his shoulders. He wore a faded flannel shirt that had probably once been red. The color suited his dark good looks.

"You're doing a wonderfully thorough job," Julia said. He had covered all the furniture with old sheeting and had already scrubbed three walls. There was a painter's brush on the windowsill that he'd used to sweep dust from crevices and ledges. Julia was beginning to feel guilty about how hard he was working. "I don't know how I'll ever repay you."

He smiled. "It's my pleasure, ma'am."

"I'll be going out to Whiskey Creek to see a lady, and then I have a few errands in town. I'll leave you and Mossy something to eat."

Gib gulped down the rest of his coffee. "I'd appreciate that."

Julia returned to the kitchen and prepared scalloped potatoes and ham for the evening meal. After setting out a cold luncheon for Gib and Mossy, she hitched Biscuit to the buggy and headed for Doubletree Gulch.

The rain had stopped and the sky had brightened a bit, but a damp chill still hung in the air. It made Julia yearn for the hot summer sun, for wildflowers and birdsong. She wondered if Gib would enjoy a picnic in the meadow.

Mercy, that was a foolish thought. In a week or so he'd be gone, no doubt relieved to see the end of housework. Julia felt a strange pang of regret and decided not to think that far ahead.

By the time she drove down Doubletree Gulch to the Chapman place by Whiskey Creek, the sun had broken through, warming the air. Julia climbed down from the buggy, tied the lead to the fence, and took Edward's medical bag from under the seat.

"Yoo-hoo, Mrs. Chapman!" she called as she made her way along the flat stones that led to the front door.

Chickens pecked and squawked in the yard, and bearded goats chewed their cud and stared from a wire pen. The house, little more than a cabin, was made of lumber that Otis Chapman had scavenged from abandoned mines in the nearby hills. He'd built a covered porch, its roof held up by bark logs, where Mrs. Chapman sat in her rocker on fair days, shelling peas and darning socks.

"Mrs. Chapman! It's Julia Metcalf here."

The door opened. Vera Chapman stood on the sloping threshold, one hand on her hip, the other on a broom. Her huge belly bulged under a faded Mother Hubbard.

"Look at you, now," she called. "Still wearing them dreary black things. It's about time you brightened yourself up."

"Not for another few months," Julia said cheerily. Mourning was a tribute to Edward as well as a welcome protection against the attentions of suitors—especially Harlan, who might be tempted to cross the line.

Mrs. Chapman waved Julia inside, then gave the rickety front porch a brisk sweep with her broom. "Life is for the living, as I always say. You'd honor your husband by getting on with things."

Inside, brightly hued rag rugs covered the board floor, and white curtains were tied back at the windows. A calico partition divided the cabin into a sitting room and a bedroom. The sweet smell of baking wafted in from the lean-to kitchen.

Julia set her bag on a straight-backed chair and gave Mrs. Chapman a critical look. She was a tall, big-boned woman, her brown hair streaked with gray. The tragedy of losing two girls to diphtheria had lined her face, but pretty dimples danced at the corners of her mouth.

"How are you feeling?"

"Right as rain." Mrs. Chapman flicked her broom at a corner of the long mirror hanging on the wall, destroying a spiderweb.

"And how is Mr. Chapman?"

"That man can't sleep for worrying. I tell him worrying won't change a blessed thing. The Lord giveth and the Lord taketh away, I say, just like he took our little girls, God bless them."

Last winter Mrs. Chapman had come to Julia complaining of the dropsy. Julia had discovered that she was pregnant, a surprise to both of them, since at age forty-eight Mrs. Chapman had gone through the change.

"A miracle," Mrs. Chapman had declared. "A special gift of Providence. God's way of making up for my little girls."

Julia had had to agree, though she didn't want to depend on Providence to see Mrs. Chapman through her pregnancy. She'd instructed her to rest her aching back and painful legs and to stop chopping wood and carrying heavy pails of water. But Mrs. Chapman was a whirlwind around her little cabin, and she'd shrugged off Julia's advice. Even a talk with Otis was fruitless, since Mrs. Chapman brushed aside her husband's views when they didn't correspond to her own.

"Are you resting every afternoon?" Julia asked.

A fly buzzed over to the wall. Mrs. Chapman swatted it with the broom. "When do I have time for resting? Now you just set yourself down. I've got some nice tarts fresh from the oven and hot water for tea."

"You mustn't go to any trouble," Julia began, but Mrs. Chapman had disappeared behind the calico partition, leaving it fluttering in her wake.

Julia took off her hat and suede gloves and sat down at the small table. It was the bane of female practitioners that patients didn't take them seriously, she thought. Her half brother Randall, a Chicago surgeon, had warned her as much when she'd told him of her intention to treat Edward's patients.

"What patient is going to listen to a woman?" Randall had demanded. "Especially a *young* woman who doesn't have a medical degree?"

Mrs. Chapman returned with a tray of apple tarts and two steaming mugs of tea. She set the tray on the table and lowered herself onto a rush-seated ladder-back that creaked and swayed beneath her weight.

"These tarts are Otis's favorite."

Julia took one from the plate. It was warm from the oven. "They smell heavenly."

She sipped her tea and munched on the tart while Mrs. Chapman beamed with approval. "Won't hurt for you to fatten up a bit, Mrs. Metcalf. Why, now that Doctor is gone, God bless him, you'd better start thinking about a new husband for yourself, a younger man who can give you babies."

Julia meant to give a dismissive laugh, but instead she blushed. "Oh, gracious," she said and hurried to change the subject. "I expect we'll have a new doctor in Stiles this summer."

"How's that?" Mrs. Chapman asked. "Surely you don't mean that horse doctor from Dillon."

"No, I mean a real doctor. My brother teaches at Rush Medical College in Chicago. He thinks that one of his students will agree to come to Stiles to practice. It would be a good experience for a young doctor and an adventure to come west."

"I should say," Mrs. Chapman agreed. "My goodness,

there's doctors all over your family, aren't there? Your poor husband, your brother, yourself."

"I'm not really qualified," Julia said quickly. "I'm only filling in until the new doctor arrives."

"Now, Mrs. Metcalf, don't speak low of yourself. I'd never let a man that's not my husband touch me. I birthed my two girls on my own, and if it wasn't for you worrying, I'd do the same with this one."

"I'm grateful, Mrs. Chapman, but surely when the new doctor comes—"

"When the new doctor comes, that will be fine for other folks. But I'll still expect you to look after my baby, if need be."

"Well, then," Julia said, pleased by Mrs. Chapman's confidence in her. "Perhaps I'd better take a look at you."

Mrs. Chapman heaved herself to her feet. "I don't mean to be rushing you, but I've got gardening to do and goats to milk, and Otis'll be expecting his dinner."

Julia picked up her bag and followed Mrs. Chapman behind the calico partition. Sunlight spilled onto the plain iron bedstead and dresser and an oversized trunk, all hauled overland from Illinois after the war.

Julia spread a clean sheet over the bed's patchwork quilt, patting smooth the rustling corn-husk mattress. While Mrs. Chapman prepared for the examination, Julia took a glass bottle from her bag and went out back to the wash bench, where she mixed carbolic acid with water and scrubbed her hands. Edward had been a believer in Dr. Lister's antiseptic system; he never touched a patient without first washing his hands and his instruments in the carbolic solution.

When Julia returned, Mrs. Chapman was lying on the bed in her chemise. With her stethoscope, Julia listened to the quick fetal heartbeat. Pressing with her fingers, she located the baby's position. It was heavy and low in Mrs. Chapman's womb and firmly fixed, just as it should be in the ninth month.

The baby gave a hard kick. "My goodness, isn't he impatient."

"Just like my girls," Mrs. Chapman said proudly.

An internal examination showed no sign of labor. "My guess is it will be another week yet," Julia said as she put her stethoscope back in its case. "You should eat plenty of milk and eggs. And stewed fruit. It wouldn't hurt to drink beef tea twice a day, three ounces at a time, to build up your strength."

"Pshaw, Mrs. Metcalf," Mrs. Chapman said, struggling to her feet. "I'm as healthy as a herd of cattle."

She gasped suddenly and fell back on the bed, looking pale and surprised. Julia grabbed for her, her heart thudding with alarm.

"It's nothing," Mrs. Chapman said, pushing Julia's hands away. "A little light-headed, that's all."

"No pains?"

"Pains! Why, I never have pains. My girls were born in an eye's blink. They didn't give me time to have pains." She was on her feet again, getting into her clothes. "Now, don't you worry. I'll be just fine."

Julia fastened the straps on her medical bag and followed Mrs. Chapman through the partition to the front of the cabin. If only she had Edward's authority, she thought. When Edward gave orders, patients obeyed.

"I think Mr. Chapman should stay close to home until the baby comes."

Mrs. Chapman's mouth fell into an impatient line. "I don't want Otis underfoot all day. And if that poor man starts thinking something's amiss, he'll be worrying all the more."

Julia knew that additional advice would get her nowhere. She put on her hat and took up her bag and gloves. "When you feel the first pain, I want you to send word to my place, anytime, day or night. If I'm not at home, Mossy will know where to fetch me." She gave Mrs. Chapman's arm a squeeze. "If this baby comes as fast as your little girls, I may miss out on it altogether."

Mrs. Chapman tied on her apron, her dimples dancing. "Why, I wouldn't have you miss it for the world, Mrs. Metcalf. Not at all."

CHAPTER

5

THE BUGGY BOUNCED along the trail back to town, climbing and dipping, skirting outcroppings of rocks and stands of trees. The hills and ravines were coming alive with green grass and silvery new leaves. The warm breeze filled Julia's nose with the earthy smell of spring. High in the clean blue sky, the sun coaxed the season along, and clouds billowed soft and white.

Julia saw babies in the spring clouds, fat milk-fed babies with sweet faces and dimpled legs, born in the new season, like lambs. Julia studied the clouds, trying to make out the Chapman baby, and felt a bit silly for her fancy.

Images of babies brought back Mrs. Chapman's admonition: "You'd better start thinking about a new husband for yourself, a younger man who can give you babies."

When Mrs. Chapman said those words, Julia had had a thought that was utterly preposterous, that made her question her own good sense.

Now out in the fresh air, with God's springtime masterpiece unfolding before her eyes, she was thinking clearly again. She reminded herself that Gib was just passing through town, and fortunately so. A handsome, tender-eyed man with a footloose nature and a dubious past could get a lady into a good deal of trouble.

The sudden whir of a sage grouse made Biscuit shy. The buggy lurched, and Julia pulled on the reins, calling out soothing words. When Biscuit regained her pace, Julia forgot the clouds and Gib and focused her attention on driving.

In town, traffic on Main Street was heavy. Julia maneuvered through the congestion of freight wagons and buckboards to Lee Tabor's livery. As she drove into the yard, a team pulling an army wagon splashed by, leaving her splattered with mud.

"Damnation!" She brought Biscuit to a halt, set the brake, and reached into her carpetbag for a handkerchief.

"Ma'am?" One of Lee's young muckers was grinning up at her, no doubt having enjoyed hearing her swear.

"Tell Mr. Tabor I want to see him," Julia said, wiping mud from her cheek.

"Yes'm."

Lee came out, his somber face made more so by his drooping yellow mustache. "Morning, Julia."

"A good morning to you, Lee." Julia had always liked Lee Tabor, though she felt sorry for him, being Harriet's son. "Mossy noticed a crack in the right shaft. I thought I'd leave the buggy with you while I did my errands."

Lee ran a hand down the mud-spattered wood. "It won't take an hour."

"That will be fine."

Julia gathered up her carpetbag, but before she could climb down, Lee was beside her, taking the reins. "I'll drive you where you're going. No need for you to walk through all this mud, carrying your things."

"Why, thank you. That's very kind."

He kicked off the brake and slapped the reins. "Where to?"

"The *Sentinel* office, if you please."

Lee drove in silence. He'd never been one for talking. Julia thought his steady, quiet nature implied a certain depth of character. It seemed a shame that such a good man had ended up pinned beneath Harriet Tabor's thumb.

"How is your mother, Lee?"

He nodded his sweat-stained tan Stetson. "Fine as can be, thank you." He glanced at her. "Gib behaving himself?"

"Oh, yes. He's a wonder. I don't think there's anything he's not capable of doing."

A little smile tugged at the corner of Lee's mustache. "Ma sure gave me an earful about him doing your cleaning."

Julia winced. It was embarrassing to think of the things Harriet Tabor was saying. "It's only cleaning."

"That's what I told Ma."

Julia appreciated Lee's sympathetic tone. "To tell the truth, I feel I'm taking advantage of Mr. Booth."

Lee looked so surprised that Julia felt obliged to elaborate. "The man is working like a drudge for no pay other than a few hot meals. He probably offered to help me just to be polite, and now he has no choice but to see it through."

Lee pulled up in front of the *Sentinel* office. From his expression, he seemed to be trying hard not to grin. "Gib don't do anything he hasn't a mind to."

"He hasn't complained to you, then?"

"About you working him too hard? Nah." Lee jumped down and came around to help her out of the buggy. "I think he likes it."

"Well, that's a relief." Julia hopped onto the boardwalk and wiped at the spots of mud on her skirt.

"He can be a devil, though, so keep your eyes open."

Julia stiffened at this new warning. "He has been a perfect gentleman."

Lee's grin broke through. "He can be that, too. See you later, then." He touched his hat brim and climbed back into the buggy.

Julia watched him drive off, feeling a bit unsettled. It was one thing for Harriet and Harlan and even Dottie to raise the alarm, but Lee Tabor was Gib's friend. Now even he seemed to imply that Gib was not to be entirely trusted.

Well, she couldn't say she hadn't been amply warned, Julia thought as she opened the *Sentinel*'s glass-paned front door.

The newspaper office smelled of grease and pipe tobacco. Newsprint and bundled papers were stacked on the floor, and front pages from past issues of the *Sentinel* hung in neat frames on the walls. Behind the counter, Walt Stringer, the ink-smudged editor and publisher, was tinkering with the huge black press, a meerschaum clamped between his teeth. When he saw Julia, he wiped his hands on his leather apron and came over to the counter.

"Morning, Julia." He took the meerschaum from his mouth and placed it on a pipe rack. "I see you're early, as usual."

"I try to be." Julia took her ventilation article from her carpetbag and handed it over.

Walt skimmed the first page, his inky fingers leaving prints on the white paper. "Fine and dandy," he said, turning to the next page.

Julia waited. She felt an unspoken kinship with Walt, since they'd both lost their spouses during the past year. The ordeal had taken its toll on Walt, who looked gray and lined beyond his years.

"Did I get any responses to my advertisement?" Julia asked.

"I believe one came yesterday." Walt went to a row of pigeonholes and pulled out a letter.

Julia took it eagerly. She'd placed an advertisement in the *Sentinel* for a live-in housemaid after Mary Hurley left for Butte. The responses so far had proved disappointing. One woman had three children; the second, a young girl, was apparently running away from home; and the third was a lady of low character who had worked in a parlor house in Three Rivers.

Julia tore open the letter and scanned it. "Gracious. It's from a man."

Walt leaned over the counter. "Is that so?"

"Oh, gracious!" Julia crumpled the paper, her face afire. Her heart started beating in double time.

"What is it?"

"Rudeness, that's all. A man amusing himself by writing rude letters."

Walt frowned. "Give it here. I'll turn it over to the marshal."

"He didn't sign his name." Julia stuffed the letter into her bag. The last thing she wanted was to have Walt Stringer and Marshal McQuigg reading a letter to her in which "an ardent gentleman" made indecent proposals to "the lady of the house."

Walt scratched his graying head. "This has never happened before."

"I want to discontinue the advertisement," Julia said. She would rather get along without a housemaid than be obliged to read another such letter. Come to think of it, she probably didn't need a maid at all. Once the new doctor arrived, she would have plenty of time to do her own housework.

"I'm awfully sorry about this, Julia."

"You mustn't be sorry, Mr. Stringer. It's not your fault. I'll see you in a few days when I deliver my article on proper lighting."

Back on the sidewalk, Julia paused to recover herself. As she looked around, she noticed an abundance of loungers on the street—muddy-booted, coarse-looking men, who all seemed to be staring at her. Then she realized that it was she who was staring at them, wondering if the "ardent gentleman" might be among them.

You're being ridiculous, she told herself. She was taking seriously something meant as a joke.

She headed down the sidewalk to the pharmacy. As she entered the shop, a little bell rang over the door. Mr. Redfern, the pharmacist, was leaning on the mahogany counter conversing with a red-faced young cowboy, whose hushed tones made Julia suspect that he was discussing a male complaint, most likely something unmentionable he'd contracted during a night of revelry.

Julia nodded to the ladies being waited on by Mr. Redfern's clerks, then occupied herself at a glass showcase that held perfume bottles.

When the cowboy left, Mr. Redfern greeted her. "What can I do for you today, Mrs. Metcalf?" He was a short, pudgy man with a neatly trimmed beard and hair so black Julia figured it was dyed.

"Good afternoon, Mr. Redfern. I have my list. I'll return for the order later in the day."

Mr. Redfern took the list and fumbled for his spectacles. "What have we here? Stomach bitters, anti-pain plaster, salicylic acid, belladonna . . . Busy with patients these days, are you, Mrs. Metcalf?"

"Not too busy," Julia answered, eyeing the well-stocked shelves of patent medicines. "Other than my ladies and children and the occasional emergency, most people prefer to see Dr. Keene." The horse doctor from Dillon used the pharmacy's back room as an office when he visited Stiles.

"Soon you won't have to bother with any patients at all." Mr. Redfern's eyes danced. "I received a letter from Dr. Beacham."

"Dr. Beacham?" Julia had never heard of the man.

"Our new physician from Chicago. The one your brother arranged to send our way."

Julia's momentary surprise was buried by sudden hurt feelings. A man had been chosen, and no one had thought to inform her. "Why, I . . . I didn't know."

"He has a mind to open his office right in this building." Mr. Redfern rapped his knuckles on the counter. "A pharmacy and clinic operating together would be a capital idea. Financially rewarding for both of us."

Julia couldn't think of a thing to say. She stared at Mr. Redfern, feeling childishly left out.

"Dr. Beacham writes that he'll arrive within the month," Mr. Redfern went on. "He says he'll be taking your husband's office furnishings and equipment. Books, too."

Julia was stunned. "He said that?"

Mr. Redfern reached into his inside coat pocket and extracted a long white envelope. He pulled the letter from the envelope and handed it to Julia.

She stared at the neat tight script, but her eyes blurred and she couldn't read a word. She handed it back to Mr. Redfern with a trembling hand. "It's wonderful," she said faintly. "Wonderful that we'll have a new doctor."

Mr. Redfern beamed over his spectacles. "Yes, indeed."

Julia managed to say good-bye. She walked to the door in a daze.

"Your order will be ready in about an hour," Mr. Redfern called as the door bell tinkled.

Outside, Julia sat down on a bench, clutching her carpetbag. She told herself that she should be delighted by the news. She had worked for months to find a new doctor for Stiles. She'd implored Randall to look among his students for a bright young man willing to take on a practice in a remote western town. She'd even persuaded the town council to pay the new doctor a small stipend to make the position more attractive.

But the doctor she'd had in mind would have conferred with her; he would have solicited her advice, even her assistance. Instead, he'd ignored her. He planned to set up a partnership with Mr. Redfern and stock his office with Edward's equipment, his furniture—even his books!

"Soon you won't have to bother with any patients at all," Mr. Redfern had said.

And she should be glad of it, Julia told herself sternly. No more emergencies waking her up in the night, no more overnight stays at remote cabins and ranches waiting for babies to be born. No more heartbreaking vigils at the bedsides of desperately ill children or trying to comfort mothers exhausted from too many pregnancies and too little help.

Why, she could get on with a normal woman's life. Housework, entertaining, her ladies' committees.

Despite her rationalizing, Julia felt a lump rise in her throat. When she got up and started down the boardwalk, her eyes were burning with tears.

Gib had moved the living room furniture and was pulling tacks out of the carpet when the buggy drove in. He heard Julia in the hallway, a soft padding sound, as if she'd taken off her shoes. There was a little squeak and gasp, like a sob.

Gib sat back on his heels and rubbed his chin. What the hell—was she crying? He got up, wiped his hands on his trousers, and went into the hall.

The door to Doc's study was open. The study was the one room Julia had told him not to clean. "There are so many books and papers, you'd never know where to begin," she'd said.

Gib had been just as glad; he was getting fed up with cleaning.

He entered the study cautiously. An Oriental rug covered the floor, and a big desk sat by the window. Opposite the desk hung a portrait of President Lincoln and a framed diploma. There were books all over the place. The room had a smell of medicine and learning that reminded him of Doc.

The door to the adjoining surgery was open. It was a small room, sunny and starkly clean. There was a long table, lots of drawers and shelves, and a white glass-fronted cabinet filled with bottles.

Julia stood by the window in her stocking feet, her topknot askew. Her back was to him, but from her posture and her little sniffing noises, Gib figured she was crying.

He thought about leaving her alone—whatever ailed her was none of his business—but something kept him rooted to the spot.

"Ma'am?"

She turned from the window, startled. "Oh, Mr. Booth." There were smudges of dirt on her cheek and chin, and her eyes were wet. She dabbed at them with a crumpled handkerchief.

"Anything I can do?"

"No, thank you," she said. "It's nothing."

"It doesn't look like nothing to me."

Her black dress drew his eyes to her face—delicate cheekbones tinged with pink, lips a little swollen, those aquamarine eyes polished by tears. He'd always thought of women as pretty or homely or good sports whose looks didn't matter. Julia was different, but he hadn't yet figured out how.

"It's good news, really . . ." She started in again with the handkerchief. "Oh, heavens, don't mind me."

"Do you always cry at good news?" Gib asked, trying to lighten her mood.

She managed a slight, quivering smile that quickly faded. "The new doctor is coming from Chicago. Mr. Redfern received a letter from him."

Gib waited. With women it usually took awhile to get the whole story.

"He's joining forces with Mr. Redfern. They'll have a clinic right in the middle of town. A medical office and a pharmacy."

Gib thought she'd been looking forward to the arrival of a new doctor, and the idea of a clinic made sense to him. But apparently she didn't see it that way.

"Where does that leave you?" he asked.

She took a breath that trembled a little. "I don't know."

Since they seemed to be having a discussion, Gib stepped into the surgery and propped himself up against the long table.

"Of course, I'm pleased about it," she said, not looking at all pleased. "It will be wonderful to have a qualified doctor. But he . . . he wants to take all of Edward's things. Even his books."

"Now, hold on a minute." Gib wasn't following Julia's logic, but he was beginning to smell a double deal.

"Dr. Beacham is setting up his first practice," Julia said. "He needs supplies, and I want to be cooperative."

Gib opened his mouth to tell her that she was too softhearted for her own good, that she gave everyone the benefit of the doubt, which meant that anybody could come along and take advantage of her. But he decided that kind of talk might start her thinking about his motives, too.

He tried a different approach. "Your new doc is trying to get something for nothing. Let him buy his own supplies."

"But he's forgoing a lucrative city practice to come here. Once he takes over, I certainly won't be needing anything . . ." Her voice trailed off, and fresh tears welled up in her eyes.

Crying women drove Gib crazy, but that was because they were usually crying over him. Julia's tears bothered him in a different way; they made him want to punch this Dr. Beacham in the nose.

"He's not getting any of Doc's things, and that's that," Gib said. "If you don't set him straight, I will."

Julia stared at him, as if absorbing his words. Gib waited for her to tell him to mind his own business; instead, he saw the glimmer of a real smile. "You're very forceful, Mr. Booth," she said. "And very kind."

Gib shrugged off the compliment, although it pleased him. "It comes on me once in a while. And call me Gib."

"Then you must call me Julia."

"Ma'am, it would be a pleasure."

The last of her tears dissolved into a big, bright smile. It was the sort of smile that could bring out the tender side of a man, if he had one.

"May I confide in you?" she asked.

"Shoot."

"I would like to continue taking care of ladies and children and helping out in emergencies."

She wasn't telling him any secrets, Gib thought. She wouldn't have been crying about giving away Doc's things if she hadn't wanted to keep on doctoring. "Why don't you, then?"

"Oh, goodness, most people disapprove of women practitioners. My own brother is a surgeon, and even he thinks it's unnatural for a woman to practice medicine."

She watched him expectantly, as if she might set some store by his opinion. Gib put on his thoughtful face and tried to frame a response that wouldn't offend her. He agreed with her brother about lady doctors, although he wasn't about to say so to Julia—not when his aim was to stay on her good side.

"Here's the way I see it," he said at last. "Men don't care for women besting them at anything. That's why they make sure men's work is separate from women's."

Julia seemed to think that over for a minute. Then she gave him a sly smile. "Housecleaning, for example."

Gib laughed out loud. By God, she'd set him straight on that quick enough. "You've got me there."

"I'm only joking," she said. "You've been wonderful to take on all this cleaning."

There was hardly any trace of tears left; she looked downright happy. Knowing he'd cheered her up made Gib feel damned good. She made him feel some other things, too—things he knew he'd better put out of his mind.

"So, Lady Doc, how much business do you get?"

"Enough to keep me busy." She reached up with both hands to fasten a few strands of shiny brown hair back in place. Her black jacket pulled open, but not enough to show anything. "I get children with broken bones and coughs and chicken pox. All sorts of female complaints. The serious cases I send to Helena or Butte. Men won't come to me unless it's an emergency."

Gib didn't blame them. He sure would've felt strange having a lady doc snooping around him.

Suddenly he had a terrible thought. What happened when a mining stiff or a cowboy came down with a case of Old Joe? Did he come to Julia for help? The idea of her dealing with men's diseased privates so disturbed him that he forgot it real fast.

"I'm especially partial to delivering babies," Julia said. "It's such a joyous event, a miracle, really."

Gib stared at the floor. Birthing was another thing he didn't care to think about.

"How would you like apple pie for supper?" He could tell from her voice that his embarrassment amused her.

"Sounds good to me."

"Gib," she said.

"Ma'am?"

"Nothing." She smiled. "I'm just practicing."

Julia took a jug of warm water upstairs and washed the smudges of dirt from her face and hands. She changed from her muddy clothes to a dark skirt and starched white shirtwaist, then tied a black velvet ribbon at her throat so it wouldn't look as if she'd forgone mourning.

The truth was, she didn't feel mournful. Not in the least. The mirror told her she didn't look mournful, either. Her eyes had a startling shine to them, and her mouth seemed to curve upward of its own accord.

Julia glanced down at the portrait that rested on the white marble dresser top, and it dawned on her that Gib was a lot like Mama. They had the same cheerful nature, the easy laugh, the generous heart—even the hint of scandal in their past.

"Mama," Julia said. "You'd love him. He's the most attractive man you could imagine."

It wasn't just his looks that were appealing; it was the way he lifted her spirits, made things seem not quite so bad. Gib saw through what she said to what she felt, and he was willing to take her side. She thought of what he'd said of the new doctor—"Let him get his own supplies"—as if she was free to do whatever she might well please.

After she pinned up her hair, Julia opened the window and stepped over the sill onto the narrow balcony. She scuffed at dried leaves and dirt on the floorboards. The balcony could use a good sweeping after a winter of neglect, she thought, and a coat of paint, too.

Resting her arms on the railing, she scanned the bright horizon. Down the road, Main Street's hodgepodge of false fronts rose above roofs both peaked and flat. In the distance, wagon traffic moved sedately; plumes of woodsmoke drifted lazily out of chimneys. Up the hill to the east, the elegant shingled gables of the Williver house looked down on the sprawling town with haughty pride. Only the thump of the stamp mill disturbed the late afternoon calm.

Things had certainly changed since Edward brought her west from Chicago, Julia thought. Ten years ago Stiles had been a booming mining camp, shocking to a city girl for its mud and chaos and outright sin. Disreputable characters had drifted around town, and road agents had lurked in the hills. People had told stories about Gib Booth, the trouble he'd caused, his escapades with women, how he'd shot a man in '72 and been run out of town.

The stories had made Julia shiver. An outlaw, she'd

thought, a wild young man. She hadn't been curious, but disapproving and a little frightened.

Now she wasn't frightened in the least, and she was more than just curious. She was hungry for every tidbit she might learn about Gib Booth and his past.

"Gib, I think Edward would have wanted you to have his gold watch."

Gib nearly choked on a mouthful of supper. "Ma'am?"

"Yes, I think he would." Julia looked pretty in a high-necked, spanking white shirtwaist with pleats that puffed out around her bosom, making it look bigger than it was. "Don't you agree, Mossy?"

Mossy's heavy brows went up and down a couple of times as he considered Julia's question. "Yes'm, I'd say so."

Gib put down his fork. "I don't think it's such a good idea."

"Why do you say that?" There was a faint smile on Julia's lips.

Gib squirmed in his chair. He remembered trying to old-soldier Doc at sick call, complaining of some made-up ailment so he could get light duty. Doc used to finger that shiny gold watch, snapping the case open and shut as he eyed Gib. "Nothing ails you but a case of lazies, Private," he'd say before sending Gib back to his company.

"I'm not worthy of it, that's why. You keep it, ma'am. Someday you'll have a son and you can give it to him."

Julia lowered her eyes. "It's high time I cleaned out Edward's room. I'll donate some of his things to the church fair, but first I want you both to take whatever you like."

Gib returned to his supper. Scalloped potatoes and ham was one of his favorites, but he didn't appreciate it as much as he had a few minutes ago. Julia wanting to give him that watch didn't sit well.

"Not many of Edward's clothes would fit either of you, I'm afraid," Julia said. "You're not tall enough, Mossy, and Gib, you're too big."

Gib looked up from his plate. "No offense, ma'am, but

Mossy and I would look pretty silly going around in Doc's black suits and tall hats."

Julia smiled. "Perhaps you're right."

Later when he and Mossy were scrubbing the living room walls, Mossy said, "She's right about that old stem-winder, Gib. Doc would want you to have it."

"Hell, Moss, Doc was down on me for years."

"It ain't so."

Gib cursed the water than ran down the brush handle and up his arm. For the first time since arriving in Stiles, he wondered if he'd made a mistake coming back. He was getting damned sick of being a housemaid, and he was having some bothersome feelings. Remembering Doc wasn't all that pleasant, especially when he was thinking about Doc's wife in ways he shouldn't.

"He ran me out of town."

"He run you out because if you'd stuck around there'da been a trial and maybe a hanging," Mossy said. "Doc made that deal for your own good."

Gib answered with a cold scowl. He didn't care to think about all the ways he'd disappointed Doc.

"Excuse me, gentlemen."

Gib jumped at the sound of Julia's voice.

"Gib, I wonder if you would ride into town while it's still light and pick up my order at the pharmacy. When you get to a stopping place, that is."

He could see from the curious expression on her face that she'd overheard his exchange with Mossy. Every goddamn word. He tossed down the scrub brush and wiped his wet hands on his pants. "I'm at a stopping place right now."

"Mr. Redfern will put it on my account."

"Yes, ma'am." Gib rolled down his sleeves and took off for the kitchen, anxious to be gone.

In the shed he pulled on his jacket and muddy boots and tugged his hat low over his eyes. As he stepped out into the early evening light, he told himself he'd better watch what he said around Julia. He sure as hell didn't want her thinking there was more to him than met the eye.

* * *

A few moments later Gib led Lucky out of the barn and mounted up. Julia watched from the kitchen window. When he rode off, she let the curtain drop. She removed her apron and went down the hall to the living room, her heels clicking on the bare wooden floor.

"I'm not worthy of it," he'd said at dinner. And then to Mossy, "Doc was down on me for years."

Gib projected a good deal of confidence, Julia thought, but she was beginning to doubt it ran very deep.

She looked into the living room. "Mossy."

He was scrubbing the wall without much enthusiasm. His pallor made him look sad and exhausted. "Ma'am?"

"Come have some coffee. I want to ask you a few things."

CHAPTER

6

IN THE KITCHEN, Mossy sank heavily into a chair. Two of his suspender buttons had popped off, leaving his rumpled trousers hanging below his belly.

"If you give me those trousers, I'll sew on the buttons," Julia said, filling a white enamel mug with coffee.

Gratitude showed in his red-rimmed eyes. "I'd sure appreciate it."

Julia sat down and ran her fingers over the creases in the fresh white tablecloth. "Mossy, I'd like to know more about Gib. Would you tell me about him?"

Mossy rubbed his wrinkled jowls. "Why, I thought you knew all about him. The shooting, the women—beg your pardon, ma'am—everything else. Everyone around here's heard about Gib Booth."

"Ladies never hear everything."

He looked embarrassed. "I don't know, Mrs. Metcalf. I ain't comfortable discussing some things with ladies."

"Could you just tell me about the man he shot?"

"That was Bob Hockett."

Julia leaned forward, encouraging him. "Bob Hockett."

"Yes, ma'am. Bob was a rough character. Ran with a rough gang. They stirred up a lot of trouble in the old days. Even killed some folks. There was talk they was road agents, but it never was proved."

Mossy looked into the distance. "I'll have to start back some, back before the shooting."

"Take it back as far as you like." Julia pinched a few wilted blossoms from the vase of wildflowers. The kitchen was warm and cozy and fragrant with the smell of coffee. Mossy settled back in his chair, seeming to relax.

"Gib was a hell-raiser, that was sure. He'd go down by Cottonwood Creek and practice his fast draw with that old double-action Army .44 he favored. He'd whip it out and go into a crouch fast as a finger-snap—it sure was something to see. Pinecones, bottles, tin cans, wood chips—all jumping to beat the band."

Julia stopped her flower arranging and listened attentively.

"He was a good-looking young pup. Knew it, too, and he liked to show it. Why, he always practiced his fast draw with his shirt off."

"Did he?" The unbidden image of Gib without a shirt jumped into her mind.

"Yep. He'd wear his pants low and his gun belt strapped on, and those dusty old boots of his, spurs with rowels the size of silver dollars. He was on the skinny side, but built just fine, burned brown as a nut, with that big shock of hair on his head. And—would you believe it, ma'am?—the young ladies used to flock down there to the cottonwood grove just to watch him."

"Goodness." He must have looked wonderful, Julia thought, lean and young and handsome.

"Till their mamas and daddies found out, that is. Then there was hell to pay—'scuse me, ma'am." Mossy chuckled. "Nah, everybody stopped by now and then to have a look."

"I can't imagine Edward approving," Julia said.

"You're right about that. Doc didn't want nothing to do with guns. Hated them. That's because he saw the harm they caused. I'd say Doc turned into what you'd call a pacifist, a man that don't believe in war and killing and shooting."

Mossy stopped talking and looked mournful as he always did when he thought of Edward or the war. Julia took a moment to imagine Gib among the cottonwoods, dusty and sun-browned and naked to the waist. Suddenly Bee landed in her lap, bringing her back to the present.

"How did Gib come to shoot Bob Hockett?"

"Well, it was like this," Mossy said. "It was election day, '72, and everybody was out and about. In those days I was working for Dellwood Petty at the Bon Ton, sweeping and swamping out the barroom, carrying out empty bottles, cleaning the spittoons.

"The saloon was closed that day, but I was working nevertheless. I'd just stepped out onto the sidewalk with my broom, and I see Bob Hockett tying his horse to the hitching rail in front of the Regal. Bob was a mean son of a gun. Whipped a boy in the face with his quirt once, and done worse to a few ladies, I heard. He never bothered me, though I knew enough to stay out of his way.

"Anyway, there was Bob Hockett tying up at the Regal when along comes Skinner Sam, colored feller that drove a team of mules for Hidy Jones—don't suppose you remember Hidy, ma'am."

Julia shook her head.

"So next thing I know, there's Bob going up to old Sam, saying, 'You going to vote, colored boy?' And here's Sam, a man about forty years old, saying, 'Yassa.' Sam knew to be polite, especially to a sesech like Bob Hockett. And Bob says, 'Votin' for the party of Lincoln, is you, colored boy?' And old Sam says, 'Yassa.'"

Mossy paused and scowled at his coffee mug. "Then I couldn't believe my eyes, ma'am, but Bob says, 'No you ain't. You ain't votin' for nobody.' And he pulls out his gun and shoots old Sam right between the eyes."

Julia's hand flew to her mouth.

"Well, I'm standing there, holding my broom, staring at

old Sam laying in the dust, dead as can be, while Bob holsters his gun. He's looking pleased with himself, as if he done everybody a favor. Then I hear this yell that just about curdles my blood—a Reb yell like from the war—and I see Gib flying down the boardwalk, tearing his clothes off."

"His clothes? Why on earth—"

"Yes, ma'am. His hat went in one direction and his coat in another—this is November and danged cold—and then, would you believe it, he pulls his shirt off. He's got no undershirt on, neither. It's as if he can't do his quick draw with his clothes on. He jumps into the street right in front of Bob, half naked now, and gets into position and says, 'Draw, you god'"—Mossy hesitated—"'blasted sesech ba . . .' You get the idea, ma'am. Bob looks at Gib with that scornful look Bob had and says, 'It's about time somebody shot you, too, you pissant little cock—' 'Scuse me, ma'am, but I'll leave off the rest."

Mossy squirmed a little and cleared his throat. "Well, I see Bob reach for his holster and then there's a flash of steel and Gib's in his crouch, his thumb on the hammer, blasting away, every shot right to the heart. Old Bob was dead before he even started to fall."

"Oh!" Julia pressed her hand to her mouth.

Mossy shook his head. "I don't favor guns myself, ma'am. The war wasn't easy for me, and I got a little upset there, seeing Bob shoot Sam and then Gib shoot Bob right before my eyes. Brought back a lot of bad thoughts."

He worked his mouth a little, remembering. "When I come to, there was a crowd of folks gathered, yelling and making a commotion, and Lee Tabor was in a fight with somebody—Lee was Gib's friend, stuck together like glue. And would you know? Gib's standing there with his old Army Colt still in his hand, his head down, crying. Couldn't believe it. Never saw him cry through the whole war, and there he is shivering in the cold without his shirt on, holding his gun, crying like a little kid."

Julia stared at Mossy, seeing the scene as clearly as if she'd been there herself. "Why did he cry?"

"I don't know for sure. Maybe he was scared of what

would happen to him, or maybe he was sorry for what he done. Or maybe it had to do with old Skinner Sam. You know, Sam had been a slave once, and Gib had this idea that he personally helped free the slaves. That's what carried him through the war. Of course, he was just a boy, fifteen or so, when it all ended, and maybe a kid can fool himself into thinking all that waste and death is worthwhile for something.''

"What a terrible thing!"

Mossy shrugged. "I think for Gib, seeing a sesech like Bob shoot old Sam just brought back the war.''

Julia stroked Bee. She felt shaken by Mossy's story, yet impatient to hear more. "What did Edward do?"

Mossy cleared his throat to continue. "In those days Doc's office was next to the *Sentinel* building. By the time he got there to check on the bodies, the marshal'd taken Gib away. Locked him up. Had to lock up Lee Tabor, too, cool him down—till his ma marched into the marshal's office and raised holy hell.''

"How long did they hold Gib?"

"I'm getting to that. After the marshal took him away, the crowd kind of broke up. I see Gib's clothes blowing around in the street, so I gather them up and go down to the jail. Marshal lets me in to see him, and there he is, wrapped up in a blanket. He wasn't crying, but he looked like a scared old pup, shivering there in his cell. I give him his things and he says, 'It ain't worth it, Mossy.' And then he says, 'Nothing's worth it, d'you know that? It ain't even worth trying.' And I didn't know what he meant, but I says, 'Now, Gib, that's not so. Some things are worth something and some things ain't,' and he says, 'Nope, none of it matters when you come right down to it.' "

Julia tried to imagine what Gib had meant, but she couldn't even guess.

"Doc shows up, looking pretty grim. He asks me to leave, says he wants to speak to Gib alone. So I says so long, and you know, I never saw Gib again. Not till he showed up here. Seems Doc worked out a deal with the marshal to let Gib go if he left town right that night. Never said good-bye to a soul, not even to Lee Tabor. Lee was like to go through the roof—he looked up to Gib in a big way. But that's another story."

Julia's fingers had stilled on Bee's silky fur. She felt lost in the story, as if she'd gone back in time.

"I think I'll just pour myself another cup of coffee, ma'am, and head on out to the barn."

Julia looked up. "Of course, Mossy."

After he was gone, Julia continued to sit there thinking of Gib, wondering what lay beneath all that clever banter and easy charm.

Gib stepped onto the porch of Charlie Soon's general store and brushed his fingers against the wind chimes, making them tinkle. He stuck his head inside the weathered door hinged with strips of cowhide.

"Hey, Charlie, you in there?"

The click-clack of the abacus stopped, followed by an exclamation of surprise. "Aiyah. Boss come back." It was Charlie's rapid-fire voice. "I see you come back."

Gib ambled inside, blinking in the dim light. The store was crowded with baskets and barrels and great earthenware jars. Behind the counter where Charlie sat, crude wooden shelves sagged under the burden of tins and bottles and gaudily wrapped packets.

"Long time no see, Charlie." Nothing had changed, not even the smell. Gib would have known Charlie Soon's place just by breathing in that noseful of herbs and incense and Oriental mystery.

"Long time, so." Charlie hurried out from behind the counter, his loose blue trousers and tunic flapping. He wore a square little cap and heelless slippers. The glossy pigtail was still black, the bullet eyes keen, his gold teeth gleaming. He looked as if he hadn't aged a day.

"Little boss big boss now," Charlie said, looking Gib over. "Rich man."

"Rich, hell," Gib said. "You're the rich one."

Charlie was a foreman of some sort, holding money for local Chinese woodcutters and miners. Gib had also heard that owners of China Alley noodle shops and laundries paid Charlie for the privilege of staying in business. No doubt he took a cut from the brothels and gambling joints, too.

"Rich, so." Charlie laughed gleefully. "Cholly never tell. No, sir. You wait one minute, we talk." He scurried behind the counter and bent once more over his ledger and abacus, which started clicking away.

Gib had forgotten how hard it was to get anywhere with Charlie. Just like with women, you had to let him talk in riddles for a while; then if you didn't act too curious or impatient, you usually got the whole story.

Gib lifted a tin cover and stared into a crock of what appeared to be stewed chicken claws. He replaced the cover, then removed his Stetson and tried on a straw coolie hat. "Hey, Charlie. Doc's wife wants some ginger water and a couple bottles of rice wine."

Charlie looked up from his calculations and beamed. "Doctor lady know Chinese medicine. Ginger water good for wind." He went back to his clickety-clack.

Gib gave the hat a spin and thought about last night. When he delivered Julia's package from the pharmacy, he'd told her he was going down to China Alley this morning before he showed up for maid duty. She asked him to pick up a few things at Charlie's. Then she'd asked him to come in for a piece of apple pie. He'd made up some excuse and headed back to the Bon Ton.

It was crazy for a man to worry that a good-looking woman might like him too much, Gib thought, especially when she was the woman whose money he was after, but it worried him a good deal. For his plan to work, Julia had to trust him, which meant she had to get to know him. But he didn't want her to know him too well. And he sure as hell didn't want to get mixed up with her in a way that would make him sorry later.

He'd have to walk a damn fine line, that was sure—make her like him, but not enough to hurt her feelings when he left.

In the distance Gib heard loud male voices and the clatter of mah-jongg tiles. He spun the coolie hat and stared at long colorful scrolls of calligraphy hanging on the wall. Charlie always made him wait. When he and Lee used to come around in the old days, Charlie would pretend they weren't there. When he finally acknowledged them, he'd say, "Ghosts. White ghosts," which was what he called Caucasians.

"Come, boss, have tea." Charlie slammed the ledger closed. He yelled something in Chinese, and a voice answered from the back room. "Girl make tea," Charlie said. "Talk business. Talk snakes."

"Snakes? Don't tell me you heard about the snakes." Charlie seemed to know everything before it happened.

"Sure, I hear." Charlie headed to the back of the shop, his slippers slapping.

Gib took off the coolie hat and followed. In the back room, hangings of fringed satin decorated the rough walls, along with a couple of framed portraits. The furnishings were sparse and plain. A wooden table was set with two cane mats and teacups painted with little red flowers. It looked to Gib as if he'd been expected.

Charlie motioned him to sit. "Cholly honored big boss come do business."

"Cut out the big boss talk," Gib said. Charlie was as bad as Dellwood, making fun of him.

A girl with straight-cut bangs put down a pot of tea and a plate of little cakes.

"How much you want, snakes?" Charlie asked.

"I don't want anything. Just get rid of the damned things."

The bullet eyes narrowed, disbelieving. "How much you want, boss? How many dollar?"

"I'm giving them to you, for God's sake." Charlie liked to negotiate. An outright gift was disappointing.

Charlie looked thoughtful for a while. "Old Brown shoot. Go get snake—bang! Cholly dead."

"Rawlie won't shoot. I guarantee it."

"Snakes make Cholly rich. What you want, boss?"

Charlie couldn't seem to get it through his thick Celestial skull that Gib didn't want anything. Gib had never been fussy about how he made money, but selling snakes out of a mine didn't seem right.

"Nothing, Charlie. No money."

Charlie's gold teeth flashed. "My cousin San Francisco, that one big boss. He know you boss get very big gold."

There was a moment of silence while the girl poured fragrant tea. Gib stared at the pale brew and told himself he shouldn't be surprised that Charlie knew everything. He had a tribe of Celestial cousins in San Francisco, each one some sort of head man.

When the girl went away, Gib leaned his arms on the table. "Look, Charlie, forget about that money, hear?" The last thing he wanted was Julia getting wind of it and putting two and two together.

Charlie grinned. "I do boss big favor one day."

"Do me big favor now and get those snakes out of the mine. And forget about whatever you heard from San Francisco."

Charlie picked up his thimble-sized cup. "Good time get snakes. Snakes cold. Not move." He snapped his fingers. "Easy."

Gib agreed. Spring was a good time to go after rattlers, though it was already a little late. "When'll you go, Charlie?"

"Three day. Friday."

"I'll meet you there," Gib said. "I don't want Rawlie to get excited and shoot your whole gang."

They sipped their tea. The tiny cakes were filled with nuts and dusted with sugar. They sure were tasty, Gib thought, and took another.

"Doctor wife," Charlie said, his eyes disappearing into smiling slits. "You like?"

With Mossy's help, Gib finished cleaning Doc's bedroom, the upstairs hall, and the living room. It took them all afternoon to wash the windows, mop the floors, and polish the furniture. After they'd moved things back in place, Mossy went out to the barn to rest. Gib brought the small summer rugs down from the storeroom to lay in the living room, and Julia hung some filmy white curtains. From Doc's study she brought an oil painting of rocks and water. The Isle of Capri, she said, someplace in Italy where Doc had traveled before the war.

Gib held the picture against the wall until she settled on the spot where she wanted it. He hammered the nail and hung it up.

"It's perfect there," she said.

Gib stepped back to admire the blues and pinks in the sky, the curls of white on the waves. The colorful painting and the white curtains sure cheered things up.

"Everything looks beautiful," Julia said gazing around. She wore a big apron over her shirtwaist and skirt. She'd had two patients in the surgery while he'd been working, a screaming child who'd fallen and bitten her tongue and a boy who'd cut his foot. Gib had been alarmed at all the racket and had gone in to see if she needed help. She didn't. It was hard to get used to the idea of a lady like her dealing with things that were best left to men.

"If it's not too chilly, we'll have coffee out on the porch after supper," Julia said. "Edward and I always did that in good weather. Unless you have other plans."

"Nope, no plans."

Gib was glad to see no trace of yesterday's curiosity. The last thing he wanted was Julia digging into him, trying to figure out what made him tick.

"Supper will be ready as soon as you wash up and call Mossy."

Gib went out back to the wash bench. Despite the cool air, he felt hot and sticky from working. Hungry, too. He'd smelled rice pudding baking and yeast rolls and some sort of hot stew. He peeled off his shirt and stuck his head under the pump. The cold water and air felt good on his sweaty body.

"Hey, Mossy," he called out. "Rise and shine. It's time for supper."

Julia heard him from the kitchen. She filled the china tureen with a thick soup of beans and potatoes and lean chunks of bacon, then went to the window. She watched Gib soap the back of his neck, watched the light gleam on his wet, work-sculpted arms. Water ran down his chest and dampened his trousers.

She tried to envision the hotheaded youth practicing his fast draw by Cottonwood Creek, but she saw only the man, his body filled out with muscle, his manner easy and slow.

Gib picked up his shirt and started to wipe himself dry. Julia realized she'd forgotten to give him a towel. She went out to the shed door and called to him. "I'll get you a towel."

He looked up. "I'd be obliged."

She hurried upstairs to the linen chest, telling herself she was foolish to spy on him like a schoolgirl and even more foolish to feel so stimulated by the sight of a man's bare torso.

With towel in hand, she went into Edward's room. She took a white shirt from the drawer and closed it with her hip. It was a simple task, fetching a towel and a clean shirt for a man, but doing it for Gib took on an intimate aspect that left her a little breathless.

She went back downstairs and into the yard, where the ground was soft but no longer muddy. Patches of grass near the barn were turning green. Gib waited, shivering in the late afternoon chill.

"It sure isn't summer yet," he said, taking the towel from her.

Julia glanced at his thick-veined arms, the hard curve of his shoulder. "You should have washed indoors. There's plenty of hot water."

"Too much hot water and sweet soap makes a man go soft. I'll be roughing it up at the Rattling Rock." With the towel, he rubbed his wet hair. Tight muscles bulged beneath smooth dark skin. Julia's gaze slid down the front of him, over the broad mass of crisp curls, the solid rib cage, the little fuse of hair that disappeared into damp, clinging trousers. She looked at the bulky outline, then quickly away, shocked at her explicit thoughts.

"Rawlie Brown's mine?" she asked.

"Yup," Gib said from under the towel. "I'm throwing in with him."

Julia's heart went still. "You mean you're staying in Stiles?"

"That's the plan." Gib pulled the towel off his head, leaving his hair standing on end.

Julia stared at his bronzed cheeks, the lively gray eyes, the faint indentation in his chin. He smiled at her. "Wish me luck."

She managed to return the smile. "Good luck." She tore her eyes away from him and busied herself shaking out the shirt and holding it up for inspection. "I brought you one of Edward's shirts. It might be small."

"I'll try it." He tossed the towel over the pump handle. "Sure is fancy."

It was a dress shirt with pleats down the front. Gib pulled it on over his head. The fabric had to work to cover his wide shoulders and muscular arms, and his wrists stuck out of too-short sleeves. He rolled back the cuffs. "What would Doc think of this?" he said. "Me dressing up in his best shirt."

Julia wondered the same thing. She reached out and touched the shirtfront, smoothing the pleats on Gib's chest. "He wore it last August when he addressed the Medical Association in Helena."

She recalled the occasion, how fine Edward had looked in his black tailcoat with silk lapels. She'd helped him prepare his paper on diphtheria epidemic treatment; it had been wonderfully well received.

Suddenly Julia noticed Gib watching her, amusement in his eyes, and she realized what she was doing. She snatched her hand away, as if he were on fire. "Oh, goodness, forgive me."

He grinned. "It must be mighty strange seeing another man wearing Doc's shirt."

"Yes, it is. I mean . . . Oh, heavens!" She was lovely in her embarrassment, her cheeks bright, her eyes wide with dismay. Gib noticed a pin sliding out of her shiny brown topknot. He rescued it and, taking her hand, pressed it into her palm. She stared at him and swallowed, a gentle bob of her throat.

"Supper," she said softly. "It's ready anytime you are."

She pulled her hand away and hurried back to the house, slipping a little in her haste. Gib ran his fingers through his wet hair and watched her go. It didn't surprise him, her touching him like that or letting him hold her hand, either. He'd heard that widows went a little crazy, missing what a man could give them.

Gib started to wonder how Julia might have liked that part of marriage. Then he thought of the separate bedrooms. Not much, he decided.

He unfastened his trousers and tucked in Doc's shirt, turning his back to the house in case she was watching.

At supper Gib talked about the Rattling Rock mine and how Charlie Soon was going to clear the rattlesnakes out of the shaft so he could get it back into operation.

Julia listened, thinking how clever he was to have come up with the scheme. Everyone seemed to benefit—Charlie got his snake oil, Gib got his mine, and Rawlie got some company. "It will be good for Rawlie to have you there," she said. "He's too old to be on his own."

"Sarabeth goes up now and then," Gib said. "Keeps an eye on him."

Julia thought about Gib living at the Bon Ton and Sarabeth working there as a hurdy girl. The possibility that he might be taking advantage of his proximity to ladies of loose character made her feel vaguely unsettled.

"So, Gib, you got enough of a grubstake?" Mossy asked as Julia ladled more soup into his bowl.

Gib didn't answer right away. In the brief silence, a thought came to Julia's mind that made her pause in mid-serving and look at him.

"Sure I do, Moss," Gib said. "Don't need much, not right off." He reached for another yeast roll. "Rawlie and Digger had quite an operation up there. It'll take me a while to get it back to where it was."

"Suppose so," said Mossy.

"This sure is good soup, ma'am." Gib smiled at Julia.

"I'm glad you like it," she replied.

She finished filling Mossy's bowl and returned to her own meal. Gib's response to Mossy's question hadn't been much of an answer. It made her wonder how much of a grubstake he really had. He would need to invest thousands of dollars to make a success of the Rattling Rock.

Julia chewed a chunk of potato and remembered Harlan's warning: "He intends to win your trust, then strip you of your money and your reputation." She glanced across the table at Gib, who was busy buttering another roll.

Ridiculous, she thought. He had refused to take a cent for doing her spring cleaning; as a matter of fact, he'd seemed more than a little offended by her offer to pay him.

"I'll be going, ma'am," Mossy said. "Thanks for supper."

He wiped his mouth on his napkin and scraped back his chair, reclaiming Julia from her thoughts. "I'll have coffee ready in a few minutes, Mossy," she said. "And there's rice pudding."

"Thanks anyway. I'm heading to town."

Julia looked at him in surprise. Mossy never went into town unless he was doing an errand for her. Now she noticed that he was wearing a string tie with his best shirt, and his thinning hair was slicked back with grease. He had on his churchgoing trousers, too. She was curious about his evening plans, but didn't think it her place to ask.

"I sewed on your suspender buttons. I left the trousers on your shelf in the shed."

"Thank you for that, ma'am." Mossy picked up the coat draped on the back of his chair. "Good night, then. See you later, Gib."

When the door closed, Julia turned to Gib. "What in heaven's name is he up to?"

"I talked him into a game of billiards at the Bon Ton the other day. He enjoyed himself so much, he decided to go back for more."

It was hard for Julia to think of Mossy being sociable. He usually spent his evenings out in his room, drinking. "You don't think the saloon crowd might get him into trouble?"

"Mossy's not a fighter," Gib said. "Better he drinks with a crowd than by himself."

Julia got up from the table and put on her apron. "I guess you're right."

Gib insisted on helping her clean up, so while Julia washed the dishes, he put the rolls in the bread drawer and took the milk and butter out to the icebox. He wiped the plates dry and put them away, all the while keeping up a stream of stories about Rawlie Brown's obsession with claim-jumpers. He was so entertaining that Julia forgot her embarrassment outside by the pump and her uneasiness about his finances.

While they waited for the coffee to boil, Gib said, "You know what I'd like?"

She smiled at him. "Rice pudding?"

"I'd like to hear you play the piano."

"Would you indeed?" Julia was pleased. She used to play for Edward almost every evening; lately, however, she'd only played for herself, and then rarely. "I suppose you're entitled, since you polished the piano so nicely." She took off her apron and rubbed some lemon cream on her hands.

Twilight had fallen, and the living room was nearly dark. Gib lit the lamps and the candle by the music rack.

Julia sat on the stool and raised the piano lid. She unbuttoned her cuffs and pushed her sleeves up above her wrists, which she flexed a few times.

"What is your pleasure, Mr. Booth?"

"Anything you like."

"Surely you have some favorites."

Gib thought. "'Annie Laurie,'" he said, "and 'Blue-eyed Nell.' I like 'The Red, White, and Blue' and 'Raise up the Banner.'"

"I think I can manage all of those." Julia struck a few chords. "Are you going to sing?"

"No, ma'am. I'm going to sit right here and listen."

Gib took a seat on the horsehair sofa. As Julia began to play, he expelled a long breath of relief. He'd had a damned close call back there at dinner. When Mossy mentioned a grubstake, Gib could have sworn she started wondering about his money—if he had any, and if he didn't, if he might be after hers.

Gib stretched out his legs and folded his hands behind his head. Julia might have something of a weakness for him, but she was no slouch in the mental department. He'd better not forget it.

CHAPTER

7

THE SWEET STRAINS of "Annie Laurie" had a soothing effect on Gib, shaking his thoughts loose from possible snags in his plans. He watched the movement of Julia's arms as she played, the gentle dip of her head. It sure was nice, he thought, to sit in a clean and tidy parlor after a good supper and listen to a pretty woman play your favorite songs.

He looked around the room with a critical eye. The walls had lost two shades of gray, the floor and furniture gleamed. He'd lined up Julia's books, their spines as straight as soldiers, and on the whatnot the marble busts of the poets shone from a rubbing with linseed oil.

Gib decided he liked this house better than any bonanza king's mansion he'd ever imagined. Part of it was Julia, the way she made him feel at home. She was always praising him, calling him a "treasure" or a "wonder" or a "whirl-wind." Gib knew he shouldn't take the compliments too much to heart, but the truth was, her praise made him feel better than he'd felt in a damned long time.

He glanced at the window, dark behind the white curtains. If this were his house and Julia his wife, about this time he'd be taking her upstairs to that bed with the flower-colored quilt. That idea started his imagination going, but he shut it down fast. She was Doc's wife. The two of them were perfect for each other, decent and moral, doing their best by folks. It was crazy for him to think of being with her, Julia being such a lady while he'd never amounted to much.

Crashing chords jolted him out of his reverie. Julia launched into the vigorous marching cadence of "The Red, White, and Blue." When the last pounding notes faded away, she spun on the piano stool, her face flushed, her white shirtwaist glowing in the lamplight.

"That was fine," Gib said. "About the best I ever heard."

"I'm glad you enjoyed it." She looked so pleased that he decided to compliment her some more.

"I'd say you're good enough to play in a concert hall."

"Oh, heavens, listen to you," she said, laughing. "My mother was the musical one in my family."

Gib waited for her to say more, but her expression changed and she jumped to her feet. "The coffee! Heavens, I hope it didn't all boil away."

Gib got up and stretched, almost popping his chest out of Doc's shirt. "We're going to sit on the porch, remember?" He'd been looking forward to sitting out there and talking.

Julia hesitated and glanced at the window. "It's dark."

Gib saw that she was worried, afraid he might have something improper in mind. "I'll be on my way in a minute or two. I want to see how Mossy's doing at the Bon Ton."

That seemed to reassure her. "You go on out," she said. "I'll bring the tray."

Gib took his buckskin jacket and hat from the hall rack and stepped out onto the porch. A half-moon cast silvery light onto the shadowed hills. The wind whispered in the cottonwoods, giving the air a bracing chill. Gib pulled on his jacket and thought about the kind of life Doc and Julia had had—a lot of piano playing and book reading and talking about medicine. He remembered the song on the piano rack the first day he came to visit: "In Tears I Pine for Thee." It made him feel a little melancholy, thinking about the two of them and their happy years together.

He held the door open while Julia carried out the tray. She put it on the round porch table.

"Sit down, Gib."

There were two cane-bottomed rockers. One had probably been Doc's. "I'll sit right here on the top step." Gib sat down and leaned his back against a post.

Julia gave him a bowl of pudding. He balanced it on a bent knee and ate a few mouthfuls. The princess might not like to clean house, he thought, but she was a damn good cook. Ma used to make rice pudding like this, firm and sweet and full of raisins.

"It sure tastes good."

"I'm glad you like it." Julia rocked slowly, making the chair squeak. She was wrapped in a dark shawl. Her hair and the white of her high collar shone faintly in the moonlight.

It crossed Gib's mind as he watched her that Julia was Doc's second wife. He'd been married before the war, lost his wife and children somewhere along the line. That thought started Gib wondering how the devil Julia had hitched up with Doc, why she'd married a man old enough to be her father and moved way the hell out to Montana.

Since she hadn't taken offense at anything he'd done so far, Gib decided to ask her. "It's none of my business, but how did you and Doc get together?"

She finished a spoonful of pudding before answering. "I'm afraid it's not a very exciting story. We met when he came to a meeting in Chicago in '73. Edward was a medical school classmate of my brother, Randall—my half brother, really. Edward stayed with us for a month, first at the meeting and later for a visit. At the end of the month he and I were married, and he brought me here to Stiles."

A month, Gib thought. Pretty fast work for Doc, considering he'd never been one for the ladies. "I guess your folks didn't mind you marrying so quick and Doc being so much older."

"My parents had passed away by then."

Gib was sorry he'd asked the question. Before he could think of a way to change the subject, Julia started talking again.

"Mama died of typhoid in the summer of '71, and that fall the Great Fire burned the city. Rush Medical College was totally destroyed. Father held the chair in anatomy. All the specimens he'd spent a lifetime collecting were lost. The shock of it killed him."

Gib wished he hadn't opened his big mouth, but at least he'd gotten his answer. It was no wonder Julia had been in a hurry to marry—both her parents dead, one right after the other.

"I'm real sorry to hear that," he said.

"I was just sixteen when they died, and terribly lonely. Mama had been my dearest friend, beautiful, young, full of life." Julia paused and smiled a little as if recalling a happy memory. "I went to live with my brother, Randall, and his wife, Helen, but they were both busy. . . ." Her voice trailed off. "Tell me about your family."

Gib's mind stopped cold. How the hell had she gotten to that subject? Then he remembered that he was the one who'd started prying.

"Are they still back east in Massachusetts?"

Gib put aside his dessert bowl and stretched one leg down the porch steps, flexing his knee to work out some stiffness. "I didn't have a family. It was just Ma and me, and she's long gone." He said it curtly, hoping Julia would take the hint and not ask anything more.

The rocker squeaked, and she got up. She fussed at the tray for a minute, then came to him with a cup of coffee. To Gib's surprise, she made a move to sit down beside him. He took the coffee and slid over to give her room.

Julia rested an elbow on her knee and put her chin on her hand. The breeze blew silky strands of hair around her face. "You said she hired out to do cleaning."

Blinking hell, he thought. "Yeah, she did."

"She certainly taught you well."

Julia's gaze was direct, her voice full of warmth. It occurred to Gib that she was the kindest, most accepting woman he'd ever run into.

"Ma wasn't strong," he said. "She broke down sometimes. My pa passed on when I was a baby, and she never climbed out of her grief. I had to look after her some."

Julia's pretty eyes went soft with sympathy. "How sad for a boy to have that responsibility."

Gib drank his coffee. He'd never thought of it as responsibility; it was just taking care of Ma.

"Where in Massachusetts did you live?"

Jesus, he thought, she was nosier than he was. "A place called North Adams. It's on the Hoosic River, a mill town. Some rich folks with big houses, and others like us who just got by."

"Your father worked in the mill?"

"He farmed. Ma and I kept a few chickens and cows."

Julia was silent. Gib hoped she didn't have any more questions. She was easy to talk to, but some subjects were best left alone.

"What did your mother think of you going off to war?"

"Huh?"

"Your mother. Since you were all she had, she must have regretted your going."

"She was dead by then." Gib put down his cup and rubbed his hands on his knees. He didn't want to talk about Ma and the war; he didn't even want to think about it.

"You were very young when you joined up. Hardly more than a boy."

"Nobody cared how old I was." Suddenly Gib had to get away. He stood up and picked his hat off the newel post. "I'll go along now, ma'am. I sure appreciate your hospitality."

Julia got to her feet, holding the shawl close about her. "Forgive me for prying, Gib. Really, I shouldn't be so curious." She looked stricken, as if he were the king of England and she'd just spilled tea in his lap.

"Not at all, ma'am." He gave her a smile to let her know

he wasn't bothered. "Tomorrow I'll be heading over to Virginia City to file on the claim. I'll be back in a day or two."

"I hope I didn't offend you with all my questions."

She looked so lovely in the moonlight with her hair blowing around that Gib knew if he didn't get going pretty damned quick he'd take her in his arms and kiss her. "Ma'am, you couldn't offend anybody if you tried." He tugged at his hat brim. "Good night, now. Thanks for dinner."

"Good night, Gib."

He went down the steps and around back to the barn to get Lucky. When he rode out of the yard, Julia was still standing where he'd left her, her arms wrapped around the porch post, watching him.

The Bon Ton was filled with men, day-shift gangs from the mines, cowboys and mill hands and a few footloose townsmen. On the dance floor some heavy steppers were pumping arms and legs to the piano's rinky-dink tune.

Gib leaned on the bar and watched the scene through the haze of tobacco smoke. He kept an eye on Mossy, who was busy at the billiard table. It was good to see Mossy enjoying himself instead of lying around sucking on a bottle of tanglefoot.

"Say, Gib, you want to dance?"

It was Sarabeth Brown, small and shapely in her hurdy girl's outfit of red satin and feathers and striped black stockings. Every time Gib saw her, he got kind of a shock. With her Blackfoot mother's strong features and glossy Indian hair—you had to look hard to see any trace of Digger—she looked like a cross between an Indian maiden and a Kansas City whore.

"Nah. I'm too tired to do much more than look around."

"Hard day housecleaning?"

"Don't start on that, Sarabeth." Gib was sick and tired of being teased. If it wasn't Dellwood or Lee, it was the mahogany miners who spent their days and nights bellied up to the Bon Ton's bar instead of working.

"Whatever you say." She settled against the bar beside him. "I'll be heading up to the mine one of these days."

"You ought to see Rawlie more than you do," Gib said. "He's your own uncle."

"I go up there every goddamn week."

Sarabeth was an expert at swearing. Stiffs who didn't know her took one look at her pretty dimples and her firm little backside and started to slobber. But let one of them get on her wrong side, and Sarabeth unwound her tongue like a bullwhacker's whip.

"He says you haven't cleaned his place in five years."

"Five years, my assbone."

"That's what he said."

"Maybe it has been five years." She shrugged. "Hell, why don't you clean it? You're the housemaid." She rapped on the bar. "Hey, Dellwood! How about a whiskey for old Gib here? He's had a hard day scrubbing floors."

Dellwood came over and swabbed the bar. He gave Gib one of his droopy-eyed scowls. "You paying for Sarabeth's time or what? I don't let my girls sit around jawboning. They got to earn their quarters dancing."

"Get him a drink," Sarabeth said.

"Why, ain't you heard?" Dellwood said. "Gib's gone temperance. He's keeping himself pure for the widow."

Gib had had just about enough. "Goddammit, Dell, I'll take my business down to the New Gaiety if you don't quit ragging me."

"What business? You don't spend a cent in this place, just stand around taking up room."

Gib turned his back and watched Mossy line up his shot. The only place he got any respect these days was out at Julia's place.

"You sparking the widow for her money?" Sarabeth asked.

"How about minding your own business?"

"Well, aren't you ugly as Sunday?"

Gib ran a hand over his face. "Sorry, Sarabeth. I'm planning to open your daddy's old mine, that's all."

"I'll drive ore for you."

"Hell, I'm not . . ." He stopped before he said that he didn't plan on there being any ore to drive. Once he got his hands on Julia's investment, he'd hop the first train out of the territory.

"I used to drive freight for old Levi Tabor," Sarabeth said. "I'm plenty strong."

Gib had overheard her talking haulage roads and freight rates with the teamsters, but he didn't know she'd been one of them. "Maybe a woman can drive freight, Sarabeth, but driving ore's man's work."

"Is that a fact?" She gave him a look that would have treed a wolf, then proceeded to skin his hide with cuss-words. Gib winced and took it, although he didn't see what he'd said wrong. Sarabeth was as tough as rawhide, but she was a woman, and women didn't drive ore. Simple as that. Nevertheless, he decided not to press the point.

"You want to give up being a hurdy girl?"

She cocked a hip, making the flesh above her bodice jiggle. "You think I like showing this off? Only good thing about being a hurdy is the pay. Driving's what I want to do. Just me and the team and my double-action Winchester, looking at the scenery. I used to go over to the depot in Dillon and pick up supplies."

"Why'd you quit?"

"Levi passed on, and the old lady got rid of me." Sarabeth made a face. "A few of the fellers here let me ride with them sometimes. Drive, too. It sure feels good."

"What about Lee?"

She stared at him. "What about Lee?"

"You two were sweethearts back when."

Sarabeth sucked on her lip and looked thoughtful. Gib could have sworn her eyes got misty. "That's pretty high-falutin talk for what we were."

A miner passed by, stumbling a bit. "Hey, jackleg," Sarabeth called. She grabbed the man's sleeve and pulled him toward the dance floor. The miner started grinning and pawing. With a few expert slaps, Sarabeth calmed him down, and they began pumping arms to the piano's tune.

As Gib watched her dance, he thought of Lee and how

smitten he'd been. Sarabeth had been a pretty girl with an earthy way about her that drove Lee crazy. Mary, Digger's Blackfoot wife, was dead by then, and Rawlie and Digger didn't seem to notice that Sarabeth had an eye for the liveryman's son. Gib remembered the dazed look on Lee's face after a spell in the woods with Sarabeth. He'd said she was wilder than a Mexican mustang.

Thinking of the old days made Gib a little melancholy. They'd had some good times up at the Rattling Rock, Gib talking to Rawlie and Digger about outcroppings and gold assays while Lee and Sarabeth played in the woods. Now Digger was dead and Rawlie half gone. Gib was planning to open up the Rattling Rock, not to find gold but to get Doc's widow's money. Poor old Lee lived with his ma, and Sarabeth sold what she used to give him for free.

Times sure did change.

Two nights after her conversation with Gib on the porch, Julia was awakened from a sound sleep by the surgery bell. It was Mr. Chapman. His wife had gone into labor.

Julia dressed warmly, since the midnight air was breezy and cold. She took her overnight bag, which was packed and ready, and Edward's medical bag, and went outside.

Mossy had hitched Biscuit to the buggy and tied Mr. Chapman's horse to the rear. Ten minutes after Mr. Chapman arrived, he and Julia were crossing the bridge spanning Cottonwood Creek.

"I could tell she was feeling poorly all evening, Mrs. Metcalf, but she didn't say nothing. You know Vera—had to get dinner fixed and the chores done, and then she sits down and says, 'It's coming, Otis, and it's about time.'"

Mr. Chapman, as lean as his wife was large, normally had little to say. But tonight he couldn't seem to stop talking. "So I says, 'The least you could do was give me some warning,' and she says, 'There's nothing you can do about it anyhow, so what does it matter?'" He tugged at the thick gray mustache that drooped over his upper lip and down the sides of his meager chin.

"Your wife has a strong mind, Mr. Chapman." Julia slapped the reins, urging Biscuit to pick up the pace.

"You suppose everything'll be all right?"

"I don't expect any problems." Prospective fathers, Julia had learned, tended to ask questions that couldn't be answered.

"Losing our girls just about killed her, and she's got hopes for this one, though she don't never say so." Mr. Chapman paused, as if struggling with his next thought. "Truth is, ma'am, it's her I'm worried about. A baby's fine and all, but if I lost Vera—why, I'd about lose my mind."

"You mustn't worry, Mr. Chapman," Julia said. "Leave things to your wife and me."

As for her, no matter how anxious she might be during a woman's pregnancy, when it was time to deliver, Julia always felt the same—excited, a little impatient, and decidedly optimistic. The beginning of a tiny soul's journey through life was nothing short of a miracle. God intended the birthing process to go smoothly; her job was to see that it did.

They climbed into the ghostly hills, following the freight road toward Dillon, then picked up the trail to Doubletree Gulch where Mr. Chapman had his diggings on Whiskey Creek. The landscape was lovely in the frosty moonlight, the hills the texture of velvet. Trees cast eerie nighttime shadows, and shreds of clouds floated like veils past shimmering stars. As they headed down the grade into Doubletree Gulch, Julia could hear the rustle of new leaves on the cottonwoods and the rushing sound of the creek swollen by melted snow.

It was a perfect night to be born, she thought. Spring meant renewal, the beginning of life; a baby born in the spring followed the rhythm of the seasons.

When they reached the cabin, Julia jumped from the buggy, leaving Biscuit to Mr. Chapman. In the front room she found Mrs. Chapman sprawled on the easy chair, her rough hands rubbing her belly.

"I tried to keep to my feet," she said. "But my legs are feeling bad."

She had lost her bustling confidence. Her face was pale and anxious; damp hair stuck to her scalp.

"Are your legs numb?" Julia asked. "Cramped?"

Mrs. Chapman nodded.

"The baby's head is pressing down. Has your water broken?"

"Not yet." She licked her lips. "It's not as easy as it was with my girls."

"You're having a normal labor for a change. I'll have you more comfortable in no time."

Julia prepared the bed. She covered the mattress with blankets and quilts to make a firm, level surface, then added an India rubber sheet, which she pinned at the corners. A cotton sheet followed, then a second small rubber sheet, and finally a sheet folded into four thicknesses. She helped Mrs. Chapman into a fresh nightgown and eased her down onto the bed.

"There's hot water on the stove, and coffee's made," Mrs. Chapman said. "If you've a mind to eat a bite . . ." She grimaced and a low groan came from her throat.

"That's kind of you," Julia said. "But now you mustn't give me a thought."

She mixed up a carbolic acid solution and scrubbed her hands. She raised Mrs. Chapman's legs and draped a sheet over her bent knees. "Let's see what that baby of yours has in mind."

Mrs. Chapman tensed during the examination. "Is it coming right?"

"Yes. The baby's in a perfect position."

"Will it be long?"

Mrs. Chapman was not yet fully dilated. "Patience," Julia said. She took out her stethoscope. "You'll have plenty of time to rest." She listened to the heartbeats of mother and baby, then put the stethoscope away. "Everything is fine."

Mrs. Chapman licked her lips. "I could use a drink."

"I'll get you some water."

It could be hours yet, Julia knew. She hoped Mrs. Chapman would sleep a little. She intended to catch a few winks herself so she would be alert when the time came.

She took a tin cup from a shelf over the bed and stepped outside into the chilly night. "Mr. Chapman?" She wanted to assure him that all was well and ask that he stay nearby.

There was no reply, no human sound at all, only the rushing creek and the tinkling of goat bells. In the distance a coyote yipped, and its mate answered. All around was the spicy scent of juniper.

Julia dipped icy water from the rain barrel and went back inside. Mr. Chapman had built fires in the two stoves, and the cabin was toasty warm.

The pains were increasing in frequency, leaving Mrs. Chapman panting and perspiring. Julia turned her on her side, placed a pillow between her knees, and rubbed her back.

"Where's Otis got to?" Mrs. Chapman asked.

"He's outside," Julia said, wondering where on earth the man had gone.

"It's best that way. He's not strong enough for this."

Julia had wanted to ask Mr. Chapman for a board to lay across the foot of the bedstead where Mrs. Chapman could press her feet while bearing down. She took a lamp and went out to the woodpile, hunting there until she found a plank that would do. On her way back to the cabin, she held the lamp high and looked around.

"Mr. Chapman?" She heard a sound, but it was only Biscuit, blanketed and tethered.

Back inside, Julia set up the footboard and folded a long towel lengthwise. She fixed the puller to the bottom of the bed and tested it with a few good yanks. From the front room, she brought in a low table, covered it with a cloth, and laid out scissors and twine, clean linens, and soft flannel wrapping for the baby.

Mrs. Chapman watched, her eyes drooping with fatigue. "I might just take a nap."

"First I'll see how things are progressing," Julia said. She scrubbed and performed another examination. The passage had dilated further but was not completely open.

She adjusted the sheets and gave Mrs. Chapman more water. "I'll be right here."

Julia dozed in a chair through the early morning hours, rising now and then to assist the laboring mother. The cabin was gray with dawn when Mrs. Chapman's water finally broke.

"Now we're getting somewhere," Julia said. She changed the sheet and helped Mrs. Chapman into a fresh nightgown. She added wood to the stoves and made fresh coffee in the small lean-to kitchen. Her eyes felt sandy and hot.

As the contractions came closer together, Julia pressed the heel of her hand into the small of Mrs. Chapman's back and made hard circular motions. When the pain eased, she wiped her patient's forehead with a cool damp cloth and offered her sips of water.

"This is nothing like it was with my girls," Mrs. Chapman said between gasps.

"Then it must be a boy."

A little before seven, Julia prepared for the delivery. She propped pillows under Mrs. Chapman's head and shoulders. She scrubbed her hands pink and donned a fresh apron.

Mrs. Chapman bore down, panting and moaning. She jerked on the puller so hard that the iron bedstead shook. She threw back her head and yelled. "Babies," she gasped. "It's for young women."

"Nonsense," Julia said. "You're an expert." But she hoped it would soon be over. Mrs. Chapman was wrung out with exhaustion.

During intervals between contractions, Julia placed warm wet cloths on the perineum to soften the skin and make it more elastic.

"I see it. Don't push hard now."

Julia held the head firmly back and massaged the area with oil and a little belladonna ointment. "You do this so well, Mrs. Chapman. I wish all mothers were as easy."

Mrs. Chapman attempted a laugh, then gasped and strained. "Tell the rascal to hurry."

"He's almost here. Yes, now! Here he comes!"

The head emerged without any tear to the surrounding tissue, then the anterior shoulder, and the baby slithered into

Julia's waiting hands. She quickly cleared the infant's mouth and nose.

"We were right!" she exclaimed. "It *is* a boy! And good heavens, such a *big* boy!"

"That's why it took so long," Mrs. Chapman said, just as her baby let out an indignant yowl.

CHAPTER

8

GIB STEPPED ONTO the landing of the Bon Ton's outside staircase and assessed the morning. The sun had yet to climb over the hills, but the sky was blue and brimming with light. Beyond the sprawl of Stiles, the hills, made green by recent rains, rolled off toward western peaks.

Gib tucked a bundle of digging clothes under his arm and pounded down the wooden steps to the street. As he hopped onto the boardwalk, he whistled a chorus of "The Red, White, and Blue." He would stop by Julia's place before heading out to the Rattling Rock. She wasn't expecting him, but he'd been gone for two days, and he felt a need to see her.

The smell of coffee and sweet baking wafted from the Pickax. Gib slowed down, trying to make up his mind whether or not to go in for breakfast. Suddenly a cloud of dust came his way, sprinkling dirt on his trousers and boots.

"What the hell?" Gib stopped in his tracks and looked around. I. Z. Blum leaned on his broom and glared over spectacles perched halfway down his nose.

"Blum," Gib said, "you call that friendly?"

"So who's friendly?" Blum came over and swept off Gib's boots. "Who doesn't bother to say hello? You tell me." He jerked his head toward the open door of his grocery. "Come in."

Gib hadn't seen Blum since he'd been back; he was surprised at how the man had aged. His thinning hair was streaked with gray as was his once-black beard. His posture was more stooped, too, but his glare could still wither a man where he stood, and his tongue had lost none of its sting.

"What did I do?" Gib followed Blum into the fragrant gloom of the store. It smelled of tobacco and cheese and fresh-ground coffee. Slabs of bacon and ham, cooking pots, and lamps hung from the ceiling. In the rear stood the potbellied stove where loafers chewed the fat in the winter and munched on crackers from the barrel.

"You're too good now?" Blum untied his long white apron, hung it on a hook, and reached for his coat. "You come back to town and now you're too good to say hello to old friends?" He adjusted his sleeves, then turned his back on Gib and started waving a feather duster over shelves of red-labeled canned goods.

Gib leaned an elbow on the counter and exchanged looks with the young clerk. "Time was, Blum, you thought I wasn't good for much of anything."

The grocer shuffled along, dusting, ignoring him. Old Blum always had to needle him about something, Gib thought. "All right, I'm sorry. I'd have come by sooner or later."

Blum put the duster aside, indicating he'd accepted the apology. "What are you up to? That's what I'd like to know." He gave Gib a critical once-over. "A boy like you isn't stupid. You should have made something of yourself by now."

"Too late for that." Gib laid down his bundle, took off his hat, and tossed it on the counter. "How's your daughter, I. Z.?" In the old days, he'd teased Ruth plenty, mostly to make her father mad.

Blum's eyes narrowed. "You think I'd tell a no-good like you?"

"Too good, no-good, which is it?"

"She's got a husband."

"*Mazel tov.*" He remembered one of Blum's sayings.

Blum didn't crack a smile, but Gib saw something sparkle in his eyes. He reached for a jar of peppermint sticks. "Have some candy. No charge."

"Thanks, I. Z., don't mind if I do."

Blum wrapped up a handful of sticks. Gib stuck the package in his coat pocket for later. "How's your wife?"

Blum shrugged. "See for yourself." He shuffled toward the rear of the store, indicating that Gib should follow.

"Look, I. Z., I've got to get going."

"You've got to eat, don't you? Renate," he called out. "Look who finally decided to say hello."

Mrs. Blum came in from the store's back room. She was younger than her husband, a handsome woman of slender proportions with smooth skin and lively dark eyes. Gib had heard that she came from a well-off Philadelphia family, which explained why she didn't share her husband's crusty nature and Old World accent.

"Gib." She came to him, shaking her head as if she didn't believe her eyes. "Don't you look wonderful." She reached up and put cool palms on his cheeks, then moved to his shoulders and chest, smoothing and patting.

"Morning, Mrs. Blum." Gib felt a little embarrassed. Renate Blum had always liked him, tried to mother him, too, and offer advice, but he'd made sure none of it stuck. "You haven't changed a day."

"And you, so big and handsome. Such a handsome boy and now such a handsome man." She blinked a couple of times, then took out a handkerchief and blew her nose.

Gib looked at Blum. "I guess that means I pass inspection."

"Come sit down," Blum said gruffly.

Renate took his arm. "I'll fry some eggs."

The back room was plain and barely furnished except for the cookstove, a table, and some chairs. There was a barrel of whiskey and a tin cup by the door, refreshment for Blum's regulars. The living quarters were upstairs. Gib had been up there a time or two. He remembered the place being full of heavy furniture and framed pictures and thick rugs.

They sat at the table covered with a lace cloth. While Gib ate, he told the Blums about his arrangement with Rawlie Brown and Charlie Soon. "Charlie's got a gang going up to the mine today to clean out the snakes."

Blum listened, his face severe. "Everybody wants a gold mine. Then they find out it isn't so easy. This one's full of snakes, that one's full of water, this one caves in, that one blows up." He shrugged and sighed. "I guess you don't need a grubstake."

Gib stopped eating, surprised that Blum would offer him a loan. "Thanks, I. Z., I'm all set."

"If you need money, you know where to come."

Gib grinned. "I figure you'd just as soon throw money in the stove as give it to a no-good like me."

Blum exchanged glances with his wife. "You think we forget? You think we'd turn our backs on you?"

Mrs. Blum patted Gib's arm. "We haven't forgotten what you did."

For a minute, Gib didn't know what they were talking about. Then it became clear. "You mean Hockett?"

Blum glared. "What else?"

Gib returned to his breakfast. Funny how it had slipped his mind. Bob Hockett and his gang hadn't cared for Blum's accent and religion any more than they'd cared for Skinner Sam voting. The gang had ransacked the store a couple of times, and they'd gotten hold of Ruth. Roughed her up some, thought she was a curiosity, being crippled as she was. What almost happened to Ruth had scared Blum so bad he'd sent her to Helena to live with relatives.

"That was a long time ago," Gib said. He finished his coffee and stood up. "I'm obliged, ma'am."

"Ruth's coming to stay with us," Renate said. "She'll want to see you."

Gib glanced at Blum. "I thought she was up in Helena, married."

"She is married," Renate said, her face bursting into a smile. "She'll be with us until her baby is born."

"Well, that's real fine," Gib said. It was nice that Ruth could have a husband and a baby like any other woman.

Blum went with Gib back through the store. It was almost eight o'clock, and business was brisk.

"We had a talk," Blum said. "Now I know what you're doing with yourself. If you need a grubstake, you let me know."

Gib put on his hat and picked up his bundle of digging clothes. "I. Z.," he said. "You're the limit."

Down at the livery, Lee crawled out from under a wagon and nodded a welcome. "Gib."

"Morning, Lee."

"Heading out to the widow's?"

"Maybe." Gib ignored Lee's grin.

"Folks are talking."

Gib fished a toothpick out of his pocket and stuck it in his mouth. "Good for them." He hoped Julia didn't mind gossip. If she got it into her head that he shouldn't come around anymore, he'd have a real problem on his hands.

"Don't let her take advantage of you, now." Lee chuckled.

"Go to hell, Lee."

Gib went into the dim, pungent stable to get Lucky. He fed him one of Blum's peppermint sticks, then slipped the bridle over his muzzle and cinched the saddle in place.

Outside, Lee was still working on the wagon. "She ain't at home this morning. In case you're wondering."

Gib swung into the saddle and leaned a forearm on the pommel. "What's that supposed to mean?"

"It means she's out at Whiskey Creek. Been out there all night delivering a baby for Otis Chapman's wife. Jim Ferry saw them heading out Bridge Street about midnight."

Gib was disappointed. He'd looked forward to seeing her, even for a minute. His disappointment must have shown, for Lee started grinning like a fool. "It ain't too far out of your way, if you're heading up to the Rattling Rock. The old Whiskey's right down Doubletree Gulch."

"Damn you, Lee, I know where Whiskey Creek is." Gib gave Lucky a nudge with his heels and took off down Main Street.

* * *

Gib headed west into the hills. The air was as clear as glass, the leaves jeweled with dew. All around, wildflowers rippled in the breeze, flashing their spring colors. Off in the distance, purple and gray peaks soared upward in a jagged chain, their ridges still decorated with snow. Gib took in the clean tangy beauty of the landscape. It was strange how Montana country could make a man feel humble and powerful at the same time.

Half an hour outside of town, he left the trail to the Rattling Rock and angled down to Doubletree Gulch. Whiskey Creek wasn't far out of the way, and he wanted to make sure Julia was all right. If he didn't stop, he'd probably wonder about her all day.

He followed wagon tracks to a sturdy little cabin with a neat fence and a goat pen. Julia's buggy was parked out back. Nearby, her buckskin mare munched grass.

"Hello, the house," Gib called. He dismounted and looped the reins around a fence post. Aside from a plume of smoke coming out of the chimney, there was no sign of life.

He went up the front walk, wiping his hands on his trousers. At the door he paused to take off his hat and smooth down his hair.

Julia opened the door to his soft knock. "Why, Gib." She gave him a smile that cheered him; he'd been afraid she might think he was butting in where he had no business.

"I'm heading up to Rawlie Brown's place," he said. "I thought I'd stop by and see if everything's all right."

She reached out and took his arm, drawing him inside. "Let me show you something."

"What's that?"

She closed the door and put her fingers to her lips. "Mrs. Chapman's sleeping."

She disappeared behind a calico partition. Gib looked around at the whitewashed walls, the simple furnishings, the wood floor decorated with rugs. It was a cozy place, he thought. Not bad at all.

Julia returned carrying a bundle wrapped in white flannel. She pulled aside the blanket, and Gib stared at a tiny, exhausted face with eyes like slits and a little cap of silky brown hair.

"You're the first person to meet him, aside from his mother and me," Julia said.

"Well, I'll be." Gib had never been one for babies, couldn't remember if he'd ever seen one so new. For Julia's sake he tried to look appreciative. He reached into his pocket and took out Blum's packet of peppermint sticks. "Maybe he'd like one of these."

Julia smiled. "That's a lovely thought, but he's too little. He hasn't had a drop of anything yet, not even his mother's milk."

Gib started to put the packet away. "How about you, then?"

"I'd love it." Julia took the candy and sucked on it, rolling her eyes in appreciation.

She looked tired, with dark smudges under her eyes, but happy, holding that baby. Looking at her made Gib happy, too; she always seemed glad to see him.

"Would you like some coffee? I just made it."

"Sure would." He decided a brief delay wouldn't hurt.

"Would you like to hold the baby?"

Gib tapped his hat brim against his fingers. "I don't think that's such a good idea."

"I'll just be a minute, then."

She carried the baby behind the partition. Gib hung his hat on a wall peg and sat down on a rocker. He heard Julia moving around. Then there was a muffled sound and a cry, and Julia almost screamed.

"Gib!"

He jumped up, knocking over the lamp in his haste to get to her. He flung aside the partition. Julia was at the bed, pressing down on the woman, and there was blood all over—on the sheets, trickling onto the floor. The sight of it and the heavy, salty smell made him gag.

"The napkins!" she cried. "Give them to me!"

There was a stack of linens on a table. Gib grabbed one, then another. Julia snatched them from his hand and pushed them between the woman's legs, all the while bearing down on her belly. She looked as if she'd been gutted. Gib hadn't seen so much blood since the war.

"Water! The cold water in the barrel outside."

Gib shot out the door, yanked the dipper free of its cord and scooped up the water.

"More, more," Julia said. "Get a bucket. Hurry. We haven't a minute to lose."

He found a bucket next to the rain barrel. He filled it and carried it inside, slopping water on the floor.

"Wet the napkins."

He obeyed, wringing out linens in icy water, then handing them to Julia who laid them over the woman's belly and thighs and pressed them between her legs. Gib was embarrassed by the woman's nakedness and frightened by the amount of blood. But he wanted to help Julia, to wipe the look of fear off her face.

The flow seemed to slow; finally it stopped. Gib sat down on a chair and rubbed his face. The woman's eyes were closed and she had a sickly pallor. He wondered if she was dead.

Julia felt at her wrist for a pulse. "You must find her husband."

Gib jumped to his feet. "Where is he?" He couldn't wait to get away.

"Probably down at the creek, prospecting."

Before he'd reached the door, Julia called him back. "Help me here first. I have to get her warm and dry."

Julia tended the woman, binding up her lower parts. Gib wiped blood from the floor and helped change the sheets. After Julia had covered the woman with a quilt, she took Gib's hands in hers.

"I'm so glad you were here," she said. "I couldn't have done it alone."

Gib found Otis Chapman a mile downstream where the creek bed curved and the water was wide and shallow. Trees grew thickly on the grassy sod, and the spring foliage obscured Gib's view. He didn't see the man until he rounded a bend and came right on him.

Chapman was hunkered down over his prospect pan, swirling and tilting. He'd left his outfit—a bedroll and jute sack—under a nearby cottonwood.

Gib wondered if he was finding any color in the old Whiskey. The surrounding hills were full of abandoned claims, shallow diggings that played out at fifty feet. Except for the Rattling Rock, Doubletree Gulch had been abandoned. But a man never knew when he might hit a lucky strike.

Gib remembered his business. "Chapman!"

The man took one look and scrambled for his rifle.

Gib's hand moved to the butt of his gun. "It's your wife!" he yelled over the rushing sound of the creek. "Good God, you think I'd jump this sorry claim?"

At the mention of his wife, Chapman stopped in his tracks. Gib saw fear on his face.

"She's not dead. At least she wasn't when I left. But you better get back there."

Chapman stood still, his throat working. He was a skinny little jasper with a mustache almost as big as he was. His battered slouch hat obscured his eyes, and his mule-eared boots came almost to his knees.

"Jump up behind me." Gib reached out a hand.

Chapman grabbed hold and swung up. Gib heeled Lucky and they headed back along the creek bank.

Chapman didn't say a word until he slid down in front of his cabin. "Who're you, mister?"

"Gib Booth." Gib touched his hat brim. "By the way, you've got a son."

Chapman went inside, leaving Gib to wonder what he should do next. He sure as hell wanted to get away from this place—he'd had enough of blood and babies—and he had to get up to the Rattling Rock before Charlie Soon and his gang spooked Rawlie. But he didn't want to run out on Julia. If what she'd said was true—that she couldn't have saved Mrs. Chapman without him—then he wouldn't mind sticking around to enjoy a bit more of her gratitude.

"Gib, come inside."

She was at the door, beckoning to him. Gib dismounted and tied Lucky to the fence.

"Mrs. Chapman's awake. She's nursing the baby." Julia took his hand in her cool fingers and led him inside. She sure seemed to like touching him, Gib thought, and he sure wasn't going to deny her the pleasure.

"The coffee smells good," he said.

"Sit down and I'll get you a cup."

The cabin was warm. Gib shed his jacket. Chapman was talking to his wife behind the partition. Gib could hear her faint replies. The little kitten sounds, he decided, came from the baby.

Julia brought him a steaming cup and a plate of bread thickly spread with jam. "You're probably in a hurry to get up to the mine," she said.

"I'll go along in a minute." Gib took a seat at the table and started in on his second breakfast of the day.

Julia sat down across from him. "When you finish, the Chapmans want to speak to you."

"There's no need for that." It would suit him fine never to lay eyes on the woman again.

"They're grateful to you."

"You're the one who knew what to do. I thought she was a goner."

"Postpartum hemorrhage can be very dangerous. But she'll be back to normal once she builds up her strength." Julia got up, smiling a little, and went back to the Chapmans.

A minute later she called him in. Gib set his coffee aside and stepped behind the calico partition.

Mrs. Chapman lay propped up on pillows, looking pale and listless. Her little bean of a husband sat at the bedside, tugging his mustache.

"Mr. Booth." Mr. Chapman got up and shook Gib's hand. "Me and the missus are grateful for what you done here."

Gib shoved his fingers into his hip pockets and glanced longingly at the back door. "I didn't do anything much."

"Mrs. Metcalf says she couldn't have saved Vera without your help." Chapman got choked up. He took out a handkerchief and honked a couple of times. "I meant to stay by last night, but something come over me. I had to get away."

Gib understood. If he'd known what he was in for, he would have stayed clear of the cabin himself.

"We decided to name the baby for you."

Gib's jaw dropped. He looked at Julia, but she was doing something with the baby that he didn't care to watch.

"Gilbert Otis Chapman." Mrs. Chapman's voice was faint, but her eyes brimmed with joy.

Gib felt a flush crawl up his neck; he couldn't remember ever feeling more embarrassed. "Ma'am, I'm glad I could help. But I don't think you should be naming your baby for me. I'm not exactly . . ." He stopped. What was he going to say? That he was a no-good sharper out to swindle a widow, a man not to be trusted, let alone named for?

"Mrs. Metcalf says you were a well-raised boy, a blessing to your own mother. I hope my little Gilbert turns out to be as good."

Gib stared at his boots. "Ma'am, I'm honored." There was nothing else he could say.

"Come, Gib, have a look." Julia motioned him over to the box where the baby lay all bundled up, his little mouth working like a fish's.

"Was this your idea?" Gib said in a low voice.

Her aquamarine eyes sparkled. "No, but I think it's sweet."

"Look, Julia, I'd better be going."

"Of course." She went away, leaving Gib alone with his namesake. The baby wriggled in his blanket, making grunting sounds.

Gib poked his belly. "Hello there, partner."

The baby seemed surprised at the poke. He stopped wriggling and blinked his dark blue eyes, then opened his little mouth and burped.

Gib reached the Rattling Rock just before Charlie Soon and his gang showed up hauling a big iron kettle on a flatbed wagon. The gang unloaded the kettle near the squared-off mouth of the mine and started gathering wood for a fire. Charlie took some candles and headed into the tunnel.

He came out a while later and motioned to Gib. "Hey, boss, come see."

"I'll go in when you get those snakes out of there," Gib said.

Charlie's bullet eyes narrowed. "Come see first."

Gib went into Rawlie's cabin to change into his digging clothes. Rawlie sat in his rocker, pawing his beard.

"Danged Chinamen," he said.

Rawlie's shotgun hung on the wall where Gib had ordered it parked for the day. He'd warned Rawlie, "You kill one of Charlie's gang and he'll toss you into the kettle along with those snakes."

Outside, the gang had gotten the fire going and had set up a bucket brigade from the spring. They passed buckets from hand to hand, yelling at each other all the while. Gib had to admire the Celestials; they sure weren't ones to lie around doing nothing.

He followed Charlie through the mine entrance. The tunnel smelled cool and damp in the darkness. Gib heard the distant drip of water, the sound of a falling rock. He concentrated on keeping his footing on the crumbly debris. He didn't want to grab on to a rocky crevice and find himself shaking hands with a snake.

As he made his way along, Gib held his candle so he could study the tunnel's face. He stopped to pick up ore samples and put them in his pocket. The Rattling Rock had been a small operation—hell, it was little more than a prospect hole. He wondered what Rawlie and Digger would have found if they'd brought in some shaft sinkers from the Comstock or from California and gone down a hundred feet. Veins that were profitable at the surface grew less so at depth; still, the Rattling Rock's twenty-foot shaft was hardly a scratch in the ground.

When they reached the shaft, Charlie stuck his candle in his hat and started down, holding on to crevices in the rock. Gib, his spine prickling, watched him descend. He could smell the snakes; he could almost feel them. A month ago those snakes would have been as stiff as boards, too cold to bite. Now it was May, and they'd be thawing out fast, ready to enjoy the spring sun.

A few feet from the bottom, Charlie held out his candle, illuminating the depths. "Lookee, boss." His excited voice echoed up the shaft. At the bottom Gib could see a mess of snakes the size of a hogshead, writhing together. There were probably more down the lower drift, hiding in crevices.

"Beautiful, Charlie," Gib said. "They're all yours. See you outside."

He went back through the tunnel and out into the bright blue day. Charlie's gang had the water boiling. Rawlie had dragged his rocker outdoors. He sat there, gumming his pipe stem, watching the Celestials at work.

Gib headed down the slope of the clearing, past the two cabins. There were still patches of snow under the fir trees, and the air was sharp with the scent of pine resin. He breathed deeply to get the stink of snakes out of his nose.

Looking down at Whiskey Creek, sparkling in the distance, he thought of Otis Chapman washing gravel. Fifteen years ago, Rawlie and Digger had found good panning down on the old Whiskey. They'd climbed through timber in search of a likely outcropping of quartz, then sunk test holes until they found a vein. They'd dug a fifty-foot tunnel and sunk the shaft themselves, hitting a two-foot-thick pay zone right on the button. The ore was high-grade, assaying at around eighty dollars a ton before the vein ran off into the wall.

Other hard-rock claims had been staked in the hills around Doubletree Gulch, but the strikes hadn't caused much excitement, not like Cottonwood Gulch, where bonanza ore had made Stiles a boomtown.

Gib wondered if Chapman was sinking test holes, looking for a lode. The man had a family to support; he shouldn't be wasting his time on land that had been prospected years ago and abandoned.

Gib hunkered down on his haunches and took out the rocks he'd pocketed in the tunnel. As he studied the milky quartz, he patted his coat, searching for his tobacco pouch. Then he remembered he'd given up smoking and muttered a few curses. It was times like this, when his mind was trying to sort through a mess of ideas, that he needed to roll a fat one and suck on it for a while.

He spotted a pink wildflower, plucked it, and stuck the stem in his mouth. He chewed on it while he studied the rock and thought of Rawlie and Digger's vein that had run into the wall. The two old coots had probably hit a block of no-good ground between ore bodies and got lazy. They were prospectors by nature, not developers. They'd only settled in Doubletree Gulch because they'd acquired a family— Digger's Blackfoot wife and the little girl, Sarabeth.

Gib thought about sticking around and really working the mine, at least for the summer. The idea was tempting. He knew ground and he knew ore; there was gold down in the Rattling Rock. He'd bet on it.

He headed back uphill to the old toolshed. The shed was falling down, boards had rotted, and weather had gotten inside. Gib poked through a wheelbarrow full of junk—battered wide-brimmed hats, a pair of stiff yellow gummed leggings, an assortment of gloves, ropes, files, and rubber tie boots. There were pickaxes of various sizes lying around on the ground, rusted shovels, single jacks, felt hats, old prospect pans, snowshoes. Off in a corner was a set of scales and weights. Under a tarpaulin he found scythe stones, a whipsaw, axes and extra handles, drill bits, and a bucket of pitch.

As he sorted through the stuff, Gib thought about sinking the shaft deeper. If he found a new ore body, he could sink a second shaft and open a crosscut between drifts to get air circulation. He'd hire men and lay track for ore cars. Get Sarabeth to transport ore to the mill—even if she was a woman.

Suddenly he stopped himself. Jumping blue hell, what was he thinking of? He already had a plan—to open the mine just enough to get Julia's grubstake, then skip town. He'd have a tidy sum to play with for a good long time.

Gib closed the toolshed and went back to the mine to see how things were going with the snakes. Charlie was pulling them out of his gunnysack one at a time, milking their venom, then tossing them into the kettle. His gang took care of the rest, skimming the scum off the brew.

"What do you think, Rawlie?" Gib asked.

Rawlie took his pipe out of his beard. "Craziest thing I ever did see. A bunch of Chinamen boiling snakes." But Gib heard admiration in his voice.

CHAPTER

9

JULIA DECIDED TO stay at Whiskey Creek overnight to be sure her patient was out of danger. Mrs. Chapman was weak, but she was able to nurse little Gilbert. The room behind the partition took on the sweet-sour scent of baby.

From the springhouse Mr. Chapman brought a rump steak from which Julia made a Chinese concoction of herbal wine and beef tea, administering three ounces every hour to build up Mrs. Chapman's blood. To guard against further hemorrhage, she dosed her with ergot.

After a supper of fried potatoes and venison, Mr. Chapman did some outside chores, and Julia went out on the front porch to get some air. The sun was sinking behind the mountains, casting shadows over the gulch. She listened to the rushing creek, felt the cool breeze on her cheeks, and snuggled deeper into her shawl. Her eyes were dry and her body heavy from too little sleep—she would have loved a hot bath and her own warm bed—but she couldn't help feeling a sense of exhilaration and, beneath it, a quiet contentment. Mrs. Chapman had a fine healthy boy. Gilbert.

Julia thought of Gib's look of dismay when he learned that the baby would bear his name. She'd expected he would be pleased or even amused, but apparently he wasn't. The Chapmans wanted him to be a sponsor at Gilbert's christening. Julia doubted he would be pleased about that, either.

She leaned against the porch pillar and thought about Mossy's story of Gib shooting Bob Hockett and his banishment from Stiles; she thought of his womanizing and mischief. Harlan said Gib was a confidence man, but somehow the label didn't fit. Praise embarrassed him; he worried that he'd failed Edward, and for some reason he didn't care to talk about his mother.

To her way of thinking, Gib was too transparent to be anything other than what he appeared—an extremely kind and attractive man.

She heard a distant "yahoo!" Looking up the hill, she saw a dark-clad rider coming down the trace on a black horse. A ray of sun flashed off the metalwork on the rider's hat. Julia knew it was Gib, even though she couldn't see for sure. As he came closer, she made out the wide strong shoulders, the familiar slouch in the saddle. She hugged herself in her shawl, feeling a sudden luminous happiness as clear as the evening air.

Gib pulled up at the fence. "How's everyone?" He was grinning.

Julia smiled back. "Come in and see for yourself."

He thumbed up the brim of his hat and glanced at the sky. "I shouldn't linger." But he dismounted and came up the walk. He wore miner's clothes—muddy boots and coarse, none-too-clean trousers. A sweat-stained bandanna was tied around his neck. He took off his hat and ran a hand through his hair. "How's that little fellow?"

"Gilbert."

Gib's eyes softened. "Yeah, Gilbert."

His shirt was unbuttoned at the throat, showing a small vee of crisp dark hair, and his jaw bristled with whiskers. He looked rough and masterful, except for his eyes. They rested on her gently, with an expression that was warmer than polite.

"Gilbert is learning how to sleep."

Julia couldn't think of anything more to say. It seemed that Gib couldn't, either. He just looked at her as if he was pleased to be there.

After a minute he shoved a hand into his pocket. "I brought him some rocks."

His hands looked as if they'd been digging. Dirt was ground into his skin and half-moons of black showed under his nails. Julia took the chunks from his open palm.

"I thought they were pretty," Gib said. "Gilbert hasn't seen rocks before."

Julia turned the milky quartz in her fingers. "I'm sure he'll like them." A handful of rocks for a baby. The gift moved her in a strange way. "Come inside and see him."

"I'm not fit for calling." He rubbed his unshaven chin with dirty fingers. "I just wanted to stop by."

"Did you take care of the snakes?"

"Charlie did. His gang boiled them down and bottled the oil like French perfume, didn't waste a drop. At the end they boiled down the leftovers and bottled that, too. Then they went in and mucked the place out. Left the shaft clean as a whistle."

"So you'll start working there soon."

"As soon as I finish up at your place."

Julia drew her shoulders together, shivering a little in the chilly twilight. It pleased her to think of him working the mine, staying near Stiles. "You've done enough for me, Gib. You should get on with your own work."

His gray eyes sparkled. "Ah, princess, you won't get rid of me so easy."

Julia stared at him. "Princess?"

He ducked his head, his face dark with embarrassment. "Sorry. It doesn't mean anything. It just slipped out."

"What on earth . . . ? Why 'princess'?"

He shrugged and looked off into the distance, clearly not wanting to explain.

"Gib." Julia made herself sound stern.

He didn't look at her when he spoke. "Dellwood Petty said Mrs. Williver was the queen around town and you were the princess, the second-in-command."

Julia pressed her fist to her mouth to keep from laughing out loud. She wondered if Louise would be flattered or insulted.

Gib glanced at her and saw the smile. He raised his eyebrows, teasing her. "It suits you."

"Don't be silly."

"I'd tell you why, but it might go to your head."

He was flirting. Julia felt a rush of attraction, something light and joyous that must have shown in her eyes, for Gib's face changed from playful to serious.

"Do you want me to drive you back to town?" He looked at her mouth, and she knew he wanted to kiss her.

"I . . . I can't leave yet. I'll be staying the night here." To her own ears, the words came out wrong—too abrupt.

Gib didn't seem to notice. He took hold of the porch post and leaned close. "Julia." His voice was whisper-soft with a hint of a tease. "I could guess your name just by looking at you. You know why?"

Julia stared at him, her hand clenched tight on the rocks. His nearness made breathing impossible. "Why?"

"Because your eyes are like jewels. As clear and pretty as jewels."

He watched her for a moment, then leaned down and kissed her, a warm, gentle kiss without haste or passion, and then again, more firmly, a kiss so sweet that Julia felt an odd sinking in her belly, and her knees went weak.

He pulled back. "I'd better go. Do you have everything you need for tonight?"

Julia nodded. Her mouth had gone dry, too dry to speak.

Gib's eyes were tender; the lines around his mouth made him look as if he was smiling. "I need to speak to Chapman for a minute. Is he inside?"

Julia opened her mouth and words came out. "Around back, I think."

He stepped away from her, and she felt a tug at her hand.

She was clutching his sleeve. Embarrassed, she released him and retreated into the porch shadows.

She didn't remember him saying good night, only that he was gone, vanished in the twilight. A longing settled over her as gently as a mist.

The next morning, Gib had breakfast at the Pickax. The place was crowded and noisy, the windows clouded with steam. All around was the smell of tobacco and coffee and frying bacon. Gib took a chair at a corner table, where a couple of sullen-looking cowboys were eating beefsteak and eggs and drinking coffee from thick mugs. Hung over, Gib decided, when they didn't answer his greeting. Just as well, since he wasn't in the mood for jawboning.

While he waited for his order, he folded back a copy of the *Sentinel* to page four: "The Importance of Proper Lighting in the American Home," by Mrs. Julia Metcalf.

"All flames used for the purpose of giving light should be surrounded by glass chimneys or some sort of shade," he read. "A flickering, unsteady flame is injurious to the eyes."

Gib grinned and roughed his hair. He'd never known a woman who wrote newspaper articles.

"The practice of bringing the lamp close to the face to economize on fuel is a bad habit, as heat is injurious to the eyes. It is far better to burn a larger flame and keep it at a greater distance."

By golly, Gib thought. Julia wrote articles for the newspaper, delivered the Chapmans' son, and saved the mother's life while hardly batting an eyelash. It wasn't every woman who could manage to do all the things she did.

The waitress brought coffee and a plate of eggs. Gib folded the paper and rolled up his sleeves.

As he ate, he thought of last evening on Chapman's porch, Julia's welcoming smile, those admiring eyes. She sure did like him. Made him feel better than he deserved, too, like a square shooter, instead of what he was—a piss-poor sharper who'd always been slightly windward of the law.

The cowboys finished their breakfast, belched, rolled their cigarettes, and departed, trailing smoke. Gib pushed their plates aside, laid the paper flat on the oilcloth table cover and read Julia's article again.

When he finished, he looked off at the windows and thought about kissing her. He shouldn't have done it, but she'd looked so pretty and seemed so damned happy to see him that he couldn't resist. The problem was, that kiss had made him think some pretty dangerous thoughts; old Adam had given him one hard case of trouble all night.

"Mr. Booth?"

A man stood across the table, resting his hands on the back of an empty chair. He was a big man with a heavy face, handsome but kind of pasty.

"Who's asking?"

"The name's Hughes. Harlan Hughes. I'm superintendent at the Continental."

He looked like a mine superintendent, Gib thought. Dark slicked-back hair, duded up black suit, gold watch chain hung with a nugget charm. Hands going soft. Gib had never trusted men like him; he didn't plan to start now.

"What's on your mind?" he asked.

"I thought I'd introduce myself. I'm president of the mining association. I hear you're throwing in with Rawlie Brown."

"You heard right."

"How do things look up at the Rattling Rock?"

Hughes was smiling, but it seemed to take some effort. He had big white teeth like tombstones and an extra chin or two.

"Too soon to tell," Gib said. "I'll keep you posted." Like hell he would. When he started shaking the bushes up at Doubletree Gulch, the mining association would be the last to know.

"You've had quite a career, Mr. Booth."

Gib stopped chewing his bacon. "What do you know about it?"

"I read the *Engineering and Mining Journal.*"

"You've never seen my name there."

Hughes had given up smiling. The man looked about as cordial as a viper. "I read about union trouble on the Washoe. You were with the gang that stirred things up at the Last Chance in Nevada. As I remember, the superintendent turned up missing."

Gib returned to his breakfast. "Only for a couple of weeks. We brought him back. Got our back pay, too."

"Eight-hour shift. Four dollars a day. It's robbery."

"Depends how you look at it. I say it's honest pay for honest work." Gib glanced up from his plate. "Don't worry, Hughes. I ain't planning to kidnap you."

"You're a tough nut, Booth. You manage to get by without really working."

Gib took a gulp of coffee. "You read that in the *Mining Journal*?"

"Salting worthless claims, high-grading, stock fraud, card cheat. I hear at one time you were the shell game king of the Idaho mining camps."

"Idaho's a harvest ground for suckers. Thimblerigger can make a fortune."

"Everybody in Stiles knows you wear a loose gun."

"I've swatted a lot of flies in my time, too. Better call the marshal." God Almighty, Gib thought. Hughes was sniffing around like a dog smelling a post. How in hell did he know so much?

"We don't want trouble around here."

"Don't plan to cause none." For some reason, talking to know-it-alls like Hughes made Gib's grammar get sloppy.

"What are your intentions toward Mrs. Metcalf?"

Gib put down his fork. He might have known this bag of hot air had designs on Julia. The idea of it stuck in his craw. "None of your goddamn business."

Hughes stared, his eyes steady and unblinking. He looked like a pig about to eat its young. "I believe it is my business."

"Is that so?" Gib lounged back in his chair and stuck a toothpick in his mouth. "Well, in that case, I'm cleaning her house. Shutters need fixing, too. Then I plan to steal a kiss and take off with her money."

Hughes's eyes narrowed. "Listen, scum. Julia Metcalf is a decent woman. If you're looking to get your gun off, take it out Two-Mile Road, Miss Lavinia's Parlor House. It'll cost you two dollars—three, if you want something fancy."

Gib felt his hackles rise. He could smell trouble in the air; it stank like gunpowder. "Let me tell you something, mister," he said. "When it comes to getting my gun off, Mrs. Metcalf suits me just fine. And it don't cost me a goddamn cent. She even throws in dinner."

The words just rolled out of his mouth, shocking even him. He saw Hughes's face turn dark, the muscles in his neck start to work, and before Gib could react, Hughes reached across the table and grabbed his shirtfront, yanking him up and over the table. Gib regained his balance and brought his arms up between Hughes's, thrusting them wide, breaking his grasp. He gave Hughes a hard shove backward and watched him crash to the floor, taking the chair with him.

The crowded café went silent, save for Hughes's thunder-blue cussing. He hauled himself to his feet, looking mad enough to burst. Strands of pomaded hair swung in front of his face like seaweed.

"You son of a bitch! I'll see you hung."

Gib fished some coins out of his pocket and tossed them on the table. "Easy does it, friend. I might take that as a threat."

He picked up his hat and coat and, without so much as a glance around, strolled out the door.

Gib started feeling bad before he'd gone ten feet down the boardwalk. He thought of what he'd said about Julia and hoped she wouldn't hear about it. Hughes wouldn't tell, not in the exact words, but he'd be sure to report that Gib had spoken loosely.

The more he thought, the lower he felt, until he decided the only way to forget about it would be to treat himself to a few whiskeys and a smoke. A card game might also improve his spirits.

Just outside the Bon Ton's batwing doors, he heard someone call his name. Barnet Cady was hurrying down the sidewalk, arms pumping, his black lawyer's coat flapping. He was walking so fast he had to put one hand on his bowler hat so it wouldn't fly off his bald head. From his expression Gib figured he'd already heard about the scene at the Pickax.

Barnet grabbed Gib by the arm. "I want to talk to you."

Seeing Barnet angry made Gib feel even worse, for Barnet was about the fairest, most even-tempered man in town. The most respected, too, after Doc. And like Doc he'd been a master at seeing through Gib's flimsy explanations.

"We'll talk in my office," Barnet said.

Gib went along meekly, past the jail and Blum's grocery, not saying a word. He stopped at the plate glass window, decorated with faded gold scrollwork: "Barnet Cady, Esq., Attorney-at-Law."

Barnet unlocked the door. Inside the office, he tossed his hat onto a rack and motioned Gib through the sparsely furnished outer office and into a small book-lined room. The room had a long table and chairs enough to seat six.

"Sit down."

It was more a command than an invitation. Gib sat. "How's Dottie?" he asked, delaying the inevitable.

Barnet leaned back in his chair and crossed his legs at the knee. His gaunt, sharp-featured face was tight with anger. "Dottie's very well. But you're not in very good odor with her these days."

That hurt Gib's feelings, since he'd always liked Dottie Cady. She wasn't nearly as stiff as the other ladies in town.

"I hear you had some outrageous things to say about Mrs. Metcalf."

Gib squirmed. "Did Hughes tell you that?"

"We're not talking about Harlan. We're talking about you."

"Hell, Barnet, it just came out. I didn't mean any

disrespect. I wouldn't have said it if Hughes hadn't provoked me."

"What exactly did you say?"

Gib slumped down in his chair. "I didn't say anything. I implied it."

Barnet's fingers drummed the tabletop. "What exactly did you *imply*?"

Gib's eyes roamed the room while he thought of the best way to answer. He ended up staring at the decorative tin ceiling. "I guess I implied I'd been with her in an intimate way."

Barnet said nothing. Gib slumped farther. He felt like a kid again, trying to talk his way out of trouble. The only difference was now he knew he'd done wrong and wished he hadn't; back then he hadn't cared one way or another.

"I'm real sorry, Barnet."

"If you don't want to take guff from Harlan, that's your business. Go out and fight him, I don't care. But when you bring a woman like Julia into it, implying that she's a . . ." His voice quavered with rage. "Bragging that she . . ." He pressed his lips together so hard they almost disappeared. "You're way off the reservation, mister."

Gib's chin sank to his chest. He wished Barnet would just get out the whip and thrash him instead of giving him the third degree.

"She's the widow of a man who saved your hide on more than one occasion. She thinks the best of you—God knows why." Barnet shook his gleaming bald dome of a head. "A woman of Julia's intelligence should see right through a smooth operator like you."

"Are you going to tell her what I said?"

"Of course not. For her sake, not yours. I told Harlan not to mention anything, either."

He'd gotten a reprieve. Gib tried not to let his relief show.

But Barnet wasn't finished. "I don't know what you're up to, Gib. But I have a pretty good idea. And if it's what I think, you'll have plenty of folks to answer to."

Gib returned to contemplating the ceiling. It seemed

everyone in Stiles thought he was after Julia's money except Julia.

"I looked over the papers on the mine," Barnet said after a minute. "They seem to be in order."

Gib straightened up. They were back on safe ground.

"You don't have to make Sarabeth part owner," Barnet said. He went to a wooden filing cabinet and unlocked it with a key from his watch chain. "The claim's not patented, and Rawlie hasn't done any work on it in years. By rights, you can claim it for yourself."

"Sarabeth deserves her share," Gib said. "Her pa owned half. Rawlie's my partner."

Barnet took out a thin file. "That's up to you. She'll need to come by and sign some papers. Rawlie, too."

"I'll take them up to him."

Barnet sat down and started looking through the file. "Where's your grubstake coming from?"

"I've got a little cash," Gib said. "Rawlie does, too." As if that old buzzard would dig up one cent of his buried treasure.

"It takes more than a little cash to open a mine."

"It's a hell of a good investment, Barnet. We got the snakes cleaned out. Maybe you want to stake me."

Barnet wasn't in the mood for jokes. "Watch your step, Gib. There's not a man in town who'll stand for Julia Metcalf being swindled."

When Gib left Barnet's office, he felt somewhat better. He decided to make up for the things he'd said about Julia by going out to her place and finishing the inside cleaning. It was still early in the day; he could have the place shipshape by the time she got back from the Chapmans'.

At the house he got a fire going in the range, roused Mossy out of bed, and cooked him some breakfast. While Mossy did the barn chores, Gib worked on the front hall and staircase, polishing the dark walnut newel posts and banister and washing the pretty stained-glass window at the landing. Together with Mossy he scrubbed the dining room walls, polished the table and the china cabinet, then gave the kitchen a going-over. He finished up by scalding the sink with hot lye and washing the oilcloth floor.

From the barn, Mossy brought out some wooden window frames filled with wire screens. By the time Gib put them up and finished sweeping the porch, it was four o'clock.

Waiting for Julia to show up made him jumpy. He wondered if she would behave differently after last night's kiss; maybe she'd be embarrassed, more standoffish. Maybe she'd just pretend it hadn't happened. And he was still bothered by what he'd said to Hughes. The windbag would be sure to tell Julia everything about his past—the labor trouble, the swindles, the gambling. She'd lower her opinion of him after hearing all that, a prospect he hated to contemplate.

Gib decided his best course of action would be to tell her everything. Ladies liked to hear a man confess and repent. He just wished he hadn't let Hughes get under his skin. If Julia found out what he'd said about her, she would never forgive him.

"How about a few hands of cards, Mossy?" Now that the chores were done, Gib figured he might as well kill some time waiting for her.

"Sure, Gib."

Gib pulled a pack of greasy, well-thumbed cards from his pocket. He and Mossy settled in at the kitchen table. They played hearts for a while, then twenty-one.

"I hear you're a real sharper," Mossy said.

Gib licked his fingers before he dealt the next hand. "Where'd you hear that?"

"At the Bon Ton." Mossy's broad, fleshy face looked troubled. "Some feller said you belly-shot a man in Denver who shaved an ace of diamonds."

"Hell, Moss, you believe I'd belly-shoot anybody?"

Mossy thought. "Naw, I guess not."

Where had that story come from? Gib wondered. He bent his hole card up and studied it. "You want a card, Moss?"

"I'm okay. You ever use a ring shiner, Gib? Or percentage dice?"

Gib took a card for himself and laid it face up. "There's a lot of suckers, Mossy, just begging to be taken."

"A card cheat . . . I don't know."

Gib tried two more cards and broke twenty-one. He flipped his cards over and leaned back in his chair. "I cut it out."

"Yeah?" Mossy looked doubtful.

"I sat in on a game of stud in San Francisco with some fellers who turned out to be professional. This is after I'd been outslicking Mexicans for a couple of years, thought I was about as smart as they come. I was using a vest hold that night—you can hold out an entire hand with it. Then all of a sudden I found three fancy San Francisco gun barrels pointed at my breadbasket. I got religion fast. I was lucky to get off with a beating."

"You quit sharping?"

"That very night. Hell, I'm good enough to win playing it straight if I stay off the professional circuit. Can't make much, but enough to keep me going."

Mossy looked relieved. "You gave up drink, too, and tobacco?"

"Gave 'em up cold." Gib gathered the cards.

"Mrs. Metcalf's a Methodist."

Gib grinned. "Hell, Mossy, I'm so clean these days, I could be a Methodist myself."

Evening was falling when Julia returned from Doubletree Gulch, exhausted. Gib came out of the house, and she forgot she'd barely slept for two days and nights.

"I'll change clothes and scramble up some eggs for supper," she said as he helped her down from the buggy.

"I got a fire going," Gib said. "There's plenty of hot water. I'll fix you a bath."

"That sounds heavenly."

The bathing room adjoined the kitchen just behind the stove. It was fitted with a large zinc-lined tub, a mirror, and hooks for towels and clean clothes. With the stove going, the room was warm, even in winter.

Julia sank into the hot water. After a long soak, she

scrubbed herself from hair to toes. Once dried, powdered, and dressed, she combed out her hair and spread it out on her shoulders to dry.

The house was nearly dark. Julia lit the hall lamp. Gib's black hat hung on the mirrored stand along with his jacket. The newel post and banister gleamed with polish.

She opened the frosty-paned door to the dusky evening. Gib sat on the top step, his feet on the step below, gazing off at the darkening heights.

"Gib."

He got to his feet and slid his hands into his back pockets. The look in his eyes and the warmth of his smile brought on a rush of affection.

"You put up the screening," she said.

"I helped Mossy."

Julia held the door for him to step inside. She'd long ago decided that thoughtfulness was a man's most attractive trait. Edward's thoughtfulness had made her love him despite the difference in their ages and the feeling that she didn't quite deserve all he'd done for her.

"You did more cleaning, too," she said.

"I'd say it's just about finished."

Out of the corner of her eye, Julia glimpsed the two of them reflected in the mirrored hat stand—Gib large and dark-clad, she slender beside him, her damp hair loose and bright about her shoulders. Too loose for propriety, she thought. She reached back and gathered it into one hand, searching her pocket for hairpins.

"Don't do that."

His request startled her.

"Let it hang there," he said. "It's so pretty."

He looked at her with eyes as clear and soft as rainwater. Julia felt a quickening beneath her ribs, and a flush sprang to her cheeks.

"Do you mind?" He sounded apologetic.

"No. Of course not." She ran her fingers through her hair, smoothing it out on her shoulders, painfully aware of his nearness and her own excited heart.

"I'm not one for fancy talk, but you sure are a pretty

lady," he said. "You've got more than a few brains, too. I read your articles in the *Sentinel*."

Julia busied herself with a hairpin, bending and twisting. Gib was flirting with her, but there was nothing practiced about him, no artifice or false charm.

"I call that singing for your supper," she said.

He laughed and gave her a wink. "Then what do you say we eat?"

CHAPTER
10

GIB BROUGHT IN eggs and milk from the shed icebox.
While Julia set the table and started dinner, he emptied the
bath. Julia glanced at him going back and forth through the
kitchen, aware of his heavy tread, the easy strength of his
movements. When he came in after emptying the last
bucket, the smell of frying ham filled the kitchen.

"Supper's ready," she said.

"Mossy's not around. Gone to town, I guess."

They would be alone, Julia thought. She felt awkward
suddenly and a little jittery.

She took off her apron, and they sat down. Bowing her
head, Julia murmured the grace, asking a special blessing
for little Gilbert Chapman. She peeked at Gib and saw that
his eyes were closed tight. At the amen, she spread her
napkin on her lap and nodded for him to begin.

They ate without speaking. She felt Gib's eyes come and
go, although she didn't know for sure, since she dared not
look up. She felt the weight of her hair on her back, the

brush of fabric along her leg, her corset's firm embrace. Each time she took a breath, she felt a pressure on her breasts.

"Things sure taste good," Gib said.

She heard a quiet undertone in his voice, as if he was having the same feelings as she. Julia immediately told herself she was being ridiculous; Gib was merely enjoying his meal.

"I'm glad you like it," she said.

After a few moments she risked a glance at him, the handsomely sculpted face, the muscles rounded beneath his shirt. She imagined his mouth on hers, his strong arms holding her close. She wondered what it would be like to abandon all caution, and her limbs turned to jelly.

Gib got up to get the coffee pot from the stove. He poured them each a cup. When he sat down, he stared at his plate, as if sorting through his thoughts.

"How the devil does Chapman make a living?"

Julie gathered up her wayward emotions and forced them aside. Gib had brought her back to reality, and just as well.

"Gold from his diggings, I assume," she said. "And Mrs. Chapman sells things in town—baked goods, canned goods, jams, goat's milk. She does mending, too."

Gib ate without further comment. When he finished, he sat back in his chair. "Chapman says he's not finding color. Doesn't surprise me, not on the old Whiskey as far downstream as he's working."

"He worked at the Continental for years," Julia said. "He was among the first to be laid off when operations slowed down. He and his wife didn't want to move away, because their little girls are buried here. I guess he's taking a chance on striking gold in Doubletree Gulch."

"He's wasting his time."

Suddenly Julia had an idea. "You could hire him."

"Huh?"

"You could hire Mr. Chapman to work at the Rattling Rock." Julia couldn't keep the excitement from her voice. "You'll need some men once you get under way." It was a wonderful plan, she thought. The Chapmans lived near the mine, Otis was a steady worker, and heaven knew he and Vera could use the income.

Gib didn't appear to share her enthusiasm. He looked at her with a puzzled expression as if he didn't know what she was talking about. "I have a ways to go before I can meet a payroll."

It came back to her in a flash—the question of his finances. Julia's excitement faded. She thought of Harlan's warning: ". . . win your trust . . . strip you of your money." She pushed food around on her plate, her heart in her throat; she couldn't bear the thought that Gib might have ulterior motives.

"Do you need money, Gib?"

He shifted in his chair. The moment seemed to stretch on and on. Julia held her breath.

"No," he said at last. "I don't need any."

Julia finished her dinner flooded with relief. Dottie, Louise, Harriet, and Harlan—they all were wrong. They believed the worst of Gib and they were wrong.

Bee walked into the kitchen, tail high, meowing impatiently.

"Well, look who's here," Julia said. "It took you long enough to smell dinner." The cat rubbed against her legs, purring. "Here are some nice pieces of ham for you."

She put scraps on a plate and crouched down on the floor, stroking Bee's silky back. She looked up at Gib and smiled. "Bee's usually in the kitchen the minute I start cooking."

He didn't meet her eyes. "I'd better be going." He got to his feet. "You've had a rough couple of days. You need some sleep."

He went down the hall to get his jacket and hat. Julia began clearing the table, struggling with disappointment, wondering why he was leaving so soon. He probably thought she'd been prying again with her question about his money.

He came back to the kitchen wearing his jacket. "Good night, ma'am."

"Ma'am," Julia thought. Last night, it had been princess. Princess with a kiss.

"I'll take care of the shutters on Monday," he said. "You've got some loose slats, and a few boards on the porch need replacing." He fingered his hat brim, his eyes trained over her shoulder. "That should about finish things up here."

Julia didn't want him to go. She wanted to see his smile, the softness in his eyes. She wanted to feel his lips on her face.

"The Chapmans want you to be a sponsor at Gilbert's baptism," she blurted. "You and me both."

As soon as she said it, she wished she hadn't.

Gib looked stunned. "What does that mean?"

"It means we all stand up together when the baby's baptized." Her words came out in an anxious rush. "And we'll see that he's kept under the guidance of the church until he's confirmed."

Gib eyes traveled the room. He rubbed his chin, crossed and uncrossed his arms. This was the wrong time to bring up the christening, Julia thought miserably. First her question about his money, now this.

"When'll that be?" he asked. "When he's confirmed?"

"Twelve or thirteen years."

"I won't be sticking around for twelve or thirteen years."

"It's a formality, Gib. An honor."

"I don't think I can do it." He met her eyes, then quickly looked down.

He didn't want the responsibility, Julia thought. She should have known; she should have broached the subject more carefully.

"Good night, ma'am." He put on his hat.

"Good night, Gib." Julia managed a smile, but the door closed before he could see it.

Gib dismounted at the livery. He loosened the bridle, removed the bit, and led Lucky to the trough.

Lee's night man came out. "I'll put him to bed, Gib."

"Thanks, Fred. I thought you'd be closed up."

"Hell, it's early. Besides, I'm here all night."

Gib went down the boardwalk to the Bon Ton, passing

through pools of light cast by streetlamps. It wasn't as late as he'd thought. Stores were just closing, and the saloons were just cranking up. He heard a cowboy yipping in the distance and the sound of smashing glass.

At the Bon Ton, Gib climbed the outside stairs to the second floor and went inside. The narrow lamplit hallway smelled of tobacco smoke and hair oil. Dellwood let rooms by the night or the week—occasionally by the hour, although that was against the town ordinance. Gib could sleep through most anything, save gunfire, so the jiggling beds and sounds of passion didn't bother him.

His room, on a front corner overlooking the street, was furnished with an iron bedstead, a dresser, and a washstand. The wallpaper, once yellow, had turned a dirty gold. Long strips had begun to peel off.

Gib lit the lamp and sat down on the bed. It had been a long, hard day starting with Hughes at the Pickax, then Barnet's lecture, and a whole lot of housework. He should have been dog tired, but he wasn't.

He scaled his hat onto the bedpost and lay back, one boot on the floor, one on the blanket. He stared at the tacked-up picture of a variety actress. Her face blurred into Julia's. He saw the spread of damp, shining hair, those dazzling eyes, and the smile that sprinkled him with warm light. Sunshine, Gib thought. It was like basking in sunshine, the way she made him feel.

Christ, he didn't like what was happening. Last night on the Chapmans' porch he'd started something that had crossed the line from wanting Julia's trust to wanting a whole lot more. The thought of it scared him to death. It scared him even more than the prospect of sponsoring little Gilbert Chapman in church.

Gib got up off the bed and went to the washstand. He threw water on his face and rubbed his eyes. The sooner he got out of town the better. That meant he had to steer his mind back to business, think with his brain instead of his privates.

He pulled out his watch: half-past nine. He stretched out on the bed and put his hat over his face. Julia had taken him by surprise, asking about his money; she'd put him right on the spot.

But it wouldn't be simple. He'd have to win her over without ending up knee deep in trouble with Doc's wife. He had another problem, too—he needed money for a start-up grubstake, and he needed it fast.

Gib decided to catch a few winks. Then he'd head out to the Tabors' house and see if he could rouse Lee.

Gib jumped one-handed over the picket fence gate and landed soundlessly on the grass. He scooped some gravel off the walk and trotted across the yard and around the side of the frame house. He squinted up at the rear second-floor window.

It was from that window that he and Lee had tried to launch a hot-air balloon. They'd lit a sponge soaked in kerosene to heat the air. The balloon had gone nowhere, but the curtains had caught fire and the room had been gutted before the fire brigade put out the flames.

Everybody had blamed Gib. He hadn't minded, since he'd expected to be blamed for most everything. To pay for the burned-out room, he'd worked for old Levi for three months. Then he and Lee had tried the balloon again, this time incinerating Mrs. Tabor's prized lilac bushes and the whole back porch. After that, the old lady had forbidden Gib to set foot on her property.

Gib tossed a few pebbles. They pinged against the window. He kept throwing in a steady rhythm, careful to keep it soft. If the old lady caught him, he'd end up with his britches full of buckshot.

There was movement at the window, the sash went up, and a head popped out. It was too shadowy to see for sure, but Gib hoped it was Lee.

"Hey, Lee," he called in a loud whisper. "Get your bustle down here. I've got to talk to you."

"Gib?"

"Yeah. Front porch."

"Don't wake Ma."

"You think I'm crazy?"

Gib loped back to the front porch and sat down on the top step. He took a toothpick out of his pocket and chewed on it. The night was spooky and quiet. Thinking of the old lady coming after him with a shotgun gave him the willies.

The front door opened, and Lee tiptoed across the porch. He wore a coat over his long johns, and his fair hair was rumpled. It was strange to see Lee with a mustache; to Gib he would always be a smooth-faced kid.

"Thanks for coming out, Lee."

"Keep it down. Ma's got ears sharp as razors." Lee sat on the top step beside him.

"Lee, I need money to get me started at the Rattling Rock. I'll pay you back real soon. I've got something lined up, but the money won't come through for a while."

Lee started tugging on his mustache. "I don't know, Gib."

"Charlie got the snakes out. I'm ready to start blasting. I need another man and cash to pay him. Need supplies, too."

Lee didn't respond. Gib shifted on the step. He didn't like putting Lee on the spot, but he had no choice. To look serious about the mine, he'd have to hire a man. Julia had made him realize that.

"A couple of hundred, Lee, that's all I need for now."

"It ain't easy, with Ma looking at the books every day."

Jesus, Gib thought, Lee was on a tighter leash than he'd thought. "I'll pay you back with interest. Give me a month."

Lee's hesitation started Gib thinking about I. Z. Blum's offer. Blum had said he'd grubstake him, but he would be asking for an accounting every minute. And he'd figure out pretty damned quick that Gib's plans for the Rattling Rock didn't amount to anything more than separating Julia from her inheritance.

"Is it true you broke jail in Salt Lake?"

Gib looked at Lee in surprise. "What're you talking about?"

Lee draped his arms over his bent knees and stared at his stocking feet. "That's what they're saying."

"Who's saying? God Almighty, there's a wagonload of tall tales going around about me."

Lee gave him a skeptical glance. "From what I've been hearing, you're crookeder'n a dog's hind leg."

"I never broke jail—never been *in* jail. Except for a few short spells and once with you. Never in Salt Lake."

Lee sighed. "I'll get you the money."

Gib was relieved. He clapped Lee on the shoulder, gripping hard. "Who's spreading these stories about me?"

"You hear them all over—saloons, the livery, the Pickax, the newspaper office. I don't know, Gib. Don't know what to think."

Gib thought of Harlan Hughes. More than likely the gasbag was behind the stories, aiming to turn Julia against him, get her and the money for himself. The idea of it roused his temper.

"I'll tell it to you straight," Gib said. "I've fleeced a fair number of stiffs in my time, but I never held up a legitimate business or conned an honest man. The only man I shot dead since the war was Bob Hockett, and that's the truth."

Lee smiled faintly. "If you say so."

Gib didn't know if Lee believed him or not, and that bothered him. For all the dust he'd kicked up, he'd never been what he would call a liar. To his way of thinking, there was a world of difference between outright lying and pulling a fast one, which took some imagination.

"Say, Gib," Lee said. "D'you see much of Sarabeth?"

Something in his voice made Gib take a second look. "You still sweet on her?"

Lee shrugged and squinted into the distance, which Gib took to be a pretty clear yes. He thought of Sarabeth in the old days, running through the hills and draws of Doubletree Gulch, flushing rock chucks and cottontails with Lee hot on her trail. Back then she'd seemed as much a part of nature as the meadowlarks and timber lilies. Now she was pretty well used, but she still had plenty of the old spark.

"She's a handsome woman, Lee."

"She's a whore."

Gib squirmed, feeling uncomfortable. Not all the hurdy girls took customers, but he wouldn't have bet on Sarabeth.

"I got her started," Lee said. "We couldn't stay away from each other, first up at Rawlie and Digger's place and then when she was driving for Pa. When Pa passed on, Ma got rid of her. That's when she took up the life." He pulled a handkerchief from his coat pocket and blew his nose.

"If you're soft on her, why don't you marry her?" Gib asked.

Lee hunched up his shoulders. "Ma."

Gib wasn't surprised by the answer, but he couldn't help feeling impatient. "You're thirty years old, Lee. Maybe it's time you did what you wanted."

"She'll take the livery away from me. Sell it. After Pa died, she threatened to do it unless I stopped with Sarabeth."

Gib could hardly believe that any woman would be so mean as to take away the things her son loved best. The old lady had chased Sarabeth off, and she'd fixed things at the livery so Lee was nothing more than a hired man.

"Back when you and I used to run around, Ma said I'd be the death of her," Lee went on. "She used to say if she died, it'd all be on my conscience. She still talks like that when I do something she don't like."

Gib wondered if old Levi's death bothered her conscience any; she'd had him hog-tied and branded his whole married life.

"Sarabeth'll have money one day," Gib said. "She's part owner of the Rattling Rock, and Rawlie's got a stash hidden away. She'll be rich enough to buy you a new livery."

Lee shook his head. "I'd never take money from a woman. That's one thing I'd never do."

Gib's knee started a nervous jiggle. He sure wished Lee hadn't said that.

"Guess I'd better get some sleep," Lee said. "Ma'll be wondering tomorrow why I'm so tired."

Gib thought of old lady Tabor staring at Lee across the breakfast table, giving him the third degree. Then he thought of his own ma going easy on him whenever he got out of line. Anger begets anger, she'd say, love begets love.

Not once in his memory had she raised her voice against him.

Gib figured that was one reason he'd turned out so bad.

Julia spent Monday morning sorting through papers in Edward's study. There were cabinets filled with record books and medical notes that Dr. Beacham could use, and files of correspondence, much of which could be thrown out.

Julia had begun the task of cleaning out the study shortly after Edward's death, then abandoned it. What had stopped her was the discovery of a hatbox filled with bunches of ribbon-tied letters. They were from Edward's first wife, who along with their children had perished in a cholera epidemic.

Edward had never once mentioned his wife and children to Julia. She knew only what Randall had told her—that Edward had lost his family, then gone to war to escape his grief. During her marriage, Julia had felt no desire to pry. Her instincts had told her that while she might be Edward's helpmeet and friend, she would never be a wife, not like the woman he'd married as a young man.

Her instincts had been confirmed after Edward's death, when she'd read a few of the tender, intimate letters. For months afterward, Julia hadn't touched any of his papers, fearful of what else she might find.

Mossy knocked on the study door and brought in the mail: an issue of the *Medical Record* and two letters.

"Gib's come to work on the shutters."

Julia started to get up. "I didn't hear him arrive."

"He says no need for you to come out. He'll see to things."

Julia sat down again. Her thoughts flew about aimlessly—Gib's kiss, his intimate glances, his reluctance to stand up for Gilbert, his abrupt departure Saturday night— the same thoughts that had kept her awake into the small hours of the morning.

"I'll hitch up Biscuit," Mossy said. "You'll be heading up to the Continental?"

"In a few minutes." It was her day to call at the mine and visit the miners' families.

When Mossy left, Julia opened the mail. A letter from Randall informed her of Dr. Beacham's decision to take over Edward's practice. Randall wrote that the citizens of Stiles should be grateful that such a gifted young physician had agreed to set up practice in so remote an area: "I have no doubts, my dear Julia, that you will accord him every courtesy and provide him with any of Edward's furnishings and equipment he might need."

He concluded, as he did every letter, with regards to Harlan, whom he'd met when he'd come to Stiles after Edward's funeral. The letter was signed, "Your affectionate brother, Randall Frye, M.D."

Julia gazed out the window. In a few weeks Stiles would once again have a physician with excellent credentials. The doctor from Dillon could go back to his livestock, and she could decorate her house.

Julia made a wry face. Louise would be pleased. The two of them could take that shopping trip to Denver.

She tore open the next letter and unfolded a sheet of cheap yellow paper. The crude style of printing was familiar. Before she even read the salutation, her heart began to pound. Her eyes dropped to the signature. "An ardent gentleman."

"Dear Lord," she whispered.

She told herself not to read it, even as her eyes flew over the words. The correspondent lamented that she had not contacted him after he'd answered her advertisement for a maid, but he was glad that her spring cleaning was going well. He complimented her on how well things looked, especially in her bedroom where . . .

Julia crumpled the paper and flung it into the wastebasket. Words, she told herself. Words printed on paper could do her no harm. But her heart was racing and her stomach felt queasy. The first letter she'd dismissed as a prank, but this one was different. Its foul sentiments showed that someone was purposely trying to frighten her.

Julia wiped her fingers on her skirt; just touching the letter made her want to wash her hands.

She went upstairs to change into her driving costume. As she buttoned her high-collared black bodice, she wondered who would send such a hateful thing, and for what purpose?

She stuck hairpins all around her topknot. The sound of hammering came from out back where Gib was working on the shutters. Suddenly Julia had a terrible thought.

Gib.

She stared at herself in the mirror; she was visibly pale. He couldn't have had anything to do with either of the letters, she told herself. The idea was too preposterous to even consider. Then she remembered that she'd received the first letter shortly after he'd arrived in Stiles.

She put on her veiled driving hat, took up her gloves, and went downstairs and outside. The day was breezy and brisk. Gib was working near the barn where he'd set up a makeshift workbench on boards laid across two sawhorses. When he saw her, he stopped his hammering and pushed up his hat brim.

"Morning, ma'am."

"Good morning, Gib."

There was the usual welcome on his face, the faint disarming smile. Julia looked at him closely, trying to see a more sinister man, but she saw only the one she knew — vigorous good looks, an easy stance, gray eyes as clear as pebbles in a stream.

"I'm on my way to the Continental," she said. "I'm afraid you and Mossy will be on your own for lunch."

"Going to see Hughes?"

"I'm making medical calls. But yes, I'll be seeing Harlan."

Gib took her bag and put it under the buggy seat, then handed her up. As she settled herself, he rested a hand on Biscuit's withers and gave her that smile again, laden with manly charm.

"I'll get the shutters up this afternoon and fix the boards on the porch."

"I appreciate all your work."

He touched his hat and returned to the shutters.

Julia curled the reins in her fingers and gigged Biscuit to a trot. As the buggy bounced out of the yard, she thought of Gib's generosity, his kindness to Mossy, his anxiety about sponsoring baby Gilbert. It was inconceivable that one man could have two completely different sides to his nature.

CHAPTER

11

THE CONTINENTAL MINING Company was located nearly five miles from Stiles, up a switchback road rutted by heavy ore wagons. The immediate landscape was scarred with abandoned mines and tumbledown shacks, but off in the distance the hills and mountains appeared gloriously pristine, the sky shone a hard spring blue, and the air was scented with pine.

As Julia drew nearer the mine's plain wooden structures, sounds grew louder—shouting men, grinding metal, banging ore cars, and slamming doors. There was a faint low rumble—dynamite blasting somewhere deep underground. She stopped the buggy before the long building that housed the superintendent's headquarters and the assay office. Almost immediately the door opened and Harlan came out to greet her. He wore shiny patent leather boots and a thick watch chain, hung with a gold nugget charm. His dark hair, slicked back smooth, gleamed with pomade. Harlan always managed to look perfectly groomed, even in the midst of the Continental's mud and chaos.

"There's not many to see you today," he said, helping her down.

"That suits me just fine," Julia said. While she didn't mind dealing with miners' ailments, she preferred visiting their families.

Inside, she turned the small bare room off the superintendent's office into a makeshift dispensary. She assembled her instruments—stethoscope, thermometers, tongue depressors, lances, and probes—and set up her small copper sterilizing pan.

Once she was washed and ready, the men trooped in one at a time. Julia listened to coughs, lanced boils, treated sprains and ulcerated sores. For rheumatism she prescribed salicylic acid; for bursitis, immobilizing the arm. Edward had taught her to believe in the body's natural tendency to heal, so she handed out medicine sparingly and instead preached her gospel of healthy habits.

After an hour she packed her bag, washed up, tidied her hair, and joined Harlan for dinner.

The unpainted dining room contained simple furnishings and possessed an unattractive view of the tailing dump. By contrast, the table was lavishly set with bright linen and china.

"So elegant," Julia said as Harlan held her chair. "Surely you and Edward never dined like this."

"My dear Julia, you are not Edward." He gave her shoulder a gentle squeeze.

Julia quickly opened a new topic of conversation. "Have you had any luck at number four level?"

"Not yet." Harlan settled across from her. "But we're blasting. I've got a crew down there timbering as we speak."

"I hope you turn up something soon. In the meantime, we should be grateful for the ranchers in the valley." With the troubles at the mine, the stockmen provided Stiles with much of its business.

Harlan made an impatient sound. "Blasted stockmen are a nuisance, if you ask me. There's more of them in the legislature every session."

He motioned to the cook, Lee Chung, who bustled to the table, bowing and smiling. Harlan snapped off an order, and Lee Chung hurried away in his humble crouch.

"Mining is the lifeblood of the territory, not cows," Harlan went on. "You know it, I know it, and the politicians know it."

Julia didn't want Harlan to get started on politics, but anything was better than the subject nagging at her—the latest indecent letter and her vague suspicions about Gib.

Lee Chung brought out platters of food—a roast oozing juices, potatoes, boiled beans, delicate rolls. "Doesn't this look wonderful!" Julia exclaimed. "Lee Chung, you've outdone yourself."

The cook understood little English, but he beamed as he held the platters for her.

When the meal had been served and Julia had said grace, Harlan cleared his throat. "I have a small announcement to make. I'm thinking of running for delegate to the constitutional convention next January."

"Why, that's fine news!" Julia pretended to be surprised, even though Dottie had told her about Harlan's plan two weeks ago. "We've all been speculating about when you'd declare yourself for public office. Running for delegate is a wonderful idea."

Harlan forked a chunk of potato into his mouth, making his cheek bulge. He chewed vigorously, then swallowed with an audible gulp. His table manners, Julia had long ago decided, were not the best.

"Once a Democrat gets into the White House, there's no telling how far I'll go," he said. "There's plenty of men in the party who'll back me all the way to Washington."

"With your connections, you're bound to succeed."

Harlan looked pleased. "I'll show those old mossbacks in Congress a thing or two." He stuffed a dripping slab of beef into his mouth, then wiped his greasy lips on a napkin and gave Julia a meaningful look. "There are other declarations in the offing, and not about politics."

She smiled vaguely, hoping he wouldn't bring up the subject of getting on with her life, which was so dear to Dottie's heart.

"Your year of mourning will be over in October. Just before the election."

"Really, Harlan—"

"I have a grand future, Julia." He stopped eating and focused his attention on her.

Julia was embarrassed by his intended meaning. Even if she felt some affection for Harlan, she couldn't imagine coping with the hectic political scene in Helena or back east in Washington City, the life he planned for himself.

"Edward has been gone scarcely six months," she said.

"Almost eight," he corrected her.

Julia fingered the buttons on her black silk bodice and tried to think of a diplomatic way to move on to a new topic of conversation.

"This is not a formal proposal," Harlan said. "I'm only making my intentions clear. I don't want there to be any misunderstandings later on."

They ate in silence. As was his habit, Harlan had made his point and left her to consider it. Julia well knew what marriage to him would mean: entertaining his colleagues, socializing with their wives, currying favor with various constituencies, devoting herself to his ambitions. She wondered if she was being selfish, wanting a life for herself.

"There is something else I must discuss with you," he said.

Julia looked up expectantly, hoping for a less distressing subject.

"I had a run-in with Gib Booth Saturday morning at the Pickax. He said things about you that were most insulting. I was forced to resort to physical force."

Julia froze. She stared at him, trying not to betray her alarm.

"He bragged that you and he had . . ." Harlan glanced

away. "Forgive me, my dear. He said he'd been intimate with you."

The words hit her like a slap. She drew back, dropping her fork with a clatter.

"It's painful for me to relate such a thing," Harlan said. "I know you think the best of him—it's in your nature to think the best of everyone. That's what makes it so despicable, that a man you trusted, a man you allowed into your home, a man Edward befriended, should so sully your reputation."

Julia's mind floundered in disbelief. She couldn't believe that Gib, with his good manners and tender smile, could have purposely compromised her. Surely Harlan was mistaken. "What did he say?" Her voice sounded quavery. "What exactly did he say?"

"My dear, I can't tell you that. He was simply too crude."

Julia's head filled with echoes—Dottie's voice, Harlan's, Harriet Tabor's: "You'd better watch out." "He's not the sort of man a respectable lady would allow inside her house." "The man hasn't a decent bone in his body."

Suddenly she thought of the letters. "I have received letters." Tears burned her eyes and slid down her cheeks. She wiped at them with a shaking hand.

Harlan frowned. "What letters?"

"L-letters that were indecent." She struggled to compose herself. She felt betrayed and frightened, hurt beyond bearing.

"You must take them to the marshal." Harlan's face turned red with fury. "Booth has a twisted mind. He's downright dangerous."

Julia was aware of Lee Chung whisking away plates. Then a cup of fragrant tea appeared before her.

"I threw the first one away." She was gulping back sobs. "It came in response to my advertisement for a maid. Walt Stringer was there when I opened it. The second one arrived this morning. I—I threw it in the wastebasket."

Harlan reached over and covered her hand with his. "When you get home, retrieve it and take it to the marshal. Will you promise me that, Julia?"

She nodded, trying desperately to master her tears.

"And be sure to lock your doors. I don't mean to frighten you, but Booth is an outlaw, a murderer. He's been involved in high-grading and kidnapping, not to mention various gambling swindles. Wherever he goes he stirs up trouble."

Julia tried to make sense of Harlan's words. Was she such a poor judge of character that she'd seen no hint of Gib's true nature? Had her infatuation so blinded her to reality?

"There, now, my dear," Harlan said patting her hand. "Drink your tea. It will soothe your nerves."

Julia drove through the landscape of tangled brush and jutting rock. Her heart felt empty, as if she'd lost something precious and there was nothing to take its place. She lifted her eyes to the western horizon where purple mountains towered skyward. God's work was wondrous, she reminded herself, a bulwark against the folly of man. But the vast beauty only made her feel worse.

Harlan had been wonderfully understanding, just as he'd been a tower of strength when Edward died. Maybe she could grow to love him, Julia thought, just as she'd grown to love Edward. Perhaps she could learn about politics just as she'd learned about medicine, and find satisfaction in her husband's career.

A mile or so below the Continental, a settlement of miners' homes lay strewn across a sloping grassy plain. The plank cabins, their whitewash worn away, looked tired and flimsy. Each had a woodpile, a few chickens, a haphazard garden. Smoke floated from chimneys, bringing to Julia's nostrils the scent of burning wood.

She stopped the buggy before a rickety fence. A little girl with tight pigtails and dirty cheeks stood in the yard, her fingers in her mouth.

"Hello, Tilly," Julia called. "Tell your mama Mrs. Metcalf's here."

The girl turned and scampered into the house, bare feet flying. Julia got down from the buggy, took her medical bag, and opened the gate. Mrs. Ames stepped outside to meet her. She was a thin woman with sand-colored hair and a delicately boned face. She reached back to fasten her hair, and Julia saw with a start that she was pregnant again.

"How are you today, Mrs. Ames?"

"Well enough, but Jimmy's foot got worse."

"You should have called me. I'd have come up."

"He's afraid of being cut," Mrs. Ames said. "And Ab couldn't get away to fetch you. He's working a longer shift now."

That news surprised Julia. She wondered why Harlan would have some men working long shifts when he'd laid off so many others.

Inside, the cabin was gloomy, nothing like Mrs. Chapman's bright, cheerful home. Greased paper covered the windows, filtering out sunshine, and gunnysack rugs lay on the dirt floor.

Julia's eyes adjusted to the dimness. The Ameses' furniture consisted of a crude table, a few chairs with rawhide seats, and a straw mattress on a board bed for the parents. They'd once had a better home, but it had burned down, leaving them nothing but their lives. It was a pity, Julia thought, that four children, soon to be five, had to live in a one-room shack and sleep in a loft.

Jimmy lay on a pallet by the heating stove. "Light the lamp, please, Mrs. Ames."

Mrs. Ames brought the kerosene lamp. "I dosed him with quinine like you said, and put on the salve."

"Hello, Matt." Julia smiled at a wide-eyed boy who sat on a stool, gaping at her. "Before I leave, I'll give you a lemon drop."

Matt wriggled with pleasure, then popped a thumb into his mouth. Julia remembered what a big baby he'd been and how Mrs. Ames had suffered through her labor.

She crouched by the pallet and smoothed Jimmy's hot forehead. He had his mother's sandy hair and freckled complexion. "How are you feeling, Jimmy?"

"It's hurtin.'" He stared at her with frightened eyes.

"Let's see if I can fix it."

"You going to cut me?"

"I'll look at it first."

She unwrapped the bandaged foot. Mrs. Ames had tended it well; the bandage and the foot were clean, the cut treated with carbolic salve. But the wound was red and pulsing. Julia knew it would have to be enlarged and drained before poisons got into Jimmy's bloodstream.

"It's like a toothache in my foot," Jimmy said.

"It looks sore. I'm going to take you home with me."

"Will you cut me?"

"I'll give you something to make you sleep. You won't feel it."

"Will I wake up?"

"Of course you'll wake up. Can you ride in the buggy with me?"

"Yes, ma'am."

"I'll finish my calls and come back for you."

Julia distributed lemon drops to Tilly and Matt and the littlest, Virgil, then took Mrs. Ames outside. "I'll have to drain the infection. It's better I do it at my place, so I can give him chloroform and watch him for a few days."

"Bless you, ma'am. I've been so worried."

Julia glanced at her faintly rounded belly. "You're expecting again."

Mrs. Ames looked away, her pale cheeks reddening. "I love my husband, Mrs. Metcalf. I can't say no."

"There are ways to prevent babies without saying no."

Mrs. Ames looked embarrassed. "I'd be grateful if you'd tell me. This one'll have to be the last.

"We'll talk about it soon. I'll be back to pick up Jimmy."

Jimmy didn't peep all the way to Stiles. He sat beside Julia, tight-lipped and pinched-faced, his throbbing foot extended. At the house, Julia was relieved to see no sign of Gib.

Mossy came out of the barn. "Why, lookee there, it's Jimmy Ames."

"Jimmy's foot is still sore," Julia said. "Do you think you could carry him into the surgery?"

"Shoot, I'll carry Jimmy anywhere."

Jimmy climbed onto Mossy's back and hung on to his neck. "She's gonna cut me."

Mossy hitched Jimmy higher. "If anyone was to cut me, I'd make sure it was Mrs. Metcalf. She wouldn't hurt a fly."

Julia went upstairs to Edward's room and made up the big walnut bed with fresh sheets. She remembered Gib whistling while he scrubbed the walls, and she had to fight back tears. Each time she thought of what he'd said to Harlan, she felt a fresh wave of despair.

When she went into the surgery, Jimmy was sitting on the operating table listening to Mossy tell Gib's breakfast story about the train crossing the trestle. Julia tried not to listen. Remembering the magical morning when Gib had first charmed her was almost too painful to bear.

"Gib finished the shutters," Mossy said. "He says to tell you he'll be up at the Rattling Rock. Won't be back till later in the week."

Julia thought of her promise to Harlan. "I want you to take something down to the marshal for me, Mossy. I'll give it to you after I take care of Jimmy here."

She looked at the wide-eyed boy. "Now let's talk about what we're going to do with that foot of yours."

Gib emptied Digger's cabin and built a bonfire for all the junk—moldy blankets, stinking animal skins, ten years' worth of newspapers, old socks, and broken-stemmed pipes. There were a few things of Blackfoot Mary's, which he set aside for Sarabeth. Then he swept out the cobwebs and insects, washed the place down, replaced some broken windowpanes, and scraped food off the sheet-iron stove.

When he finished, he kicked at the tables and chairs that weren't too far off kilter and decided the cabin was more than livable; it was downright homey. Cleaning a place was like mining a claim—it made a man feel possessive. Maybe that was why he felt at home at Julia's place—all that cleaning made it seem part his.

"When're you going to start digging?" Rawlie asked.

"Soon as I lay in supplies."

Rawlie was about as excited as Gib had ever seen him. For two days he'd followed him around in his long Confederate coat, his beard blowing in the breeze, commenting on Gib's every move. The old man was lonely, Gib figured. Digger's dying must have been real hard on him.

"I'm going to hire on Otis Chapman," Gib said. "He's been panning the old Whiskey since the Continental gave him his time and sent him down the hill."

Rawlie pawed his beard. "That so?"

"Yep. That's so."

"Otis worked powder at the Continental," Rawlie said. "He's laid track. Timbered, too. Don't make no sense, laying off a good man like Otis."

"He's got his own place down the gulch. Just got himself a new baby boy."

"Well, I'll be."

Gib thought about Gilbert Chapman and realized he'd pretty much forgotten what the baby looked like. Maybe he'd ride down this evening and pay the Chapmans a visit.

The sun was slipping toward the horizon as Gib headed down the trail. When he rode into Doubletree Gulch, the landscape was bathed in a warm late-afternoon glow. He listened to the rushing sound of water and the singing of birds and thought about Gilbert growing up here in the shadows of the mountains, close to the earth and wild things. The boy could hunt for rabbit and grouse and wild berries, and farther up in the hills he'd see puma and bear. Thinking about it pleased Gib. With nature close by and his hardworking parents to look after him, the boy was sure to grow into a fine upstanding citizen.

At the cabin Gib heard the whack of an ax. He dismounted and went around back. He stood for a minute watching Chapman chop wood. The man was as skinny as a cornstalk, but he had a wiry strength and an easy swing. Rawlie said Chapman was a good man with a single jack, and he knew how to handle powder, too — could load holes so the ground broke just right.

"Evening, Chapman."

Chapman looked up. His droopy mustache lifted into a smile. "Why, Mr. Booth. It's mighty kind of you to stop by." He tossed a few splits onto the pile and took out a handkerchief to wipe his hands. "You come to see the baby?"

Gib felt a little embarrassed. "I wouldn't mind."

"The wife'll be pleased."

Gib followed Otis inside, wiping his feet before he stepped in. The cabin was warm from the stove and smelled of woodsmoke and dinner. Gib realized he was damned hungry.

"Vera, look who's come."

Mrs. Chapman stuck her head out from the lean-to kitchen. "Land sakes, Mr. Booth, I was just thinking of you."

Gib was surprised to see her up and about. Julia had said she'd be in bed for a few weeks. He glanced at the cradle on the floor where the baby lay bundled up in a white blanket.

"There, now," Mrs. Chapman said. "You want to hold the baby, I can see that plain enough."

Gib felt a jump of alarm. "I'll just look, if it's all the same."

"Nonsense. Otis, you take Mr. Booth out front and give him Gilbert. I'll set another place at the table. Will you stay for supper with us, Mr. Booth?"

"Thank you, ma'am. I'd be pleased to."

Mr. Chapman followed Gib into the front part of the cabin, carrying Gilbert.

"I think I'd better just look," Gib said in a low voice.

"He's asleep," Mr. Chapman said. "Even when he's awake, he don't wriggle so's you'd drop him."

Before Gib could protest further, the baby was in his arms.

He seemed heavier than Gib expected, a good solid weight. Gib looked at his face, plump and pink, slits of eyes like a kitten's. His little fists were curled at his cheeks—tiny fingers, miniature nails—and his hair was a silky cap. Gib took in all the details; he'd never looked closely at a baby.

Mrs. Chapman came in with a steaming dish. "Isn't that a nice picture," she said. "Such a big man and such a tiny baby."

Gib grew braver and gave Gilbert a jiggle. The baby's eyes opened and he emitted a little sound. Gib froze and looked at Mrs. Chapman.

"You're doing fine, Mr. Booth. Just fine."

He didn't jiggle the baby again, and Gilbert's eyes closed. Gib was relieved when Mrs. Chapman took him away and they sat down to eat.

"We'd be honored if you'd sponsor Gilbert at his christening," Mrs. Chapman said after they'd finished bowing their heads for grace.

Gib rubbed his hands on his knees. "Ma'am, I'm not sure—"

"Reverend Dudley's circuit brings him to Stiles the second Sunday of the month."

Gib wished he could think of a polite way to decline. "Mrs. Metcalf said something about watching over the boy till he was twelve or thirteen," he said. "I'll be pulling up stakes before then."

Mrs. Chapman laughed. "Heavens, you've no obligation. Just keep Gilbert in your prayers and send him a letter now and then."

Plates were passed and filled, and Gib took a few mouthfuls of dinner. The fish was fresh out of the creek—it just about melted in his mouth—and the stewed tomatoes were spiced just right.

"You are a Christian, Mr. Booth?"

The Chapmans were looking at him as if they wondered why he was so ignorant about baptisms. "My people were Quakers," he said, and immediately wished he hadn't.

The Chapmans exchanged glances. Chapman's eyes dropped to Gib's belt line where his gun hung under his jacket. Gib remembered he should have removed it before sitting down to eat.

"Quakers," Chapman said. "Well, what d'you know?"

"Such simple, peaceful people," Mrs. Chapman said. "We had Quaker neighbors in Illinois."

It was too late to take it back, so Gib just sat there and suffered. The Chapmans would figure him for a man with no character, raised as a Quaker and wearing a gun. They'd get themselves another sponsor, change Gilbert's name, too.

"I'm sorry, ma'am."

But Mrs. Chapman didn't seem the least bit upset. "Why, there's no need to be sorry, Mr. Booth. Otis and Gilbert and I will expect to see you at church on June the tenth."

CHAPTER

12

JIMMY AMES LOOKED small and tired lying in Edward's big bed. His head was propped up on pillows, and his sore foot stuck out from under the covers. He'd had another bad night with pain. Julia had given him a small dose of laudanum to help him sleep, and he was still a bit fuzzy.

"How about a piece of cake, Jimmy?"

"Yes'm." He held Bee in his arms. The cat seemed to give him comfort, and Bee, purring loudly, enjoyed the attention.

"Tomorrow you can move downstairs and sit in the front room. It's sunny there. I'll play the piano for you."

"I can hear ladies down there."

"It's the Civic Betterment Committee." Julia broke off a piece of cake and popped it into Jimmy's mouth. "We meet every few weeks to talk about how to make Stiles a better place to live."

"I wished I lived down here. Then I wouldn't have to walk all that ways to school."

"I want you to wear your shoes from now on. You hear

me?" Julia put on a stern face that made Jimmy smile. "Mossy cut down a crutch for you. You can start hopping around on it soon."

Julia left him and went back downstairs. In the living room, Harriet Tabor was holding forth on violations of town ordinances, the topic for that day's executive committee meeting. Harriet was puffed full of indignation, her abundant bosom stretching every black silken pleat in her bodice.

"If you ask me, the Bon Ton ought to be closed down. 'Hurdy girl' is a fancy name for 'common prostitute,' and Dellwood Petty is nothing but a purveyor of women."

Julia winced. "Please, Harriet, keep your voice down. Jimmy Ames is upstairs."

Harriet gave Julia a long look through her pince-nez. She had behaved coolly since their confrontation about Gib in Louise's living room. "The New Gaiety is bad enough," she went on in a less emphatic tone, "what with whiskey and cards. But at least there's no faro or females of low character."

"Having the Bon Ton on Main Street brings in business," Renate Blum said. "I'd say all the storekeepers would oppose closing Mr. Petty down."

"Money," Harriet sniffed. "That's all you storekeepers think about."

Renate raised her perfectly arched brows. "Now, Harriet, we're just as concerned about social evils as everyone else. But Mr. Petty is a good neighbor, although he does drink whiskey now and then when he's sitting out front."

Dellwood's public drinking led to a squabble between Dottie and Harriet. Then Louise, a festival of henna and bright blue silk, raised the question of boys peeking through the saloon's batwing doors to glimpse the hurdy girls' scanty costumes.

Julia tried to get the discussion back on course. "The faro table is clearly a violation of the ordinance."

"Marshal McQuigg doesn't seem inclined to do anything about it," Dottie said.

Louise looked thoughtful. "Nor do any of the men on the town council. I've brought up the subject with George any number of times, but he seems to think that what goes on behind closed doors is best left alone."

"Disgraceful!" Harriet held her teacup high, taking angry little sips. "If the men in this town don't have the courage to stamp out sinful behavior, then the ladies had better." She glared around the room. "I want that game closed and the prostitutes run out of town. If the council won't do it, I'll force the marshal to take action."

She got to her feet, brushing cake crumbs onto Julia's freshly beaten summer rug. "Weak-willed women, every one of you. I cannot abide weak-willed women. Good day to you all."

With that, Harriet threw up her chin and sailed out of the living room, leaving the other women gaping. It took Julia a moment to gather her wits and go after her.

"Harriet, you mustn't run off. We're not disagreeing with you; we're simply having a discussion."

Harriet stood before the hall stand straightening her hat. "You, Julia Metcalf, are a perfect disgrace. No sooner has Edward passed on than you're consorting with that . . . *man*!" She jammed a pearl-tipped hatpin through black felt.

"Harriet—"

"Don't think I haven't heard what's going on between you two. It's all over town." She snatched up her black kid gloves and opened the door. "I'm afraid I'll have to reconsider our association." The door slammed, rattling the frosted-glass panes.

Julia stared after her, stung to the quick. The story was all over town. Everything Gib had said in the Pickax Café was now grist for the gossip mill.

With sadness she realized that Harriet had been right all along. Gib had taken advantage of her hospitality and damaged her reputation. She should have been terribly angry with him, but she felt only sorrow and bewilderment. What had he gotten from her, other than one small kiss and a few meals? No money, and certainly no sexual favors.

She heard the murmur of women's voices, and Louise called her name. Julia returned to the living room.

"You know how Harriet speaks out of turn," Dottie said.

They all looked sympathetic, ready to comfort and console. But Julia's feelings were too private for public airing; she would come to terms with her humiliation quietly and alone. "We were discussing the faro game at the Bon Ton." She stood with shoulders erect, her mouth firmly set.

Louise and Dottie exchanged glances. "Barnet gave Gib a good talking-to," Dottie said.

"He did a marvelous job of cleaning," Louise said, looking around the room. "I couldn't get George to pick up a rag, not that I've ever tried."

"I don't care to discuss him," Julia said, taking her seat. "If you don't mind."

"Of course we don't mind, dear," Louise said quickly. She gave the room another glance. "You really should wallpaper, you know."

"Louise," Renate prompted.

"Back to business." Louise opened her notebook and licked the point of her pencil. "Now that Harriet's gone, I can resume my rightful place as head of this committee. I declare, that woman speaks her mind and the devil take the hindmost." Her exasperated tone made everyone laugh, dispelling the tension.

The discussion returned to the prohibition against banked games. It was decided that the faro table would have to close; its continued operation would undermine the force of the town's other ordinances.

Louise proposed that as committee chairman, she should meet with the marshal. Julia had another idea. "Since I'm the acting public health officer until Dr. Beacham arrives, perhaps I should approach Mr. Petty. He might be more receptive if we raise the gaming table as an issue of public health rather than legality. It will give him the chance to do the right thing of his own accord without any confrontation."

After a brief debate, her suggestion was adopted, although with some reluctance, Julia noticed. "We'll expect your report at our next meeting," Louise said, jotting something down in her notebook. "The next agenda item is the Bon Ton's violation of the ordinance against prostitution."

By law, the vice was confined to designated areas—Two-Mile Road and China Alley—where no respectable woman would set foot. Hurdy girls could work in saloons as long as they limited their activities to dancing and serving food and drink.

"How in the world does Harriet know what's going on at the Bon Ton?" Julia asked.

"She doesn't," Renate said. "Her outrage has to do with Sarabeth Brown. Harriet wants Sarabeth out of town and away from Lee."

Louise and Dottie murmured agreement. Julia was surprised. "I thought Lee gave up Sarabeth long ago."

Another round of looks was exchanged, as if the ladies were deciding who should break the bad news.

"It all comes down to Gib," Dottie said. "Now that he's back in town, Harriet's afraid Lee will fall in with him again and with Sarabeth, too, just like in the old days. With Gib opening the mine, going partners with Rawlie, living at the Bon Ton where Sarabeth works—why, it's Harriet's worst nightmare come back. At least that's the way I see it."

Julia thought of Lee's glum demeanor, his air of melancholy. It was a shame he couldn't have the girl he wanted, even though she wasn't the most respectable girl in town.

"Be that as it may," Louise said, "we have to decide what to do about the hurdy girls. Shall we demand an investigation?"

"I could mention it to Mr. Petty when I talk to him about the faro table," Julia said.

Louise gasped. "Don't you dare mention any such thing!"

"But it relates to the public health."

"If any one of us brings up the subject, it will not be you," Dottie said firmly. "You'll be opening yourself up to all sorts of insinuations. And if you want my opinion, I think it would be best if you didn't speak to Mr. Petty at all—about anything." She cleared her throat and added, "Under the present circumstances."

Julia looked from one lady to another, seeing agreement

in every face. Suddenly it became clear to her how seriously Gib's bragging had compromised her. Not only had her personal reputation been tarnished, but her moral authority as the town's doctor and public health officer had been undermined as well.

She must have appeared as distressed as she felt, for Dottie said comfortingly, "Now, don't you worry one bit. It will all blow over in good time."

"Of course it will," Louise added, but there was a note of doubt in her voice.

Renate lingered after the other ladies departed. She stood before the hall hat stand, smoothing her lustrous dark hair. As always, Renate was the picture of spare elegance, her face a perfect oval, pearl earbobs her only adornment.

"My daughter's coming home on Friday," she said. "Do stop by and see her."

"Of course I will," Julia said. "And I'll give Ruth a scolding. I don't favor train travel and stagecoach rides for expectant mothers."

She thought Ruth had shown bad judgment by deciding to have her baby in Stiles, although she couldn't fault her motives. Ruth's husband had been called east on business, and Ruth wanted to be with her mother.

"I would have gone to Helena," Renate said, "but I. Z. can't seem to manage for a minute by himself. And we've heard such wonderful things about this new Dr. Beacham."

"I'm sure Ruth will be in good hands," Julia said. She certainly hoped the new doctor would be well trained in obstetrics.

Renate adjusted the clasps of her violet silk jacket. "Speaking of Ruth, did you know Gib saved her?"

Julia felt her cheeks flush. "Please, Renate, I'd rather not discuss him." She'd quite had her fill of Gib.

"Of course. Forgive me."

Renate put on her hat, taking time to adjust the tiny veil and the stylish little feathers. Julia watched her, growing more curious as the silence stretched on.

"Saved her from what?" she asked.

"From Hockett and his men."

Julia felt a chill down her back. "I didn't know."

Renate lifted her chin, and her expressive dark eyes suddenly glistened. "They were outlaws of the worst sort. Night riders. Twice they broke into our store. Rode their horses right through the front door, smashed the display counters, helped themselves to whatever they pleased. It was because of our faith and I. Z.'s accent. They killed an Italian in McAllister and hanged two Chinese boys right here in Stiles, just for the sport of it."

Recalling the terrible events clearly upset Renate. She took out her handkerchief and dabbed at her eyes. Julia waited in horrified expectation.

"They wore hoods over their faces when they made their raids and did their killing. But they didn't have to hide when they tormented a crippled girl. They called Ruth names right in broad daylight."

Julia gasped. "How dreadful!"

"She came home from a school party one night after dark. She left her friends at Wallace Street. Hockett and his gang grabbed her near the New Gaiety. They dragged her down the alley and pulled up her dress. They said they wanted to see how a crippled girl was made."

Julia's hands flew to her mouth. "Oh, Renate!"

"Gib and Lee were out prowling, up to their usual mischief. When they heard her scream, they ran down the alley and got her away from Hockett and his outlaws. I don't know how they managed, the two of them against four rough men. After that, we sent Ruth to Helena to live with my cousins."

The vision of Gib pulling his gun on that cold November morning and shooting Hockett right in the heart flashed through Julia's mind. She had the feeling that she would have done the very same thing.

"As far as I'm concerned," Renate said, "nothing Gib can do will ever turn me against him. Lee Tabor, either."

The clock bonged the hour, and in the distance the stamp mill thumped. Julia turned Renate's words around in her mind. She thought how strong were the emotions Gib aroused; people saw him as good or wicked, nothing in between.

As for her, she simply didn't know her own heart anymore. She wanted to believe in him, but doubts loomed like shadows. And deeds spoke for themselves.

"Underneath everything, he's a decent man," Renate said. "Remember that before you judge him."

Gib rode into Stiles Friday evening. He left Lucky at the livery and went directly to Dick Cramer's barbershop for a bath and a shave. After he'd cleaned up, he hoofed it down to Chinatown with a bundle of clothes for Huat Lee's laundry. The laundry was little more than a hovel made from flattened tin cans and tar paper, but the place smelled steamy clean, and shirts came out of there looking better than new.

China Alley was busy. Something was going on at the meeting hall—mah-jongg, from the sound of clattering tiles and raised Chinese voices—and in the distance, a celebration was under way, accompanied by the thin wail of a fiddle.

A woman passed by with a baby strapped to her back. Gib looked at the baby's fat little face and decided to stop by Charlie Soon's store and buy Gilbert Chapman a Chinese toy.

After he finished at the laundry, he tickled the wind chimes at Charlie's place and went inside. The light of kerosene lamps cast the room in spooky shadows. At the far end of the counter, Charlie and a couple of other Celestials had their heads together. Their silky shirts and skullcaps gleamed in the light.

When Charlie saw Gib, he sent his visitors scurrying out the back way.

"Hey, Charlie," Gib said, tossing down his hat. "How's the snake oil business?"

Charlie didn't smile. "You boss big trouble."

"Me?" Gib was surprised. "What did I do?"

Charlie's eyes narrowed. His expression gave Gib the

willies. He'd bet the other Celestials paid attention when Charlie got his dander up.

"You boss send doctor lady letter."

"Letter? What letter?"

"Boss say he and doctor lady do . . . ?" He made a gesture with his fingers that needed no words.

A wave of heat crawled up Gib's neck. Jesus Suffering Christ, he thought. Instead of saying it to Hughes, he might as well have printed it in the newspaper.

Charlie seemed to read guilt in his face, for he suddenly came to life. "Aiyah! You stupid boss. Dead snake! You dead white devil." He threw up his hands in disgust.

"Yeah?" Gib shouted back. "Well, watch what you call me!" He slammed his fist down on the barrel of chicken claws, making the tin cover rattle. "What the hell business is it of yours what I say?" He didn't know what made him madder—Charlie's outburst or the realization that what he'd said at the Pickax was all over town and that Julia might have heard about it. "Next time I want to be insulted, I'll know right where to come." He grabbed his hat off the counter and headed for the door.

"Mine boss ask doctor lady marry. Mine boss no good man. Ugly toad. Son of a bitchee."

Gib stopped in his tracks, feeling a fresh surge of alarm. "What did she say?" He asked the question before he realized how scared he was of the answer.

Charlie studied Gib grimly, as if considering whether or not to respond.

"What the devil did she say?" Gib demanded.

"Too soon. Husband doctor too soon dead."

Gib stared at Charlie, thinking the unthinkable. What if Julia cared for Hughes? What if she intended to marry him when her mourning period ended?

"How do you know so much about her business, Charlie?"

Charlie looked mysterious. "Cholly know."

"Cholly beat around bush," Gib snapped. The smell of pickling spices and camphor and God knew what else was suddenly overpowering. He kicked open the door.

Charlie yelled after him. "Next time you be smart, boss."

Outside, Gib retraced his steps toward Main Street, his nerves rubbed raw. As he passed the fire-breathing dragons carved on the doorway of the Chinese meeting hall, he imagined stuffing Hughes down a dragon's throat. His fat carcass would melt into wax, fit punishment for spreading the story about Pickax and wanting to marry Julia.

Main Street's lamplit boardwalk was busy with cowboys and miners. Gib climbed the outside steps of the Bon Ton and went into his room. He dropped onto the bed and stared at the pattern of water stains on the ceiling. He thought for a while, trying to regain his usual easy detachment. He told himself that Julia was just another mark waiting to be taken. He was after her money, nothing more; once he got his hands on it, he'd turn up missing. If she decided to marry Hughes, it was none of his concern.

But thinking of her with the gasbag made him feel as touchy as a set trigger. She'd been married to Doc, for God's sake, the most decent man in the world. She deserved better than a busybody know-it-all like Hughes.

Gib sat up on the edge of the bed and rubbed his hands over his face. The truth of it was, she'd done something to him; just thinking about her unsteadied his nerves. It was the craziest thing that had ever happened to him, getting suckered by a gentle heart and a pretty smile, but there it was. For a man with his savvy, he'd sure come to a sorry pass.

Noise from the saloon came up through the floor; music and stomping made the bed throb and the pictures jump. Maybe Mossy was down there, Gib thought. Mossy would know if Julia had heard what had happened at the Pickax. As Charlie said, if she'd heard about it, he was one dead snake.

Gib got up and grabbed his hat. In the hallway he met Clara, a copper-curled hurdy girl, with a man in tow.

"Evening, Clara," he said.

She gave him a bright smile. "Evening, Gib."

Clara had sweet-talked him on more than one occasion.

When he'd let her know he wasn't interested, Clara pinched his cheek and said, "I guess you have bigger fish to fry."

He hadn't asked her what she meant, but it probably had to do with Julia. It was beginning to bother him that everybody suspected he was up to no good.

He descended the stairs into the boisterous racket of the saloon. The air was foggy with tobacco smoke. Gib didn't breathe for a minute. It always took awhile to get accustomed to the saloon smells of unwashed bodies, spilled beer, and old puke.

"Hey, Gib!"

Mossy put down his cards and lunged up from a chair. He stumbled toward Gib, grinning.

"What d'you say, partner?"

"I'm on a streak, Gib. Hotter than a stove top."

Gib glanced at the table where three men sat hunched over their cards. One was a sharper for sure in his black funeral togs and gold watch chain. Beside him was Bert Scobie, a slack-jawed loudmouth who rubbed everybody the wrong way.

"Nice friends you've got, Mossy."

"They're all right."

"How's Mrs. Metcalf these days?"

"She's got Jimmy Ames back at the house. Had to cut open his foot."

"She seem happy enough?"

Mossy's face fell. "Down in the dumps some. She might be missing you."

Gib's spirits lifted. "Yeah?"

One of the men yelled at Mossy. Gib clapped him on the shoulder and aimed him back to his game. "You enjoy yourself, Moss."

Gib wandered over to the door of the adjoining room where the faro table was getting some play and all the poker tables were full. Sarabeth, in her skimpy red satin dress, decorated the lap of a man who looked to be sleeping off a load.

"Say, Gib," she hollered. "How're them snakes?"

Gib turned two thumbs up. Then he pushed his way back

to the bar and leaned there thinking about what Mossy had said. If Julia was missing him, maybe she hadn't heard about the Pickax. He hoped to God she hadn't, not just for his sake, but to save her from embarrassment. He sure wished he'd kept his mouth shut when Hughes started ragging him.

"What'll it be, Gib, lemonade or daisy punch?" Dellwood bellied up to the other side of the bar, whiskers bristling, buttons straining, a towel slung over his shoulder.

"I'm dry as dust. Draw me a beer."

Dellwood's droopy eyes widened. "Holy blue hell, I'm going to tell your Sunday school teacher."

"Beer don't count as drinking," Gib said. "I want a sandwich, too. A big one."

Dellwood picked up a schooner and pulled the beer tap. The wall behind him was all mirror and whiskey bottles. Above the mirror hung a painting of a reclining lady, stark naked.

Dellwood set the mug on the bar. "You hear about your widow friend getting them letters?"

"What letter's that?" Gib dug two bits from his pocket and slapped it on the counter.

"The kind of letters ladies don't like to get. Gamy stuff, from what I hear."

Gib's heart thudded against his ribs. He remembered Charlie saying something about a letter. "What the hell?"

"First one came to the *Sentinel* office last week," Dellwood said. "The second one came to her house a few days ago. She turned it over to the marshal." He stuck his thumbs in the waist of his apron and looked Gib up and down. "Some folks think you wrote them. I say it ain't your style. One thing I got to hand to you—you never stooped to dirty tricks to get what you wanted from a woman."

Gib took a gulp of beer and backhanded the foam from his mouth. Something was going on, something more than Hughes spreading stories, and he didn't like it one bit.

"I hear you been bragging she primed your pump."

Gib stared at the suds in his glass and shook his head,

despising himself for his careless words. "Shut up, Dell. I don't like that kind of talk."

"Suit yourself. I'm just telling you what I hear." Dellwood turned to the backbar and started throwing meat and cheese on slices of bread.

Gib picked up his beer and moved to the quiet end of the bar where he could think. The more he thought, the more bothered he got. Hughes was out to make him look bad. He'd told everybody about the Pickax, and he was probably behind the letters, too. No question about it, the gasbag was doing everything in his power to get him away from Julia and get her for himself.

"Say there, feller. Didn't expect you'd still be around these parts."

It was the stage driver who'd driven Gib in from Dillon.

"Will Crutchfield, in case you don't remember." The driver wiped his hand on his leather vest and extended it. "Thought you'd have lit out by now."

"Evening, Will." They shook hands. "How's things?"

"Can't complain." Crutchfield was an anvil-shaped man, all shoulders and arms and short stubby legs. He aimed a stream of tobacco juice at a brass spittoon and hit it square. Streaks of brown in his graying beard showed that his aim wasn't always so true. "How about yourself?"

"Fair enough." Gib drained his mug of beer and put it on the bar.

Crutchfield bellowed for Dellwood.

"Hold your water!" Dellwood shouted. He hurried down the plank behind the bar, carrying a thick, lopsided sandwich. He threw it on the bar in front of Gib. "What'll it be, Will?"

"Gimme a bottle of whiskey and an extra glass for my friend here."

Dellwood smirked at Gib. "He ain't drinking hard liquor these days. Smoking, neither. The gent's courting a lady."

"That so?" Crutchfield looked at Gib. "You sure work fast, boy."

"Gib don't waste time when it comes to ladies," Dellwood said. "He's been caught bare-assed more times than any man in the history of the world."

He went off after Will's whiskey. Crutchfield tugged at his ear and gave Gib a sideways glance. "You aim to settle here in Stiles?"

Gib examined his sandwich. The bread was as stiff as a shingle, and the cheese had patches of blue fuzz. "Not a chance."

"Booth. That's your name, right?"

Gib looked at the driver, sensing something was up. "What's on your mind, old-timer?"

Crutchfield glanced around the crowded saloon, then leaned close. "I run into a couple of fellers up yonder. They just come down from the Breaks, running with a bad bunch up there, the Sontag brothers. Rustling, I heard. They put the word out they was looking for you."

CHAPTER

13

THE MOLDY SANDWICH had killed most of Gib's appetite; the news about Wylie and Trask finished it off. "You talked to them?"

"Yep. They heard I was a driver and asked me special. Gib Booth, they said. Tall, dark-haired feller in his thirties. Hard-rock stiff, fast arm with a single jack. Shell game artist. A real ladies' man."

Gib eyed the backbar mirror, as if Wylie and Trask might suddenly burst through the door, shotguns blasting. He reached inside his coat and touched the butt of his Colt. "What'd you tell them?"

"I told them Sam Dang nothing. Wouldn't wish that pair on nobody."

Gib pushed away his sandwich.

"Tall one's a cold-eyed sumbitch," Crutchfield went on. "Wears one of them long duster coats. The other's ugly as Sunday. Got a queer-looking ear."

Dellwood returned with a bottle and a glass for Crutchfield. He looked at Gib. "What's up, long face? Your mule die?"

Gib splashed some whiskey into his empty beer mug and took a gulp. The liquor burned all the way down. "Keep me posted," he said to the driver. "If I'm not around, leave a message with Dellwood here."

"Sure thing, young feller."

Gib pushed the sandwich at Dellwood. "Maybe you can find an old sow who'll eat this thing." He started for the stairs and his room. He had some serious thinking to do.

"Booth!"

Gib spun on his heel, reaching for his gun.

Thank God he didn't draw. Marshal McQuigg stood a scant ten feet away, revolver cocked and aimed.

"Put your hands up. Real slow."

The piano plinked and fell quiet. Men put down their cards and stared. Gib eased his hands away from his gun belt, his heart hammering. "You come up on a man's back, Marshal, you've got to expect he'll go for his gun."

McQuigg came over to Gib and yanked the Colt from its holster. "Wearing a gun's against the law in this town." The marshal was a tall man, whip-hard, with a graying mustache and small dark eyes. A tin star the size of a tea saucer hung on his black frock coat. "This time it'll cost you ten dollars. Next time you're in jail."

"You've got one too many laws here, Marshal. A man's got a right to bear arms. It's in the Constitution."

"Take it up with the President. Now get over to my office and pay your fine. I've got more to say to you in private." He glanced around the saloon. "At ease, men."

A buzz of talk started up, then the piano, and in an instant, the saloon was humming again. Gib looked at Dellwood behind the bar. Dell put his hands on his hips and shook his head.

"Gib." Mossy was at his side, riffling through some bills. "I got plenty here if you need ten."

"No, thanks, Moss. I've got it." He had Lee's two hundred, although he didn't want to waste any of it on a shakedown.

"You coming, Booth?"

Gib followed the marshal out into the cool night air. They crossed the street at an angle and hopped up on the boardwalk. Under a sign that said Jail, McQuigg unlocked the door and pushed it open.

"After you."

The office area was small and warmed by a stove. Tacked-up wanted posters decorated the whitewashed walls. A gun cabinet held rifles and shotguns, chained together like prisoners.

Marshal McQuigg unloaded Gib's gun and tossed it on his kneehole desk. "Sit down, Booth."

Gib thumbed back his hat and pulled up a wooden armchair.

"Coffee?" McQuigg went over to the potbellied stove and picked up the pot.

Gib shook his head no.

The marshal returned to his desk, steaming cup in hand. He flipped the tail of his frock coat, sat down in his swivel chair, turned to Gib, and gave him a long look.

"I don't like you, Booth."

The feeling was mutual, but Gib said nothing.

"I've heard about the trouble you caused here. Woman trouble, gun trouble. Robbery. Murder. Marshal Early ran you out of town. I'd have done the same."

Gib crossed a leg over one knee and began scraping dried mud off his boot.

McQuigg's foot swung up, kicking Gib's boot off his knee. The force of the blow nearly knocked him out of his chair.

"You've got the manners of a mule, boy."

Gib settled back in his chair, both feet on the floor, and tried to look sorry. There was something about a lawman that always brought out the worst in him.

"I hear you're pretty good with a gun, Booth."

"I was once."

"How many men've you killed?"

"Don't rightly know, there's been so many."

McQuigg ignored his sarcastic tone. "You've built quite a reputation as a gunfighter."

Gib looked hard at the marshal, trying to figure out what he was driving at. "You mean Bob Hockett?" Shooting that son of a bitch hardly made him a gunman.

"I mean Lincoln County, New Mexico Territory," the marshal said. "Eighteen and seventy-eight. The Murphy-Dolan gang. Innocent people killed, peace officers. Men shot down in cold blood."

"Hold it, Marshal." Gib started to rise. "You can't pin that on me."

"Sit down! I've been hearing stories about you."

"Let's see your proof."

"You can read about it in the next issue of the *Sentinel*."

"You're bluffing."

McQuigg leaned back in his chair, his gun belt creaking, a smug look on his face. "Gunfights, kidnappings, high-grading, confidence games. The citizens of Stiles have a right to know what sort of man is in their midst."

Gib felt like punching him in the face. Then he thought of Julia. A newspaper story like this would finish him off with her.

"They're lies." At least most of them were.

"You deny everything?"

Gib didn't reply. McQuigg was out to get him, and there was nothing he could do about it.

"This isn't the Wild West, Booth. Stiles is a law-abiding community with law-abiding citizens. They're doing their civic duty by informing me about you. My advice to you is to get out of town."

A silence settled between them, tense and heavy. Gib looked longingly at his gun; he imagined picking it up and putting a bullet between McQuigg's eyes.

"What if I don't go?"

"You swindled Rawlie Brown out of his claim. With a cloud on the title, you won't be doing much mining up at the Rattling Rock."

"There's no cloud on the title. I filed in my name and Rawlie's. Sarabeth's, too, since her pa owned half. Rawlie even signed a quitclaim."

"That don't make it legal."

"It's legal, all right. Barnet Cady looked over the papers."

For a minute McQuigg didn't look so sure of himself. "Folks don't like you snooping around Mrs. Metcalf."

Gib laughed out loud. "You've got a heap of laws around here, but I didn't hear mention of one against talking to particular ladies."

The marshal's left eye started twitching. "You've written her letters. Spread stories that hurt her reputation. If she says the word, I'll string you up for taking criminal advantage."

Gib shifted in his seat, avoiding the marshal's glare. "Let's see the letters."

McQuigg leaned down to open the bottom drawer, not taking his eyes off Gib. "She destroyed the first one."

Gib took the letter and scanned it, wincing at the blunt prose. It was crudely printed, but the writer had a flair for words. Seemed to spell well, too—a lot better than he did. Then he thought of Julia reading it and started to get mad all over again.

"Son of a bitch."

"Recognize it?" the marshal asked.

"That's not my handwriting, in case you're interested. And the spelling's too good."

"We'll see about that. Now get out of here."

"How about my gun?"

"It stays here. Claim it when you leave town."

Suckered again, Gib thought. Plenty of men carried concealed weapons.

He stood up and tossed a golden eagle on the marshal's desk. "There's your fine."

Outside, he walked along the darkened boardwalk, cursing. The whole time he'd been in Stiles, he'd behaved like a model citizen—no drinking, no fights, no whores. He was about to sponsor a baby in church, for God's sake. Yet McQuigg was talking about getting up a necktie party with him as the honored guest.

He sat down on the bench outside Blum's store to think things through. McQuigg had nabbed him for wearing a gun in town, but Hughes was behind everything else. Hughes was the one who'd dug up his past; he was the one the marshal said was doing his civic duty. That lily-livered coward was trying to pin on him every crime since the Crucifixion, just to get him out of the way so he could get his hands on Julia. And there wasn't a damn thing Gib could do about it. The only question was what would happen first—would he get away clean with Julia's money or get chased out of town by the marshal? Or would his old partners ride into town with their stubby double-barreled shotguns and blow him to fossil bones?

Gib got up and stretched. He was in a pickle, all right. He had Wylie and Trask on his tail, McQuigg trying to run him out of town, and he'd yet to see one cent of Julia's money. One thing was sure, if he ever found proof that Hughes was behind that letter, he would crack the gasbag's crust wide open.

He headed across the street to the Bon Ton. Before he was halfway up the outside stairs, the sound of gunfire roared into the night, followed by yells and screams. Gib threw himself flat against the wall of the building. His hand moved to his holster. Empty. God damn McQuigg.

There were two more shots in quick succession, skull rattlers. Gib realized they'd come from inside the Bon Ton. He ran around to the front of the saloon. Light spilled out of the windows and door. Men were shouting on the board-walk; feet pounded.

"Get the marshal!"

"Bring a wagon around!"

Inside, the Bon Ton was a mess of overturned chairs, broken glass, and panic. Men and hurdy girls were running in and out, cursing and yelling, and the place smelled of powder smoke. Gib saw Mossy hurrying in his direction.

"Get Doc before he bleeds to death."

"What?"

Mossy was shaking, his eyes glassy. "Got to get Scobie to Doc. He pulled a knife on Buell, and Buell shot him."

Gib followed Mossy outside. "You're taking him out to Julia's? Jesus, Moss, it's late."

"Coming through." The marshal elbowed his way toward the saloon. His presence seemed to calm the crowd of milling men.

Mossy was talking to a mounted rider, telling him something about Doc's place. Gib grabbed his arm. "Mossy, what the hell are you doing?"

"Got to tell Doc so he'll be ready."

"Are you crazy?" He couldn't believe that Mossy expected Julia to get out of bed and tend to some outslicked loser who'd stepped in the way of a bullet. Then Gib saw that the horseman was Sarabeth dressed in her driving garb. "Where are you going?" he shouted at her, but she rode off without answering.

"Got to tell Doc so he'll be ready," Mossy said again.

Mossy didn't look too steady on his pins. Gib realized that he was slipping back in time, confusing Julia and Doc. "Doc's dead, Moss," Gib said. "Get ahold of yourself."

He sat Mossy down in one of Dellwood's rickety outside chairs and went back into the saloon.

A crowd had gathered around Scobie, who was lying on the floor, babbling and crying. Someone had wrapped a towel around his shoulder and another around his ribs. There was blood all over the place. Scobie started screaming for his ma.

"Shut up, Scobie," Dellwood said.

Scobie yelled louder. "Where's the doc? Jesus Christ, I'm dying!"

Chilling memories rushed at Gib: men on the battlefield pleading for their mamas, for Doc. He went outside into the fresh night air and sat down beside Mossy. "You all right, Moss?"

Mossy nodded. "Nerves got rubbed a little thin."

The marshal came out with the cardsharp in funeral clothes, his wrists in iron cuffs. The sharp was carrying on about self-defense.

McQuigg gave him a shove. "Tell it to the judge, Buell."

A flatbed wagon pulled around to the front of the saloon. A gang of men brought Scobie out on a plank and loaded him into the wagon. He was moaning and swearing, sounding lively enough for a man who claimed to be dying.

Gib watched, feeling a little shaky. Gunplay made him nervous, especially when he was unarmed. As the wagon pulled away, it dawned on him that these saloon roosters were heading out to Julia's place, and she was all alone.

He jumped up from his chair. "Hey!" He ran after the wagon and vaulted onto the bed.

The ringing surgery bell woke Julia. She struggled awake and managed to light the lamp. She blinked at the clock, trying to focus her eyes. It was just after midnight.

The bell rang again. She heard a shout. "Wake up, ma'am. A wounded man's coming."

Julia pushed Bee aside and fumbled her way into her slippers and robe. By the time she got downstairs, her brain was awake, ready to deal with the emergency.

At the surgery door, she found Sarabeth Brown, her hat pushed back on her head, her hurdy girl's paint garish in the lamplight. She wore men's clothes, hastily put on, from the look of her misbuttoned shirt.

"A man's been shot at the Bon Ton. Name's Bert Scobie. He got fleeced in a card game. Sharper pulled his coat gun and shot him. The wagon's on the way."

"Come in, Sarabeth."

Whenever there was a casualty at the Bon Ton, Sarabeth assisted Julia in surgery. It was a partnership that had developed quite by chance. Shortly after Edward's death, a gambler had been wounded in a knife fight, and Sarabeth was handy by. She'd proved to be unflappable, not in the least squeamish, and willing to obey instructions, unlike the male assistants Julia had recruited, who either fainted or tried to take over.

Julia spread a sheet over the examining table. While she set out pans and sponges and a pack of sterile instruments, Sarabeth built a fire in the little stove and started water boiling.

"How badly is he wounded?" Julia asked.

"Hit in the left shoulder and side. I bound him up and belted him. Last I saw, he was yelling like thunder."

"Is he drunk?"

"As a skunk. He puked, too. Not much in his stomach."

Julia needed that information to determine how much anesthetic to give him.

In the surgery's tiny anteroom, she bound her hair into a snug braid. She turned down the sheet on the patient's cot and laid out blankets. Rolling up the sleeves of her bulky woolen robe, she went back into the surgery. She put on an apron that covered her from throat to ankles, then washed her hands and arms. As she dried off, she heard men shouting.

"Good heavens, listen to that racket."

"Sounds like a big crew," Sarabeth said. "Nobody wants to miss the fun."

Sarabeth shed her jacket and refilled the scrub pan. Julia glanced over her strong, pretty figure clad in shirt and trousers meant for a man and thought of Lee, too timid to stand up to Harriet. Sarabeth wasn't the sort of girl a respectable man like Lee was expected to marry, but she was the perfect girl to give him backbone.

A moment later a crowd of heavy-booted men tramped into the surgery, smelling of whiskey and cigar smoke. They were all talking at once, speculating about whether Buell had cheated Scobie or vice versa, who had drawn his weapon first, and why Buell's aim had drifted off its lethal course.

"You can't beat a pocket Smith and Wesson thirty-eight for indoor shooting," someone said.

"Shee-it," came the response. "For close range it's the Colt New Line forty-one any day of the week. Why, how-de-do, Sarabeth."

Julia heard the splat of tobacco juice. "No spitting please," she called out.

"Christ Almighty, jackleg," Sarabeth yelled. "This is a surgical area. Don't you know nothing?"

They had Scobie on a plank, one leg hanging off, his shoulder and waist bound with blood-soaked towels.

"Put him here on the table," Julia said. She bent over the wounded man, who was gasping and sobbing, his long, lopsided face contorted with pain. Julia recognized him as one of the miners she'd treated at the Continental.

"There, Mr. Scobie. Try to calm down."

Scobie was unloaded onto the table, squalling like a cat. "Goddammit, I'll kill that son of a bitch Buell!"

"Shut your mouth, Scobie, or I'll do it for you."

It was Gib, pushing his way through the press of men. He looked around the surgery, incredulous. "This is crazy. Get another doc to take care of him."

"There isn't another doc." Julia put some snap in her voice to let him know she didn't tolerate being given orders in her surgery.

Scobie's belt held a towel at his waist, making an effective compress. When Julia loosened it, he squeezed his eyes closed and cursed at the top of his lungs.

Gib made a threatening sound and pushed closer.

Julia nudged him with her elbow. "Get out of my way, Gib." She examined Scobie's mouth for false teeth, tobacco, and anything else that might impair breathing.

"You're going to let this tinhorn talk to you like that?"

"Yes, I am." Her temper was hanging by a thread. "Sarabeth, I want all the men out of here. And that includes Mr. Booth."

"Haul your freight, jacklegs!" Sarabeth shouted.

Gib grabbed Julia's arm. "Not on your life am I leaving you with that piece of scrub."

"You heard the lady, Booth." Marshal McQuigg stood in the doorway, his tin star gleaming.

"Thank you, Marshal," Julia said. "Things are a bit out of control."

McQuigg surveyed the room through narrowed eyes. "All right, men, march. Let the lady do her work."

The men began shuffling out. Gib gave Julia a quick, dark glance before he dropped her arm and turned away.

"I'll stop back later, ma'am," McQuigg said. "After I escort these fine gents back to town."

"There's no need, Marshal. I'll be keeping Mr. Scobie through the night."

"If you're sure, then. By the way, I brought Mossy home. The shooting shook him up some."

"I appreciate it."

McQuigg stroked his mustache. "And if Booth bothers you, just give me a holler. Men like him ain't fit to be around ladies like you."

Julia held a cup of water to Scobie's lips. "Good night, Marshal."

When the men were gone, a blessed silence descended, broken only by the faint sound of boiling water and Scobie's deep-throated groans.

"The more ornery the man, the more punishment he can withstand," Julia said, checking Scobie's pulse and respiration.

Sarabeth snorted. "Then it'd take a whole lot to kill Scobie."

Julia prepared a solution of morphine sulfate, alcohol, and distilled water and drew it into a hypodermic syringe. The narcotic would deaden Scobie's pain and support his system in case of shock. It would also prolong the chloroform narcosis.

"I'm going to give you an injection, Mr. Scobie. It will make you more comfortable."

He yowled when the needle went in, but his struggle was feeble. With her shears, Julia cut away his shirt, wrinkling her nose at his gamy odor. She opened his trousers and hitched them down over his hips to expose his hairy belly. Bullets had torn flesh from his side and chipped bone in his shoulder.

"He's fortunate Mr. Buell was such a poor shot," Julia said.

"Hear that, Scobie?" Sarabeth said. "You're one lucky buck."

Scobie ground his teeth. "Son of a bitch."

Julia draped a sheet over his lower regions to preserve his modesty, then removed his boots and eased his trousers and long johns down farther.

Scobie smiled dreamily. "I'm in heaven."

The morphine was taking effect. "Not quite yet," Julia said.

She scrubbed her hands again and sterilized the surgical

area with a spray of carbolic solution. "Sarabeth, open the windows a bit, please. We need some fresh air."

She dripped chloroform onto a dampened cup-shaped sponge and held it close to Scobie's nose and mouth.

"There, now, Mr. Scobie. I'm giving you a whiff of chloroform. Breathe normally, no deep breaths."

Scobie hummed softly to himself. Julia moved the sponge closer to his face, her fingers on his pulse.

"There he goes." She waited a few moments more before taking away the sponge.

She went to work, digging into bloody flesh for bone fragments while Sarabeth held the pan. It was important to remove all the bone chips; any left behind could lead to infection.

When each wound was clean, Sarabeth pressed a bandage over it to stanch the bleeding, exposing only enough skin so Julia could sew up the edges. Scobie's pulse remained steady, his respiration even. From all appearances, the man had the constitution of an ox.

By the time she had taped the last bandage in place, Julia's eyes ached. She gave Scobie one last whiff of chloroform to keep him asleep, then took off her bloodied apron and arched her shoulders, digging her hands into the small of her back.

"Sarabeth, you're a wonder. Go home and get some rest."

Sarabeth looked around the room. "We better clean this place up."

"I can't face cleaning right now. I'm going to sit down for a moment." Julia sank into the easy chair and rubbed her temples. "If you don't want to go back to town, you can sleep here. I've got folding cots upstairs."

"Thanks anyway. I better take back the horse I borrowed before the jackleg who owns him decides to shoot me." At the door she hesitated. "Don't be too hard on Gib, ma'am."

Julia closed her eyes. "Good night, Sarabeth."

CHAPTER

14

JULIA STARTED AWAKE. She looked around, her ears straining for the sound that had disturbed her. She glanced at her watch; it was nearly two-thirty. Scobie lay on the table, his breathing normal. Taking the lamp, Julia hurried upstairs to check on Jimmy Ames, who was sleeping soundly.

She returned to the surgery, put on a fresh apron, and began cleaning. She set aside instruments to be sterilized, emptied pans of crimson-tinged water, and gathered bloody sponges that needed to be boiled clean. The floor was soiled with mud and tobacco juice. Tomorrow she would scrub everything with carbolic solution.

Scobie groaned. She should get him to the cot in the anteroom, Julia thought. She would have to get Mossy to help her.

She opened the surgery door and stepped outside. Light from inside spilled onto the small porch, illuminating the dark shape of a man sprawled on the steps.

"Oh!" Julia clutched her robe with sudden fright.

The man groped himself upright. "It's me."

"Gib! You frightened me half to death."

He got unsteadily to his feet. For a moment Julia thought he was drunk. Then he rubbed his eyes, and she realized he'd been sleeping.

"Where's Scobie?" He ran both hands down his face and shook his head as if to waken himself.

"He's in the surgery. Come help me move him."

Gib followed her inside where Scobie lay on the table, covered with blankets, his shoulders bare, save for bandages and tape.

"God Almighty, he's buck naked!"

"He's not naked," Julia said in a harsh whisper. "And please be quiet. He needs a good long sleep."

She went to a storage closet and brought out a stretcher. "Lift his legs. Gently, please."

Scobie was a wiry man and not too heavy. They got him into the anteroom and onto the cot. Julia put hot-water bottles at his feet, then covered him and set a cup of water on the bedside stand.

"I'm staying the night," Gib said. "I'll sit right here and make sure that son of a buck doesn't start roaming around."

Dear heaven, Julia thought. Scobie couldn't even crawl, let alone roam the house. "I gave him chloroform and morphine. He's dead to the world."

"I'm not leaving you alone. There're stiffs all over town, blowing off steam, and you've got them coming and going all hours of the night."

Gib's jaw was set; Julia had never seen him so adamant. She pushed him out of the anteroom and closed the door halfway. "I help people, Gib," she said. "No one intends me any harm."

"What about when they're puking drunk and remember you're a pretty woman, all alone?"

Julia turned on him, exasperated. "I practice medicine. A wounded man came here tonight, and I treated him. I will continue to help patients until there is someone qualified to take my place. Now, you can stay or you can go—I'm too tired to care one way or the other—but I won't have you interfering in my surgery."

She picked up the bottles of chloroform and morphine and put them into the glass-fronted cabinet. "And since you are so concerned about my safety and reputation, perhaps you'll explain why you told Harlan Hughes certain slanderous stories about me."

Gib's face turned to stone. He backed up against the wall and stared at the floor. Any doubts Julia might have had about his guilt abruptly vanished.

"From what I hear, you told him we'd been intimate. I would appreciate your telling me exactly what you said."

He mumbled something, his voice so low she could barely hear it.

"If you don't tell me, you can leave my house and not come back."

His head shot up, a surprised look on his face.

"Well?" Julia was tired and annoyed, not in the mood to deal with a bullheaded man.

"First I'll tell you what Hughes said."

"I don't care what he said."

"You better care, because he's the one who started things."

Stubborn, Julia thought. Stubborn and prickly, as if the entire business were Harlan's fault—or hers. "All right, then. Tell me."

"He told me to stay away from you. He said if I wanted to visit a lady, to go out to Two-Mile Road. It'd only cost me two dollars."

Julia met his gaze full on, dreading what would come next.

"I said when it comes to visiting ladies, you suit me just fine. You don't charge me nothing, and you throw in dinner."

Julia flinched. It shocked her to hear him say the words, so vulgar and hurtful, so terribly crude.

Gib crossed his arms, his big hands dark against seasoned buckskin. "I didn't like the way he was talking. Telling me to keep away from you."

"Other people's taunting is no excuse for rude behavior."

He jerked his chin, not wanting any lectures. It crossed Julia's mind that Harlan might have purposely provoked him. Perhaps he was to blame for what Gib had said.

Rubbish, she told herself. She might as well argue that the words had been forced from him under torture.

She started stacking clean linens in a pile, then decided she'd had enough of Gib's company—better she keep an eye on her patient. "If you'll excuse me, I'm going to sit with Mr. Scobie."

As she took off her apron, she remembered the letters. She looked at Gib, uncertain if she should mention them. She opened her mouth, faltered, then tried again. "I've been receiving indecent letters."

Gib's eyes didn't leave hers. "The marshal already tried to pin them on me. Along with everything else he could think of."

"Did you write them?"

He tilted his head, a bitter smile on his mouth. "What do you think?"

Julia flushed a little and wished she hadn't asked. Words uttered in anger were one thing, vile prose quite another. "No, I don't think it was you."

"Tell me something else," he said. "Are you going to marry Hughes?"

"I'm still in mourning. I have no thoughts of marrying anyone." She hung the apron on a peg, went into the anteroom and closed the door.

Julia sat in the armchair beside Scobie's cot, her eyes closed, her exhausted mind turning. Gib had damaged her reputation with his careless remarks to Harlan; he'd made her the subject of gossip and hadn't even said he was sorry. She should end their association, send him away. There was no reason for him to come around anymore, no reason at all.

Her thoughts drifted, and she dozed, slipping into a half-dream of the golden evening on the Chapmans' front porch. Gib brought rocks to baby Gilbert; he leaned down and kissed her warmly, tenderly. Abruptly his words intruded: "When it comes to seeing ladies, you suit me just fine . . ."

She jerked awake. Her body was leaden with fatigue; her mind longed for sleep. She got to her feet and checked Scobie, making sure she could leave him and go to bed.

The surgery was dark, Gib nowhere to be seen. Julia went through the study and into the hallway. At the foot of the stairs, she noticed the front door ajar. She opened it wider and held up the lamp, spilling yellow light over pots of geraniums Louise had given her.

"Gib?"

He was standing in the darkness, leaning on the porch railing.

"I didn't know you were still here," she said.

"I told you I'd stay."

Julia stepped outside into the cool night breeze. Gib wasn't wearing his jacket. His sleeves were rolled back, showing silky dark hair. He slid his hands into his back pockets and watched her warily, as if expecting some new reprimand.

"Aren't you cold?" she asked.

"Nah, I'm all right. How's Scobie?"

"He's sleeping."

The night was cloudy and moonless, dark except for the small pool of light where they stood. Julia wondered what Gib had been thinking, standing there alone.

"Gib, I think it would be best if you didn't come around here anymore."

A flicker of emotion crossed his face, almost a wince of pain. He took off his hat and studied the inside of it. When he lifted his eyes to hers, his expression was so grave, so utterly repentant, that Julia wondered if she was being too harsh.

"I'm as sorry as a man can be about what I said to Hughes. If I could take it back, I'd do it in a minute."

His apology made Julia weaken a little. "People are talking."

He took the lamp from her and gestured toward the steps. "Sit down for a minute."

Julia hesitated. She knew she shouldn't linger, but to be fair, she decided she should give Gib a chance to explain himself. Tucking her robe about her, she sat down.

He sat beside her, forearms on knees, hat brim pushed up. He stared at his boots, as if trying to decide how to begin. "The marshal said Walt Stringer's running a story on me. A lot of it'll be lies."

Dear heavens, Julia thought, a story in the newspaper. Harriet would have a field day. "Walt Stringer doesn't print lies, Gib."

He turned his head to look at her. "He might if he believes who's doing the telling."

"What kind of lies?"

"He's saying I was a gunfighter in Arizona Territory. Lincoln County. That I ran with the Murphy-Dolan gang, shot innocent folks."

The Lincoln County wars. Julia searched his face, trying to see cold-blooded cruelty.

"I'm no saint, but I'm no killer. The gunman's life isn't for me."

Julia laced her fingers around her knees and held on tight, wondering where this conversation would lead. "You should tell Walt your side of the story."

"How about I tell it to you?" He gave her a questioning look.

She wasn't sure she wanted to hear it. Thinking about Gib's past made her uneasy, not so much for what he'd done as for how it would make her feel. Contrary to all good sense, she still wanted to think the best of him.

"All right. Tell me."

He shifted on the step and cleared his throat. His voice was hesitant at first, gathering assurance as he warmed to the story. He told about starting out as a mucker on the Comstock, loading one-ton cars, sixteen to a shift, till his back nearly broke. As time went on, he learned the drill, loaded powder, timbered, laid track. He became a real hard-rock miner, moving around the West—Colorado, Utah, California—staying only four or five months at a job.

"Always underground," he said. "I never cared for surface mining."

He elaborated on the misdeeds Harlan had mentioned. At one camp he'd been involved in a kidnapping; the miners had held the superintendent until they'd received their back pay. Later he'd earned money as a gambler, making the rounds of mining camps, working a game that involved sleight of hand.

"I got so I could take the shine off a four-flusher's teeth faster than any man west of the Divide." He glanced at her, watching for a reaction. "I cheated any tinhorn crazy enough to take me on. Drank till my ears turned blue. Didn't tame down when it came to the ladies." He paused. "I guess you've heard about that."

The ladies. Everyone said he'd pursued girls relentlessly in the old days. Renate thought he'd been looking for comfort after all he'd been through in the war.

"I've had enough of all that. Since I came here, I've been as pure as soapsuds, except for a little cussing and saying those things to Hughes."

He was trying to work his way back into her good graces, Julia thought. He'd violated principles she held most dear—honesty, sobriety, moral rectitude—and he wanted her to excuse him.

"You said you were in Mexico."

He looked startled. "I did?"

"You said your experience going over the railroad trestle reminded you of the earthquake in Mexico."

He stared into the darkness. "It wasn't much of a quake. A few shakes, some falling rock."

"What were you doing there?"

"I spent a few years in the Sierra Madre."

"Mining?"

"Yeah, mining."

He didn't have anything more to say on the subject, and Julia couldn't think of more to ask. She slipped her hands into the sleeves of her robe and shivered with exhaustion. She shouldn't be sitting out here on the porch, she told herself; she should be upstairs in her own warm bed.

"I'm sorry I made a case about you taking care of Scobie," Gib said. "I've got no business interfering, especially seeing how you know so much." He took off his hat and tossed it a few times. "I'd say you're the savviest lady I ever ran into. Savvier than most men I've known, for that matter."

Julia snuggled her hands deeper into her sleeves. She'd never heard such praise from a man, even from Edward, who thought her clever for a lady, although he believed that men by nature were the more intelligent sex.

"Do you really think so?" she asked, feeling flattered and a little embarrassed.

Gib gave her his soft-eyed smile. "I sure do."

Looking at him, Julia thought of Mama with her abundance of charm and her scandalous past. Mama used to say that women had at least as many brains as men and a good deal more common sense.

"You remind me of my mother," she said.

Gib stared at her, taken aback. "Your mother? Me?"

"She had the kindest heart, but everyone disapproved of her, especially my half brother, Randall, who's as stuffy as an old couch." Julia paused, remembering. "Mama was an actress before she married Father. She'd been divorced, too. Father and I adored her."

Gib gave his hat another low toss. "An actress. Well, I'll be."

"She was a grand success in New York. She played Castle Garden and Barnum's Museum and the Bowery Theater. She was featured as Lady Amaranth in *Wild Oats* and played the lead role in *Jenny Lind in America*. I used to spend hours looking at her old theater programs." Julia glanced at Gib, wondering if he was at all interested. "That's her picture on my dresser."

A tender expression touched his mouth. "You look like her. I bet you have her color eyes, her hair, too."

"Mama had curls."

"Ah. There's the difference."

Dawn had chased away the night; the lamp lost its glow. Birds were chirping, the breeze plucked at Julia's hair. Gib reached out and smoothed a strand. His handsome face was starkly outlined in the breaking light, every detail crisp.

"Do you mind if I kiss you?"

Julia felt a soft rush of anticipation. For all his shocking stories and unbridled ways, there was something in his nature that was able to reach her forgiving heart. "Last time you didn't ask."

"You're right, I didn't."

His arm circled her shoulders, drawing her close. He leaned down and touched his lips to hers. Julia closed her eyes; warmth flooded her senses. His lips shifted and parted, stealing her breath, making her heart pound. She reached out and touched him, feeling soft flannel and the hard muscles of his chest.

He pulled back. "Look at me."

She did as he asked. His fingers loosened her braid and drifted through her hair, spreading it on her shoulders. "There, now," he said. "You sure are a beautiful sight."

"You're shameless, Gib."

"I sure am."

He pulled her close and kissed her again. Warmth turned to heat, pleasure to desire. Ladies' man, Julia reminded herself, trying to keep her head. But before she could think again, his tongue skimmed her lips, and the earth seemed to drift. Caution disintegrated, spinning off into nothing. He explored her mouth with slow, sensual thoroughness, with rough sounds of pleasure. Julia spread her fingers wide on his back and kissed him in return.

He drew away slowly. "Well, now." His voice was soft with surprise, his eyes alight.

Julia gripped his shoulder, solid beneath dark fabric. She wanted to feel more of him, but she was too shy to do anything except slide her hand down his arm. Suddenly she stifled a yawn. She was shivering from fatigue and excitement. She pressed her knees together to keep them still.

"You'd better go to bed," Gib said. "I'll keep an eye on Scobie."

"Jimmy Ames is upstairs in Edward's room."

"I'll take care of him, too." He gave her waist a squeeze. "Now, get!"

After Julia went up to bed, Gib looked in on Scobie, got a fire going in the stove, and started a pot of coffee. Out back, he doused himself at the pump, finger-combed his hair, and went upstairs.

A freckled-faced boy lay in Doc's big walnut bed, curled around the cat. He was blowing in the cat's ear, watching it twitch.

"Are you Jimmy Ames?" Gib asked.

Jimmy rose up on an elbow, his sandy hair tousled from sleep. "Who're you?"

"Name's Gib Booth." Gib went over to the bed and stuck out his hand. Jimmy seemed pleased to shake it. "Mrs. Metcalf's asleep, so I'll look after you this morning." He glanced down the short length of the boy. All his limbs seemed accounted for. "What ails you, soldier?"

"My foot swelled up. She had to cut me." He stuck the bandaged foot out from under the blanket. "Mossy's taking me home later."

Gib looked around for Jimmy's clothes. "You need help getting dressed?"

"I can do it."

Jimmy managed well enough with his crutch, but accepted Gib's offer of a ride down the stairs.

While Jimmy went out back, Gib brought in eggs and milk from the shed and started breakfast.

"I heard a whole lot of noise last night," Jimmy said when he came back inside.

"A fellow got shot." Gib found some leftover biscuits in the bread tin and put them in the oven to warm. "Name of Bert Scobie. Mrs. Metcalf fixed him up."

"Bert Scobie got shot?" Jimmy's ears turned an excited pink. "He works at the Continental, the same shift as my dad. Who shot him?"

"Sharper named Buell." Gib poured himself a cup of coffee. He offered some to Jimmy, who declined in favor of milk.

"Why'd he do it?"

"A misunderstanding about cards, I'd say."

Gib set a place for Mossy, who had yet to appear, then joined Jimmy at the table. They dug into eggs and biscuits and raspberry jam.

"What shift is it your dad works?" Gib asked.

"Number four level. They're drifting and timbering, looking for a lead." Jimmy licked raspberry jam off his lips. "Dad says I'm old enough to work as a tool nipper. I'd rather do that than go to school."

Gib looked at the boy's bright face and thought of him spending his growing years underground. "If it was me, I'd take school."

He finished his breakfast thinking about the trouble at the Continental. From what he'd heard around town, they'd been drifting for more than three months on the new level with no pay in sight. They were mostly Cousin Jacks down there—Cornishmen, a clannish, close-mouthed sort, but the best in the business. If anybody could find high-grade ore, they could.

While Gib washed up the breakfast things, Jimmy asked more questions about the shooting at the Bon Ton. Then he hauled the cat out on the porch to play. Gib went upstairs to check on Julia.

He stepped softly through the open bedroom door. Julia slept curled on her side, her hair strewn across the pillow. The white ruffle of her nightgown sleeve lay beneath her cheek. Gib glanced at the picture on the dresser. It was about the craziest thing he'd ever heard, a man reminding a woman of her mother.

"Gib." Her eyes were open.

"You awake?" He was embarrassed to be caught spying.

She smiled sleepily. "I guess I am." But her eyes blinked and fell halfway closed.

Gib sat down on the coverlet of purple and yellow and blue, bracing his arms on either side of her. He looked at her creamy cheeks, her soft, full mouth, and thought of the way she'd kissed him, tender and willing, letting him take all the liberties he wanted. She'd let him do it because she was lonely for a man, he decided, that was all. As for him, he'd had to do some fast talking and some faster romancing to get back on her good side. It was the only way to move his plan back on track.

He knew he was bulling on both counts. She'd kissed him because she liked him—he could tell that easily enough—and he'd kissed her because he couldn't help himself.

"Go back to sleep," he said, smoothing her forehead.

Julia opened her eyes again and lifted her arms to his neck. "Is Jimmy awake?"

"Yeah. I've seen to everything. Even Scobie."

"Gib, you're a treasure."

He tried to appear unmoved. "Does that mean you won't chase me away?"

The answer was in her smile and the gentle pressure of her fingers. He leaned down to kiss her, intending nothing fancy, just a good, grateful, wake-up kiss. Then her arms tightened and her tongue shyly probed, and suddenly Gib lost all memory of the past, all sense of the future. He was swallowed up in some new, absorbing emotion that was deep and honest, that came from a place he couldn't name. It took a while to bring himself back to earth.

"We'd better quit doing this," he said, drawing away, "before it gets to be a habit."

CHAPTER

15

SCOBIE CAME INTO the kitchen, leaning on Mossy. His right side bulged where his arm was bandaged to his side, and his forehead glistened with sweat. He sat down, groaning and whimpering. "Ma'am." He screwed up his face as if he was about to cry. "I think I better stick around here today. So's you can tend to me."

It was late morning and Julia was finishing a quick meal of cheese and soda crackers and a bowl of applesauce. "I don't do nursing here, Mr. Scobie," she said. "Mossy will take you down to Mrs. Kitchen on Spring Street. She'll look after you very well."

"But, ma'am—"

"I'll stop by to see you tomorrow."

"I was thinking I'd best stay here, ma'am."

Gib came in from hitching up the buggy, trailed by Jimmy Ames. "You heard the lady, Scobie."

Scobie stared at Gib. "What the hell are you doing here, Booth? Oh, yeah, I heard you was sparking the widow."

A thunderous look crossed Gib's face. Julia put down her teacup and quickly got to her feet, catching a few cracker crumbs that fell from her black bombazine lap. "Come, Mr. Scobie, I want to talk to you privately."

She assisted him down the hall and into the study. Once inside, she closed the door. "The charge for treatment, Mr. Scobie, is five dollars."

"Five? Ouch! Why, ma'am, no disrespect, but you ain't even a real doctor. You're just a lady."

"Lady or not, I expect to be paid. The charge includes visits to follow your progress till you're well."

"Hell, I heard you're the richest lady in town, and now I can't work."

"If you have enough money to gamble and drink at the Bon Ton, you can surely pay your doctor's fee."

His wheedling expression turned into an unpleasant sneer. "Ladies take money for only one thing I know of, and it ain't for doctoring."

Julia had heard that comment before. In her experience, men were grateful to the point of tears until it came time to pay their bills. "I would suggest, Mr. Scobie, that you're associating with the wrong sort of ladies. The wrong sort of men, too, from the look of things last night."

Scobie reached into his pocket and clapped a gold piece on the corner of the desk. He pulled open the door and stomped out, grumbling and swearing.

Julia followed him down the hall. She watched from the front door as Mossy loaded him into the buggy and drove out of the dooryard.

When they were out of sight, she went into the living room and sat down at the piano. She struck a series of chords, cocking an ear for Jimmy and Gib, who had earlier been fixing a leak in the rain barrel by the barn.

Certain she was alone, she retreated into herself, playing hymns and ballads, allowing her mind to wander among rich new feelings. Simply by summoning the memory, she experienced it all over again—a passionate kiss, a strong embrace, a tender smile. The rest of it she could only wonder about—raw male hunger, and how it would feel to be possessed.

Julia took her fingers from the keys and bowed her head, trying to calm herself. Gib made her feel reckless, a bit out of control; he made her want things she'd never known, let alone craved. If she had a shred of good judgment left, she would send him away.

But she couldn't do that, not with her heart so fond of him.

She started playing again. Earlier, when she'd come downstairs, she'd found Gib in the living room, browsing through a guidebook that Edward had used on his European travels. When she offered him the use of the library, he'd looked startled, as if reading were a newfangled idea.

"It's been a long time since I did any book reading," he'd said.

Julia softly sang the words of a Scottish ballad. She thought of her life with Edward—books and learning and challenging discussions. With Edward, she'd always been striving to be worthy of his esteem, always trying to measure up. With Gib, she just felt like herself. She didn't have to prove anything to him. In his opinion, she was savvier than most men; from the way he kissed her, she knew he thought she was entirely a woman.

When the notes of the ballad died away, Julia heard voices on the porch. She went out into the hall and looked through the screen door.

Gib and Jimmy sat on the top step, legs outstretched, a spread of cards between them. With a sweep of his hand, Gib slid the cards into a deck and squared it. He cut and shuffled, riffling the cards together with a swish and a snap. His hands began to move. Cards flipped and slid, appeared and disappeared, quicker than the eye could follow. Gib kept up an easy banter while Jimmy stared and exclaimed, his ears flushed pink.

Julia studied Gib's profile, the straight nose, the strong chin, the dark stubble of beard. She looked at his long spread legs, the thick shoulders, the quick hands. She leaned her forehead against the screen, and a thought came to her as clear as a voice: She wanted him to love her, to live with her, to father her children. She wanted him to wake her with kisses every morning and be a husband to her every night. She wanted him to tell her that she was one savvy lady, and she wanted to hear the admiration in his voice.

"Gee whiskers," Jimmy said, "I wish I could do that."

"All it takes is a deck of cards," Gib said, "and a lot of practice."

"Will you teach me?"

"It'd be an honor."

Julia came out of her daydream with a jolt. "Jimmy, I don't think your mother would approve of card tricks."

Jimmy looked at the screen door, his face falling. "But tricks isn't gambling."

She opened the door and stepped out into the fragrance of the day, warm and sweet with blossoms, on the cusp of June. "Your mother might disagree."

Gib scooped up the cards and got to his feet. He helped Jimmy onto his crutch, pushed up the brim of his hat, and looked at Julia. "That piano music was real nice."

"I'm glad you enjoyed it."

He looked tall and tough in his Levi trousers and worn black shirt. "I'll be heading up to the mine today." He ducked his head and scuffed his boot. "I'll be back, though."

"When?" She said the word too quickly.

Gib gave her a squinting smile that made her blush. "As soon as I can." He glanced at Jimmy. "See you, soldier."

"See you, Gib."

He grabbed his jacket from the porch rail and went around back to get his horse. Jimmy looked up at Julia. "Gee whiskers, Mrs. Metcalf, he's just about the best man I ever met."

Julia left Jimmy playing on the porch with Bee and a ball of yarn and went into the study to resume her chore of sorting through Edward's papers. She took out a file of correspondence and newspaper clippings relating to Dr. Joseph Lister's visit to the United States in 1876. Edward had gone to Chicago to attend Lister's lecture and to visit with Randall and Helen. Julia had stayed home. For her, Chicago held too many sad memories.

She turned pages, scanning old letters from Edward's colleagues. A piece of lined paper slid from the file and drifted to the floor. Julia picked it up. It was a page torn from a record book, a list of soldiers' names in Edward's handwriting, along with their next of kin. Julia glanced down the list, recognizing a few men Edward had mentioned.

Suddenly she stopped. "Morris Swain—Tewksbury." And beneath his name, "Ada (wife), Beth (daughter), Morris, Jr. (son.)"

Julia laid the paper on the desk and stared at it in wonder. She remembered Gib's story about Mossy burning his letters from home, tears running down his face. "Mossy's life is his own business," Gib had said. "None of yours or mine."

But Julia couldn't dismiss this discovery. Mossy had a wife and family in Tewksbury, Massachusetts. They'd sent him off to war and had never seen him again—probably never knew what had become of him. Julia wondered if Ada Swain still lived in Tewksbury, or if she still lived at all.

She heard the door slam, the sound of hurrying feet. "Mrs. Metcalf!"

Mossy burst into the study. He was wide-eyed and sweating, his breath coming in heavy puffs.

"Good heavens, Mossy."

"It's Gib. Marshal's clapped him in jail."

Julia stood up, feeling a rise of alarm. "Jail?"

"Somebody broke in at the livery during the night, cracked old Fred on the head. Busted open the safe with a drill and a crowbar. Mrs. Tabor went right to the marshal, blamed it on Gib."

Julia's mind raced through last night's events. "What time was the robbery?"

"Fred said he looked at his watch a little after four. Next thing he knows he's waking up with a bass drum in his skull."

Gib had been nowhere near the livery at four this morning. "He was here, Mossy. With me."

Mossy gulped and wheezed, trying to catch his breath. "Ma'am, you can't say that. You can't tell the marshal that Gib spent the night here."

"Of course I can. I'll get my hat and gloves. You stay with Jimmy."

Mossy followed her down the hall. "It don't look right, Gib staying here all night."

Julia stopped before the mirrored hat stand. She swept a few strands of hair up off her neck and pinned them in place. "I don't care whether it looks right or not. It's the truth."

She glanced at Mossy's reflection as she fastened her black curl-brimmed hat in place. "For heaven's sake, stop wringing your hands. Nothing improper happened. Gib helped me with Mr. Scobie, then sat out on the porch all night."

Mossy shook his head. "It still don't look right."

Julia marched out onto the porch, letting the screen door slam. Jimmy hopped on his crutch. "Gib's in jail? Did he shoot somebody?"

Julia hurried down the steps. "Of course he didn't shoot anybody."

She climbed into the buggy, grabbed up the reins, and kicked off the brake. It was unfair the way Gib was being treated. Harriet, Harlan, the marshal—they were all intent on thinking the worst of him.

Main Street at noon on Saturday was busy with pedestrians and wagon traffic. Julia left the buggy in a shady spot by the *Sentinel* office and hurried down the boardwalk. When she reached the jail, her black worsted and silk dress was damp with perspiration.

The marshal's office was in an uproar. Harriet was carrying on at the top of her voice like an angry crow while Lee stood by, head hanging. Buster Caine, the young deputy, leaned against the wall, cracking his knuckles.

"He's always been a menace!" Harriet shrieked. "This isn't the first time he's broken into that safe."

Marshal McQuigg waved his hands in an attempt to calm her. "Mrs. Tabor, kindly quiet down for a moment."

"Ma," Lee said, "Gib never broke into the safe."

"Don't you defend that criminal!" Harriet cried. "*I* counted the money! *I* know what he stole."

"It was open. Pa left it open—"

"Don't contradict me! Gib Booth has been a bad influence on you since the day he arrived in this town."

"Marshal McQuigg," Julia said.

Her voice silenced everyone; they all turned to look. Harriet clamped her pince-nez onto her nose.

"Good afternoon, Mrs. Metcalf," the marshal said. "What brings you here?" His eyes narrowed, as if he sensed her purpose.

"Mr. Booth did not rob the livery," she said. "You saw him in my surgery shortly after midnight. From two-thirty until eleven o'clock this morning he was at my house."

McQuigg grimaced. It was obviously not news he wanted to hear. "You're saying he spent the entire night at your house?"

"I am. He helped me with Mr. Scobie."

A soft hissing sound came from Harriet. The marshal didn't take his eyes off Julia. "You're prepared to swear to that?"

"Of course I am." How ridiculous, Julia thought. A man was being treated for a gunshot wound and all they thought of was illicit goings-on. If any man other than Gib had been assisting her last night, no one would have batted an eye.

Harriet moaned. "The doctor's own wife and that . . . safe robber!"

"Gib didn't need to break into the safe," Lee said. "I gave him two hundred dollars. I'd have given him more if he'd asked." He glanced around as if startled by his admission. Almost immediately he began to look guilty; his face got red, and he started tugging at his mustache.

"Lee," Julia said, "are you saying you lent Gib money?"

"He's my friend. Always was. He was down to his last few dollars."

Suddenly Harriet was gasping. Her pince-nez fell from

her nose, and she clutched her chest, her face drained of color. "My heart . . . My heart."

Julia rushed to her side and supported her to a chair. "Lee, get your mother a glass of water." She undid the buttons on Harriet's dress and felt for a pulse at the neck.

"She does that to get her way," Lee said.

"For heaven's sake," Julia said, "your mother is ill."

Harriet's pulse was steady. When Julia pressed an ear to her chest, she heard a strong heartbeat. There didn't appear to be any immediate danger.

"Ma's dead set on framing Gib, that's all," Lee said. "She wants to see him locked up for good." He picked up his hat and wiggled it down onto his head. "Guess I'll head back to work."

When the door slammed behind him, McQuigg exchanged surprised looks with his deputy. "Well, what do you know?" Caine said.

Julia fastened up Harriet's clothing. It was remarkable to see Lee stand up to his mother, but more curious still was his lending Gib money. Gib had assured her he had a grubstake when in fact he was apparently all but broke.

"Booth's a troublemaker." McQuigg was back to business, his frock coat flung open, hands planted on hips. "I wouldn't put anything past him."

Julia pushed Harriet's spell and Gib's grubstake out of her mind and focused on the marshal. She could see that he was trying to convince himself that he had a criminal on his hands.

"I've told you where Mr. Booth was last night," she said. "You have no evidence that he had anything to do with the break-in at the livery."

"Evidence!" Harriet snorted, suddenly restored to good health. "I have plenty of evidence."

Julia ignored her. "There's nothing to justify holding him."

McQuigg stopped his pacing and fixed her with his beady stare. "Don't tell me how to do my job, Mrs. Metcalf."

"I wouldn't think of it, Marshal. I just want to remind you that this town is full of men who are down on their luck and who know how to use a drill and a crowbar. Any one of them could have broken into that safe."

"I am well aware of that fact, ma'am." From the marshal's resigned expression, he appeared ready to give in.

"I would like to speak to Mr. Booth, if I might," Julia said.

McQuigg gave her a skeptical look, then nodded at Deputy Caine. "Take Mrs. Metcalf back to see the prisoner."

Caine grabbed a ring of keys from the wall. "Come along, ma'am."

Julia followed the deputy through the door and into the jail, leaving Harriet to resume her harangue about Gib's past sins.

The jail was hot and musty. A dim hallway separated four cells, two on either side. Gib was in the last cell on the right. In the meager light filtering through the small barred windows, Julia saw him lying on a wooden bunk against the back wall.

"Booth," the deputy said, "you've got a visitor." To Julia he said, "Just a few minutes, ma'am," and headed back to the office.

Julia peered into the dim cell. "Gib."

There was no answer. Julia called his name again, louder.

The figure on the bunk stirred. "Go home, Julia," he said. "You shouldn't be here."

There was a sound of throat-clearing behind her. Julia looked over her shoulder to see a sleek-haired man in the cell across from Gib's. He gave her a leering smile. "Your lady friend's damn pretty, Booth. If you don't want to talk to her, I'll be pleased to oblige."

"Shut up, Buell." Gib swung his feet to the floor and came over to the bars. His black shirt and undershirt were unbuttoned, revealing a chest covered with crisp dark curls. He wiped a sleeve across his perspiring brow. "What the devil was all that racket out there?"

"Harriet Tabor arguing with Lee." Julia grasped the bars and spoke softly. "I told the marshal you were at my house last night. I'm sure he'll release you soon."

210 ELIZABETH DeLANCEY

Gib hung his head. "You shouldn't have said that. Everybody'll be talking again."

"It's the truth, for heaven's sake. Why should you be in jail for something you didn't do?"

In the shadowy cell his shoulders were massive, his unshaven face fearsomely attractive. But there was a brooding, dispirited look in his eyes that touched her heart.

"You'll be free in no time," she said. "The marshal knows he has no cause to hold you."

"Yeah. Then he'll figure out some way to lock me up again." Gib wrapped his hands around the bars, just above hers. "Go home, princess. This is no place for you."

Julia thought of Lee's words, that Harriet was set on seeing Gib in prison. She felt a fierce anger at Harriet and at the marshal, too, for his misguided complicity.

Then she thought of Lee lending Gib money. "Come to the house as soon as you can," she said. "I need to talk to you."

Gib shook his head in an emphatic no. "I'm going up to the mine."

"It's important, Gib. It's about Mossy."

As she expected, that got his attention. He looked at her closely. "What about Mossy?"

Julia glanced over her shoulder at Buell, who was watching them. She rose up on her toes and whispered to Gib, "I think I've found his family."

Gib's brows drew together. "What the devil . . . ?"

"I'll tell you when I see you. Please come."

"All right," he said. "I'll be there."

"Ma'am?" Deputy Caine stuck his head in the door. "Marshal says time's up."

"I'm coming, Buster." She gave Gib a quick smile and a touch on his hand.

At midafternoon, McQuigg turned Gib loose. He went back to the Bon Ton and packed up his gear. He would stop at Julia's and see what she'd found out about Mossy, then head for the Rattling Rock, hide out there until Gilbert

Chapman's baptism. After that, he'd ride out of town and never look back.

He was fed up with Stiles. The marshal sure as hell wasn't going to leave him alone; he'd said as much: "Next time, mister, it'll be the penitentiary at Deer Lodge." Wylie and Trask and their stubby-barreled shotguns were most likely still in the territory, and his plan for Julia was as good as dead. He just couldn't see a way to get that money. He might as well give it up.

Gib loaded his saddlebags onto Lucky, tied on his war bag and bedroll, and mounted up.

Julia's porch was bright with geranium blossoms. Fat yellow flowers decorated the shrubs in front of the house. As Gib rode up, she came out the door, looking so happy to see him that his heart jumped a little. It sure was nice to be appreciated. If he hadn't been dirty and unshaven and reeking of jail, he might have swept her into his arms.

"What's this about Mossy?" he asked.

"Come sit on the porch for a minute. I'll get you something to drink."

She made him sit in Doc's rocker and brought out some lemonade. He drank it down, and she poured him some more. The cat jumped onto his lap and started to purr.

"Mossy's taken Jimmy home," Julia said. "I want to show you what I found before he gets back."

She gave him a paper with the names of Mossy's family. Gib studied it awhile. It sure brought back memories. "Ada Swain," he said. "I saw her once."

"Tell me."

April 18, 1864. The day the regiment left Camp Wool, Massachusetts, and headed south. The regimental colors fluttered in the breeze. The fifers and drummers played "The Girl I Left behind Me."

Gib told her about it, surprised at how much he remembered. "When we boarded the train, a lot of families were there to see their men off. I felt like I was going off on some sort of an adventure. Mossy cried."

Mossy had hung out the train window, his arms full of

food packages, while a plump woman with two clamoring youngsters tried to embrace him.

"Why didn't he go back to them after the war?" Julia asked.

Twenty years, Gib thought. Every man in the 57th had changed during the southern campaign of '64. When it was over, some of those with no ties drifted west, but most went home. Mossy was the only one Gib knew who didn't return to his family.

He sat back in the rocker and stroked the cat and wondered how much he should tell her. Mossy's reasons were his own affair, but Julia had known him all these years, and Mossy thought the world of her. Gib decided it wouldn't hurt for her to know.

"I'll tell you what Mossy said once. He said he'd come from a good Christian home, had a good Christian wife. He said he'd seen things nobody should've seen, done things nobody should have done. The war had spoiled him. He said he never could get the smells out of his nose and the sounds out of his ears. And the sights . . ." Gib shook his head.

He told her about the Battle of the Wilderness. Three weeks after they left Camp Wool, the regiment had its first encounter with the Rebs in Virginia. The carnage and terror of battle were horrific, the fighting so intense there was no way to retrieve the dead and wounded. The woods were as dry as kindling. It didn't take much for small ground fires to turn into an inferno. The screams of the wounded men caught in there were like a double-quick march into hell.

"I had nightmares for years afterward. Mossy hasn't been right in the head since."

Gib didn't look at Julia. He was glad she didn't say anything. "Mossy said the war had rotted him out. He had the idea that he'd stink up his own place, that he'd bring the war home and spread it to his family." Gib stared at the paper in his hand. "I used to think it was pretty strange thinking, but I guess it made as much sense as anything else."

They were quiet. Gib finished his lemonade and scratched

the cat's chin. It sure made him feel low, talking about the war.

"What shall I do, Gib?"

He wasn't sure. Mossy had loved Ada, but who knew what he felt now? Twenty years was a long time, and nobody was getting younger.

"Talk to him about it. Tell him you'll be glad to write to her, to say he's well."

"Would you rather do it?"

Gib considered it. All those dark, writhing memories of war—the smell of smoke, the flash and crack of guns as men fired blindly, the roaring sounds that left him dazed. It had all faded in his mind over the years. He didn't want to bring any of it back.

"It'll be better if you do it," he said.

They sat not speaking, both deep in their thoughts. Inside, the hall clock bonged five o'clock. Gib picked the cat off his lap and set her on the porch. "I guess I'll head for the mine."

Julia looked at him. "Gib, I want to invest in the Rattling Rock."

CHAPTER

16

GIB LISTENED AS Julia handed him his plan on a platter. She told him she knew about the money he'd borrowed from Lee. It was nowhere near enough for the equipment and men he would need to develop the Rattling Rock. She said that Doc would have wanted her to help him. She spoke with nervous haste, as if she was afraid he would refuse her offer.

Gib didn't give her any chance for second thoughts. "It won't be cheap."

She moistened her lips and nodded.

"I know a yard in Salt Lake that sells used equipment," he said. "Decent stuff from mines that closed down. Figuring in all the development costs, hiring a crew, surveying . . ." He paused, not wanting to look at her. "A complete outfit for a fifty-foot shaft and an exploratory crosscut will take about seventy-five thousand."

He heard her gasp. "Dollars?"

"That's a pretty big chunk of foliage."

He let her think it through. If she went for it, he could get out of town with half of her inheritance—an even split, just as he'd planned. Her feelings would be hurt for a while, but she'd get over it.

"I'll instruct Mr. Coolidge at the bank to advance you the money using my portfolio as collateral." She sat up straight in her rocker, trying to look sure of herself. Gib figured she didn't know a damn thing about finances.

"It's probably more than you can afford," he said, offering her a chance to whittle it down.

"No. Edward left me a great deal of money."

The deal was done. Gib got up and put on his hat. "I sure am obliged."

"I'll speak to Mr. Coolidge tomorrow. He'll open an account in your name."

Gib went down the porch steps, feeling lower than a heel.

From Julia's, Gib went to Williver's General Merchandise to pick up powder and fuses and various lengths of drill steel. Then he stopped by I. Z. Blum's for supplies. He leaned on the counter, scribbling a list.

"It's about time you started digging," I. Z. said in his disapproving tone.

"Nice of you to point that out," Gib said.

In truth, he couldn't have agreed more. As long as he had the chance, he'd do his damnedest to find a decent pocket of ore before he left Stiles. If he did that, he could feel he'd accomplished one worthwhile thing.

"Ruth's here, in case you're interested," Blum said.

Gib looked up from his list. Ruth stood at the break of the counter, wrapped in a paisley shawl. She was small and pretty, just as he remembered, but grown into a lovely woman.

"Hello, Gib."

"Well, I'll be." The counter and shawl hid some of her crooked shape, but Gib could see from the way her arms were folded above her belly that she was expecting. "You look mighty fine, Ruth."

Her cheeks flushed a little. "Thank you. So do you."

"Kind of you to say." Evidently she didn't mind a man unshaved and uncombed and fresh out of jail. But then, Ruth had always had a soft spot for him. He used to tease her about it, too, but in a way that made her laugh. "I hear you've got a husband."

Her eyes were dark and lively, a lot like her mother's. "Jack and I have been married for two years now. He's gone back east on business. That's why I came to stay with my folks."

It pleased Gib to see that a crippled girl like Ruth could have a regular life. "Mrs. Metcalf will take good care of you when the time comes. She did real fine by Otis Chapman's wife."

"The new doctor will be here by then," Blum said. "The fancy one from Chicago. You can't go wrong with a doctor like that."

Beacham. Gib had forgotten. It burned him up all over again to think of Beacham waltzing into town, taking Doc's things, and putting Julia out of business.

He went back to his list, trying to figure what he'd need to feed himself and Rawlie for the next couple of weeks.

"I hear the marshal locked you up," Blum said.

Gib gave him an impatient look. Now that he was sticking around, he'd have to put up with Blum's ragging for a while—Dellwood's, too. "He thought I busted into the livery safe. Turned out he was wrong."

"Lucky you had a good alibi."

Gib glanced at Ruth. He wasn't surprised that word of his overnight stay at Julia's had already spread. "She had a wounded man out there. I had to keep an eye on things."

"So that's what you call it," Blum said.

Ruth laughed. "Oh, Papa, don't be so hard on him." She leaned on the counter. "Julia stopped by to visit yesterday. She told us about you doing her spring cleaning."

"Turns out I'm a first-rate maid."

Blum started tallying the bill. Gib dug in his pocket.

"Never mind," Blum said, waving at him. "I'll put it on account."

"I've got the cash."

Blum slid his glasses down his nose and gave him a hard look. "Count your blessings."

Gib gave Ruth a wink. "It's up to you, I. Z." He hoisted an armful of packages. "I've asked Sarabeth Brown to drive the rest of the stuff to the mine." He'd made the arrangements earlier when he stopped by the Bon Ton. "Ruth, it's been a pleasure."

"Come back soon, Gib. Stay for supper."

Outside, Gib unbuckled the saddlebags and stuffed in his supplies. He checked the straps holding the white wicker baby basket behind the saddle. He'd bought the thing at Williver's; it was lined with pockets of blue satin and had little pink and blue bows on the outside.

As he swung into the saddle, he spotted Walt Stringer coming out of the Pickax, heading for the *Sentinel* office.

"Hey, Walt," Gib shouted. "Get over here."

Stringer ambled down the board sidewalk and leaned on the hitch rail. "What's up, Gib?"

"I hear you're running a story about me."

Stringer took his pipe from his mouth. "Had a good one about you breaking into the livery safe. Now that the marshal's let you go, it won't be near as interesting."

"Where are you getting your information? Hughes?"

Stringer seemed to find the question amusing. "In my business, everybody's a source of information." He thought for a minute. "Speaking of Hughes, I could have printed a story on your dustup with him at the Pickax, but I didn't want to embarrass Mrs. Metcalf."

Gib had to give him credit there; a man of another stripe might not have been so considerate. "I'd sure like to know what lies you're planning to spread about me."

Walt chuckled. "I thought I'd let it be a surprise."

"Yeah? Well, you'll be surprised when I give you a thrashing."

"Cool off, Gib. It won't be that bad."

Lucky snorted and sidestepped, impatient to be going. Walt squinted at Gib's cargo. "What in hell are you doing with that baby basket?"

"It's for Otis Chapman's boy. They named him after me."

"I heard about that. Now, there's a real story."

"Baptism's two weeks from Sunday." Gib touched his hat brim and gave Lucky his heels. "See you in church."

Gib hurt from his neck to the soles of his feet. Swinging a hammer all day long wasn't easy work, especially in a narrow stope where he had to fold himself into cramped positions. His knuckles were scraped raw, and his striking arm was sore, not to mention his head, which he bumped against rock a dozen times a day. But he was glad to be doing something that made demands on his body and occupied his mind.

He and Chapman worked by candlelight that flickered each time they moved. They drilled at all angles, settling into a rhythm of about forty strokes a minute. When there was room enough, they worked partners, double-jacking, Gib swinging the long-handled eight-pound hammer while Chapman turned steel.

An hour underground told Gib he hadn't gone wrong hiring Chapman. After a week he decided the man was one of the best hard-rock stiffs he'd ever run into. Chapman knew how to point drill holes, knew how to load powder and fire it, too. After each round, the ground broke the bottom of the hole perfectly, leaving a clean square face.

They loaded holes twice a day, taking a noon break after the first round to let the dust settle, firing the second at quitting time. It became routine—drilling, loading, firing, mucking out the round. Day after day. At night Gib fell exhausted into his bedroll in Digger's cabin. Each morning after he built up a fire and got the coffee started, he stepped out into the vigorous air, sniffed the resin-scented woodsmoke, and stuck his head in a bucket of cold water. While he dried off, he watched the sky brighten, outlining distant big-shouldered mountains splashed with white.

Sarabeth came up now and then to visit and talk about teamstering once they started hauling ore. She seemed to light a fire under Rawlie, who spent most days sitting in his rocker waiting to jaw with Chapman or Gib. Sometimes Sarabeth took him hunting. The old man couldn't see well enough to shoot a bear if one tapped him on the shoulder, but he usually managed to bring home grouse or squirrel or rabbit when she was around. Sarabeth skinned and cleaned the game; then Gib made a stew with potatoes and onions and greens. It sure was tastier than hash out of a can.

Some nights Gib went down to Whiskey Creek for a visit with little Gilbert. While Mrs. Chapman prepared supper and Otis did chores, Gib took the baby outside and showed him the creek bubbling over the rocks and the shadows on the mountains.

"Say, Gib," Chapman said one evening after supper, "you ought to enter the drilling contest on Independence Day. There's an open-for-all contest on double-jack drilling. Five hundred dollars prize money to the winning team."

They were sitting in the front room, listening to the evening rain. Mrs. Chapman was behind the partition, nursing Gilbert, who made eager little noises.

"Some boys from Butte will be coming down," Chapman said. "They've got some of the best double-jack teams in the country. I'd sure like to see you go up against them."

The prospect of a drilling contest interested Gib. At one time he'd been half of the best double-jack team on the Washoe. He'd drilled forty-nine inches into black granite in fifteen minutes, sixty strokes a minute, and had a jam-up good time. Won a pot of money on wagers, too.

"What do you say, Gib?"

It suddenly occurred to him that if everything went according to plan, he wouldn't be around for the Fourth. The baptism would be over, and he'd be long gone, with Julia's money in his pocket and Stiles no more than a memory.

He decided not to think that far ahead. "You want to pair off with me?"

Chapman chuckled. "I'm too small. You want to partner with some big feller from the Continental."

"I don't know any of those stiffs except Bert Scobie, and he's all shot to pieces." Gib wasn't going to add that he wouldn't have paired off with that loudmouth if he was the last stiff on earth.

"There's a feller named Ab Ames who's hard-core. You

two drill on changes, you'll be a match for any of them
Cousin Jacks from Butte."

On changes the partners took turns, one swinging the
hammer while the other turned steel. Even drilling on
changes with a strapping big partner, Gib wasn't sure he had
what it took to win a contest against a team of Cornishmen.

"Ab'll most likely be in church next Sunday," Chapman
said. "You can see him then."

Gib squirmed in his chair. He wished Chapman hadn't
mentioned the baptism. Just thinking about standing up in
front of a church full of suspicious townfolks made him
jumpy. But he'd do it for the baby. He had the feeling little
Gilbert would appreciate having him there.

Gib rode back to the mine in the rainy twilight. Along the
trail, larches and cedars stood gloomy and silent. Branches
brushed against his hat, sending raindrops drumming down
his slicker. Lucky's hooves made a soft, lonely sound on the
wet ground. It was the kind of night that made a man long
for a woman's company, preferably in a horizontal position
under a nice warm quilt.

After the cozy cheer of the Chapmans' place, Gib felt
stone-cold alone. Talking about the baptism had reminded
him of Julia, made him think how much he missed her. For
more than a week he'd kept her at the back of his mind,
because thinking about her was too unsettling. Now he let
her slip into his main thoughts, a poor substitute for the real
woman.

He thought about her smiles, her kisses, the gentle way
she got mad. When he kicked up a fuss about her taking care
of Scobie, she'd put her foot down all right, but in a way
that hadn't hurt his feelings or made him feel low. She'd
even forgiven him for the things he'd said to Hughes. It was
hard to walk away from a woman who treated a man so fair.
When the baptism was over and he had the money, Julia
would be the one thing holding him back.

Gib told himself his thinking didn't make a lick of sense.
He wasn't a man to settle down; he didn't want anyone
depending on him, expecting things of him, which was what

women usually started doing as soon as a man said hello. He wanted a fast, exciting life, a life with loose rules, a life without ties. He'd had it, too, ever since the war, and it suited him just fine.

At the clearing Gib dismounted and led Lucky into the shed. He unsaddled him, rubbed him down, and poured oats into the tin trough. Rawlie was in his shack enjoying a before-bed pipe. Gib stopped long enough to say good night and headed for his own cabin. He stripped off his damp clothes, dabbed some salve on his scraped elbow, and climbed into his bedroll.

Sleep usually came easily, but not tonight. He stared into the darkness and thought about sitting on the porch with Julia, undoing her hair, kissing her lips. He thought of flipping cards with Jimmy Ames in the sunshine while the soft tones of the piano drifted through the open door.

Then he was sitting there with his own son, teaching him card tricks.

Gib fumbled on the shelf beside the bunk and struck a match. It sizzled, and the lamp puffed alight, making shadows leap on the walls. He swung his feet to the floor and sat on the edge of the bunk, his heart pounding, wondering if his mind was slipping its halter.

Seventy-five thousand dollars, he reminded himself. And a life free of cares.

Gib nearly blew himself up the next day. The backfire of a spit fuse put out his candle, and he couldn't get his matches to light. He had to feel his way out of the tunnel and up the shaft with eight holes fired, ready to blow him to kingdom come.

Chapman told him he was getting careless, that he needed a break. Feeling hot and jumpy, Gib headed down to the old Whiskey to cool off. When he rode into the gulch, he saw Julia's buggy in front of the Chapmans' place. The sight of it made him feel even hotter and jumpier.

If he hadn't smelled as rank as a billy goat, he'd have gone straight down to the cabin. Instead, he headed south to the bend in the creek under the cottonwoods where the water bubbled and sang, and the rocks were worn smooth. While Lucky drank, Gib stripped off his digging clothes and waded in. The icy water numbed his feet and legs. He lay down and let the water flow around him till he was frozen all through. Then he dried off, put on his black shirt and pants, mounted Lucky, and rode back up the creek.

Julia's buggy was still there.

Gib dismounted in front of the cabin and wrapped the reins around the fence. He stood there scratching his whiskers, wishing he'd shaved. Suddenly the door opened and Julia came out.

He was lost in a blizzard of color—dress the color of violets, shining nut-colored hair, blazing blue-green eyes. He stared at her, gaping like a beached fish.

"Gib. How are you?"

He wasn't good. He felt as green as peas and twice as tongue-tied.

She came toward him, holding the baby in her arms. Gib's senses filled with springtime perfume, with birdsong and breezes and bright blossoming silk.

"Are you surprised?"

He found his voice. "You look sweet enough to melt in the sun."

She laughed and cuddled Gilbert to her cheek. "What a nice thing to say."

He soaked her up with his eyes. In black she'd been lovely, but a little distant. Black said, "Keep away." A man had to look hard to see the shape of a woman in black. But a soft-colored dress that clung to her breasts and showed a bit of shoulder made seeing damn easy.

She turned around. "Do you like it?"

He looked at her slender back, a waist curved to invite a man's hand, hips gently hidden.

"I sure do."

It was a pretty fancy outfit to wear out to Doubletree Gulch, Gib thought. Then it occurred to him that her new dress might have something to do with him. The idea of it made him light-headed.

"Eight months I've been in black. I think Edward would have said that was enough."

She was telling him it was time to move on with her life.

"Gilbert's getting fat." She jiggled the baby and motioned Gib to have a look. Gilbert's eyes were wide open, the color of heaven. He blinked and waved his little fists, and Gib would have sworn he smiled.

"Hello there, Gilbert."

Gib followed her inside. Mrs. Chapman fussed over him, but he didn't pay her much attention; he couldn't keep his eyes off Julia.

Mrs. Chapman took the baby. "You two go on outside. Enjoy the spring air."

They walked along the creek in the afternoon sunshine, down to the bend where the cottonwoods grew. Birds were singing all around, and the creek made a rushing sound.

Gib felt big and awkward. Julia's smile seemed to push him off balance, and when she asked him about the mine, his answers got stuck in his mouth. He couldn't get up enough steam to utter a whole sentence.

She tilted her head. "Is something wrong?"

"Nah."

She stopped to pick a creamy wildflower. "You're so quiet. You've hardly said a word."

Her smile reached out and embraced him, offering affection like water to a dying man. Until now Gib hadn't realized he was dying, but standing with her, wanting her so bad, he knew that his soul was parched.

"I guess I'm out of practice. Chapman's not big on jawboning."

She glanced at his hands. "He says you've been working hard."

His knuckles were scraped and scabbed, his palms thick with calluses. "Hard enough." He hid his hands in his pockets.

She stood close to him and stuck the flower in his shirt. He stared at the curve of her cheek, the slipping strands of hair. The neckline of her dress was trimmed with a pretty ruffle.

"I've missed seeing you, Gib."

His throat closed up tight. His whole body ached. "Princess." He leaned down and kissed her cheek. He looked at the blush on her face, the gold in her hair. Her eyes were like the tropical sea, warm and languid, blue tinged with green. He kissed her cheek again.

She turned her head so her lips met his. A light, sweet pressure, an angel's kiss. Gib felt a knife go through his innards, sharp and clean, right to the core. She whispered his name against his mouth, not pressing, just there. Her fingers touched the back of his neck, no more than a tickle.

Gib took her in his arms and held her close. Tender, yielding lips opened to his. Sweet tastes, sweet fragrances, her hands in his hair. He kissed her and caressed her, all down her back. He felt her breasts against his chest, and when he drew her hips to his, her arms tightened, and her tongue delved deep.

He crushed her to him. She gave a little cry of passion or surprise, jolting him to his senses. He pulled back abruptly. Her eyes were shining, her lips full and moist, and Gib realized that what was going on between them was getting downright dangerous.

"We shouldn't be doing this." His head was buzzing like a swarm of bees, and his heart pounded hard.

She plucked the ruffle at her neck, smiling a little. "I should go back."

Gib walked her to the buggy through new grass and scattered wildflowers. He helped her up, not knowing what to say. He felt hot and lustful, yet befuddled by tenderness. What he wanted with Julia went beyond his male urges; it had to do with happiness, with giving it to her and finding it for himself.

"I've spoken with Mr. Coolidge," she said. "He's set up an account in your name."

For a moment Gib didn't know what she was talking about. Then he remembered his plan. He tried to steady himself by thinking about it. "Thanks," he said. "Thanks for getting me out of jail."

She touched his sleeve. "Don't forget Gilbert's baptism next Sunday."

"I'll be there."

Julia drove off, up the trace, the buggy rocking and bouncing. Gib stared after her and tried to gather up the bits and pieces of his mind.

"Good manners and good character are two quite different things, Julia."

Harlan was furious, she could tell. They were waiting in the Regal Hotel lobby, warm with the smell of cigar smoke and noontime cooking.

"The man has no discernible character at all."

Julia put on a cheerful face for the gentlemen who tipped their hats and addressed her by name. She felt as fresh and new as the season in a smart buff-colored two-piece dress. Randall's wife, Helen, had sent her the costume from Chicago last summer, together with a brown hat decorated with feathers that nearly matched Julia's hair.

"I think good character and good manners rather go together," she said.

Along with a good heart, she added to herself. Gib had given Mrs. Chapman a baby basket for Gilbert. And when the weather was good, he took the baby outside and showed him the mountains. Mrs. Chapman said he talked to Gilbert as if the baby understood everything he said.

The head waitress led them into the noisy dining room, decorated with rose-colored wallpaper and gilt-framed mirrors. Julia followed, wending her way around dining tables and potted ferns. She didn't wait for Harlan, who paused to greet a group of men.

Whenever he was in town, Harlan stayed in his suite at the Regal and took his meals in the dining room, usually with Barnet Cady or other members of the town council. Today he had requested her company. "To discuss some very important matters," he'd said.

Harlan arrived and took his seat, flipping his coattails. His eyes swept the room, making sure he hadn't missed anyone. He was in his element, surrounded by important men.

"What shall we eat?" He tried to sound jovial, but his heavy face was flushed with irritation.

"The lamb chops are excellent," Julia said.

When the waitress departed, Harlan started in again. "I'm concerned about you, Julia. I'm concerned about this whole business with Booth. The man spread scandalous rumors about you, bragged about certain intimacies—"

"I think you might have provoked him into saying those things."

Harlan waved aside her interruption. "You provided him an alibi when he robbed the livery safe. You allowed him to stay the night at your house. Now you've abandoned your mourning. You're flirting with scandal, Julia. You leave all of us at a loss."

A plate of soup appeared before each of them, glistening with fat. "I think we have discussed Mr. Booth quite enough," Julia said. "As for my decision to stop wearing black, Edward never favored mourning. He said a short memory was far better for one's mental condition than dwelling on the past."

Harlan gave a disparaging snort. "That's ridiculous."

Julia tasted her soup. She had debated long and hard about retiring her mourning attire. She knew it would cause raised eyebrows, but dragging around in black when all of nature was bright and fresh had seemed like a misplaced gesture.

In her heart, however, she knew that Gib was the real reason for her decision. She remembered the expression on his face when Mrs. Chapman put Gilbert in her arms and all but pushed her out the door. Standing there in her best lavender silk, so inappropriate for an afternoon's visit to the gulch, she'd experienced the heady feeling of rendering a man speechless. The rest she relived every night—his hungry kisses and the almost brutal strength of his embrace.

"Surely you can't be thinking of Booth as a suitor."

Julia touched the napkin to her lips, careful to maintain a neutral expression. She couldn't help feeling some sympathy for Harlan. She'd tried not to encourage him, but he continued to assume that their friendship would lead to something more.

"If you're asking whether he's declared his intentions, the answer is no." She thought how furious Harlan would be if he knew about the money she'd invested in the Rattling Rock.

"I can give you a life any woman would envy. Material comfort, social standing, worthy friends. Think about that before you get mixed up with a disreputable man bent on taking advantage of you." Harlan tore into his bread, his lips thin with anger. "This isn't the first time you've had a lapse in judgment."

Julia lowered her spoon and looked at him. "What do you mean by that?"

"It's not necessary to go into detail. I think you know very well what I mean."

Julia sat quietly, waiting for him to say something that would dispel her sudden feeling of dread. But he remained silent, chewing his bread, not looking at her, and it crossed her mind that this was one of the things she most disliked about him—the way he used silence to show his disapproval.

"I think you'd better explain yourself," she said.

Harlan glanced up, a triumphant gleam in his eyes. "Edward did you a great favor by marrying you, didn't he?"

CHAPTER
17

JULIA LEFT THE Regal angry and shaken. Randall, her own half brother, had betrayed her. Of course, he wouldn't have seen it that way; he probably thought he'd done the honorable thing. But it was clear to Julia that he had violated her trust.

According to Harlan, during Randall's visit to Stiles last fall, Harlan had alluded—most inappropriately, Julia thought—to his hope of winning her hand. In response, Randall had felt obliged to mention the stain on her past.

What he'd done was beyond Julia's comprehension; he'd revealed a shameful episode she'd long since put behind her, a secret that could very well destroy her. Yet shocking though his actions were, Julia knew she shouldn't be surprised. Randall had always been critical and self-righteous. Despite his brilliance as a physician, he had little tolerance for human failings, especially the failings of women.

She set off down the boardwalk toward the Bon Ton, medical bag in hand. There was no point in dwelling on

Randall's treachery, she told herself; she couldn't undo what had been done. She was thankful that Harlan had been sympathetic. After his initial annoyance he'd listened attentively as she explained herself. He'd promised that everything she said would be safe with him. Julia could only pray he would be as good as his word.

The sun was bright, the street dusty. A wagon clattered by, raising a cloud, forcing her to put a handkerchief to her nose. At the Bon Ton, she climbed the outside stairs and entered the dim second-floor hallway, echoing with female voices and a few masculine rumbles. Julia kept her eyes straight ahead. She didn't want to see anything that involved hurdy girls and their male companions.

Suddenly a door opened, and Sarabeth Brown stepped into the hallway, followed by a man. Julia dropped her gaze and backed up against the wall, pressing herself there, hoping to be invisible.

"Howdy, Mrs. Metcalf."

Julia forced herself to look up. "Good afternoon, Sarabeth—" Her voice caught. Standing beside Sarabeth, looking painfully embarrassed, was Lee Tabor.

Julia stared at him in astonishment. "Why . . . Lee."

He mumbled something, then slunk back into the room.

"Don't mind him, he's shy," Sarabeth said. "You looking for Bert Scobie?"

"Why . . . yes. I heard he'd taken a room here after he left Mrs. Kitchen's care."

"Second door from the stairs, on the left," Sarabeth said. "He seems hale enough, except for drinking himself half to death." She gave Julia a grin and followed Lee back inside, closing the door behind her.

Julia took a moment to recover herself. Lee was calling on Sarabeth in her room at the Bon Ton—and they certainly weren't crocheting doilies!

She proceeded down the hallway, glancing at each closed door, wondering what surprise might emerge next. At Scobie's door she knocked softly and called his name.

"It's open," bellowed a voice from inside.

Julia opened the door to find him sprawled on an untidy

bed, wearing the sullen look of a man with too great a fondness for whiskey.

He waved a bottle and belched. "Guess I'm still getting my five dollars' worth."

Julia wrinkled her nose at the smell of sweat and spirits and unwashed clothes. "So you are, Mr. Scobie."

She helped him off with his shirt. Her examination showed that despite his abominable habits, his wounds were healing. "I'd say you could start back to work," she said. "Short hours, but work nevertheless. You want to get that shoulder moving again."

"Ain't got a job. Hughes gave me my time and sent me down the hill. He says I'm no good if I can't swing a jack."

"I'm sorry to hear that," Julia said, but she wasn't surprised. What with all the other layoffs, it was no wonder that Harlan had let go a man who couldn't work a full shift.

"He'll be sorry," Scobie said. He flexed his fingers and buttoned his shirt.

"And why is that?" Julia asked.

Scobie rolled his rheumy, red-rimmed eyes. "You'll hear in good time. You'll all hear in good time."

"It might be to your advantage to go to Butte," Julia said, fastening the buckles on her bag. "There's plenty of work there."

Scobie gave her a sly grin. "That's what Hughes said. But I ain't interested in Butte."

On Saturday, the day before the baptism, Gib took his best duds into town. He got his hat cleaned and blocked and his suit brushed, then stopped at the barbershop for a shave and haircut. When he went out back for a hot-water bath, there was a line of cowboys and miners. He'd heard that Miss Lavinia wouldn't let a man in the door of her parlor house unless he'd had a recent acquaintance with soap and water.

After supper at the Pickax, Gib stopped by the Bon Ton. The place was full up with the Saturday night crowd, so Dellwood told him to park his bedroll in the storage room.

"Want a drink?" Dellwood had to shout over the din.

Gib hoisted his foot onto the brass footrail. "Nah, I'm due in church tomorrow." He felt a little proud saying it.

"So I heard." Dellwood shook his head. "I hope that little bugger don't turn out as bad as you."

The comment stung. It must have shown in Gib's face, for Dellwood added, "'Course, I've seen worse." He pulled a rag out of his belt and started swabbing the bar. "You heard about Sarabeth and Lee?"

"What about them?"

"They're back keeping company."

"Is that a fact?" Things sure had been happening in the two weeks he'd been at the mine, Gib thought.

"Lee's in here just about every night, looking moon eyes at her." He jerked his head in the direction of the gambling room. "Go see for yourself."

Gib was about to do just that when the sound of crashing glass broke over the plink of piano and banjo. He whirled around to see a table thump onto its side and roll a few turns, scattering glassware and cards onto the floor.

"Christ Almighty," Dellwood muttered. He hurried out from behind the bar.

Scobie, one arm in a sling, was swearing a blue streak. A cowboy hopped around as if the table had landed on his foot.

"I swear, Scobie," the cowboy hooted. "You're dumber than a stump."

Scobie pushed up against him. The two men stood chin to chin, hurling insults.

"That's enough, you two," Dellwood said.

Gib had a vision of the cowboy laying Scobie out on the floor and Julia having to patch him up again. He hotfooted it over to the men and stepped between them. Scobie pushed at him blindly, trying to get at the cowboy.

"Cool off, Scobie," Gib said, giving him an elbow. "You're in no shape for a fight." The smell of whiskey rose off him like steam off a bog.

Scobie took one look at Gib and lost interest in the cowboy. "Well, lookee here. If it ain't Mr. Gib Booth." He wavered on his feet, his eyes glassy. "How's the widow? You still riding that filly?"

Gib's fist hit Scobie's jaw, sending a jolt of pain through his hand and halfway up his arm. Scobie staggered, then fell to the floor in a loose sprawl.

Men gathered around in bunches, whooping and shouting. Gib's blood was pounding, making waves in his head. He reached down and hauled Scobie up by the sling. His eyes were rolling around, his jaw hanging, his panting breath foul.

"Lay off, Gib." Lee's hand was on his shoulder.

Gib thrust his face at Scobie. "You keep talking like that, mister, and you'll be breathing out your belly."

"That sounds like a threat, Booth."

The marshal's voice sent a chill down Gib's back. He let go of Scobie and turned around. McQuigg stood with his hand on his six-gun, his mustache waxed into tight little curls.

"Take it any way you want," Gib said.

He looked around. The room was silent except for Scobie's whining. He remembered Julia's warning about not letting men taunt him into trouble. Hell, he didn't want a fight. Not tonight.

"Maybe I'd better take you across the street," McQuigg said. "A spell in a jail cell will cool you off."

Gib's gut clenched in panic. "I'm due in church tomorrow morning."

There was an instant of silence. Then the men began to laugh. Their laughter rose until they roared and hooted and banged their fists, until the very walls seemed to throb with hilarity. Even the marshal was leaning back, hands clapped to his vest, howling.

Gib hung his head. He wished he could strike a cocky pose—grin and strut, as if he'd made a joke. But the men's laughter made him feel too low. It reminded him of who he was—a smooth-talking sharper out to bluff a woman who trusted him.

The hilarity died down, fading into talk. McQuigg was

staring at him, still grinning. "You can always do your praying in jail," he said.

"Another time," Gib said.

He walked across the saloon, past knots of grinning men, and through the swinging doors. As he stood on the dimly lit boardwalk, he imagined the whole congregation staring at him tomorrow, thinking the worst. They'd probably laugh when he stood up with Gilbert, whoop and holler like the men in the saloon. They'd have good reason, too. For him to sponsor a baby in church was laughable.

He decided to head back to the Rattling Rock. He'd spend tomorrow deep in the mine, blowing up rock.

The saloon doors creaked. "Say, Gib."

It was Lee. The sight of him lifted Gib's spirits a little. "Say, Lee."

"It don't mean nothing, them laughing like that."

Gib didn't want to discuss it. "Hell, let them laugh." He punched Lee on the shoulder. "I hear you're back with Sarabeth. That's real good news."

Lee rested a boot on one of Dellwood's chairs and took out his tobacco pouch. "I got you to thank for it."

"Me? How's that?"

Lee shook a line of tobacco into a paper and started to roll. "That night we talked on the porch started me to thinking. Here I am thirty years old, giving up the best girl in the world just so's I can keep the livery. I decided it wasn't worth keeping if I can't have Sarabeth."

Lee struck a match with his thumbnail. As he drew on his cigarette, he looked at Gib expectantly. Gib nodded to let him know he understood.

"When Ma tried to frame you for busting into the safe, I decided I'd had enough of her danged interfering. The way I look at it, she's just plain selfish." He took another drag and watched the smoke curl. "After I left the marshal's office that day, I came straight down to the Bon Ton and saw Sarabeth."

Lee studied the tip of his cigarette and smiled a little. From the expression on his face, Gib figured Sarabeth hadn't made him cool his heels long.

"You two getting hitched up?"

"Already did. Barnet Cady tied the knot last week. Dottie stood up for Sarabeth." He gave Gib a long, squinting look. "If it hadn't happened so fast, I'd have gone up to the mine to get you, but Sarabeth was afraid I'd change my mind." He took another pull at his smoke. "I'd have liked you beside me, Gib. For old times."

Gib had to swallow a couple of times to get rid of the lump in his throat. It pleased him to see Lee happy; it pleased him even more to know that he'd wanted him by his side. "That's mighty kind of you to say, Lee."

"Hell, Gib. You know I think the world of you. Always did."

Gib had never heard of two grown men standing around getting sentimental, though it felt kind of good. "Guess I better shove off," he said. "Tell Sarabeth she's a damned lucky woman."

"Keep it under your hat. Ma don't know about it yet."

"Not a word."

Gib untied Lucky and swung into the saddle. As he headed down Main Street toward the bridge, he decided he'd better let Julia know about tomorrow's change of plan. He didn't want her worrying when he didn't show up in church.

Julia sprinkled flour on the pastry cloth and rolled out a batch of cookie dough. Tomorrow after the service, the ladies would serve refreshments in the churchyard. She was contributing her thin, crisp molasses cookies, a favorite at socials and bake sales. Later Harlan would drive her to the Willivers' for Sunday dinner; Louise had planned a welcome for Dr. Beacham, who had arrived today on the late stage.

Julia plucked at the dough stuck to the rolling pin. Thinking of Harlan made her uneasy. She'd seen him twice since their dinner at the Regal, and he'd behaved perfectly well; he hadn't said a word about the unpleasantness they'd discussed. But she'd begun to wonder if by bringing up her past, he might have been trying to intimidate her. Perhaps he wanted her to be more receptive to his suit. Or perhaps he was using it as a threat to force her to stay away from Gib.

Nonsense! Julia told herself sternly. Harlan might be disappointed that she hadn't responded favorably to his overtures, and he might be angry about her association with Gib, but he was a gentleman. Surely he had no wish to expose her shame.

Julia went back to her dough rolling and turned her thoughts to tomorrow. Gib was probably worried about standing up in church. She imagined him by the baptismal font, fidgeting with fright, and she couldn't help but smile.

The surgery bell clanged, jolting her from her thoughts. Julia looked at the clock. Ten-thirty. She hoped an emergency wouldn't keep her up all night.

She wiped her hands and removed her apron. Taking a lamp, she went into the hall, through Edward's study, and into the surgery. The bell rang again. She smoothed the pleats of her white shirtwaist and opened the door.

"Why, Gib." A lovely tingle slid up her spine. "What are you doing here?"

He gave her a quick glance, then stared at his boots. Right away Julia knew something was wrong.

"I'm heading back to the mine," he said. "I won't be in church tomorrow. I thought I'd better let you know."

Julia opened her mouth to protest, then stopped herself. From the look of him, he was suffering from more than a case of jitters.

"Come in for a moment," she said.

He fingered his hat brim. "I don't think I'd better."

She sniffed the air. "The cookies. Oh, heavens!" She reached out and gave his sleeve a tug. "I'm baking molasses cookies for the social after church tomorrow. You must try a few."

He shook his head. "Thanks—"

"I have a nice pot of tea, Chinese tea. Charlie Soon carries a wonderful array." She retreated, lamp in hand, trying to lure him inside with her chatter. "I feel as if I've been running from one thing to another all day long. An Independence Day fair committee meeting at Louise's, medical calls, errands in town, finishing my article for the *Sentinel*. That's why I'm up so late baking."

She reached the study door. "Come, Gib," she said. "Keep me company. Just for a while." She smiled entreatingly. "Please?"

He put a foot over the threshold, looking uncertain, then stepped inside. "Just for a while."

Julia led the way through the study and down the hallway into the kitchen, wondering what she should do. Bullying, she knew, would only make him defiant. She had to find a gentler way to get him to church.

In the kitchen she moved the mixing bowl and the jug of molasses, clearing a place for him at the table. "You should eat something if you're riding up to the mine," she said. "How about some beef stew?"

He hung back at the doorway, turning his hat in his hands. "Thanks just the same. I had supper at the Pickax."

Julia turned up the lamp over the table, the better to see his face. She noticed that he'd gotten a haircut, and he looked freshly shaved.

She put on her apron and started arranging cookies on the plate. "When I was a girl, these cookies were my favorites, especially in winter." She opened the oven door, pulled out a finished batch, and set the cookie sheet on the shelf above the stove to cool. "I used to chew up molasses cookies and spit the juice out, pretending it was tobacco juice."

She glanced at him, expecting a smile or at least a questioning look, but neither was forthcoming. Gib kneaded his hat, his face solemn, his body tense.

"I used to fill my mouth with cookie juice and spit it all over the snow," she said. "I thought it was great fun, like being a man. Father was disgusted, but Mama thought it was hilarious. She laughed so hard she cried."

Julia saw it then—a break in his reserve, the faintest trace of a smile. "It's hard to imagine," he said. "You spitting."

"I still get the urge, when I've just baked a batch and there's a fresh snowfall."

She started cutting dough with a tin cookie cutter, dropping circles onto the baking sheet. The kitchen odors were sweet and thick, and all around was the cheerful clutter of baking. Watching her, Gib imagined a fair-haired girl in a snug winter coat and hat, warm gloves. A neat, trim little girl, who'd grown into a neat, trim-figured woman. Gib's eyes skimmed over her. She wore the shirtwaist that puffed out around her breasts.

"There," she said. She picked up the cookie sheet and pushed it into the oven. "The last batch."

She pinned up a few stray locks of hair and motioned to a chair. "Sit down, Gib."

He shook his head. There was no point in sticking around; he'd told her what he'd come to say. The trouble was, Julia wasn't easy to leave, especially when he remembered the afternoon at Whiskey Creek and how she'd felt in his arms.

"I wish I could change your mind about tomorrow," she said.

He shrugged. "It's no use, me going to church. I can't do anything for that baby."

"Of course you can. You can help him grow into a fine young man."

She looked like a pretty schoolteacher with her high collar and slender posture, her hands neatly clasped. Her feelings for him made no sense, Gib thought. She knew about his past—the gambling and the girls, the shell games and the shooting. The things he'd said to Hughes no woman should forgive. Yet there she was, admiring him with those pretty jewellike eyes.

"You don't know me, Julia."

She smiled a little. "I think I do."

Gib stared at the floor. It was enough to make a man crazy, he thought, a woman who wouldn't quit believing him. "I got into a fight with Scobie at the Bon Ton tonight. He said something along the lines of what I said to Hughes. I hit him. The marshal wanted to put me in jail. When I said I was due in church tomorrow, all the men laughed like a bunch of loons." He glanced at her. "I don't have any business in church, or sponsoring a baby, either."

Julia's face registered no change of expression, not even a

quiver of disapproval. "Is that why you decided not to go? Because the men laughed at you?"

The way she asked the question made Gib think she'd probably understand everything he might tell her—even the truth about the money and his plan to ride out of town.

"Yeah, that's why. I'm not cut out for church. When you come right down to it, I'm not cut out for much of anything that folks around here set store by."

She regarded him thoughtfully. "Surprise everyone, then. Do what they least expect." A mischievous light brightened her eyes. "Especially Marshal McQuigg."

Gib hadn't thought of it that way. If he stayed away, he'd be giving McQuigg plenty of satisfaction.

"Besides," she said, "I know you love Gilbert."

Gib punched at the crown of his hat and thought of those baby eyes staring at him, big as poker chips. He knew every detail of Gilbert's face, every curl in his hair, every wrinkle on his hands. When he left town, he'd sure miss that little nipper.

Gib wiped his sleeve across his nose. "He's a good fellow."

"So there," Julia said. "Go to church tomorrow and stand up proudly."

Her gentle assurance warmed his soul, easing the gloom that went deeper than blood and bone. The thought crossed his mind that she might love him. Why else would she treat him so kindly and allow him so many liberties?

"I guess I'll be there," he said.

"Good."

She turned away and opened the oven, pulling out more cookies. Tin banged against iron as she scraped cookies off the baking sheet. Gib looked at her, all down the back, from shoulders to waist to the hem of her skirt. He recalled how worried he'd been that she'd get too fond of him. Turned out the joke was on him. He would never get her out of his heart. Remembering the feel of her in his arms, the taste of her mouth, the scent of her hair, brought on a surge of longing that made his eyes sting. What he'd hardly dared think about, he now wanted to do—had to do, if she would let him.

Gib put down his hat and went to her. He put his hands on her waist. "Julia."

She stopped her scraping and stood still. He slid his hands around the front of her, cautiously, awaiting her reaction. She dropped the pot holder and spatula and leaned back against him, giving him his answer.

He tightened his arms under her breasts. He kissed her neck, smelling lemon and the spice of cookies. "I didn't come here for this. I want you to know that."

"I know you didn't."

The room was dead quiet, the very air mysterious. Gib nuzzled her hair, kissed her ear, making her sigh. He hungered for her. He wanted her love, to know it just once, to feel the wholeness of being in her arms.

He slipped his hand inside the bib of her apron, feeling the fabric of her blouse, the rise of firm flesh. No corset, nothing other than a few layers of flimsy cloth. He fumbled in the pleats, caressing her.

"I need you, Julia."

She turned in his arms and reached up to embrace him. He pressed his lips to hers, hesitantly at first, then harder, deeper, kiss after hungry kiss, tasting every bit of her mouth. It was his dream come true, his nightmare. She was soft and light, a confection of womanly sweetness, kissing him back with a shivering delight that he felt all through him. Suddenly he was frantic for her, pressing against her, his hands fumbling at buttons and hooks, pulling at apron strings, getting nowhere.

"Wait."

Gib stopped, his heart thundering in his chest.

She took his face in her hands and whispered against his mouth, "Come with me."

She left his arms and removed her apron. She turned out the overhead lamp and picked up a smaller one. Taking his hand, she led him down the hallway and up the stairs. Her bedroom brightened in the lamplight—shining furniture, cozy pillows, the flower-colored quilt. Julia set down the

lamp and started to fold the coverlet back. Gib wanted to ask
her if she understood what she was doing, giving herself to
him. He wanted to tell her that he might not be a gentleman,
not with her, although he would try.

Then he had a thought that checked the beating of his
heart. Julia was Doc's wife. Doc hadn't even been dead a
year, and now he was going to take her to bed.

"I . . ." He faltered. "What about Doc?"

Julia glanced at him. "It wasn't like this with Edward and
me, Gib. With us there was nothing."

He stared at her. "What do you mean, nothing?"

She smiled, a grave, lovely smile tinged with regret. "We
managed for a while. He thought I expected it, I suppose.
Then we stopped. We didn't discuss it, but I think he never
got over losing his wife."

"You were his wife."

"Not really. Not like his first wife."

Gib was dumbfounded. He'd never been disappointed in
Doc, but he was disappointed right now. A man had no right
to marry a woman if he wasn't going to be a husband to her,
no right at all.

"I was happy with him," Julia went on. "You mustn't
think otherwise." She leaned over and began spreading up
the quilt. "You can leave now if you want to. I'll understand."

The sadness in her voice plunged right to his gut. Gib
took off his jacket and stripped off his shirt. When Julia
straightened up from the bed, he was beside her, his hands
on her waist.

"Forget about Doc," he said. "This is between you and
me."

CHAPTER

18

HIS BODY WAS hard, well used, every bulge and sinew tight. Julia touched sculpted flesh and springy hair, a scar here, a scrape there, and down by his trousers, pale places the sun hadn't reached.

He stood beside her, his arm at her waist, his lips near her cheek. "That's nice, princess," he said softly. "That feels real nice."

The lamp flickered, caressing him with golden light, making his eyes shine. She felt taut muscles rise and fall, and the heat of him beneath her hands. For the moment he was hers. This would happen once or a hundred times. But the future didn't matter, or the past; only now, with him.

He unbuttoned her blouse with bent head and clumsy fingers. He pulled it off and eased down her shift. As he looked at her, something raced along her nerves, a light tingling spark that hopped all over her body, trying to set her afire. Gib touched her breasts and the spark caught, making her shimmer and melt.

"Beautiful," he said. "I knew you would be."

"There's not much of me."

"A perfect handful."

He leaned down and kissed her with open mouth and sliding tongue, and all inside she felt the silky warmth of wanting him. She ran her hands over rough denim. She touched his thigh, then higher, where he was hot and straining.

"Julia . . ."

He fumbled at the fastenings of her skirt. She pushed his fingers away, finding the hooks herself. His mouth didn't leave hers; his hands were everywhere—on her hair, her breasts, her skirt, grabbing at fabric. He pulled her toward the bed. She tripped, and he caught her in a desperate embrace, tugging her. They fell back together, sinking into feathered softness, his weight pressing her down.

His mouth and hands were all over her. She felt hunger and heat, and his mouth, oh, his mouth. Face, lips, hands—she'd known they would be kissed. But not her throat, her shoulders, her breasts. He sucked and licked, making ravenous sounds. She dug at his hair, his back, hard, damp flesh. He shifted over her, raising her skirts, pushing fabric aside. He grasped the waist of her drawers, pulled and tore. Ribbons and lace, all torn away, then his hand seeking, finding.

"Oh, Gib."

He stroked her with delicacy and care, creating sensations she'd never imagined, and deeper desires that made her hips move and her eyelids tremble. She heard her own quick gasps and his labored breaths, soft words in her ears.

"My God, Julia."

Desire grew to a deep, trembling hunger. "Gib, I can't bear it."

He rose off her, fumbling at his trousers. Then he was pushing against her—flexing hips, vulnerable flesh, rough hands gripping. Hot, mingling kisses silenced her cries. He thrust into her with a deep, driving power that made her frantic, that took her near to fainting. She clung to him, trying to contain this terrible pleasure, but he'd swept her into a swift-flowing current that was carrying her high and fast. Suddenly, too soon, it swallowed her. Breath left her; time stopped. She rode silent waves of ecstasy, clutching him deep within her. She felt him stiffen, heard his hoarse cry, and his mouth crushed hers.

He stayed with her, his heartbeat thumping through his body. Sensations lingered, then receded, leaving behind a reality both undeniable and profound. Whatever Gib had been or might become, he was the man she wanted for life.

"Princess, you awake?"

She stirred. "Yes."

"I was rough on you. I didn't mean to be."

She brushed a hand across his chest, giving the hair a little tug. It felt damned good, like everything else she did.

"You weren't rough."

They lay together, her head on his shoulder, his lips pressed to her hair. Gib knew he should take stock of the complications he was creating for himself, but it was hard to get beyond the moment, being here with Julia in the bed with the flower-colored quilt.

"You sure I didn't hurt you?"

She looked up at him, her face radiant in the lamp glow. There was a warm tint to her skin, and her hair shone with streaks of gold. "It was wonderful."

Her words pleased him, though her satisfaction probably had less to do with him than with not having had a man's attention her whole married life. He knew he'd gone after her like a madman—not what he'd intended at all.

"You sure curled my hair."

She laughed. "It still looks straight to me."

He couldn't take his eyes off her. She was alive with loveliness, prettier than ever—and she was his. For tonight. He'd heard the new doc was in town, so he wouldn't have to worry about low-grade stiffs dropping by her surgery day and night. The money was in the bank, ready and waiting, and tomorrow the baptism would be over. There'd be nothing in Stiles to hold him.

He played with a sleek strand of her hair. "Did you write to Mossy's wife?"

"A week ago. He was upset when I first brought it up, but later he said he wouldn't mind."

Gib was glad for that. He didn't like leaving Mossy. Lee, either. But Lee had Sarabeth. Mossy had no one, other than Julia.

She shifted a little under the sheet. "I was thinking about the war after you told me about Mossy. I wonder why some men had a bad time of it, like him, and other men didn't."

Gib folded an arm behind his head and considered her question. "Every man had a bad time, Julia. Some managed to shake it off better than others."

"What about you?"

He looked down at her curious face. It was strange how questions he'd never wanted to think about were easy to answer when she did the asking. "I shook it off pretty well. Took a lot of hell-raising to do it, though."

"Were you wounded?"

"Nah. Sick as a dog a few times, but I never got a scratch." He thought back. "I figure I was too scared to die. I was afraid I'd have to face Ma in the afterlife."

Julia tilted her head questioningly. "Why was that?"

"She was a Quaker." He said it without thinking. "She raised me as a Friend."

He quit talking and waited for her to say something—be surprised or shocked, show some sort of reaction. She didn't, so he went on. "You asked me once about Ma and the war, what she thought of me going."

"The night we sat on the porch," she said.

"Rice pudding."

She smiled.

Damn, she was easy. With her, words just spilled out. "When the war came, I wanted to fight in the worst way. Ma knew what I was thinking, and she knew she was dying. Before she passed on, she pleaded with me to be faithful. She said that it wasn't for us to enter into deadly strife. She said the war would turn me to vice and evil company. I told her I wouldn't leave the Meeting. I swore to it."

It still lay like a bruise on his memory, how he'd let Ma down, how he'd broken his word. He talked, more slowly, trying to express things he'd kept to himself all these years. "I was fourteen when she died. I was sent to a strict home. Ma'd been easy on me. I couldn't stand the new place, so I ran off and joined the army."

Julia was silent. Gib didn't know what she was thinking, but he doubted it was bad. Till now he'd never told anyone the story of how he'd broken his word. He'd been ashamed of it, figured it was proof of his low character. But Julia wouldn't see it that way; she couldn't seem to see that part of him at all.

"You comforted her at the end, Gib," she said. "You told her what she wanted to hear and allowed her to die in peace."

He squinted at the ceiling. "Ma used to say she raised me to be tender, so I'd know the grace of God. Turned out she wasted her time. In the war, when the time came, I did as much killing as the next man. Shooting Hockett was another thing. He deserved it, but it brought back Ma again, made me feel mighty low."

Julia reached across his chest and gave him a hug. "None of us can live for the dead. We lead our lives as best we can. Your mother was a fine, forgiving woman, and she loved you."

He looked at her. "You think so?"

"You carried a heavy burden for a boy. It's no wonder you turned wild."

Gib leaned down and kissed her for a long time. When he stopped, she smoothed the hair back from his forehead. "You are tender, Gib, just as your mother raised you. No matter what you might think, you're a tender man."

He looked at her breasts, cupped in shadow, and bent to kiss her there. He teased her with his tongue, then took her in his mouth, breathing in her fragrance of lemon and cloves. He heard her breath quicken, felt her fingers dig into his hair, and blood thudded through him, swift and sudden. His hand slid down the curve of her belly, into curls and heat. He wanted her, to lose himself in the comfort of her body.

He took her in an entrancing silence, her sighs like whispers against his neck, her mounting pleasure a balm to his soul. Her excitement crested with a cry, and he thrust into her with all his passion and strength until something grabbed him, tossed him high, and shook him till he saw stars.

He lingered in his stupor, aware of her warmth all around him, her softness beneath him. His mind floated to some peaceful place on the far side of memory that was clearer than imagination. There was a warm stove, a warm bed. Piano music drifted onto the porch on a blossoming spring day. Bees hummed, children shouted. A striped cat took a bath in the sun.

Julia whispered in his ear. "I love you, Gib."

He tried to shake himself out of his fog. He was getting himself in too deep. If he wasn't careful, Julia would ask more of him than he was able to give.

As soon as Julia woke, she reached for him. Instead of Gib, she found an empty pillow with a note on it. She sat up and spread the paper on her knees: "Dear Sleeping Beauty—You sure look pretty. I thought about waking you with a kiss, but I don't have the heart to bother those sweet dreams. See you in church. Yrs, G.B."

Julia read it again. "Yrs. G.B." Yours, she thought. Mine. She looked at the bright windows. Outside, the sun shone, the birds were busy at their songs. A glorious day.

She put on her robe and went downstairs to a warm stove, a pot of steaming coffee, and a full reservoir of water. Cookies were stacked on plates. Last night's bowls and spoons had been washed and dried, the table cleaned. The kitchen looked as if Mary Hurley herself had been through.

Gib, she thought. A tender touch, bewitching kisses, and the kindest heart a woman could ask for.

She took a jug of hot water upstairs. After she washed, she laid out a two-piece light wool dress in a dusky rose color with a swaglike drape on the skirt that looped up in back over the bustle. Paired rows of pearl buttons decorated the snug bodice. It was a city dress, much fancier than anything she would see in church this morning.

When she was dressed, she brushed out her hair, pinned it up, and fastened on her hat. She hummed to herself as she buttoned on her glazed kid shoes. Not until she picked up her bag and gloves and headed for the stairs did she wonder about the propriety of dressing for church with the intention of pleasing one's lover.

The churchyard was crowded with people in dark, dignified clothes. Julia looked around for Gib, then warned herself to be discreet.

Mossy helped her down from the buggy. She took the basket of cookies and headed for the long table set up for after-church refreshments. The white cloth flapped in a stiff breeze that rustled leaves and tossed up dust. Dottie Cady was laying rocks on the table to keep the cloth in place. She smiled at Julia from beneath the brim of a dark green bonnet.

"Don't you look pretty."

"Thank you, Dottie. I might say the same about you." Dottie's green and black checked dress flattered her matronly figure.

"It's a lovely day for a baptism," Dottie said.

"Indeed it is."

"Gib looks well. I've never seen him so dressed up."

Julia followed Dottie's nod to a nearby cottonwood, where Gib stood talking with Barnet Cady and Lee Tabor. He wore the dark suit he'd worn the day he first came to her door, a white shirt, string tie, the silver brocade vest. He looked virile and vigorous, devilishly handsome. At the sight of him Julia felt a flood of nervous longing.

He met her eyes with a quick, intimate smile, an admiring rise of his brow. To anyone watching, it was nothing, but it told Julia everything she needed to know. She fumbled with her basket, and a handful of cookies slid to the ground. Before she could avoid them, she stepped down on one with a solid crunch.

"Dr. Beacham arrived yesterday," Dottie said. "He seems like a nice young man. He's staying with Louise and George Williver until he gets his own place."

Julia arranged the remaining cookies on plates, all the while making appropriate comments. So glad Dr. Beacham had come. Looking forward to meeting him. To herself, she thought of the day ahead—church, socializing, Sunday dinner at Louise's, talking with Harlan, getting acquainted with Dr. Beacham, croquet on the lawn. She glanced at Gib again and wondered how she would manage to get through the day, when all she could think of was him.

Harriet yoo-hooed across the churchyard and hurried toward Dottie with a basket in her arms. As she passed Julia, she glared darkly, her eyes sweeping up and down.

Dottie squeezed her arm. "Here come the Willivers and Dr. Beacham."

Julia trudged dutifully toward the Willivers' carriage where Harlan, looking heavy and important, stood with the others.

"Ladies!" His jovial voice boomed out. Taking Julia's arm, he drew her to his side. "Julia, may I introduce Dr. Stanley Beacham. Dr. Beacham, this is Dr. Edward Metcalf's widow."

He was a small-statured young man with a goatee. Shining spectacles magnified his eyes. "Welcome to Stiles, Dr. Beacham," Julia said. "We're delighted you've come."

He took her hand and made a little bow. "Madam, I'm delighted to be here."

"Mrs. Metcalf has had a difficult time these past months," Harlan said, giving Julia's elbow a sympathetic squeeze. "After losing her husband, she felt obligated to look after his patients. The ordeal has taken a great deal out of her. She will be relieved to have this part of her life behind her."

Dr. Beacham looked appropriately sorrowful. "My deepest condolences, madam. I have heard nothing but praise for Dr. Metcalf's medical skill."

"You're very kind," Julia said, wondering where Harlan had gotten the idea she wanted to give up her practice.

As Dottie and Dr. Beacham exchanged pleasantries, Julia

studied the young man. If the goatee was supposed to make him appear older, it didn't succeed, nor did the spectacles. To her, the doctor looked too fresh-faced to be taken seriously. She glanced at his hands. They were strong and long-fingered, good surgeon's hands—the only thing about him that inspired confidence.

Julia scolded herself for being so critical.

Dr. Beacham was speaking to her again. "Later in the week I'll stop by your house and give you a list of things I'll need in my office. Your brother, Dr. Frye, said you would sort through your late husband's supplies and provide me with what I might need."

Before Julia could utter a word, Harlan said, "I'm sure Mrs. Metcalf will be more than happy to oblige."

Then Louise was fluttering her arms and scolding in her gay hostess's manner, telling everyone it was time to go inside. Dottie came up beside Julia and linked arms.

"Dearie," she said softly, "whatever has happened between you and Gib, it's written all over the both of you. Take my advice and try not to let it show quite so much."

The varnished pews were filled with sober-looking citizens, a good number of whom seemed startled to see Gib in their midst. Glancing around, he decided church was not a habit he'd want to cultivate, but it was as good a place as any to sit and think. And thinking had been his main occupation since shortly after dawn when he'd wakened with Julia in his arms, warm, naked, and beautiful. He'd looked at her sleeping face for a while, then decided to do the right thing. He'd gotten up, dressed, and gone to the Pickax for breakfast.

Now he stared at the sunlight gleaming on walnut and varnished pine and tried not to dwell on last night. Remembering made him think reckless thoughts—such as staying around Stiles. Every time the idea crossed his mind, the consequences slid right in behind it. Sticking around would mean ending up in trouble—the marshal and Hughes would see to that. Or dead—Wylie and Trask would see to that.

He looked at Julia sitting at the church piano, directly in

his line of vision, and felt something deeper than melan-choly and more than regret. It was downright sorrow over what he would lose. She was the sweetest woman a man could want, but there was nothing she could do to improve him. Old habits died hard, and his most deep-seated habit was staying on the move, one step ahead of trouble.

This morning he decided that he'd be doing her a favor by getting out of her life. Hell, she'd find a decent man to marry one day, somebody like Walt Stringer, a man with brains and character who was more her sort.

Gib swallowed a few times and shifted on the pew and tried not to think about it.

The reverend announced a hymn. Julia sounded a chord, and everyone stood up. Lee nudged him and shoved a hymnbook into his hands. Gib opened his mouth and sang, not sure of the tune. A few pews up, Marshal McQuigg turned around and scowled.

When they sat down again, Reverend Dudley droned on, and Gib looked out the window. Tomorrow the bank would be open. He'd withdraw the money, hop a freight wagon for Dillon, and head for Salt lake.

". . . Holy baptism . . . Mr. and Mrs. Otis Chap-man . . ."

Gib jerked to attention.

"Mr. Gilbert Booth . . ."

He looked at Lee, whose mustache quivered.

"Mrs. Julia Metcalf . . ."

Gib got to his feet, sweat prickling on his back. The church was dead quiet except for Gilbert's little squeaks. Gib remembered what Julia had said about standing up proudly. He tugged at his vest and strode up the aisle, trying to look the way she would want him to look. He caught Dottie Cady's eye and gave her a wink.

They gathered around the enamel basin set on a wooden stand. The minister peered over his spectacles at Mrs. Chapman, who held Gilbert in a long white dress, and at Otis, who was looking kind of jittery.

Gib folded his hands in front of him and put on his most solemn expression. It wasn't easy standing next to Julia. He felt her pull on him, as if she were a magnet and he were loaded up with iron filings. The faint lemony scent of her made him dizzy, reminding him of last night. He allowed himself a discreet glance at her profile, the clean lines of her nose and chin, the soft fullness of her lips, the gentle swell of her bosom. Her hat looked like a flowerpot turned upside down and stuck with feathers, but on her pile of shining hair, it was graceful and beautiful.

Reverend Dudley started talking about baptism, saying that it symbolized a profession of faith, that the church asked God to accept the unknowing infant as his child. He spoke about the saving grace of the Holy Spirit, the heirs of life eternal, the mark that distinguishes Christians. He talked about God noticing a sparrow's fall and knowing every single child by name.

Gib listened with interest, thinking those were mighty nice sentiments.

At last the reverend took Gilbert from Mrs. Chapman. He dipped his hand in the bowl and sprinkled some water on the baby's head. "Gilbert, I baptize thee in the name of the Father and of the Son and of the Holy Spirit."

Gilbert decided he didn't like being grabbed by Reverend Dudley or getting a shower on his head, either. As he yelled, the minister asked the sponsors and the parents if they would keep Gilbert under the ministry and guidance of the church until he was confirmed. Gib agreed, though his words were drowned out by Gilbert's yelps. The reverend started another prayer, which set Gilbert to howling even louder.

Gib kept one eye open. The problem seemed to be that Reverend Dudley had Gilbert all crowded up by his shoulder as if he were a sack of meal. Holding a baby properly wasn't that hard to learn; calming him down wasn't hard, either. Gib had found that rubbing Gilbert's belly or tickling his toes usually did the trick. Sometimes just sticking his nose in Gilbert's face was enough to quiet him.

The reverend finished praying, and it was time to sit down. When Gib got back to his pew, Lee was grinning behind his mustache. Marriage to Sarabeth had sure put the old sauce back in him, Gib thought. Normally he was too scared to say boo to a ghost if his ma was in earshot, but this morning when Gib got to church, Lee had greeted him in full view of everybody, then invited him to share a pew for the service.

"What's so funny?" Gib asked.

Lee started to shake with silent laughter. "Not a thing."

It was time to sing again. Lee was still chuckling. Down the pew, old lady Tabor was looking daggers at the both of them. Earlier, when Gib passed her in the churchyard, he'd doffed his hat and given her a good-morning. She'd swelled up like a boiled sausage, shoved her nose in the air, and huffed off. Now she shot him an evil look as if he were the devil himself.

Gib wondered what would happen when she found out that Lee had married Sarabeth. He'd sure like to be around to see that hand played out.

CHAPTER

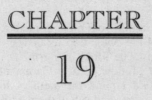

19

WHEN CHURCH LET out, Gib headed straight for the Chapmans, taking Lee with him. He wanted to say hello to Gilbert, now that he was officially named.

Folks were gathered around, offering congratulations and exclaiming over the baby. Gilbert lay in his mother's arms, his eyes closed, his little hands curled at his cheeks.

Gib bent close. "Hello there, Gilbert," he said.

"Why, Gib." Mrs. Chapman leaned over and kissed his cheek. Then she started introducing him around, embarrassing him with praise. Otis jerked his head toward a stand of trees by the graveyard where a group of men had gathered. Gib nudged Lee, and they legged it up the rise and joined the group.

Barnet Cady, hat in hand, bald dome gleaming, was wearing his stern lawyerly look. "I've heard a power of strange things in my time, but hearing Gib Booth promise to look after a baby's spiritual life is just about the strangest."

The other men grinned and chuckled. Gib shrugged,

pretending the remark didn't hurt his feelings. "His folks will see to it without me interfering."

Barnet's eyes continued to bore into him, as if searching for something that wasn't there. "Otis thinks you're doing a bang-up job up at the Rattling Rock."

"We're onto a promising lead."

"Pleased to hear it. I expected you'd have moved on by now."

Barnet might as well have added, "With Julia's money," since that was what he was thinking. Aside from Mr. Coolidge, Barnet was the only person who knew about her investment.

"No sense in running out on a promising mine," Lee said, relieving Gib of the obligation to answer. He caught Gib's eye, and his mustache lifted in a grin.

"Heard about a fellow up near Garnet a few years back," Walt Stringer said around the stem of his pipe, "bought some worthless mines and salted them with good ore. When he started shipping, the stock shot up. Fellow sold out at a good profit and disappeared. The new stockholders were left with a bunch of empty tunnels and worthless paper."

"That's about the oldest mining swindle there is," Gib said.

"You ever run it?" Barnet rocked on his heels, hands clasped behind his black frock coat.

Gib was starting to get hot under the collar. He sure was tired of folks thinking the worst of him. "I'll tell you for a fact that any fellow who wakes up wanting to get rich quick will end up a sucker by sunset."

"You should know," Walt said, making everybody laugh.

Gib was about to say something back, then decided to let Walt have his fun. When you came right down to it, Stringer was an honorable man. The story he'd run in the *Sentinel* had turned out to be pretty tame.

Otis came up the slope, bringing with him a solemn-faced man with sandy hair and a hard-rock build. "Gib, this here's Ab Ames," Otis said. "He's the Cousin I was telling you about who'll go partners in the rock-drilling contest."

Gib shook hands with a vise. "Pleased to meet you, Ames."

Ames was a fine-looking stiff, but he apparently didn't go in much for smiles. "Likewise, Mr. Booth. I've heard a fair bit of you from my boy Jimmy." There was a trace of Cornwall in the man's speech. "Otis says you're four-square."

"Foursquare isn't what we usually think of when we think of Gib," Walt said, making everybody laugh again.

"Lay off, Walt," Lee said, getting red around the cheek-bones. "It ain't Christian to rag a man on a Sunday morning."

Walt pocketed his pipe and gripped Gib's shoulder in what might have been a gesture of apology. "One thing's sure, nobody ever named a baby after me." He pulled a silver flask from inside his coat, uncorked it, and handed it to Otis. "Here's to young Gilbert growing up to make you proud."

"Your health," Otis said and took a pull.

The flask passed from man to man. Gib was surprised that they would drink so close to the church, even out of sight of the ladies; but then, this was a special occasion. When Barnet offered him the flask, he didn't decline.

Once they'd had their nips, the conversation turned to territorial politics, next year's constitutional convention, and Harlan Hughes's prospects for winning a political office. None of it much interested Gib; he was mainly glad that Hughes wasn't standing there under the trees.

He glanced at Ab Ames, who was poking at dirt with the toe of his boot, apparently as bored as he was. "How's that boy of yours?" Gib asked.

Ames nodded down the slope to the churchyard where sandy-haired Jimmy raced around with a pack of other boys. "His foot's healed up fine. He speaks of you, Mr. Booth, tells me you offered to teach him cards."

"He seemed real interested."

"That's my wife yonder, with young Virgil and Tilly."

Gib followed his gaze to a woman with a baby in her

arms and a bigger girl hanging on to her skirt. From the look of her, she had another one on the way.

"My wife won't have me betting on my own self in a drilling contest, Mr. Booth. It's best you don't teach yon Jimmy about cards."

Gib remembered Julia saying that Jimmy's mother wouldn't approve of card tricks; he felt embarrassed for having led the boy astray. "You can count on it," he said. "And call me Gib."

"Then it's Ab to you." Ames folded his arms before him and regarded Gib a bit more warmly. "I'll be putting up the granite two days before the contest so the men can practice. If we go partners, we'll need extra steel. I'll see if Mr. Hughes'll let me take some along."

"I'll bring steel from my outfit," Gib said. He'd have to temper it specially for granite to take into account the occasional crack or soft gouge that might raise hell with the drill.

"That's just as well, then," Ab said.

Then Gib remembered he wouldn't be in Stiles on the Fourth. He'd be back east with his seventy-five thousand dollars.

"I hear you're timbering down on number four level," he said, opening a new topic of conversation. "How does it look?"

Ab's face became guarded, his eyes a little shifty. "It don't always lie where you figure."

His mumbled answer pricked Gib's curiosity. He looked at the man more closely. "What the devil does that mean?"

"There's a fair showing of ore, but it's spotty."

"How does it assay?"

Ab shrugged and squinted off in the distance. "Fair to middling, I'd guess."

Gib took off his hat and ran a hand through his hair. There was nothing wrong with being closemouthed; Cousin Jacks usually were. But when a man shut up fast and wouldn't look him in the eye, Gib couldn't help wondering a little.

"They're saying the Continental's dead on its feet," Gib

said. "Course, you never know what's an inch farther down."

Ames said nothing.

"Otis and I are seeing some color up at the Rattling Rock," Gib went on "Not much, but it keeps us from working blind."

Maybe the men on Ab's team were high-grading, he thought, pocketing rich ore as it was shot down from the tunnel face. But it was hard to imagine a man high-grading when he was too straitlaced to lay a bet.

Gib kept on talking, telling Ames his philosophy of mining, what he and Chapman were up to at the Rattling Rock, speculating about plans for development. As he talked, his mind turned. The Continental's mill had hung up twenty stamps. A whole shift of miners in the upper workings had been given their pay and sent down the hill. A crew was digging at a new level and coming up empty. There were reports of problems with mud.

Nothing out of the ordinary there, just an old mine playing out. It happened every day.

But for some reason, Gib couldn't leave it alone. He'd always had a knack for smelling cabbage cooking, and right now he was getting a pretty strong whiff. He strained to remember things he might have heard but hadn't given any thought to.

"Jimmy said you're acquainted with Bert Scobie," he said.

Ames nodded. "We worked the number four together. Mr. Hughes gave him his time after he was shot."

That pretty much scotched his theory, Gib thought. If Hughes was trying to hide something, he wouldn't have put a big-mouth drunk like Scobie on the shift, then let him go. "They say Continental's stock's down to cats and dogs."

"I don't bother with that part of it." Ames's mouth was tight; he was not enjoying Gib's prying.

"If the mine shuts down and you're looking for work, I expect Otis'll be hiring at the Rattling Rock—if the showings get good, that is." Gib smiled, letting Ames know that he'd meant no harm by his questions.

Ab didn't return the smile. "I'm obliged, but if things pan out, I'm hoping to be shift boss. If it comes to that, Jimmy can stay in school. As it is, he'll go underground as a tool nipper next year."

Gib glanced at Ames's threadbare coat, his tired eyes. He remembered Otis saying a fire had burned the family out of their home not long back. Harlan was dangling shift boss in the face of a poor man with a houseful of young ones and another on the way.

Gib brought himself up short. Hell, his imagination was getting the better of him; if he thought hard enough, any situation could look queer. Maybe things would pan out at the Continental, and if they didn't, it was no skin off his nose. Why should he care what happened to Stiles? The town sure as hell didn't care about him.

That evening Julia sat at the piano, playing hymns. She felt raw and jittery, worried that Gib might come to her, worried still more that he might not.

She'd felt that way all day, since Dottie had told her what was written all over her. At Louise's dinner table, she'd maintained a cheerful manner. She'd allowed Harlan to respond to questions addressed to her, and Louise to make extravagant plans for a shopping trip to Denver. She'd tried to pay attention to Dr. Beacham, and through the afternoon of croquet, she'd pretended to enter into the fun.

But her thoughts had been with Gib and what the future might hold for them. She couldn't dispel the feelings that nothing would come of their night together, that she wouldn't—shouldn't—be with him again.

Her fingers strayed from "Thy Pastures Fair and Large" to "Thou Art Mine Own, Love." As the chords rang out, she imagined living with him in sanctioned bliss, raising their children.

She snatched her hands from the piano keys. Dear heaven, she was thinking like a fool. Gib had barely managed to sponsor little Gilbert in church; he could hardly be expected to take up the responsibilities of marriage and fatherhood.

The situation was simple. If she continued to carry on with him, she would be discovered—sooner rather than later—by the sharp eyes of Harlan and Harriet and Dottie. Once she was found out, her reputation would be ruined, and her friends would shun her. There would be no hope of living in Stiles, let alone continuing her medical practice.

Her mind knew all that, but her heart didn't care about consequences. If Gib came to her now, she would walk right into his arms.

She returned to the keyboard. As the last notes of "Then You'll Remember Me" died away, she heard a knock at the door. The knock came again, and she heard Gib call her name. With thudding heart, she got to her feet and went into the hall, past the hat stand that reflected her dressing gown of bright India cotton. The gown was buttoned up to the throat; the hem skimmed the floor. It was perfectly modest, but underneath it she wore nothing.

She opened the door. Gib still had on his churchgoing clothes and carried his hat in his hand.

"Gib," she said.

"Evening, Julia."

He stepped into the hallway, bringing with him the scent of outdoors. The lamplight made the threads in his vest sparkle and the metal gleam on his hat.

"I heard you playing. It sounded real nice."

"Thank you." Julia clasped her hands together and squeezed tight.

Shadows darkened Gib's cheeks and deepened the indentation in his chin. He fiddled with his hat brim, looking uneasy. "How's the new doc?"

"Young," Julia said. "A little frightened. At dinner we tried to make him feel welcome." She rushed on, tripping over her words. "Would you like to sit down?"

His eyes wandered the hallway, then came back to her. "Thanks just the same, but I shouldn't stay. I'll be heading up to the mine in the morning."

He was leaving. A small, helpless pain took root in Julia's stomach. She couldn't think of a thing to say.

Gib plucked at the studs on his hatband. "The baptism went all right."

"Oh, it did."

"Except for Gilbert yelling." He smiled a little.

"Babies do that."

The silence lengthened. He looked at her in a way that seemed to go right to her secret self, that made her aware of the whole surface of her body, naked beneath her gown.

Gib shifted his feet. "I was going to be a gentleman tonight. Stop by to see how you were, tell you I'd be going. Leave it at that. But it's not so easy."

"No," she said, barely remembering to breathe. "It's not easy."

"I tried not to come here at all."

"I'm glad you did."

He eyed her gravely. "You're sure, Julia?"

She nodded, very sure. There would be other nights when he wouldn't feel like a gentleman, and she would again answer her door.

He tossed down his hat and drew her into his arms, holding her against rough brocade and his pounding heart. "Dottie suspects," Julia said. "She said it's written all over both of us."

"Tonight's the end of it, then. Agreed?"

"Agreed." Until the next time, she thought.

She slipped her arms around his neck, and he kissed her, a long, slow tease that made her shiver and sigh. Then he bent down and grabbed her below the hips, swinging her up and over his shoulder.

Julia let out a shriek. "What . . . ? Oh, Gib! Stop!" she cried. "Oh, my heavens!" She was hanging head first down his back. She grasped frantically at his coat. "Put me down!"

"Hold on." He gripped her legs and patted her backside, then set off up the stairs. "This is the fastest way I know to get a lady into bed."

"But you're being . . . silly!" She felt an irrepressible need to laugh, which she did, all the way up the stairs and into her bedroom.

He set her down on her feet, and her laughter died, her breath steadied. They stood in darkness, their fingers entwined, their bodies touching. Gib put his arms around her, found her lips with his, and the world outside retreated.

His kisses ripened her desire, making her blossom like some nectar-laden flower. Last night she'd been starved for him; now she wanted him slowly. She wanted to feel everything, absorb it right to her heart.

She whispered against his lips, "I liked the way you touched me last night."

"So I remember." He tickled her ear with his fingers. "I'll show you some other things you'll like."

"What things?"

"You'll see."

He left her and lit the lamp, then shed his coat and boots, his string tie, the glittering silver vest. Off came the shirt, revealing his broad chest, his great, thick shoulders. He dropped his belt on the floor. At his trouser buttons, he hesitated.

Julia watched him, smiling. "Such modesty. After all we've done."

Gib looked sheepish. "A man doesn't show himself to a woman. Those were the good manners my mother taught me."

She put her hand on his waist and plucked at the top button. "That's what I like about you. You're so very mannerly."

She turned away while he removed his trousers. Then he came to her, eased her back onto the bed, and lay down beside her. His lips skimmed her face with lazy little kisses.

"How about I show you some more of my good manners?"

"Yes," she said softly. "Please do."

Gib undid her dressing gown down to her waist. He opened it, baring her, making her breath quicken. "Well, hello. There's nothing under this thing but you." He covered her breast with his hand and gave her a squinting look. "Mighty suspicious, I'd say."

Desire flowed through her in warm, restless waves. Julia

pulled his head close and whispered in his ear. "I thought of you all day, Gib. I thought of being with you. I wanted you to come."

"Ah, princess," he whispered back. "I couldn't have stayed away."

He unfastened the last button and laid her gown open around her. Julia watched the shadows play on his face and all down his body—tapered brawn and animal grace, so beautifully, stunningly male.

He caressed her breasts and thighs, his hands warm on her skin and ever so gentle. He lifted his eyes to hers. "Now I find the lady's not wearing her drawers."

"I'm not a lady when I'm with you." Her voice was unsteady, her body weak with longing.

He smiled. "You sure aren't."

He touched her with brazen hands, the softest kiss, the warm slide of his tongue—and suddenly he was taking her into a world of intimacy that respectable women didn't enter, a world that Julia had never imagined, an excitement that could scarcely be borne.

"Gib . . ."

She lay exposed and trembling, utterly helpless. He teased her, drawing out her pleasure until she was desperate for what he could give or withhold, until she thought she would die from it. She grasped at him with small, panting sobs, balanced on the edge of some vast chasm, not daring to move. Then she felt the thrust of his tongue, and his warm mouth took her all.

The world went dark. He seized her, lifted her, bore her away. It was an instant of ecstasy, an eternity; then everything shattered, bursting before her in a shower of broken stars.

Julia returned to his arms, to his pounding heart. She felt as if she existed only within his interest, as if she was meant to do nothing but receive his love. She struggled to reclaim her reason, but she felt too weak for any task more arduous than drawing her next breath.

"It's unnatural," she said. "The way I feel about you."

Gib pressed his lips to her hair. "You're beautiful." His voice cracked and trembled. "Beautiful beyond words."

She turned her head to find his mouth. She ran her tongue across his lips and deep inside. She caressed his hip, his muscular thigh, and took him in her hand.

He allowed her to touch him, then rose over her—stark and masterful, thick, splayed arms, his eyes afire. Julia took him inside her; she wrapped herself around him, filled her mouth with his kisses. He rolled her from side to side, surging into her with swollen thrusts, with harsh animal sounds. His excitement made her soar and gasp, and suddenly, unexpectedly, her body shuddered.

Then the blow hit him, felled him. Julia held him as he crashed down on her with a shout, as if to break her bones.

They lay together in a slippery tangle. When Julia opened her eyes, Gib was watching her. She touched his cheek, faintly shadowed with beard, and wondered if he felt what she did—a twining of spirits, his with hers, binding them together into a whole new being. She wanted to ask him, but something in his eyes gave her pause.

"Gib? What is it?"

He smiled at her, but without much conviction. "Go to sleep, princess. I'm going to hold you in my arms all night."

CHAPTER

20

A CLANGING BELL woke him. It was barely dawn. "What the hell?" Gib sat up, rubbing his face.

"It's the surgery." Julia was out of bed, hunting for her dressing gown.

"I'll go down." He swung his feet to the floor. "I'll tell them to come back at a decent hour."

"It's an emergency, Gib. It happens all the time." Julia pulled on her dressing gown and found her carpet slippers. "Go back to sleep."

"The devil I will."

Gib stood naked in the dusky light, yawning and stretching, puzzling over what to do. He looked at Julia, sleepy-eyed, her hair all tumbled. This was a fine kettle of fish, he thought. He'd planned a couple more rounds with her before they got up. He'd wanted to give her the whole treatment, soup to nuts, nice and slow, then show her some new tricks. But he'd slept like a bear, not even dreaming, till that damn bell hit him in the head.

Julia padded out into the hallway and down the stairs. Gib put on his trousers and looked out the window at the horse tied to the front fence. It would be one hell of a life, he thought, to have your woman yanked out of bed whenever some fool got shot.

Gib had his shirt on and was thinking about a wash when Julia came back.

"It's Mr. Kimball from the valley," she said. "Mrs. Kimball's baby is coming. I told him Dr. Beacham was here, but he said his wife wants me." Julia had stopped looking tired, and there was a purposeful gleam in her eyes.

"Do you want me to go with you?" As soon as he said the words, Gib knew he was trying to find an excuse to stick around.

"Heavens, that's not necessary. It's a ways out there, and I'll probably have to stay a few days. But thank you for asking."

She shed her dressing gown and poured water into the basin. At the sight of her slim nakedness, old Adam woke up fast. Gib thought of last night, the way he'd felt in her arms. It had been more than fireworks, more like being struck by lightning. For a minute there he'd honestly thought she'd killed him.

"I'll get the stove going."

She gave him a grateful smile. "I'd appreciate it."

Downstairs there was no sign of Kimball. That meant Julia would have to drive out to the ranch by herself. Gib built up the fire and ground some coffee. Once the pot was on the stove he went back upstairs. Julia was dressed and fixing her hair.

"Will you be all right?" he asked.

"Of course I'll be all right. I do this all the time."

Bloody hell, Gib thought. He was going to worry about her. For the rest of his life he'd worry and wonder and hope she was happy.

She looked at him in the mirror. "You're going up to the mine today?"

"Yeah." He'd make a quick stop there, and another at the Chapmans'.

Julia lowered her eyes. From the expression on her face, Gib knew she wanted to ask him to come back, but she wouldn't. She had too much pride for that.

He put his hands on her waist, narrow and firm in her black driving costume. "Remember what we agreed to last night." He was speaking as much to himself as to her. "No more of this business that can get us both in trouble."

Julia stuck in one last hairpin, then turned in his arms, giving him a kiss that went on for too long, that aroused him too much. He held her close, trying to feel her through the bunching petticoats.

"I love you, Gib."

He sighed into her hair. "I love you back, princess. More than you know."

She slipped away from him. It sure hurt to let her go.

Downstairs she drank coffee. Mossy was still asleep, so Gib hitched up the buggy and loaded her gear. He wanted time to slow down. He wanted to fix her a good breakfast, sit with her for a while, hold her hand, say a real good-bye. But she was rushing, her mind on the woman at the Kimball ranch and the baby waiting to be born.

She gave him one last kiss and climbed into the buggy. When she drove out of the dooryard, Gib stared after her, knowing he would never see her again.

The buggy disappeared around the bend. Gib turned back to the house, feeling like a tired old horse. The race was finished, his plan had worked. But he'd never felt worse in his life.

The ordeal of bringing the Kimball baby into the world tested Julia's knowledge and stamina. The mother was a large, muscular woman whom Julia expected to deliver easily. But during the second stage of labor, she realized that the woman's pelvic bones were unusually thick and the arch narrow. When the baby's head encountered the obstruction, progress slowed. The head tried to mold itself to fit the outlet, but was forced posteriorly, threatening lacerations to the perineum and rupture of the rectum.

Julia feared she would have to choose among three

harrowing alternatives: a cesarean section on an exhausted mother—a risky procedure under the best of circumstances—breaking the woman's pelvic bones, or destroying the child. As it turned out, low forceps were sufficient to deliver the baby, although Mrs. Kimball suffered dreadfully.

Once mother and son were resting, Julia spoke bluntly to Mr. Kimball, warning him that any future pregnancy would endanger his wife's life. She told him about conception preventatives such as sheaths, interrupting the act, and determining his wife's safe time, all of which nearly embarrassed him to death.

Then she drove wearily home. When she walked into the house after two nights away, she longed for a bath and a good long rest.

But no sooner had she gotten through the door and taken off her hat than Dr. Beacham appeared at the front door.

"I have come with my list of supplies, Mrs. Metcalf," he said.

It was a warm day and he was perspiring. Seeing no buggy, Julia concluded he'd walked all the way from town. She showed him to the living room and opened the windows, letting in a breeze.

"Forgive me for not having refreshments to offer," she said, bringing a glass of water from the kitchen. "I've just returned from a difficult delivery in the valley."

Dr. Beacham's startled eyes blinked behind his spectacles. Julia hurried to explain. "I told Mr. Kimball that you were in town, but he insisted I attend his wife. You see, I'd visited her during her pregnancy and know her rather well."

She motioned for Dr. Beacham to have a seat on the sofa, then settled in her chair. "Mrs. Kimball has a masculine-type pelvis. You're familiar with the condition?"

The doctor flushed a little. "I have read extensively in the obstetrical literature, but I'm afraid I've never attended such a case."

Oh, dear, Julia thought. He certainly was green. It was too bad he hadn't worked under an established physician for a few years to gain clinical experience.

"In a masculine pelvis, the pelvic bones are thick, not

narrow," Julia explained. "External measurements don't reveal the problem. Labor progresses normally until the appearance of the head, which if it cannot pass through the outlet is forced posteriorly."

Dr. Beacham sat forward with interest. "May I ask how you managed the case?"

"I delivered with low forceps. Had that failed, I would have attempted a cesarean section."

Beacham looked dumbfounded. "Forgive me, Mrs. Metcalf, but it was my understanding that you were your husband's assistant, at best a midwife. I didn't realize that you performed surgery."

"I have performed surgery when necessary," she said patiently. "With no other doctor in town, if I hadn't done it, who would have?"

"And yet you want to give up your medical responsibilities?"

The directness of his question and the curiosity in his face made Julia speak more frankly than she'd intended. "I don't want to give up my obstetric practice at all," she said. "But I'll defer to you, since you are needed in the community. I don't want to compete with you for paying patients."

Beacham scratched his knees and squirmed. He looked young and uncertain and rather silly with his goatee. "Your brother, Dr. Frye, feared that, unsupervised, you could cause a great deal of mischief. He says women often seek out midwives trained in aseptic procedures for criminal purposes."

It took Julia a moment to comprehend his meaning. When it became clear, she felt an angry rush of heat to her cheeks. "If you are implying that I am in the business of wasting infant life, Doctor, you are quite wrong. I am trained in obstetrics, perhaps not in a medical department as you were, but by a very fine doctor who happened to be my husband. When I make decisions about life and death, my decisions favor the mother. Beyond that, I take your comment as an insult."

Beacham slumped a little, his face red. He took out his handkerchief and wiped his foggy spectacles. "My apologies, Mrs. Metcalf. I shouldn't have mentioned it, but that is what I was given to understand.''

If Randall had been there at that moment, Julia thought to herself, she would have slapped his face. She looked at Beacham, utterly cowed, and felt a bit guilty for her outburst. "I'm sorry for speaking so harshly," she said. "It is Dr. Frye who is at fault in this matter, not you.''

Beacham seemed relieved by her words. He got to his feet and took a paper from his inside pocket. "These are the items I'd hoped to collect from your late husband's surgery. Perhaps I can stop by for them later in the week.''

Julia glanced over the list. "Friday will be fine.''

Beacham cleared his throat. "If my presence wouldn't be an inconvenience, perhaps you would allow me to accompany you on obstetrical calls now and then. And if I might consult with you on cases of particular interest . . .'' He hesitated, looking flustered. "I would be most grateful.''

Julia stared at him. "Why, Dr. Beacham, are you saying that you wouldn't object if I continued my practice?''

"Ma'am, I think it would be a great misfortune if you didn't. From what I hear around town, you are highly regarded, and I'm afraid I'm somewhat in need of your expertise." He offered her a hopeful smile.

Julia gathered her wits enough to respond in her best professional manner. "Then we shall be colleagues, Dr. Beacham.''

"Mrs. Metcalf, that is indeed good news.''

Julia showed him to the door and bade him good-bye, not quite believing what had just transpired. She was still in business. Not only that, but she now had a medical colleague with whom to discuss problems and exchange ideas. And once Dr. Beacham became proficient at treating gunshot wounds, crushing injuries, burns, and the results of other mishaps, perhaps she would be able to devote herself entirely to her ladies and babies.

Julia climbed the stairs to her room, unfastening her jacket as she went. If she hadn't been so exhausted, she would have felt elated—heavens, she *was* elated, tired or not.

At the open bedroom door she stopped. Two mornings ago she'd left things in a mess; now the bed was made, her slippers lined up, the dresser top neatly arranged. Resting on the bed's sunburst coverlet was a bunch of wilted wildflowers tied with a yellow ribbon.

Tears gathered in her eyes. "Oh, Gib."

She sat down on the bed and took the bouquet in her lap. There was a note folded in among the drooping blossoms.

"Dear princess," it read. "I'm no poet, but to me you're as pretty and wild as these flowers. There is plenty more I should explain, but there's not much use. You will hear that I have left town, which is just as well for you. In the end I always cause trouble. You will always be in my thoughts. Yrs. G. Booth."

Julia stared at the note. She read it again and again, as if the words and their meaning might miraculously change. But they didn't change; they only became clearer.

Gib had gone. But why? And for how long? She went downstairs, her head in a daze. She found Mossy out back, standing by a pile of split wood, ax in hand, his shirt damp with sweat.

"Mossy, where's Gib?"

He stared at the ground. "Gone for good."

A sick feeling rose in Julia's stomach. "But why?"

Mossy wouldn't look at her. He wiped his nose on his sleeve. "He said he was going, that's all I know. He said to tell you he's sorry."

Julia went back upstairs. She sat on the bed, the bouquet in her lap, the note in her hands: "I'm no poet, but to me you're as pretty and wild as these flowers." The line ran through her mind, along with other words spoken, intimacies exchanged. Julia's numbness began to thaw; the strength left her bones. Despair swelled in her chest until she could no longer contain it. It poured out of her in hot tears, in deep shuddering sobs.

Gib, I loved you. I trusted you.

She crumpled the note and covered her face. Tears leaked through her fingers, wetting her lap. After all they'd shared, the tender words, the passionate embraces, after all his kindness, his flattery, after making her love him, after taking her to the very limits of happiness—he was gone.

She heard a banging on the front door, then the knocker. Julia put her hands over her ears and curled up on the bed. She didn't want to see anyone ever again.

"Julia, we know you're here." It was Dottie's voice, muffled and distant. There were footsteps on the stairs. Julia burrowed deeper into the pillow, gasping with sobs.

"My dear child." Dottie came into the room and sat on the edge of the bed, making it sag. Julia felt a hand on her shoulder; another stroked her hair. "There, now. Look at me."

Julia rolled onto her back. Her face burned with heat and tears. "He's gone, Dottie."

Dottie took out a handkerchief and wiped Julia's cheeks, then held it to her nose. "I must say Gib has reached a new low in male behavior."

Julia licked her swollen lips. "He said he was going to the mine."

"He did go to the mine. He left papers in his cabin signing over his share of the Rattling Rock to Gilbert Chapman. Then yesterday Otis Chapman turned up at the bank with a bagful of money—several thousand dollars his wife had found in the pockets of Gilbert's baby basket."

Julia didn't understand. She started to say that Gib didn't have any money. Then suddenly she remembered that he did have money—her money.

"We know you invested in the mine, dearie," Dottie said. "Gib cleaned out the account. Mr. Coolidge said there was nothing he could do. Everything was in Gib's name."

Reality crashed down on her with the force of a club. Money and sexual favors—that was what he'd wanted from the beginning, and dear heavens, he'd gotten it all. The rest of it—her love, her very soul—had meant nothing to him. His betrayal was beyond comprehension.

"What's this?" Dottie picked up the crumpled note. She glanced at Julia. "May I?"

Julia nodded dumbly. She wanted to scream and wail and

rend her clothing, but she didn't know how. She could only lie there and silently die of grief.

Dottie smoothed the paper and read it. She looked at the bouquet of wilted flowers and shook her head. "You poor child."

"I loved him, Dot. I loved him so much."

Dottie leaned down and pressed her cheek to Julia's. Her bosom felt soft and motherly; she smelled like soap. Julia put her arms around her and wept.

After a few moments Dottie gently extricated herself. "Come downstairs," she said. "Barnet is here and Mr. Coolidge and Marshal McQuigg. They want to talk to you."

"Is Harlan with them?"

"I told him to stay away for now," Dottie said, smoothing Julia's hair. "He's furious, of course. Frothing at the mouth."

Julia remembered Harlan's warning: "Booth is a confidence man. He intends to win your trust, then strip you of your money and your reputation."

Dear God, she couldn't bear to think of it.

She got up, washed her face, changed her clothes. Going down the stairs, she had to steady herself on Dottie's arm. Her legs were weak, her mind exhausted, her emotions in ruins.

In the living room the men stood around, hats in hand, looking uncomfortable. The scene reminded her of the day Barnet and the marshal had come to tell her that Edward was dead. She hadn't fallen into hysterics then, and she wouldn't do so now.

Mr. Coolidge stepped forward. The banker was a round and rosy man in formal striped pants and a cutaway coat. "My dear Mrs. Metcalf, I'm so sorry about this."

They all sat down. Barnet explained that since Julia had requested there be no conditions attached to the account— against his advice, he reminded her—Gib was entitled to do with the money as he wished. But if he had persuaded her to give him the money under false pretenses, a case of fraud could be brought against him. If Julia chose to press charges, all her private conversations with Gib about her investment in the mine would be presented in court.

"As well as the circumstances under which they took place," Barnet added, giving her a kind but meaningful look.

Julia thought of the public humiliation of a trial. She would have to face Gib, look him in the eye, testify about their conversations. She would have to listen to his side of the story, to whatever lies he might tell, as he broke her heart all over again.

She imagined the story on the front page of the *Sentinel*, the *Helena Daily Herald*, even the *Chicago Tribune*: "Seduced and Swindled: Wealthy Widow Falls Prey to Confidence Man." A trial would make her look like an even bigger fool than she was.

"I can't do it, Barnet."

The men cleared their throats and looked at one another. "Fortunately you still have a substantial portfolio," Mr. Coolidge said. "While your loss was considerable—nearly half of your assets—it could have been worse."

Dottie brought tea. The men made polite conversation. When they departed, Marshal McQuigg lingered at the door. "He'd be easy enough to apprehend, ma'am. The freight driver who drove him to Dillon said he took the Utah and Northern to Butte. I'd have thought he'd head south, pick up the Union Pacific at Salt Lake. Be that as it may, I'll go up to Butte myself and drag that son of a gun back here—beg your pardon, ma'am. Clap him right behind bars where he belongs. You just say the word."

"Thank you, Marshal," Julia said. "You've been very kind."

She closed the door behind him and returned to the living room where Dottie was cleaning up the tea things. She watched Dottie work, feeling strangely detached, as if someone other than she had been swindled.

"Gib told Mossy he was leaving," she said.

"He told Lee, too," Dottie said. "He stopped by the livery and paid him the money he owed."

Julia ran a finger over the dusty piano lid. He'd told

everyone important to him except her. "Harriet will be pleased to hear the news. She'll be completely vindicated."

"Harriet isn't feeling pleased about anything these days," Dottie said, straightening up from the tray. "Lee just broke the news to her that he married Sarabeth Brown last week."

"Why . . ." Julia stared at Dottie, at a loss for words. "Lee and Sarabeth are married?"

"Barnet married them in our living room. I suggested they wait for Reverend Dudley's next visit, but they were in a hurry and didn't mind a justice of the peace officiating. I stood up with Sarabeth. Harriet's as mad as a jackal, doesn't know what to do. She's taken to her bed for now, and she'll likely stay there till she figures out a way to get back at all of us."

Dottie picked up the tray and headed for the kitchen. Julia followed, her muddled emotions stirring again. Lee and Sarabeth were married. She should have been happy for them, but instead she felt sorry for Harriet. Her sorrow swelled to an ache that filled her chest and throbbed in her head. Then she realized she was feeling sorry for herself, not for Harriet. Sorry for losing all the happiness she'd had with Gib, all the dreams she'd imagined.

She began to cry again.

Dottie dried her hands and put her arms around Julia, hugging her close. "Hush, now, dearie. It will be all right in time."

"He hurt me so much." Julia wiped her eyes on her sleeve. "He hurt me terribly. He made me into a fool."

"You need a nice long rest. I'm taking you right upstairs."

Dottie undressed her like a child and put her to bed, just as she'd done last October when Edward died.

"Thank you, Dottie, for not saying 'I told you so.' "

Dottie sat on the bed and stroked Julia's cheek. "Heavens, I wouldn't think of it. Now, I'm going to sit right here till you go to sleep. Louise will be out later with some supper. Renate will come by in the morning. You're not to worry about a thing."

* * *

The next morning Julia found Renate Blum downstairs in the kitchen with Ruth. The aroma of coffee filled the house, and something sweet was baking in the oven.

Julia pushed aside her heavy sadness and forced herself to put on a cheerful face. "How nice of you to come out," she said. "It's a lovely day."

Renate looked out the window at ashen skies, threatening rain. "I'm glad you think so."

"Have some coffee," Ruth said.

Julia glanced from mother to daughter. Ruth's belly swelled with the child she carried, the child of a man she dearly loved. Looking at her, Julia felt a sudden and unexpected pang of envy.

"I don't want to talk about Gib," she said.

"Of course not," Renate said, pouring Julia a cup of coffee.

"We won't mention his name," Ruth agreed.

Julia sat down at the table. Last night, lying in the darkness, wrung out with tears, she'd reminded herself that life went on; it always did. Disasters could be turned into lessons. Once before she'd been a credulous fool and hadn't learned from the experience. Now she was being offered a second chance.

"How are you feeling, Ruth?" Julia looked with a critical eye at a young woman not made for bearing children. Childhood poliomyelitis had left Ruth with a shortened leg and compensating scoliosis, and her pelvis was underdeveloped on the right side.

"I feel perfectly well."

"Have you seen Dr. Beacham?"

Ruth nodded. "He says a successful delivery depends on the size of the baby's head, how easily it molds to the passage, and the strength of the contractions. It's too early to tell, but he thinks it will pass."

Julia approved of Dr. Beacham's frank explanation, even though it sounded like a quotation from an obstetrics text. She thought of her conversation with him yesterday, his acknowledgment of her expertise. If complications arose during Ruth's delivery, Dr. Beacham would likely ask for her help.

Renate took a pan of sweet rolls from the oven; more coffee was poured. Julia tried to enjoy the rolls and the company, the distraction from her thoughts, but beneath everything ran an undercurrent of misery. She had the feeling that every waking moment would be a struggle against despair.

After a half hour, Renate got to her feet. "If you're feeling all right, perhaps Ruth and I should go." Her gentle dark eyes were filled with sympathy.

"I'm not ill, Renate," Julia said. She hated being treated like a pitiable scorned woman.

Renate exchanged glances with Ruth. "Of course you're not."

"Just three weeks until the Fourth," Ruth said cheerfully. "That's something to look forward to."

"Yes, isn't it?" Julia said, not caring in the least.

At the door Renate embraced her, not a ladylike touching of cheeks but a full, hard hug. "Dear Julia," she whispered, "I feel this is partly my fault."

Julia hugged her in return; ever-present tears burned in her eyes. "I was the fool, Renate."

When Ruth and Renate had gone, Julia retreated to Edward's study. She sat in the big leather chair, staring at the great wall of a library, thinking of Ruth. After a few moments she got up and went to the bookshelves. She took down Hodge's *Principles and Practice of Obstetrics*, then hunted until she found the other volumes she wanted.

CHAPTER

21

BUTTE WAS ONE curly wolf of a mining camp—wild and rackety and downright dangerous. It was ugly, too, spread out on a broad slope of ravaged earth beneath a hill thick with towering headframes. Each headframe marked a shaft that could go down as far as a thousand feet. Gib had heard someone say that Butte was a mile high and a mile deep. He'd also heard that the camp ran at full throttle twenty-four hours a day. Turned out he hadn't heard wrong. Saloons, cafés, and brothels never closed their doors. The scarlet district was a bedlam of pianos, hurdy-gurdy halls, roulette wheels, and noisy games of poker. Main Street reeked of whiskey and sin.

When he first arrived, Gib felt no inclination to jump into the fray. He stopped at the bank and locked up his money, then took a room at a flea-trap hotel that made the Regal in Stiles look like a palace. He spent the rest of the day stretched out on the bed, listening to the rattle and creak of wagons outside his window and thinking of Julia.

Leaving her had made a lot of sense at the time. Leaving Stiles had made even more sense when he thought of Wylie and Trask and the marshal who was out for his hide. But making sense didn't stop him from feeling low, and he felt damned low—lonely and weary and worried about Julia. He was beginning to think he'd let her down, just like Ma.

He got to his feet and kicked at the balled-up pieces of paper that littered the floor. He'd tried for hours to compose a letter to her. He was full of things he wanted to say—explanations, excuses, things she had a right to know. He wanted to tell her that his leaving had been for the best, that he wasn't a man to put down roots and take on responsibilities. But he couldn't seem to make sense of his reasoning. In his heart he wanted to live with Julia, love her, spend the rest of his life making up for all the years she'd slept alone.

Gib doused his head in a basin of water and combed his hair. He reminded himself that he'd come to Butte for a purpose, to look for a girl named Mary Hurley. Once that errand was done, he would board the Utah and Northern and head for Salt Lake, put Stiles and everyone who lived there out of his mind. That was the right thing to do, no doubt about it. Sometimes doing the right thing just meant you had to feel like hell for a while.

A racket coming from outside interrupted his thoughts—rawhiders cussing at the top of their lungs. Gib went to the window and looked down at the dusty street, teeming with men and commerce. After a moment he picked up his hat and headed for the door. What the hell, he thought, he might as well go out and have a look around town.

The Bullwhip saloon was ready for trouble. There was no bottle-filled backbar, no mirrors or pictures, and heavy wire screening protected the inside of the windows. The big round card tables were stripped to bare wood and, instead of chairs, men sat on solid sections of railroad ties that were too heavy to throw.

It was a stinking, swearing, spit-on-the-floor miners'

saloon, its clientele low-grade scrub, men who worked shifts in the tunnels on the hill. The atmosphere reminded Gib of the old days in Stiles, which meant it suited him just fine.

After pushing his way up to the five-deep bar, he managed to buy a bottle of rye. He settled in at a back table with a trio of dirt-mean muckers. Biting off the end of a cheroot, he tossed in his ante.

"Deal me in."

For the next several days the back table at the Bullwhip was Gib's roost. His life revolved around greasy cards, throbbing noise, gut-burning liquor, profane company. After seeing a tinhorn get carved up with a pocket knife, he made sure he played it straight. Occasionally he went back to the hotel to sleep off a head of booze. Down the street he found a café where the kitchen stew wasn't half bad and the coffee was strong enough to grow hair. He lived in the moment, not thinking ahead or behind. It sure felt good.

One afternoon he heard the sound of a scuffle and a familiar whining voice. The complaining rose over the whooping and stomping on what passed for a dance floor. When the whine turned into a scream, Gib looked up from his cards. Through the smoky haze he saw none other than Bert Scobie struggling with a bear of a man who seemed to be squeezing him to sausage meat.

Gib folded his cards and got up from his game. By the time he made his way through the crowd, the houseman, brandishing a sawed-off pool cue and a Remington navy revolver, had talked the bear into dropping Scobie, who lay on the floor in a gasping heap.

"Hey, Scobie." Gib nudged him with his boot. "What the hell are you doing here?"

Scobie crawled around on his hands and knees, whimpering and sniveling, trying to find his feet. Gib leaned down and hauled him up by the collar. He looked like hell. Bloodshot eyes wandered in his head, his face was bruised and unshaven, his lip cut. He stank like sin.

"Scobie!" Gib gave him a shake. He felt an obligation to

the man after all the work Julia had done patching him up. "It's Gib Booth. Remember me?"

Scobie's eyes cleared for an instant of recognition. "Sonofabitch."

Gib found a space against the wall and stood Scobie there while he went back to the table and picked up his money. When he got back to the wall, Scobie was wallowing on the floor again, yelping about his shoulder, which must have still been tender from the shooting. Gib got him upright and dragged him back to the hotel. He passed out as soon as he hit the bed.

Gib intended to go back to the Bullwhip and lose himself in another game of poker. But running into Scobie had started him thinking again—this time about Harlan Hughes and what might be going on at the Continental. The idea that Hughes was up to something sat right there in the front of Gib's mind, and the more he tried to push it away, the more bothered he got.

He slid down onto the floor and leaned against the wall, a half bottle of whiskey between his legs. He thought about Hughes's efforts to get him run out of town by spreading the stories about his past. He thought of the indecent letters to Julia, the livery robbery frame-up. He'd always figured the gasbag was behind all of it, aiming to put him in a bad light with Julia, so he could marry her and get her inheritance. Now he was beginning to think there was more to it than that. Hughes knew he was a mining stiff familiar with all the angles, a man who could smell a freeze-out a hundred feet down. When you came right down to it, Hughes wanted him out of town for more reasons than just Julia. He wanted him gone because he might figure out his scheme.

Gib took another drink of whiskey. He hated to admit it, but by leaving Stiles he'd played right into the gasbag's hands. Now that he was gone, that son of a bitch must be jumping like a herd of toad-frogs.

As night fell, the room grew dark, the whiskey bottle empty. Gib sat on the floor, arms draped on knees, his head full of worries. He thought about Hughes wanting to marry

Julia. Once, she'd said she had no thoughts of marrying anyone, but that was before she'd spent two nights in bed with a real man. Now she might think differently. Holy blue hell, Gib thought, what if he'd so whetted her appetite she couldn't think straight? What if Hughes came courting with all his oily charm and Julia said yes?

Gib couldn't stand to think about it—the gasbag sitting pretty on bonanza gold, sweet-talking the widow Metcalf into being his wife, while Gib caught the Union Pacific back east and let it happen.

By midnight, he had decided he couldn't leave Julia to the mercy of a four-flusher like Hughes. He'd just have to go back to Stiles and expose him for the no-good he was.

It took a full day to nurse Scobie back to coherence. He woke up with the shakes, and Gib gave him small doses of whiskey to calm him down. When Gib started asking questions, Scobie was too scared to talk. He said he'd promised Hughes he wouldn't say anything, that when he'd tried to get money from him in exchange for keeping quiet, Hughes had threatened to have him killed. Just talking about it made the poor bastard cry.

Gib offered him money so he could leave the territory. He gave him more whiskey. Then Scobie talked, confirming everything Gib had suspected.

Harlan sat with Julia on the porch. They rocked together into the dusk of an early summer evening.

"Things will blow over," Harlan said, clapping his hands on his belly. "In a month or so, Booth will be nothing more than an unpleasant memory."

Julia gave him a grateful smile. Harlan had been a comfort to her this past week. He seemed so pleased by Gib's departure that he hadn't lectured or gloated or said a word about the money she'd lost.

"Chapman's a hardworking fellow with a good nose for ore," Harlan said. "If there's gold up there at the Rattling Rock, he'll find it. Investing in his operation is a wise idea."

"I think so," Julia said.

She was reluctant to attribute any good motives to so coldhearted a confidence man as Gib, but she'd been relieved that he hadn't left the Chapmans high and dry. Signing over his share of the Rattling Rock to Gilbert had been a decent thing to do, as was leaving ten thousand dollars in the baby basket. After the Chapmans insisted on returning the money, Julia had decided to invest it in the mine.

Gib had left Gilbert a letter, too, which Mrs. Chapman had shown her. Julia remembered every word.

"Dear Gilbert," it said. "Take a lesson from me and stay out of trouble. Mind your schoolwork and your folks, because they know best. Doing the right thing is easier in the long run than doing the wrong thing. I will keep you in my prayers. Yrs. Gilbert (Gib) Booth."

The note was the height of hypocrisy, yet it had pleased Mrs. Chapman. Julia had the feeling neither Vera nor her husband harbored any bad feelings toward Gib.

"Well, I should be going along." Harlan got to his feet and helped Julia to hers. "My dear, you look tired." He took her hand and rubbed her fingers in his soft fleshy palms. "And you're growing thin. I suspect you're not eating."

Julia felt too exhausted to eat, and at night too wide awake to sleep. "I'm doing my best, Harlan."

He made a sympathetic sound. "Before you know it, things will be back the way they were."

Never, she thought to herself. Things would never be the way they were before. She did have one thing to be grateful for, however—her liaison with Gib had taken place during her safe time of the month. If it hadn't, she would have been nearly mad with worry.

After Harlan left, Julia went into the surgery. The room looked a bit emptier than it had, but hardly depleted. As it turned out, Edward had accumulated enough supplies and equipment to furnish at least two medical offices. Julia had sent Dr. Beacham away happy.

In the study she sat down in Edward's leather chair and

took Bee on her lap. She closed her eyes against the welling-up of tears that seemed to come on every evening at this time. She knew it was foolish to feel sorry for herself. Her friends had been extraordinarily kind. Dottie, Louise, Renate, Harlan—none of them had uttered one word of condemnation. She had more than enough money to see her through, and she was beginning a professional association with Dr. Beacham. Nevertheless, her waking hours were marked by unexpected moments of misery, and at night she thought too much and wept herself weak. She knew it would take a long time for her to gather up the pieces of her heart.

Twilight was deepening. Julia lit a lamp and forced herself to look over the notes she'd made on pelvic deformity and labor. She was growing more concerned about Ruth's case; should complications arise, she wanted to be prepared.

She found on the bookshelf Edward's sketchy translation from the German of Sänger's thesis on the use of uterine sutures in cases of cesarean section, and compared it to the Porro operation, which controlled postoperative hemorrhage with hysterectomy. Edward, she recalled, had written a paper on the early use of internal sutures by American practitioners. Moving the lamp to the corner of the desk, she crouched over the file drawer. While Bee rubbed against her, Julia rifled through papers, pulling out files that looked promising, stuffing them back when they yielded nothing of interest. As she pulled out the last one, her hand stopped in midair. Written on the file was one word: "Gib."

Her heart started to pound. She took the file to the desk and opened it. Inside were letters bearing Gib's familiar bold print. They were his letters to Edward, arranged chronologically starting in 1872, most from the early years, telling Edward where he was, what he was doing, a few descriptions. Utah, Colorado, California, New Mexico, Arizona.

Mexico. Gib wrote of a place called Batopilas and his partners—Wylie and Trask and a Mexican named Porky. Julia skimmed descriptions of Indians in breechcloths and sandals scrambling around the mine. Gib wrote that the Indians thought the ore belonged to God. He described trains of pack mules coming from Chihuahua, bandit raids, dining on boiled skunk, the earthquake. She read the letters from Mexico again, absorbed by the vivid descriptions.

She turned to the last letter. San Francisco. September 19, 1880. "Dear Doc . . ."

She read it through with mounting dismay. When she finished, she closed the file and stared at it, feeling stunned and sick, wondering what she was ever going to do.

Gib's train reached Dillon at midafternoon. He'd missed the noon stage to Stiles, so he asked around the depot for a freight wagon that might be heading that way. Somebody pointed out a yellow Studebaker that was being loaded out of the warehouse. Right away, Gib recognized the black Indian braid and the shapely hips in snug striped trousers.

He braced himself and ambled over. "Howdy, Sarabeth."

She took one look at him and started exercising her tongue. When she finished cussing, she said, "Make yourself useful and give me a hand."

The day was overcast but warm. Sarabeth was sweaty and cranky. When the wagon was loaded, she stomped off to the water barrel and took a long drink. Gib followed, trying to be conversational.

"When did you start driving freight again?"

Sarabeth wiped her mouth and gave him one of her scalding looks. "If you're wanting a ride back to Stiles, don't look at me. I don't fancy being party to a hanging."

Gib took off his hat and scratched his head. "Is it that bad?" He imagined Marshal McQuigg standing at the town limits, holding the noose.

"You'll be about as welcome as a hooker at a church social."

"I'm going back, Sarabeth, whether you drive me or not."

She looked at him as if he were some wriggling thing that had just crawled out from under a rock. "What the hell for?"

"That's my business."

She heaved her shoulders in a shrug. "All right. Let's get cracking."

The road crossed rough mountainous terrain, past broken cliffs and brush-choked draws. Sarabeth was a good driver, managing the steep grades and sudden switchbacks. As time passed, her mood improved, and Gib eased her into conversation. Right away she got down on him again.

"Everybody figures you for a no-account," she said. "Not that they thought so high of you before. Lee's about the only one in town who'll speak a kind word."

Gib had told only Mossy and Lee that he was leaving, and that was because he'd run out on them after the Hockett shooting without saying good-bye. He'd always felt bad about it; he knew they'd both taken it hard.

"I heard you're Lee's missus now, Sarabeth."

After a struggle to keep a stern face, she broke into her pretty dimpled smile. "Yep. Lee's bunking with me at the Bon Ton. Paying the rent, too, since I'm through dancing."

"How did Rawlie take the news?"

"Real good." Sarabeth squinted at Gib from beneath her hat brim. "You leaving didn't ruffle his feathers one bit. He just sat there in his rocker and said, 'Gib always comes back.'"

Gib glanced up at a jagged outcropping of rock topped by a leaning boulder. Funny how he missed the old man following him around with his misty gaze and endless jawing. "I guess he's right about that."

Once Sarabeth got talking, Gib didn't have to say much of anything. He listened to her story of the wedding in the Cady's living room and how Lee's ma had taken to her bed after hearing the news. "She won't talk to nobody. Won't eat, neither. Lee goes over there all the time, but she won't give him the time of day, just turns her face to the wall. Says how he ruined her life."

Gib remembered Lee telling him about his ma's threats to die and leave it on his conscience. There was no doubt in Gib's mind that she was bulling him. Pigs would fly before old lady Tabor would die and miss out on making Lee suffer for marrying Sarabeth.

"Lee's all tore up over it," Sarabeth went on. "I got to work real hard to keep him from being sorry for what we done. It sure is painful to see a good man worry so bad."

Thinking about Lee and his ma seemed to put Sarabeth in a low frame of mind. Gib left her to her thoughts. He turned his own to Harlan Hughes and how he was going to accomplish his goal.

Julia arrived at the Cadys' house on Wallace Street shortly after seven in the morning. She wanted to catch Barnet before he left for the office.

Dottie answered her knock, wiping her hands on her apron. "Julia, what a surprise . . . Dearie, what on earth?" She took Julia's arm and pulled her inside. "You look dreadful. Do you sleep at all? And you're getting thinner every day."

"I have to see Barnet, Dottie." Julia took off her gloves. Her hands were like ice.

Dottie opened her mouth, then shut it. "I'll make you some eggs. Barnet's in the dining room."

The Cady house had the tired but comfortable look of a home yet to recover from four lively children who had grown up and moved away. Faded wallpaper blended into woodwork, rugs showed patches of wear, and the seat of the horsehair sofa was nearly bald. The only splash of color was a crimson piano shawl that Barnet had bought in an extravagant moment on their honeymoon years ago. It must have had some significance, because Dottie still teased him about it, and Barnet still blushed.

He sat at the dining room table in shirtsleeves and suspenders, reading a folded newspaper. When Julia came in, he glanced at her over the top of his spectacles.

"Good morning, Julia." He got to his feet and pulled out a chair. "This looks serious."

Julia felt so confused she no longer knew what to think or where to begin. She started to explain, then pulled out the letter and handed it over.

Barnet read it through, running a hand over his gleaming

bald head. "Well, I'll be damned," he said when he finished. It was the first time Julia had ever heard him swear.

Dottie came in with a plate for Julia. "What is it?"

"It's a letter to Edward from Gib," Julia said. "Read it aloud, Barnet."

Barnet adjusted his spectacles and cleared his throat: "'San Francisco, September 19, 1880. Dear Doc. Things are fine with me. Hope the same for you. Ran into a windfall in Mexico. Sierra Madre are full of gold. Here is a statement of account in your name in the Bank in San Francisco. As you can see, it's $150,000. Help yourself to it.

"'I have been doing a lot of thinking. There is a lot of time for that when you're in the belly of a mountain with a couple of no-good partners for company. You did a lot for me, Doc. Saved my neck more than once. I didn't show much appreciation (none, you might say), but I always felt it. I hope this money helps make things square between us.

"'I know you are not a man for big spending, but you always liked books, so buy yourself some, or anything else for that matter.

"'I'm no Indian giver, but I might settle up with you sometime, if there's any money left for my "old age." Right now, I'm staying on the move. If anyone asks, it's better you leave my name off this deal. Say hello to Mossy.

"'Your old friend, Gib Booth.'"

Barnet folded the letter and laid it by his plate. He looked from Julia to Dottie and back again. The silence stretched on, broken by the steady tick of the grandfather clock in the hall.

Dottie pulled out a chair and sat down. "What does it mean?"

"It means he swindled me out of his own money," Julia said.

But it meant much more. All night she'd considered the implications of Gib's letter. He'd come back to Stiles to "settle accounts," just as he'd said in his telegram. When he found Edward gone and her in possession of the money, he'd concocted an elaborate scheme to get it back. He'd cleaned her house. He'd reopened the Rattling Rock mine.

He'd kissed her, flattered her, made love to her. He'd broken her heart. When all he'd needed to do was tell her the truth.

"The money is all his," Julia said. "I don't want any of it."

Barnet reached over and patted her hand. "Now, Julia, don't be rash."

"None of it, Barnet. Not one cent."

"Gib meant Edward to have it."

"It's ill-gotten. I'm sure of it."

That quieted him. He and Dottie exchanged glances. "You need that money, Julia," Dottie said. "Edward had nothing else to leave you."

"I have a small inheritance from my father."

"A pittance," Barnet reminded her.

"I'll earn my way, then. Dr. Beacham and I have worked out an arrangement. I'm going to continue my practice." The prospect of supporting herself frightened Julia a little, but it also made her feel proud. She was a professional woman in her own right, not an assistant to her husband or a temporary fill-in until the new doctor arrived. Why, she might even apply for membership in the Montana Medical Association.

"Julia, you know very well that Harlan wants to marry you," Dottie said.

"I don't love Harlan, Dottie. And I don't have to marry anyone. I can very well take care of myself, inheritance or not." She got to her feet and pulled on her gloves. "I'm going to put a notice in the *Sentinel* announcing that I'm still seeing patients."

It was twilight when the Studebaker freight wagon made its way down Main Street. Gib jumped down in front of the Bon Ton and the usual crowd of loungers. He retrieved his war bag, bedroll, and saddlebags from the rear of the wagon and said good-bye to Sarabeth.

"Come by the room later," she said. "Maybe you can cheer Lee up."

The next voice Gib heard was Marshal McQuigg's, shouting. "Booth! What in thunder . . . ?" Then, "Haul your sorry self over here, you back-hearted snake!" The marshal stood on the boardwalk in front of the jail, thumbs in his gun belt, his mustache curled and angry. "Into my office where I can speak my mind without ladies fainting."

Gib picked up his gear and headed across the street. He'd sure jumped into the kettle, he thought, coming back to Stiles. At least McQuigg wasn't standing there knotting a rope.

Inside the marshal's office, McQuigg confiscated Gib's gun, then lit into him with a tongue-lashing strong enough to take the fur off a cat. Gib sat with both feet on the floor and didn't utter a word in his own defense. He wasn't about to give the marshal any back talk, not when everything he had to say was true.

"I'd lock you up quicker than a duck comes down on a June bug, except that the money was yours all along."

Gib lurched forward in his chair, nearly falling out of it. "What the hell . . . ?"

"We know it's yours. The whole goddamn bundle. Mrs. Metcalf found a letter from you to Doc saying so. She don't want a cent of that money."

Gib's blood raced wild. "What do you mean she doesn't want it?"

"You think she wants anything from you after what you done? Take the money and clear out, Booth. The money's what you wanted, and now you got it all. So move on."

Gib's knee started its nervous bounce. Jesus, the last thing he'd wanted was for Julia to find out the money was his. That was the whole point of his plan—to leave her with a goodly share of what she thought was hers.

"I'm not going anywhere."

"You're going if I have to kick your assbone all the way to Salt Lake."

"You can't run me out if I didn't do anything wrong. And what did I do wrong—take some money that was mine in the first place?"

McQuigg's face turned crimson; he looked fit to burst. He started jabbing the air with his finger. "Damn you, Booth, if I say you go, you go!"

"I won't cause trouble, Marshal. Count on it." Gib got to his feet and picked up his gear. He had to talk to Julia, work out some sort of arrangement. "You won't even know I'm in town."

McQuigg stomped to the door and yanked it open. "Get out of my sight," he shouted. "And remember, I'll be watching you close! I'll be watching you every goddamn minute!"

CHAPTER

22

IT WAS DARK when Gib left the marshal's office and headed across the street. As soon as he pushed through the Bon Ton's batwing doors, Dellwood started insulting him. "Watch your wallets, boys!" he shouted. "Here comes the king of the shell game."

The saloon quieted down a few levels; heads turned. Gib tossed down his war bag and bedroll and leaned on the bar. "I need a bed, Dell, and a place to park my gear."

"Who'd you cheat to get that money, that's what I'd like to know," Dellwood said. He squirted a stream of tobacco juice at the spittoon and wiped his mouth on his sleeve. "Widows, I suppose, and poor little orphans."

Gib wasn't going to let the ragging get him down; he had too much to do to waste his time feeling low. "Have you got a room or not? If you don't, I'll go down to the Regal where they treat their guests like gents."

"Well, bless my backside, I guess I didn't recognize you for a gent." Dellwood tossed him a key, which Gib caught one-handed. "Your old room's right where you left it. The maid's been keeping it up real nice."

Gib went upstairs, ignoring the gawking regulars. He put his gear in his room, then headed down the hall to Sarabeth's door and knocked.

"Lee, you in there? It's me, Gib."

He heard a grunt of surprise. Lee opened the door, looking rumpled and bewildered. "Gib? What the hell—"

"Sarabeth's already told me I'm low-down scum," Gib said, stepping inside. "Dellwood, too, not to mention the marshal. So don't waste your breath."

Lee was grinning. "Hell, Gib, I'm just glad to see you back."

Gib gave him a soft belly-punch to show his appreciation. It sure was nice to see one friendly face.

He looked around the room. It wasn't the bridal suite, but Sarabeth had made it homey. An Indian blanket decorated the bed, and colored bottles at the window caught the light. Among the advertisements and pictures of variety performers tacked to the wall, Gib saw a photograph of Digger and Rawlie in their younger years, looking all spiffed up.

"You enjoying married life?"

Lee's grin widened, and his neck turned red. "You might say so."

Gib was pleased. For all Sarabeth's cussing and complaining, she'd never been anything but good to Lee.

"I hear your ma's giving you trouble."

Lee's grin faded. He worried a finger across his mustache. "She won't talk, won't eat. I'm afraid she's going to die on me."

When it came to seeing the old lady for the bluffer she was, Gib thought, Lee wore blinders the size of shed doors. "Take my word for it, Lee, your ma's not going to die. Go over there and talk turkey. Tell her she's seen the last of you till she starts behaving herself. She'll be up and about in no time."

Lee looked skeptical. "I guess I can give it a try."

"Good. Now, there's something you could help me out with."

"What's that?"

"Tell me what you know about that gasbag, Harlan Hughes."

After a wash and a shave in his room and supper at the Pickax, Gib headed for the livery. He saddled Lucky and rode out to Julia's place through the gentle sounds and easy breezes of an early summer night. He'd waited until late to be sure she was alone, and so no one would notice where he was going.

Looking at the stars and breathing in the smell of flowers and pine brought on a tender feeling in his chest. He wished he were on his way to go courting. He and Julia would sit on the porch, rocking in those chairs, talking about their future. He could almost feel the contentment that would come with planning an honest life with a woman who loved him.

Hell, he thought, his thoughts were sure running wild. If he was going to waste his time, he should imagine how smart he'd have been not to cook up his plan in the first place. When he'd learned Doc was dead, he should have tipped his hat and cut his losses. After a condolence call on the widow, he should have headed straight for Salt Lake and forgotten about the money. But it was too late for that bright idea; he'd have to think up a few better ones — such as how to persuade Julia to take money she knew was his and didn't want, and how to prove Hughes's swindle. Gib wouldn't rest easy until Julia was financially set and the gasbag was running for the hills.

The house was dark except for a light in Julia's bedroom. Gib dismounted and tethered Lucky to the fence. The sweet air and chirping nighttime sounds made him restless; they made him think of being with Julia under that flower-covered quilt.

"Gib?"

He jumped. It was Mossy, shambling out of the black shadows at the side of the house. "What the hell, Mossy? You scared the devil out of me."

In the starlight, Mossy's pale jowls seemed to hang down a mile. "I knew you'd be back. I told her you're no low-down." He took Lucky's bridle and unwound the reins from the fence. "I'll put him out by the barn."

"Thanks, partner. I won't be long."

"Sure, Gib. Take your time."

Mossy's voice had the old sadness from way back. Gib wondered if he'd heard from his wife, but before he could ask, Mossy disappeared into the darkness.

Gib glanced up at Julia's window and suddenly felt a weakness in his gut. He thought of what was to come— anger and hurt where he'd once found sweetness, a closed heart, which once had given without limit.

He mounted the steps to the surgery door, reminding himself that he'd done the right thing, leaving her. Trouble was, she sure as hell hadn't seen it that way.

Julia was half undressed when she heard the surgery bell. She rebuttoned her shirtwaist, fastened on her skirt, and tied back her hair with a ribbon. The bell rang less often since Dr. Beacham had opened his office, but she was grateful it rang at all. She needed all the business she could get, and not only for financial reasons; professional responsibilities gave her life meaning, especially now that she had little else.

She hurried down the stairs, stopping to light lamps as she went. The bell rang again.

"I'm coming!"

She opened the door.

"Julia."

The strength left her body. "Oh, dear Lord." She slammed the door and threw the bolt.

"Julia!" Gib called. "I need to talk to you."

She thought of everything she'd given him, everything he'd taken away, and felt a burst of emotion that tore at her heart and filled her eyes with tears.

"Oh, Gib," she whispered. "I can't bear any more of you."

He was at the front door now, knocking, calling her name. Julia ignored him. She retraced her steps, turning out lamps in the hall, at the top of the stairs, in her bedroom. She sat in darkness, listening to the silence. Gib had stopped knocking, stopped calling. Julia told herself she should be angry. His daring to come back should make her furious. But all she felt was a weary sadness and a pitiful kind of longing. She couldn't hate him, even after what he'd done.

There were sounds outside her open window—scrapes and thumps, a muttered curse. Julia got to her feet, pressing a hand to her chest. Gib had climbed onto the upstairs porch. He was removing the screen, raising the sash. He loomed at the starlit window, a large dark-clad form. One leg swung inside, followed by the other, and then he was standing before her, not ten feet away.

"Julia, I have to talk to you."

She should scream, she thought; she should do something. But she remained mute and still—held by his audacity, which was beyond belief, and by a deeper terror that he might find a way to reclaim her.

"Go away, Gib."

"Listen for a minute."

He stepped toward her, and Julia jumped back, bumping into the bedside table. The lamp teetered. She turned and reached for it. Gib lunged across the room, catching the lamp and righting it.

A stillness fell around them. Gib was close enough to touch, close enough to fill her senses with memories. She moved away from him, wrapping her arms around herself from shoulder to waist.

"Don't come near me."

He retreated to the vanity chair and sat down. The room seemed to shimmer in starlight, brighter than before. Julia could see his face, the wide brow, the clean line of his jaw, the mouth that had kissed her so intimately.

"I meant for you to keep half the money," he said.

The money, she thought. He was getting right down to it. "That's what you wanted from the first, isn't it? That's why you offered to do my spring cleaning."

"That's how it started."

"Why didn't you just tell me it was yours?"

He sat forward, his hands hanging between his knees. "I

didn't have any proof it was mine. I figured you were too savvy a lady to hand over your inheritance to some rawhider who rode into town claiming it was his."

Of course he was right, Julia thought. But then she wondered. If he'd told her the truth, she might have felt differently.

"If you'd known it was mine," Gib said, "you wouldn't have kept any of it, would you? Even if I'd wanted to divide it."

"No, of course not."

"Well, then," he said, as if that explained everything.

Julia sat down on the edge of the bed, trying to sort through his reasoning. In a way, his plan made sense; he'd found a way to get half of the money without her knowing it was his.

It made sense except for one thing. "You deceived me, Gib. You made me trust you, and then you ran away."

He looked at the floor. "If I were a different man with a different set of troubles, I'd have stayed with you and wouldn't have cared who the money belonged to."

She didn't believe him; she didn't dare. How could she believe a man who came and went on a whim, charming and seducing, who'd no doubt left a trail of ruined hearts from Idaho to Batopilas, Mexico?

"If I'd stayed, there'd have been trouble," he said. "A couple of hard men are looking to track me down. I don't want you mixed up in it."

"Wylie and Trask."

Gib looked up, startled. "How the devil do you know about them?"

"You mentioned them in your letters from Mexico. They were your partners."

"Doc kept those old letters?"

"All of them."

He rubbed his forehead. "Jesus."

"Your partners," Julia said. "Did you swindle them?"

"I wouldn't exactly . . ." He paused. "Yeah, you could call it that."

She felt a sinking sensation in the pit of her stomach. His

own partners. There was no limit to his treachery. "You hid the money in Edward's name so they wouldn't find it."

"Before you take their side, you'd better hear what kind of men they were. They were gunmen who worked for the Murphy-Dolan gang in the Lincoln County wars. They were killers. They got sick of it and quit, drifted into the copper camp where I was working near Good Springs in New Mexico Territory."

Gib paused, seeming to wait for some sign from her to continue. When she gave him nothing but silence, he went on anyway. "At the time the price of copper was low, so the company paid stock for wages. I'd been there awhile and had collected a fair amount of stock, but I was fed up with not earning hard cash. When Wylie and Trask showed up, I was already thinking about moving on."

He shifted a little on the vanity chair. "They didn't know scratch about digging, but they had some start-up money and they'd heard talk of abandoned mines in Chihuahua— that's a state in Mexico. We partnered up, took a boat to Topolobampo, laid in provisions. We had a complete mining outfit—powder, steel, tools, general equipment . . ." His voice trailed off. "Do you want to hear this?"

Julia's tight grip on herself had slackened; she wanted to hear every word. "Yes, I do."

He continued. "I looked up a stiff I used to know from my days on the Comstock, Porfirio Cruz, a clever little fellow from Mazatlán—we called him Porky. He was dead broke and wanted to get in on the deal, which was fine with me, seeing how the Sierra Madre was crawling with bandits and Porky knew the lay of the land. Wylie and Trask didn't like it. They thought Porky would horn in on our profits. I insisted he come."

Gib rubbed his hair in thought. "Those two pieces of scrub started celebrating before we left Topolobampo. When they finished their whiskey, they started in on *lechuguilla*, the native brew. Wylie and Trask were drunk most all the year and a half we were together."

He told her how Porky led them to an abandoned mine near the Batopilas River where they worked for months before they hit pay. "We uncovered a vein so rich we could hardly find enough rock in it to blast."

They hired Tarahumara Indians who helped work the mine. Every few months Porky and Gib took a *conducta* of pack mules down to the coast. "We took the ore to the reduction works north of Los Mochis and sold it there."

In camp there were arguments. Wylie and Trask didn't want to pay the natives a fair wage, and they didn't want to pull their weight in the mine.

"Fighting cocks, siestas, *lechuguilla*, that's all they cared about," Gib said. "They wouldn't work, and they wouldn't leave the senoritas alone. We ended up paying out gold for a lot of hurt feelings."

Eventually, the local police chief decided the payoffs weren't big enough; he wanted more gold. Gib and Porky refused, and they had a falling out with the locals. Without the chief's protection, the mine was vulnerable to bandit raids and attacks by renegade Indian bands that roamed the mountains looking to kill gringos.

"Things got so bad with the locals that Porky and I decided we'd had enough," Gib said. "We loaded the mules with ore and headed for the coast. At Topolobampo, we divided the profits we'd saved in the Banco Nacional. Porky headed back to Mazatlán to build a hacienda. I took the first boat to San Francisco."

He stopped talking. Muted sounds of the summer night drifted through the open window. A gust of breeze rattled the panes and cooled the air. When Julia said nothing, Gib went on.

"Before you decide Porky and I swindled Wylie and Trask, remember we left them a working mine. They could have made a fortune out of it if they'd put their minds to it. But all they wanted was the money they'd done nothing to earn. Now they're after my scalp."

"Maybe they went after Porky, too."

"I doubt it. He's got a family the size of an army. All I've got is my six-shooter."

Julia didn't know whether to believe Gib or not. For all

she knew, he'd told her a tall story, and Wylie and Trask were victims of his swindle, just as she was.

He seemed to read her mind. "I earned the money fair and square, Julia. Keep half of it. I won't rest easy unless you do."

"No," she said. "I don't want it."

She thought he would argue, but he didn't. After a minute he got to his feet and glanced at the window. Julia caught a glimpse of his smile. "I guess I'll go out the same way I came in."

As he started out, Julia said, "I don't know why you came back, Gib, or how long you plan to stay, but I don't want to see you. Please don't come by again."

He straddled the windowsill, a dark shape against a backdrop of stars. "If that's what you want, princess, I won't bother you. I promise."

After he'd gone, Julia stood in the darkness, wishing she could reach some understanding of who he was and what he meant to her. Then she decided it was better not to try. Her affair with Gib Booth was finished, its meaning best left to the judgment of time.

The next morning, Gib rode up to the Continental and left word with Ab Ames's wife that he was still counting on partnering Ab in the Independence Day drilling contest. Then he had a talk with Mr. Coolidge at the bank, and later stopped by Barnet's office to draw up a will.

Barnet was easier on him than Gib expected—no lectures, no eye-rolling disgust. "That was a pretty fancy trick," he said. "Getting away with your own money."

Gib told him about the mine in Batopilas, about Wylie and Trask and how he and Porky had run off with the profits. "I have a pretty good idea what'll happen if those two catch up with me," he said. "If they kill me, I'd like the money to go to Julia Metcalf and Gilbert Chapman."

Barnet did some thinking. "Wylie and Trask might not look kindly on a baby and a widow getting the money they figure is theirs."

Gib hated to consider that possibility, but he knew Barnet

was right. Those two buzzards could cause Julia and the Chapmans a whole lot of trouble. "I swear, I've never heard of money being such a goddamn problem."

"It's been known to happen," Barnet said, looking more amused than sympathetic. "Seems to me your best plan would be to sort things out with these two fellows and get rid of them."

The idea was tempting, which proved to Gib how softheaded he'd gotten. Before he came back to Stiles last May, he'd have died in a hail of shotgun pellets before he'd have considered giving Wylie and Trask the time of day, let alone a cent of the money they'd done nothing to earn.

Barnet went on. "From the way Julia's feeling about you, I'd say there's no way she'd take any of your money. Even if you bequeathed it to her."

Gib worried a hand through his hair. "Christ, Barnet, she hasn't got enough to live on—at least not enough to have a decent life."

"She's set on earning her own way with her medical practice."

"You think she can do it?"

Barnet shrugged. "She'll get by. It looks as if she and Beacham will work something out."

Gib thought of the worst possibility. "She won't marry Hughes, will she?"

Barnet leaned back in his swivel chair and tugged at an earlobe. "She says not, says she doesn't love him. Matter of fact, she says she doesn't want to marry any man. Of course, you never know what might happen."

Gib jumped to his feet. "He's one four-flushing son of a bitch if I ever saw one."

"Oddly enough, he uses the same term when referring to you."

Gib paced the office, rubbing the back of his neck. He was tempted to tell Barnet his suspicions about the freeze-out at the Continental, but he knew it wouldn't be wise. Barnet was a friend of Hughes; he'd probably think Gib was talking wild. And if he did believe him, he'd go straight to the marshal, who'd tip Hughes off so he could cover his tracks.

"I'd say the only way Julia will get anywhere near your money is if she marries you," Barnet said.

Gib stopped cold and looked at him. "What are you, crazy?

"Dottie says she's mighty fond of you."

"Was, Barnet. She *was* fond of me. She told me last night she never wanted to see me again."

"Just a thought." Barnet folded his hands behind his head. After a while, he added, "So you went out there last night."

"Yeah. I tried to explain."

"I guess she didn't think much of your explanation."

"I just told you," Gib said impatiently. "She doesn't want to see me." He slumped down in one of the chairs that surrounded the long table. He was feeling all worked up, worrying about Julia not having any money and about Hughes preying on her tender feelings. "It's just as well. I'm not sticking around here long."

"Why did you come back, then?"

Gib stared out the window. "I've got some business."

After a minute Barnet got up from his desk and went to the file drawer. He took out some papers and laid a page on the table in front of Gib. "After Julia discovered the money was yours, I took another look at Edward's will. Something interesting caught my eye."

Gib leaned forward and started to read: "I, Edward Charles Metcalf . . ."

Barnet pointed to one of the last clauses.

"I also bequeath to my beloved wife, Julia, the assets on deposit at the Bank of San Francisco and whatever legacy may accompany said assets, to do with as her heart and her good sense shall dictate."

Gib stared at the words, feeling a sudden pressure in his chest: "whatever legacy may accompany said assets, to do with as her heart and her good sense shall dictate."

He kept reading the lines over and over until he thought his eyes would fall out of his head.

He looked up at Barnet. "What the hell does it mean?"

"Your guess is as good as mine. But I figure that legacy is you."

Gib got up, grabbed his hat, and got out of there fast. He stood on the boardwalk, studying his boot toes, while his heart pounded and he gulped down some mighty strong feelings.

"To do with as her heart and her good sense shall dictate," the will said.

Doc had trusted him with Julia, in his will he'd given the two of them his blessing.

Gib remembered what Julia had said about Ma the night he'd talked about breaking his promise: "She was a fine, forgiving woman, and she loved you." Those words had come back to him more than once. They'd been a real comfort, too. He wondered if there was a chance Julia might apply them to herself.

Then he thought of what she'd said last night. She'd made it clear she didn't want him or his money. Doc's will was all well and good, but it didn't change a goddamn thing.

Charlie Soon's China Alley shop was Gib's next stop. As usual, Charlie seemed to be expecting him.

"Boss come back one time," he said gleefully, scurrying out from behind the counter. "Doctor lady know big dollar belong to boss."

"And you knew all along, didn't you?" Gib said. "You and your San Francisco cousins. Would you mind telling me how?"

Charlie waved the question away, and Gib didn't ask it again. The answer, he knew, would remain some dark Celestial secret, known only to Charlie and his head men cousins in San Francisco's Chinatown.

But there were other answers in that brain of Charlie's that Gib intended to dig out. "Let's have a talk, Charlie."

Charlie was agreeable. "Boss come have tea."

He took Gib into the back room where the girl with bangs poured tea into thimble cups and served the tiny nut-filled cakes dipped in sugar.

After they'd eaten and sipped, Gib said, "There's something queer going on at the Continental."

Charlie put down his teacup and looked at Gib, his eyes narrow little slits.

"What do you know about it, Charlie?"

"Not Cholly business what white devil do."

"Have you got a spy up there?"

Charlie's face closed. "What spy?"

Gib wished he was better at negotiating the Celestial mind. He knew that Charlie would prefer he beat around the bush for a while instead of asking direct questions, but Gib was too impatient to observe that Chinese custom.

"You've got somebody up there. Some fellow with big ears who told you the mine boss wants to marry Mrs. Metcalf. Remember? You told me yourself." Gib figured it was Hughes's cook. "Is it Cookie?"

Charlie pretended he had to think that through. "Cookie know English. Pretend dumb."

"Is he clever enough to get me into the mine office some night?"

"Aiyah!" Charlie looked shocked. "Very dangerous you go there. Very dangerous Lee Chung let you in."

"I'll pay you," Gib said. "I'll pay Lee Chung." All he had these days was money, and so far not one cent of it had done him a damned bit of good.

Charlie sipped his tea. Gib could see his mind turning. "Why you want mine boss dead snake?"

"Because he's swindling the town, and I don't want him marrying Mrs. Metcalf."

Charlie seemed to accept those reasons. "You boss marry doctor lady."

"Hell, Charlie, she won't marry me, not after the business with the money."

"Boss marry doctor lady," he insisted. "Fill her belly with happiness."

"Are you deaf?" Gib snapped. "She doesn't want me. Besides, as soon as I get Hughes, I'm heading out of town."

He ate another couple of cakes, feeling hot and jumpy. Everybody was talking about him marrying Julia—Barnet,

Charlie, even Doc, from the grave—just when she'd shown him the door.

"Charlie owe boss big favor."

Gib looked up. "Yeah? For what? The snakes?"

"Boss shoot Hockett dead."

Gib had to think for a minute before he remembered that Hockett and his men had strung up a couple of Chinese boys for the fun of it. One of the boys had been Charlie's son.

"Big favor," Charlie said again. "Boss tell Charlie when go to white devil mine. Lee Chung let him in."

CHAPTER

23

JULIA WAS GETTING ready to go into town to visit Dr. Beacham's surgery, newly opened in the rear of Mr. Redfern's pharmacy, when a buggy drove into the yard. She pulled on her shawl, a necessity on the drizzly late June morning, and stepped onto the porch.

Harlan climbed out of the buggy. Even before he got close, Julia could tell he was angry. He tramped toward the house, heedless of the mud that caked his shiny boots, and stamped onto the porch.

"I hear Booth's come back."

Julia looked at him in alarm. His fleshy face was mottled, and his neck bulged with rage. "For heaven's sake, Harlan. I have no intention of seeing him—"

"I want him out of town. Do you hear me? I want him gone." Despite the cool air, Harlan was sweating. He pulled out a handkerchief and mopped his face.

"Come in and sit down," Julia said, trying to calm him.

"Let me warn you, Julia, if he starts nosing around,

there's going to be trouble and plenty of it, and it's going to include you." He glared at her. "If you take my meaning."

His threat sent a shiver down Julia's back. She thought of the secrets he knew and drew her shawl closer. "I'm not sure that I do. Perhaps you'd better explain yourself."

"I'll be glad to." He wiped his feet furiously and pulled open the screen door. Without waiting for Julia to precede him, he went inside. She followed, feeling a sick kind of dread, as if she were about to receive some horrible news.

In the living room Harlan motioned for her to sit next to him on the sofa. He reached into his pocket and took out a photograph, which he shoved into her hands.

Julia took one look and dropped the picture into her lap. "What . . . ? Oh, dear heaven!" Shock hit her in a hot wave, then stunned her cold. "Where did you get this?"

"It came from a photographer in Chicago. His name is Harry Marcus. He wasn't hard to find."

Julia clapped her hands over the picture in a vain attempt to make it disappear. "They were destroyed," she said. "The plates were destroyed. The pictures . . . Randall had to pay . . ." She stammered as she spoke, too appalled to complete her thought.

"Evidently Mr. Marcus kept back a few. For sentimental reasons, I assume, seeing how lovely you were. He was willing to part with the pictures for a price—with the remaining plates, too."

Julia squeezed her eyes shut, trying to block out the shameful evidence that lay in her lap. But the picture pushed through all attempts to deny it—a ruffled skirt raised to the thighs, long girlish legs, a slip of a drape that hid nothing on top. A lonely smile.

Julia's throat closed tight; the pain of old memories nearly overwhelmed her.

"Last fall your brother aroused my curiosity with his confidence about your little scandal," Harlan said. "I sent an investigator to find the photographer. He remembered you well."

Julia turned her head away. Harlan was taking advantage of the girl in the picture—sixteen years old, her world shattered by grief and loss—just as Harry Marcus had done so many years ago.

"What do you want, Harlan?"

"I don't want the pictures falling into the wrong hands. I'm sure you don't, either."

A chill went right to her bones. He was talking about blackmail, she was sure of it. "What do you really want?" she asked.

"I want Booth out of town by tomorrow midnight."

Julia's heart felt trapped in her chest—wild, like a bird. "Tomorrow? But . . . I—I'm not even speaking to him. I don't know where he is."

"Then you'd better find him." Harlan got to his feet and pulled at his cuffs. "From what I understand, he was here only a few nights ago, so he couldn't have gone far."

Julia stood up, her mind careening over the impossible task of doing his bidding. She didn't understand him at all, why he was so adamant, why he would threaten to ruin her.

"The pictures," she said. "What will become of them?"

"Once Booth is gone, I'll give them to you, along with the plates."

Julia thought frantically. There was no way Gib would leave Stiles by tomorrow night. "The Fourth," she said abruptly. "He's here till the Fourth to partner Abner Ames in the drilling contest. That's why he came back." She was guessing. She knew nothing for sure, just something Mrs. Chapman had mentioned way back. "After the Fourth, he'll be gone, I'm sure of it."

"I can't wait that long."

"It's less than two weeks away." Julia twisted her hands together in an agony of desperation. "After the Fourth he'll be on his way. I'm sure of it."

After a moment's thought, Harlan seemed to acquiesce. "All right. Till the Fourth." He looked her up and down in a bold, rude manner. "In the meantime I've grown rather tired of playing gentleman to the bereaved widow."

He grasped her shoulders and dragged her toward him. Julia fell against his chest with a gasp of surprise, and then his mouth was on hers, wet and open, his tongue squirming deep into her mouth.

She struggled, but his embrace crushed her, hurt her. Then as quickly as he'd taken her, he thrust her away. Julia tried to catch her breath, staggered by the unexpectedness of his assault.

"Ma'am?" It was Mossy. He stood in the living room doorway, looking from her to Harlan. "I brought the mail."

Harlan made a sound of disgust. "I was just leaving." He snatched up his hat and shot Julia a fierce look. "I'll be back to continue this discussion."

He stormed out of the room, brushing past Mossy without so much as a glance. After a moment, Julia heard the muffled sounds of the buggy as he drove away.

Mossy stared at her in wordless amazement. Then his eyes dropped to the floor, where the photograph lay. Julia bent down to snatch it up. She shoved it into the drawer of the side table.

"Mr. Hughes and I . . ." she began, trying to think of a way to explain. "We had a . . . misunderstanding." Her face was afire, her hair slipping down. She still felt the imprint of Harlan's teeth on her lips.

Mossy shook his head, his broad brow furrowed. "From the look of it, he was forcing himself on you."

"Oh, heavens, no," Julia said. "It wasn't that way . . ." Tears swam in her eyes. She wiped at them with the back of her hand. "Oh, Mossy, swear you won't tell anyone. Please say you won't tell."

He kept shaking his head back and forth. "Ma'am, I'd never do that. I don't breathe a word about what goes on here. You know that."

Julia sat down on the sofa and tried to compose herself. She'd survived the incident at the Pickax when Gib had spoken of her so crudely. She'd survived the scandal over him running off with the money; everyone had seen her as an innocent dupe. But she would never survive what Harlan had uncovered. The shame she'd all but forgotten had returned to haunt her, and if she didn't do what Harlan wanted, it would destroy her.

"Ma'am, I got a letter from Ada. Maybe you'd open it for me. I just don't think I'm able."

Julia looked at Mossy's face, lined with hope and misery, and in an instant her worries vanished. She took the letter from his trembling hands, tore it open, and skimmed it. "She wants to come here, Mossy. She wants to see you."

Mossy pulled out his handkerchief and blew his nose.

"She says you don't have to go home with her if you don't want to. She just wants to see you, talk to you, tell you about Morris and Beth and . . . Oh, Mossy, you have six grandchildren."

Julia sat back on the sofa and stared at the letter, feeling something pure and hopeful that eased the ugliness of the scene with Harlan. A happy ending to a twenty-year tragedy. It cheered her just to know such a thing was possible.

"I'd like to see the letter, ma'am," Mossy said. "If you don't mind."

Julia folded it and pressed it into his hand. Mossy and his Ada, she thought, their early years together torn apart by war. Now they'd formed a fragile connection that could grow strong again and hold them till death.

"She loves you, Mossy," Julia said. "She never stopped."

He wiped his eyes. Mumbling words of thanks, he shuffled out of the room.

Gib rode Lucky out of town toward Doubletree Gulch in a cold, drizzly rain. After two days in Stiles, he'd decided to get away, lie low, and plan his next move. The best place for lying low and planning was at the Rattling Rock. He could work and think and jaw with Rawlie and Otis, go down to Whiskey Creek and visit little Gilbert, too, which always lifted his spirit.

Barnet had drawn up a simple will leaving his share of the money to Julia and the Chapmans should he unexpectedly meet his maker. Gib had decided he had to provide for Julia, even if she didn't want the money. As for Wylie and Trask tracking it down and causing trouble, he figured they'd been through town once last spring. With luck they'd not be back.

Gib turned his thoughts to Hughes and the goings-on at

the Continental. Scobie had told him that six months back, several rounds of shot had blown down bonanza ore on number four level. The shift boss, who was being paid off by Harlan in Continental stock, had cleaned up the rock and ordered the men to drift in a different direction— supposedly because of mud, which made timbering difficult. None of the crew said anything—they didn't want to risk losing their jobs, or worse—but Gib was sure that any stiff worth his powder knew he was working a freeze-out.

He'd asked Sarabeth to keep an ear out for talk of secret ore shipments going to Idaho or Butte to be assayed— Hughes would want to know what he had on number four before he pulled out of a payload vein with the intention of saving it for later—and Charlie Soon had agreed to get in touch with his Celestial cousins in San Francisco. Gib wanted to know how Continental stock was selling on the San Francisco exchange, and to whom. If his hunch was right, Hughes had agents buying up shares for him at bargain prices.

Gib decided he would make his move when he heard back from Charlie, probably in a few weeks. Once he exposed Hughes's scheme, he'd hop a train east and leave Wylie and Trask a stone-cold trail.

At the Rattling Rock, Gib rode past the tailing dump and the outcropping of rocks that formed the head of the mine. He gave a shrill whistle, a sign to Rawlie that he wasn't a claim-jumper asking to be shot.

He dismounted on soft, damp ground. The air was fresh and pine-scented, and in the gulch below, mist swirled around deep green trees. Gib led Lucky down to his cabin to unload supplies. He'd stocked up at Blum's—been on the receiving end of a whole lot of ragging, too, although he had the feeling I. Z. was pleased to see him back.

"Say, Gib!"

It was Chapman coming out of Rawlie's cabin, followed by Rawlie in his long Confederate coat.

"What the hell, Otis?" Gib said, unbuckling his saddle-bags. "Loafing on the job again?"

"I knowed you'd be back," Rawlie said. He walked down

the slope to peer into Gib's face. "I told Otis, 'That boy always comes back.'"

"You hungry?" Otis asked. "Rawlie and me was just having some of Vera's gooseberry pie." He was grinning so hard Gib thought his mustache would fall off. "It's mighty good to see you, Gib."

Gib felt the same way. He cuffed both men and shook their hands, then went inside Rawlie's cabin for a cup of coffee and slice of pie.

"Sarabeth's been up," Rawlie said. "She said you were back." He rocked in his chair and pawed his beard. He did a lot of scratching, too, which reminded Gib it was time for a dunking in Whiskey Creek.

Then Otis told him some surprising news. He'd hit rock that was laced with wires and chunks of pure gold. He'd kept his discovery to himself, uncertain of what to do, except to keep on working.

"I done some tests," he said. "Looks like it'll assay at about a hundred dollars a ton. We need men up here to work it, see how deep she goes." He started grinning again. "There's no telling, Gib."

Gib was pleased, but he didn't want the mine to attract attention while he was still in town. "We'll keep it to ourselves for a while," he said. "There'll be plenty of time to hire men later."

For the next week he and Chapman worked the vein, blasting and mucking, deepening the drift, sorting rock that was worth shipping. Gib brought Rawlie into the tunnel, holding the lamp so it would shine on the gold.

"By gum," Rawlie said, peering close. "That sure is pretty."

"It's part yours, old-timer," Gib said, "so take a good look."

"Say, Gib." Rawlie lowered his voice. "I got some money buried out there on the up side of Digger's cabin. If you're needing any, I could dig some up."

Gib clapped him on the shoulder. "Thanks, partner. Better you hang on to it for a rainy day."

After supper one evening in the Chapmans' cabin, Otis

started in on the papers Gib had signed turning over ownership of the mine to little Gilbert. "Now that you're back, we better fix those papers again," he said.

Gib looked at the baby cuddled against his mother's bosom. "Leave the papers be, Otis," he said. "I won't be here much longer. There's an account in your name at the bank. Use it to develop the mine or anything else you want."

Otis's face fell. He exchanged glances with his wife, and Gib knew they were wondering what he was up to, coming back after running off with money he'd pretended wasn't his. They probably wondered where the money had come from in the first place and whether they should accept it. But Gib wasn't going to explain. He didn't want Otis turning up his nose at the money, as Julia had, figuring it had been swindled. The Chapmans had had enough years mucking out a meager living, and they'd lost their two little girls. Now they had a paying enterprise at the Rattling Rock and a fine baby son. They deserved some peace of mind.

"We missed you when you were gone," Mrs. Chapman said.

Her words pleased Gib, but he tried not to let it show. "I've got some business to tend to in town. When that's taken care of, I'll be moving along."

Later, heading back to the mine in the misty twilight, Gib thought how hard it would be, leaving Stiles again. Last time, Julia had believed the money was hers, so there was no question she'd keep it. Now she didn't want it, but she had little else to live on. He was sure going to worry.

As he thought, it occurred to him that worrying about things was unnatural for him. He'd always left his problems behind—a man moved on, and his problems disappeared, simple as that. But when he'd gone to Butte, his worries hadn't disappeared; they'd gotten worse. He had a feeling the same thing would happen when he headed back east. Even if he exposed Hughes's scheme and left Julia and the Chapmans with plenty of money, he'd keep right on worrying.

It didn't take a whole lot of brainpower to figure out why. A man worried when he formed ties, when he loved a woman and started thinking about something other than his own hide.

Julia awoke shortly after sunrise on the Fourth of July. She got up and looked out the window at what promised to be a hot, sunny day.

Usually she loved the Fourth. There were sounds of church bells and cannons and the snapping of Chinese firecrackers. The town was festooned with decorations, everyone was in a holiday spirit, and the procession of patriotic floats down Main Street was glorious. The festivities never failed to make her proud to be an American.

But today her excitement was dulled by the feeling that something awful was hanging over her head, held by Harlan, ready to drop and ruin her life. Today Gib had to leave town. If he didn't go, the consequences for her would be disastrous. Julia shuddered at the thought of those pathetic pictures being passed among the men at the Bon Ton and New Gaiety.

But she had more to lose than her pride. Should Harlan carry out his threat, she would lose the confidence of her patients. Her entire practice would be gone. Respectable people didn't choose as a physician a woman who'd posed naked for artistic photographs. They would look down on her just as they did on the girls at Miss Lavinia's Parlor House.

Julia washed her face and brushed her teeth, put on her robe, and went downstairs. Mossy sat at the kitchen table, drinking coffee.

"Good morning, Mossy," she said. "Happy Fourth of July."

He got to his feet. "A happy Fourth yourself, ma'am."

Since he'd received the letter from Ada, Mossy was a changed man. He stepped more lightly, whistled through his chores, and seemed to have given up drinking. Julia suspected he would soon return east to rejoin his family, leaving her all alone, save for Bee.

"You going to the rock drilling contest?" Mossy asked. "Gib and Ab Ames are a team."

Julia poured herself some coffee. "I certainly am."

"We'll drive in together."

Mossy was being protective. The few times Harlan had stopped by the house, Mossy stayed nearby, performing tasks that Julia hadn't asked him to do—floor polishing in the hallway or shrub pruning by the porch. He hadn't mentioned the incident in the living room, but Julia knew he was concerned.

After breakfast she dressed in a red and white striped dress with a bright blue sash and a white lace collar. She wound a red, white, and blue ribbon around the crown of her best straw hat and tied it in a bow. She hummed a snatch of "Yankee Doodle," trying to boost her spirits, but all she felt was dread. She wished she had someone to confide in. But Louise would be horrified, Dottie shocked—and of course she could never mention the photographs to a man . . . except, she thought, to Gib.

Foolishness! She hadn't seen hide nor hair of him for two weeks, since the night he'd climbed in her window and told her about Wylie and Trask and the gold mine in Mexico. Even if she did see him, how could she trust him after the trick he'd played?

But the more she thought about it, the more she felt that Gib was the only person she *could* trust with her secret. He might be taken aback, but he would never condemn her. Knowing Gib, she was sure he would try to understand. Why, if she asked him to leave town, he would probably go, just to spare her embarrassment.

Julia got to her feet and gave herself a good scolding. It was ridiculous to think of confiding in a confidence man, a man who'd wooed her with sweet talk and intimate moments, knowing all along he would leave her once he'd achieved his goal.

After the parade and patriotic speeches, the crowd milled around Main Street, waiting for the drilling contest to begin. Julia had never seen the town so festive. Storefronts and houses were strung with red, white, and blue bunting. Eagles and national flags decorated windows and doors.

Families had come in from the ranches in the valley, and the mines had been shut down for the day. Every living soul for miles around, it seemed, had packed Main Street to watch the parade and the drilling contest. Rooftops were dense with people, and boys hung from every available post and tree.

While Marshal McQuigg's brass band played a rousing march, Julia nervously scanned the crowd for Harlan. With the other members of the town council, he'd ridden in the parade in a carriage draped with bunting, waving and tipping his hat. Julia wondered what his plans were for putting her pictures in the wrong hands. She tried to convince herself that he wouldn't carry through with his threat.

She hailed Lee and Sarabeth, walking arm in arm in the street. Sarabeth looked pretty in a blue checkered dress that matched Lee's shirt, her thick black braid wound around her head.

"Did Harriet come out for the parade?" Julia asked.

"Wouldn't know," Lee said. "She steers clear of me these days."

Harriet had stayed in bed for a week after Lee stopped going to see her. But then she'd emerged from her sulk and resumed her activities, although she had yet to speak a word to Lee.

"Drilling contest's about ready to start," Lee said.

He took Julia's and Sarabeth's arms as the crowd pressed forward toward a block of granite that stood in front of the town hall. The granite was surrounded by a bunting-draped platform where the drillers were shedding their shirts and preparing their equipment.

"You want to watch with us?" Sarabeth asked.

Julia declined, since some of the men in the street were drunk and rowdy. Instead, she pushed her way to the safety of the sidewalk where she encountered Walt Stringer.

"I brought this week's article for you," she said. "It's in the buggy."

Walt looked excited. "Never mind that. The contest's ready to start. I've got my money on Gib and Ab Ames." He led Julia to a chair in front of the *Sentinel* office. "Climb up here. It's a good spot for you to watch from. Gib and Ab's the last round, up against the team from Butte."

As Walt helped her onto the chair, the six-gun fired, and the sound of hammers pounding steel rang out, along with the shouts of men as they cheered on their teams. Julia stood on her perch, her heart in her throat, watching bare-torsoed men swing their hammers as their teammates turned steel. Drilling on changes took skill, speed, strength, and great concentration. A hand in the way of a hard-swung hammer would be smashed beyond repair.

After four two-man teams had competed, and the depth of their holes announced, she felt a tug at her sleeve. She glanced down at Mossy.

"Gib and Ab's next!" he shouted.

Julia's stomach filled with butterflies. She crossed her fingers in the folds of her skirt and offered up a prayer that Gib and Ab might win.

Gib slammed hammer on steel in a muscle-clenching rhythm that made granite chips fly. Despite the bandanna tied around his forehead, his face ran with sweat. He felt sweat all down his back and under his arms. As the sun beat down, he clenched his teeth and swung harder, focusing on the drill that Ab turned after each stroke.

Jim Ferry, owner of the High Top mine, called out Gib's strokes per minute — "Sixty!" — and Barnet the other striker's — "Fifty-nine!"

There was a flash of steel as Ab tossed away the used bit. Then the change was down and they shifted — Ab to the hammer, Gib to steel — not missing a stroke. They'd practiced on rock up by Ab's place. There their striking had reached sixty-two a minute, and they'd drilled a quarter inch short of the record held by the team from Butte.

Gib threw steel from the hole and rammed in the longer replacer as Ab's hammer came down. Seven drills were left, one for each of the minutes remaining in the contest, beautiful steel of graduated lengths that Gib had sharpened and tempered with care. When he'd laid them out before the contest, the other teams had come over to admire his work.

"Sixty-one!"

Again, the shift, two blows of the hammer.

"Sixty!"

It would be close, Gib thought. He'd heard sixty for the other team, but not sixty-one. He and Ab had had at least three sixty-one-stroke minutes. If the two teams were striking near an even weight, he and Ab would win.

For the remaining minutes, Gib didn't hear Jim Ferry's count. He concentrated only on striking, turning steel, the shift. Then the six-gun that had started the contest fired, ending it. The crowd cheered the contestants.

Chest heaving, pulse throbbing, Gib dropped his hammer and looked at Ab. The two of them were wrung-out wet, hair stuck to their heads, their eyes burning with pride.

Ab grinned like Gib had never seen him and threw an arm around his shoulders. "You're one hard-boiled stiff, Gib."

Gib hoisted his pants, which had slipped some, and gave Ames a jab in the ribs. "You're not bad yourself," he said. "For a Cousin."

While the judges made their measurements, Gib drank from a canteen. He tipped back his head and poured water into his mouth, letting it run over his chin and onto his chest. Then he bent down to collect his drill steel. None of it was chipped, and it had hardly dulled; he'd prepared it well.

Jim Ferry made the announcement. The Cornishmen from Butte had put their hole down forty-two and three-eighths inches, the team of Ames and Booth, forty-three and seven-eighths. Ames and Booth were declared the winners.

The team from Butte disputed the measurements, and the holes were measured again, then a third time, before the Cousins were satisfied. Still, loud arguments broke out in the crowd, and a few fights, too, among men who'd wagered the wrong way.

The purse of five hundred dollars had been put up by mining companies—the Continental, the High Top, and the smaller operations down the gulch. Gib had contributed fifty dollars from the Rattling Rock. It amused him to think he and Ab had won back his money and some of Hughes's, too.

In the crowd he saw a sandy head bouncing up and down—Ab's boy, Jimmy, trying to see over tall shoulders as he worked his way toward the drilling rock platform. When he reached the granite, Jimmy clambered up the platform steps, his eyes on his father, his freckled face bright with pride.

"Dad," he said, and Ab pulled him close, wetting him with his sweat.

Gib watched father and son embrace and felt a stab of envy. He wondered if Julia had been watching the contest. He hoped she had; he wanted her to know that he was the strongest, the best, a man to be reckoned with when it came to drilling rock.

He pulled off his bandanna, wiped his face, and put on his shirt, not bothering to button it. After the award ceremony, he collected his hammer and drill steel and climbed off the platform. As he made his way through the crowd, he stopped to talk to stiffs from other teams. He looked around, saw Lee and Sarabeth. Otis, too. Dellwood gave him a thumbs-up from his chair in front of the Bon Ton. A gaggle of boys pushed close, as if he were someone important, and a few ladies gave him the eye. Gib didn't see any sign of the one lady he hoped had been watching.

Mossy caught up with him before he'd passed the Regal. "Gib, I got to talk to you."

CHAPTER

24

MOSSY LOOKED WORRIED, but Gib didn't give it much thought, since Mossy always looked worried.

"Hell, Moss, I'm just heading down to the creek to cool off." His whole body was sticky with sweat.

"It's kind of important."

Gib glanced down the crowded street. "I sure could use a drink."

There was a line out the door at the Bon Ton, and the Pickax was the same. They headed for the town hall, where ladies were selling lemonade and cake with pink icing. Gib drank off five glasses of lemonade before he quenched his thirst.

He and Mossy went out back where things were quiet. Gib dropped down under a slender cottonwood whose shimmering leaves rustled in the breeze.

"Did Julia see the contest?" he asked.

Mossy sank down beside him, licking pink icing off his mouth. "She sure did. She had her fingers crossed for you.

She thought she had them hid, but I seen them when she was hopping around on that chair she was standing on."

Gib lay back and stared up at the lace of leaves. It pleased him to think of Julia watching the contest, her fingers crossed for him. He wondered what had been going through her mind.

"Harlan Hughes come by last week."

Gib opened one eye and looked at Mossy. "Yeah?"

"He brought a picture of her half-naked."

Gib sat bolt upright, too astounded to swear. He listened in disbelief as Mossy told about Hughes forcing himself on Julia in the living room, her being upset afterward, and the picture that had fallen to the floor.

"She put it in the drawer. I know I shouldn't have done it, but I went back to have a look." Mossy's face fell. "It was her all right. She was young, maybe seventeen, eighteen years old. She was showing her legs, didn't have nothing worth mentioning on top, either."

Blood started pounding in Gib's head. Where in hell had a naked picture of Julia come from, and what was Hughes doing with it? He couldn't imagine Julia—savvy, dignified, from a fine family, Doc's wife—posing for such a thing. It didn't make a scrap of sense.

"Goddammit, Mossy, you should have told me before. You should have told me right away."

"You were up at the mine. Hughes came back a couple of times to talk to her. I figured I'd better stick close, so he wouldn't do anything."

Gib got to his feet and buttoned his shirt. There were some mighty strange things going on, but this one sure took the prize.

"I'm going to find that bag of wind," he said. "He's got some explaining to do."

The afternoon activities were held on the flat of land just south of town by Cottonwood Creek. There were booths and tables set up, decorated in red, white, and blue, and a few games of chance. McQuigg's band pumped out an off-key tune that grated on Gib's nerves, while Harriet Tabor, very much among the living, auctioned off box lunches in a shrill voice.

Gib dismounted and tethered Lucky. He saw Sarabeth and Lee under a tree eating chicken and cold beans. "Where's Hughes running the boys' wrestling contest?" he asked.

Lee nodded his head toward a crowd. "Hasn't started yet. They're doing the sack races. Just follow the kids hollering."

Gib set off at a fast pace, flexing his fingers. He made a fist and smacked it into his callused palm. He'd do his damnedest not to get into a fight, but it wouldn't be easy. Hughes had forced himself on Julia; he'd kissed her, for Christ's sake, had a picture of her naked. Just thinking about it made him blistering mad.

At the sack race, boys were leaping and screeching and tumbling around on the dusty ground. Hughes stood on the sidelines, arms folded across his chest. He was a big hulk of a man, soft-bellied but strong. If it came to whipping him, Gib knew it wouldn't be easy.

Gib circled around in back of him, keeping his distance, thinking about what Lee had said. Hughes was a Missouri man who'd come west from St. Louis. When he first arrived, he was a big talker, fought like a backwoods brawler. In time, he polished himself into a real gent and became a favorite with the ladies, with politicians, too, but Gib figured he was still a brawler at heart.

"Hughes!"

He turned around. When he saw Gib, a look of alarm flitted across his face, then changed to a sneer. He spat on the ground. "What do you want, Booth?"

Gib ambled closer. He glanced at the folks standing nearby watching the sack race, yelling and cheering. Ab Ames was there with his pretty wife and their flock of youngsters.

"Let's talk in private," Gib said.

Sweat had beaded on Hughes's forehead, and dark patches of it showed through his shirt. He mopped his bullish neck. "Sorry I can't oblige. I'm in charge of the boys' wrestling contest."

"It'll just take a minute."

Hughes shrugged. They stepped away from the crowd and walked toward the creek, masked by willow and cottonwood and clumps of bushes. Gib could make out the spot where he used to practice his quick draw in hopes of impressing the girls.

He slid his hands into his hip pockets. "How did you come by those pictures of Julia Metcalf?"

Hughes stopped in his tracks. "None of your business."

The gasbag could sure thin a man's patience, Gib thought. "That's where you're wrong, Hughes. You'd better turn them over to me, pronto."

"Not on your life. I purchased the plates from a photographer in Chicago." He smirked. "They make up into real pretty photographs."

"You bastard."

"Get out of here, Booth. Take my word for it, leave town and no one will see the pictures. Julia's reputation will remain unspoiled."

"And after I leave, you'll blackmail her into marrying you."

Hughes raised his eyebrows and rocked a little on his heels. "I've known Julia for a long time. She's intelligent, gracious, beautiful, not given to excessive emotion. She's the perfect mate for an ambitious man like me."

Gib's blood ran like fire. The gasbag was a crude know-it-all who played at being respectable. It took all Gib's self-control not to blurt out what he knew about the freeze-out at the Continental. But now wasn't the time to tip his hand. First he had to get hold of those pictures, the plates, too, and then find out from Julia what the hell it was all about.

"I'd offer you a look," Hughes said, smirking again, "but I figure you've seen more than she's showing in those pictures. A lot more—"

Gib's first plunged into Hughes's underbelly, right where it hurt. A whoosh of air came out of him, and he doubled over, clutching himself. Gib stepped back, expecting him to go down. Instead, he charged, head down, arms drawn back, bellowing like a bull. Before Gib could step out of the way, Hughes drove his head into his stomach. Gib staggered backward, trying to keep his balance, but before he could right himself, Hughes barreled into him again, knocking him to the ground. He drew his booted foot back, aimed at Gib's ribs. Gib grabbed it, pulling and twisting, flinging Hughes onto his back, then he scrambled to his feet and reached down, hauling Hughes up by the shirtfront.

Hughes's eyes were wild; his neck bulged. He opened his arms to welcome Gib's rush, and when Gib's fists hit his belly, Hughes grasped him in a massive backbreaking hug, squeezing and grunting with rage. Gib slammed a knee into his groin, then smashed his boot heel down on his instep. Hughes yelped and dropped his arms, bending over in pain. Gib hit him with two hand-splitting punches to the jaw. Hughes fell, then rolled onto his hands and knees, his back heaving, shaking his head as if to clear it.

Gib thought the fight was over. Then Hughes moved like lightning. He ripped Gib's legs out from under him, dropping him like a sack of sand. Hughes was on top of him, fists smashing his face, dulling his senses. Gib felt blows to his ribs and tried to crawl away. Another kick—pain burst across his back, and the bottom dropped out of his stomach.

People were all around, hollering. Somebody rolled him onto his back. Sarabeth stared down. From a great distance, she shouted, "What the hell's going on?"

Gib willed himself to remain conscious. He turned onto his side, pulled himself up on his hands and knees, crawled a little, then stumbled to his feet. He swallowed bile and blood, tried not to puke. He picked up his hat and slapped dirt from his pants.

Hughes was tucking in his shirttails, smug with triumph. Son of a bitch, Gib thought. He should have given it to him, knuckle and skull, kicked him while he was down, gouged his eyes, cracked a few bones.

"You all right, Gib?"

It was Ab Ames. Lee was staring at him, too, looking

alarmed. "Yeah," Gib said. He wiped blood from his mouth. His back was afire, and his head felt the size of a bushel basket. He gave his hat a shake and put it on his head. "What the hell, it was just a little dustup."

He staggered away, down to the creek, into the willows' cool shade. The banks were dense with chokecherry bushes, and the earth smelled damp. Gib stripped off his clothes— gingerly, since the pain and dizziness made it hard for him to keep his balance—and climbed into the slow-running creek. He lay back on smooth stones, grateful for the cool water that soothed him.

He dozed a little, dreamed a little, thought of practicing his quick draw right on these banks. In his mind, past and present merged, and he was showing off for the girls, for Julia, too, bragging, shooting, stealing kisses—more than kisses when he got the chance. He thought of Julia watching him in the drilling contest, fingers crossed. He saw her eyes like aquamarines, her silky hair shot with gold, that sunshine smile. He thought of her sweet mouth on his, the way she twined around him in bed, and he wished she was with him now, naked in the water, easing his pains.

The creek burbled around him, birds chirped in the alders. Through half-closed lids, Gib saw sunlight sparkle in the leaves. Hughes, he thought. He'd get that bastard. Make him pay for what he'd done to Julia, make sure he didn't do anything more.

And then what? Gib wondered. Would he really leave her? How about the others—the Chapmans, little Gilbert, Lee and Mossy, Rawlie, Barnet, old I. Z., Charlie, too? Strange how things had turned out. Despite the raggings from Dellwood, the threats from the marshal, and Hughes trying to chase him away, Stiles kind of felt like home.

Gib slid deeper into the water and thought of the fears and failings that had kept him on the move all these years. He'd felt guilty about letting Ma down, felt scared of anyone depending on him again. He'd done wrong when he'd meant to do right—sometimes he hadn't seemed able to tell the difference—and when he ran into difficulties, he'd just moved on. Then he'd come back to Stiles. Julia had welcomed him; she'd trusted him, tried to see the best in him—hell, she'd even fallen in love with him. Because of her, somewhere along the line he started to see things differently. He wasn't sure why or how or exactly when it had happened, but like turning a kaleidoscope, his view of things had fallen into a whole new pattern.

Now he wanted to stay—with her, with all his friends. This time he didn't want to just move on. He thought of Doc's old adage: Put a man in a situation where something's expected of him and he'll rise to the occasion. That's what he wanted to do, Gib thought. He wanted Julia to expect things of him, to depend on him. He wanted to spend the rest of his life rising to the occasion.

A rustling sound in the bushes snapped Gib out of his daydreams. Jimmy Ames's freckled face popped through the foliage, followed by the rest of him clad in dusty blue overalls. He was carrying a bucket.

"Hey, Jimmy," Gib said from his spot in the creek. "What've you got there?"

"Toads, for the contest." Jimmy hunkered down on the bank, folded his arms on his knees, and stared. Gib figured he must have seen the fight but was too polite to comment.

After a moment Jimmy stuck out a hand with something in it. "You want a chicken leg?"

"Sure," Gib said. "Toss it here."

He caught it one-handed. It tasted salty and good. "Do me a favor, Jim," Gib said when he finished. "Bring Lucky on down. He's the blazed-face black with three white stockings."

"I know Lucky," Jimmy said.

"There's another errand I want you to do, if you've got the time."

"Sure, Gib." Jimmy was up and gone in a rustle of leaves, his bucket bumping his legs. Gib stayed in the water a while longer and did some more thinking. Naked pictures, he thought. Damn that Hughes.

He decided to find Renate Blum. Of all Julia's lady friends, Renate liked him the most.

* * *

It was nearly three o'clock when Jimmy Ames turned up at Dr. Beacham's surgery and told Julia that Gib was at her house in need of medical attention.

"He got in a fight with Mr. Hughes," Jimmy said.

Julia's alarm must have shown, for Dr. Beacham gave her a sympathetic look. "Go along, Mrs. Metcalf. I can manage on my own."

They were setting a boy's arm, broken when he slid from the sloping roof of the express office and landed on the hitching rail. Julia took off her apron and washed her hands, not daring to ask Jimmy about the fight.

When she drove into the yard and saw Gib sitting in one of the porch rockers, she thought of the way he'd looked this morning on the drilling platform—massively strong, beautifully sculpted, swinging his hammer with barely controlled power. Immediately she reminded herself that she didn't trust him, that he would say or do anything to achieve his ends.

Taking her medical bag, she went onto the porch. The sight of him made her gasp. "Gib, what in heaven's name happened?"

His left cheekbone was swollen and bruised, his eye dark and puffy, his lip cut. There were splotches of dried blood on his faded rose shirt and denim pants.

He looked her over with a faint smile. "Well, there, Yankee Doodle. You sure look pretty."

Julia glanced down at her dress. She felt a little silly, being so decorated in red, white, and blue. "I guess it's too much."

"I like it. You know I like you in anything."

From the expression on his face, she could tell that he was recalling something intimate. Julia hurried into words. "Jimmy Ames said you fought with Harlan."

"I took the worst of it."

Before she could ask about his injuries, Gib reached out and dragged the other rocker close to his, wincing a little. "Sit down, princess. Let's talk about those pictures."

The pictures, Julia thought. He knew about them. She sat down, smoothing red and white stripes over her knees, and hung her head, feeling the hot flush of shame. In the silence a bee droned by, fat and lazy, heading for the bushes that banked the porch.

"Hughes is blackmailing you, isn't he?" Gib said.

"He wants you out of town by midnight."

She heard him swear softly. "Why didn't you tell me about the pictures? I'd have helped you."

"I didn't want to see you after what you did. I could never bring myself to trust you again."

Gib didn't speak for a moment, as if weighing her words. "I'll get them back for you."

She gave him a desperate look. "How?"

"I'll figure out something."

She almost believed he could do it, with that too-clever mind of his that had so neatly outwitted her.

They rocked, saying nothing, as firecrackers snapped in the distance and the warm breeze drifted by.

Julia turned her head and looked at him. "Why did you come back, Gib?"

"I came back to make sure you didn't marry Hughes."

"I won't marry him."

"I'm glad to hear it." He smiled gently through his bruises. "How did you come to have those pictures taken?"

She didn't mind telling him. It would be a relief to tell someone who understood. "It was after Mama died. After the Great Fire destroyed our house and Father had his stroke. I was sixteen. I went to live with Randall and Helen. They'd never approved of Mama, and they were rather suspicious of me, too."

Randall and Helen had no children and didn't know what to do with the sad girl who'd been thrust upon them. So they ignored her. They went about their lives—Randall had his medicine, Helen her society functions—leaving Julia to her loneliness. She withdrew into herself and her memories of Mama, the gay times they'd had together, the laughter and promises of grand things to come.

"Mama loved having her photograph taken. Harry Marcus had taken hundreds over the years in his photographic studio—of both Mama and me. He flattered us, made us laugh. Mama didn't take him seriously. She teased him, but I adored him. He told me I was a little beauty, that one day he'd marry me." Julia grimaced at the memory. "After Mama died, I went to his studio alone."

She'd been seeking something—love, comfort, memories—and Harry had sensed her vulnerability. He'd given her the portrait of Mama that now sat on her dresser, since all of her cherished photographs had been consumed by the fire. Each time she returned to his studio he told her how beautiful she was, convincing her that she was too lovely not to photograph nude.

"'Artistic photographs,' he called them," Julia said. "It turned out he sold them. Someone anonymously sent one to Randall. He went to Harry, demanding the pictures and plates. They reached some sort of financial settlement, and that was the end of it."

Gib whistled. "Well, I'll be damned."

"Randall and Helen were furious. They said I was an embarrassment to them, that I'd ruined my life. I was too mortified to go out of the house. I started reading Randall's medical books; that's all I did."

She told him about Edward's stay with the family when he came to Chicago to attend a medical meeting. He'd been impressed with Julia's knowledge of medicine and had shown an interest in what she had to say. She was flattered by his attention. When he suggested she return with him to Stiles, she readily agreed.

"That's how I came here. Edward was happy to have an assistant, Randall and Helen were glad to get rid of me, and I was able to start a new life."

The rockers squeaked on the wooden porch floor. Julia rested her head on the high chair back and closed her eyes.

Gib took her hand, rubbing the back of her wrist with his thumb. "That photographer—did he take advantage of you?"

"No, not in that way, but of course everyone believed he had." She sighed. "Dear Lord, I'm so ashamed."

Gib slipped her fingers between his. "Ah, princess, it's not the worst thing in the world."

They rocked for a while, holding hands between the chairs. For the first time in weeks, Julia felt calm.

"I talked to Renate Blum," he said. "Dottie knows about the pictures. So does Mrs. Williver."

Julia sat up with a gasp. "Harlan told—"

"No, Julia. Doc told them. When he brought you out here, he told Dottie and Louise and Renate, the ladies who would be your friends. He didn't want any scandals blowing up in your face."

Julia stared at him in disbelief. They'd known all this time, all three of them, and they'd never said a word.

"Even Harriet Tabor knew, but she kept it to herself."

"Harriet?" Julia was stunned.

"That's why they were all so worried when I turned up. They were afraid you'd be caught in another scandal. Renate thinks that underneath everything, Harriet's just worried about you."

Julia sat back in her chair and thought of the welcome the ladies had given her when she arrived from Chicago. They'd helped her through her first years as a young bride and through her grief when Edward died. They'd supported her when Gib ran off with the money, and not once had they ever mentioned the pictures. Not even Harriet.

Gib squeezed her hand. "Barnet told me once, 'No man in this town will stand for Julia Metcalf being swindled.' The way I figure it, nobody will stand for Harlan passing around those photographs, either."

Julia felt a vast sense of relief. She felt something else, too, something deeper than gratitude and much more dangerous.

She removed her hand from Gib's and rested it in her lap. "You've been very kind, Gib."

He shifted a little in his chair—painfully, it seemed. "There's something else I've got to tell you." He looked embarrassed. "There's no way I can put it delicately, but you're a doc, so it probably doesn't matter. I'm pissing blood. It's got me kind of worried."

Julia brought him into the surgery. She took his temperature, felt his pulse, pressed all over his lower areas, back and front, looking for tender spots. Her hands on him got old Adam excited, which embarrassed Gib, but Julia seemed not to notice. She maintained her brisk, capable manner, as she had when Scobie got shot. She wanted to know how Harlan had hit him and the nature of his pain. She asked if he'd vomited, if he felt nauseated now. When she demanded to see the color of his piss, Gib wished he'd kept his mouth shut.

"You seem to have a simple contusion of the kidney," she told him when she'd completed the examination. "There's no indication of shock or infection or excessive hemorrhage, but I'm putting you to bed. You need absolute rest."

Gib eased himself off the examining table. "I'm not going to bed. It's not even dark."

"With kidney injuries, the symptoms don't always reflect the severity of the problem," Julia said. "What appears to be a simple case can quickly turn serious if infection sets in." She took off her apron and gave him a look that meant business. "You mustn't do anything to aggravate your condition. You're going to bed."

Gib figured an hour or two of rest wouldn't hurt him, so he went upstairs, stripped off his clothes, and got into Doc's big walnut bed. Julia came up with ice bags, which she applied to his throbbing back. They were a cold, lumpy nuisance, and he didn't want them anywhere near him.

"If you'd prefer, I can administer urinary antiseptics," Julia said. She held up a tube and explained what she would do with it.

Her explanation left Gib shaken. "I'll stick with the ice bags."

When she went downstairs, Gib started thinking about the pictures again. If word got around, plenty of folks would be scandalized, and Julia would be humiliated. He had to find out where they were—in Hughes's suite at the Regal or in his office at the Continental or locked up somewhere in a safe.

He decided the mine office would be the best place to start looking, and the best time to do it was tonight. With Julia's magic-lantern program and the fireworks set for after dark, everybody would be in town; the coast would be clear at the Continental.

He made his plans. As soon as Julia left for the flat, he would ride into town, see Charlie Soon, pick up his gun at the marshal's office, and head up to the Continental. If all went well, he'd be back in bed before she got home.

Gib folded his hands under his pillow and decided to catch a few winks of sleep.

The sun was going down when Julia woke him. She'd come in to examine him again, change the ice bags, and give him something to eat.

She was sure nice to wake up to, Gib thought. She bent over him, bringing the clean lemony scent that reminded him of kissing her skin. When her fingers pressed his belly, old Adam started in again.

Julia blushed a little. "Whatever you're thinking, you'd better stop. It's not good for a man in your condition." She helped him sit up and put the supper tray on his lap.

"I suppose you'll be leaving for town soon," he said.

"I'm not going."

"What?" He tilted the tray, almost knocking it to the floor. "Why the devil not?"

"Because I have a patient who, I suspect, might try to escape." She gave him a stern look. "While you were asleep, I asked Harriet Tabor to fill in for me as narrator of the magic-lantern show. Now eat your dinner and drink all that water. It's important for you to consume lots of liquids."

She left Gib mumbling at his supper. He would have to bolt. He glanced at the window and decided the drop to the ground was too far. Then he remembered the porch outside

Julia's bedroom window. He'd gone down that way once; he could do it again.

But before Gib had finished his supper, the surgery bell rang. A few moments later Julia came into the room looking worried.

"That was Mr. Blum. Ruth's gone into an early labor. Dr. Beacham is with her, but there are complications. I'll probably be away all night."

CHAPTER
25

AFTER PALPATING RUTH'S abdomen, Julia knew there was trouble. Once she'd taken external measurements and determined the internal conjugate of the pelvis, it was clear that Dr. Beacham's original measurements had been in error. Ruth's pelvis was dangerously flattened, measuring about six centimeters, too narrow for a child to pass.

Julia wished to heaven she'd taken over the case earlier, although it would have made no difference in the choices she now faced. As soon as Ruth became pregnant, her baby's fate was in doubt.

"Ruth," she said, smoothing the young woman's damp forehead, "your baby is healthy, but he can't come the natural way."

Ruth lay back on the pillow, her lips trembling as she struggled not to cry. "Will he die? Will I die?"

Julia believed in telling patients the truth. "We can sacrifice the baby and almost certainly save your life, or we can perform a cesarean section and take the child through an incision in your abdomen. The operation is dangerous. The chance of a mother surviving is about fifty percent."

Ruth clutched at Julia's hand. "Do the operation. Please. I can't let my baby die."

Julia squeezed Ruth's fingers, relieved by her decision. The thought of performing an embryotomy on a viable child repelled her, although many physicians chose it over the more radical cesarean surgery.

"I'll do all I can to save you both," she said. "First, I need to talk to Dr. Beacham and your parents. Rest now and conserve your strength."

She left Ruth's bedroom and went into the Blums' front room where Renate and I. Z. sat on the sofa, hands entwined, talking to Dr. Beacham. They all looked at Julia.

"I'm afraid the passage is too narrow to deliver a living child."

"I feared as much," Dr. Beacham said. "I explained to Mr. and Mrs. Blum that the child must be sacrificed to save Ruth's life."

Renate took out a handkerchief, and Julia saw she was weeping.

I. Z. put an arm around her. He looked old, Julia thought, worn with worry, his beard salted with white.

"Ruth must live," he said, fixing Julia with his stern glare. "She's our child, our joy."

Julia's heart went out to the Blums. She'd heard they had suffered terribly during Ruth's childhood illness, and they'd rejoiced to see her happily married. Losing her now would be a cruel blow.

Julia spoke gently. "Ruth has agreed to a cesarean operation, Mr. Blum."

A sound of surprise came from Dr. Beacham. "But, Mrs. Metcalf, the mortality rate—"

Julia gave him a silencing glance and addressed the Blums. "It is a risky procedure for the mother—you must understand that. But I think in Ruth's case the risk is worth taking. The baby is living, Ruth is healthy, and it's early in her labor. She wants the surgery."

I. Z. looked from Dr. Beacham to Julia, his eyes

glittering. "You say she might die? No, that I will not allow." His beard trembled with anger and grief.

"I must see her," Renate said.

Her lovely face was flushed and wet. Julia wanted to embrace her dear friend, but she didn't dare test her emotions. A physician couldn't break down and weep before undertaking a perilous operation. A physician remained stoic, keeping her mind clear for the challenge ahead.

"Go in and see Ruth, both of you," she said. "Listen to her and try to understand her wishes."

When the Blums left the room, Dr. Beacham took off his glasses and wiped them, his disapproval evident. "Surely it's more humane to perform a craniotomy and extract the fetus from the womb than to endanger the mother's life."

Julia listened as he presented the conservative arguments against cesarean section—the danger of infection, of hemorrhage, of shock and probable death. She responded patiently, drawing on readings that had stimulated much discussion in medical circles. She cited Dr. Harris's studies, which found greater success when the operation was undertaken before the onset of labor, when the mother was still strong and capable of withstanding surgery. She summarized Dr. Sänger's work on uterine sutures to control postoperative hemorrhage.

"But internal sutures can cause infection," Dr. Beacham said.

"The greater danger comes from leaving the peritoneal cavity open," Julia replied. "Sänger found that using silver wire sutures lessens the chance of infection and lowers the death rate when aseptic surgical techniques are applied."

Beacham slumped in his chair, looking resigned. "I take it you have performed the operation?"

"I assisted Edward twice," Julia said. "In one case, the mother and child lived. In the other, sadly, labor had gone on for too long, and the mother was exhausted. She couldn't withstand the shock."

Dr. Beacham wiped his brow. "I'll help you in any way I can, Mrs. Metcalf."

"Good," Julia said. "Let's go to your surgery and make our preparations. I'll explain to you exactly what we'll do."

Lee Chung let Gib into the office with "Superintendent" on the nameplate. It was a plain room, containing an open rolltop desk, a table and chairs, tall cupboards, and on the far wall a large double-door safe. Gib looked at the safe and hoped Hughes hadn't put the pictures there. Lee Chung had come up with the keys to the office, but he sure as hell wouldn't know the combination to the safe.

Gib went to the desk and set down the lamp, turning it low. He glanced through scattered correspondence and ledgers stamped with gold letters. An assay report lay among the papers. It didn't show anything interesting. Gib made a mental note to stop in the assay office next door to see if he could find reports on number four level.

A sudden flash outside the window made him jump. A shower of color filled the sky; then a boom thundered in the distance. Fireworks down at the flat. Gib worked faster, rummaging through cupboards and drawers. He found keys to a filing cabinet, but no photographs and no plates. He set the lamp on the table where more papers were stacked, and his foot bumped something. A wooden box. He pulled it out from beneath the table and lifted the top. Inside were photographic plates standing in a vertical row, a dozen of them. Gib's heart started to pound. He pulled out two envelopes that were pushed down between the plates. Pictures spilled onto the floor. He gathered them up, laid them on the table, turned up the lamp and stared.

Jesus, she was beautiful. Young and delicate, a soft gaze, the saddest smile. Small girlish breasts, long legs like a colt, her hair all spread out. Ah, Julia, he thought. Princess. She aroused him, she broke his heart. He wanted to grab up the box and race down to Stiles, take her in his arms and protect her forever.

He put the photographs back in the box, closed the lid, and fastened it. There was another burst outside the window. Gib glanced at the shower of red, white, and blue. He heard

the faint boom and snap, then the sound of the door latch
behind him.

He turned. "Lee Chung?"

"You're dead, Booth. So's the Chinaman."

Gib's vitals shriveled up. His mouth went dry. Hughes
loomed in the open doorway, pointing a nickel-plated
revolver right at his middle.

"Toss over your gun."

Son of a bitch, Gib thought. He was gallows meat now.
"Sorry, Hughes. I've got nothing to toss." Deputy Caine had
refused to return his Colt. Marshal's orders, he'd said. Guns
don't mix with Fourth of July celebrating.

"Get your hands up and move over here."

Gib raised his hands to shoulder level. He was sweating
stones. "I figured you'd be down at the flat, Hughes,
enjoying the festivities."

"And I figured you'd be here." Hughes patted him down,
keeping those mean-cut eyes right on him. "Seems I've been
outfiguring you all day, Booth." He nodded at the box. "I
see you found the pictures. I left them in a convenient
enough place. I take it you enjoyed them."

"Real pretty."

"When the marshal gets here, he'll find your dead body
right beside them. It's a shame, having to embarrass Julia
like that, almost as big a shame as having to kill you." He
gave Gib one of his smirking looks. "But what's a man to do
when he finds an intruder going through his papers?"

"Yeah," Gib said, trying to loosen up his frozen brain.
"It's a real shame."

Hughes stepped back, his pomaded hair gleaming in the
lamplight. "So long, Booth. Sorry we won't be having
another waltz."

The dry click of the revolver kicked Gib's mind into gear.
"It's a real shame about that freeze-out scheme you almost
pulled off. You came close, Hughes, but close ain't good
enough when you're working a swindle."

Hughes's face turned dark, and the muscles in his neck
started to work. "What the hell are you talking about?"

"Number four level. The assays. There's no mud problem down there. Nothing but a lode of gold."

Gib paused to let his words sink in. Hughes's thumb lowered the hammer. He looked uncertain—and scared.

Gib hurried on. "I've got to hand it to you for getting away with it this long. Trouble is, your company's on to you. That shift boss you've got on number four—the one you're paying off—he double-crossed you, wired the owners in St. Louis. He's after your job." Some of what Gib said came from Scobie and Lee; the rest he was making up as he went along. "Word is, your bosses are heading out here to wrap things up."

"You're bluffing." The hammer snapped again.

Gib's knees turned to jelly. "Fraud'll get you a few years at Deer Lodge," he said. "Murder means a long drop from a rope."

"What else do they know in St. Louis?" Hughes had the same wild look he'd worn during their fight. "Talk, you son of a bitch."

Gib looked at the gun. "Funny how I lose my train of thought when a cocked pistol's aimed at my gut."

Hughes eased off the cock. Gib knew his talk was gaining him nothing but a little time. He could tell the gasbag all the lies he could think of and still end up dead.

"Just a few questions, Hughes, before I meet up with Saint Peter. You were behind those letters to Julia, weren't you?"

"What of it?"

"Just thought I'd like a few less sins on my ledger."

"Yeah, I was behind them. Now, what else do they know?"

"How about the livery stable break-in? Did you think that up, too?"

"No, but I wish I had." He waved the revolver. "Talk, damn you."

At that moment Gib saw movement in the dark hallway behind Hughes's back. Someone was out there. His heart started to gallop. "Now that you mention it, there are a few other things. Your bosses know about the ore shipments and the secret assays." Hell, he was repeating himself. "And they know your agents are buying up Continental stock in San Francisco." He was taking a flyer on that one. "It's a classic freeze-out—everyone thinks the mine's playing out, you buy the majority stock at dirt-cheap prices, then stumble onto a million-dollar lode. Overnight you're the bonanza king of the territory."

Suddenly a huge black object came out of the hall shadows and crashed down on Hughes's skull with a sickening thud. Hughes's eyes rolled back in his head, and he wobbled to the floor. Before Gib could shut his gaping mouth, the room was filled with black silk and pigtails and Celestial chatter.

Lee Chung held a cast-iron frying pan with two hands. Charlie Soon and a bunch of other Chinese gathered around Hughes, commenting in their singsong voices.

Charlie looked at Gib. "Mine boss not dead. Get big bump." He tapped his own head.

"Where the hell did you come from, Charlie?" Gib said, although he knew there was no point in expecting an answer. "I thought I was a goner. Lee Chung, too."

The other Celestials had found a rope and were tying up the unconscious Hughes. "You boss tie up mine boss," Charlie said to Gib. "Chinamen know nothing."

Gib understood that he would have to take credit for Hughes's condition. Folks wouldn't look kindly on Charlie and his gang assaulting a white man, even if he was a swindling piece of scrub.

"I sure wish you'd stepped in earlier," Gib said. "That bastard might have shot me before I got a word out."

Charlie's bullet eyes gleamed. "I know you, boss. You good talker. You get out of tight spot."

"Yeah, sure," Gib said. His brain was swimming with relief; his whole body felt disconnected. He picked up the lamp and the box and headed for the assay office.

Gib dropped off the box of photographic plates and pictures at Julia's house and rode on into town. McQuigg was in his office, buckling on his gun belt, getting ready to make his midnight rounds.

"What do you want, Booth?"

"I'm here to report a freeze-out at the Continental."

McQuigg's mustache bristled. "Are you drunk, or did Harlan Hughes knock something loose in your head this afternoon?"

Gib was too worn out to think up a clever reply. "Take a look at this." He tossed the assay report onto the marshal's desk. "And you'd better sit down. I've got a long story to tell."

After leaving the marshal's office, Gib rode back to Julia's place. When he saw that she hadn't returned, he put down a bowl of cream for the cat, drank some water, and went to bed. He slept restlessly—his back was sore as hell, and he was anxious for Julia to come home.

He woke to the flicker of lamplight in the hallway and the sound of Julia's footsteps on the stairs.

"Gib?" she asked softly at his door. "Are you awake?"

"Yeah." He rose up on an elbow. "Did the baby come?"

"A perfect little girl. She's beautiful." He heard the excitement in her voice.

"How's Ruth?"

"I performed a cesarean section. The passage was too narrow for the baby to be born naturally, so I had to take her out through an incision in Ruth's abdomen."

Gib winced. He'd always thought cutting a baby out of its mother's belly was an old wives' tale.

"Dr. Beacham assisted." Julia came into the room and sat down beside him, nestling her hips right up against his side. In the lamplight she looked exhausted but happy, and it occurred to Gib that she'd done something extraordinary. "Mrs. Kitchen and Sarabeth were there to take charge of the instruments and sterilization and attend to the baby. There's still danger of infection, but we took every precaution. Now we have to pray for the best. Dr. Beacham was so impressed he's going to recommend that I be admitted to the Montana Medical Association."

Gib lay back on the pillow, his arms folded behind his head. "I always knew you were a savvy lady." He was glad to see her so happy. He felt a little proud, too, as if her success had something to do with him. "Doc would sure be pleased."

A wistful expression came into her eyes. "I thought of that." She raised the lamp and studied him. "Are you feeling all right?"

"No problems."

She smiled. "I should go to bed myself. It's almost four o'clock."

He put an arm across her lap and gave her a pat. "Sleep tight, princess."

Julia went to her room, still marveling at the thought of Ruth and her new baby girl. She would never forget this night—the drama of the operation, how well everyone took her direction, their quiet awe when she pulled the baby out. She thought of all the women over the centuries who had died undelivered, who'd endured destructive fetal surgery or perished from infection or hemorrhage after undergoing cesarean section. It was certainly wonderful, Julia thought, to live in an age of modern medicine.

She was in bed, ready to blow out the lamp, when her eyes fell on a wooden box pushed against the wall. She got up and went over to it. When she lifted the lid and saw the contents, she shrank back.

Dear Lord, the photographic plates.

At first she didn't understand what they were doing in her bedroom. Then she remembered Gib's words this afternoon. "I'll get them for you," he'd said.

And that's what he'd done. Tonight, when he should have been resting, he'd kept his reckless promise.

Julia felt a flood of relief mixed with a trickle of annoyance. Against her orders, Gib had endangered his health; she should give him a good scolding. But her heart overruled any such thoughts. He had retrieved the photographs and saved her from scandal. She would be indebted to him forever.

She got to her feet and went down the hall, pausing in the doorway to whisper his name.

"I'm still here," he said.

"You got the photographs."

"Yeah," he said in the darkness. "Hughes couldn't wait to hand them over."

She went in and sat beside him. Leaning down, she kissed his cheek. "Thank you, Gib."

He stroked her hair and took her face in his hands. With his lips, he found her willing mouth. He kissed her gently at first, then with more urgency, until the familiar leap of desire made something give way in Julia's heart. She pulled back, afraid of where it would lead.

"Lie down beside me," he said. "I'll tell you what happened tonight."

Julia hesitated. She felt flushed and unsteady, and her heart was beating too hard.

Gib's fingers sifted through her hair. "Don't worry, princess. I'm not up to doing anything that can get us in trouble."

She curled up next to him, her head on his shoulder, and listened as he told her about Harlan and the freeze-out, how Charlie Soon arranged for Lee Chung to let Gib into the office.

"You're not supposed to know about that," he said. "Not a word about the Celestials."

"Not a word," she whispered, too shocked by Harlan's treachery to say more.

"There's bonanza ore up there, enough to keep the Continental going for years. That's why Hughes wanted you to invest in the mine, so when the stock's value went up, you'd be richer still. The richer the widow, the better the wife."

"I wouldn't have married him," Julia said.

Gib rubbed her cheek with the backs of his fingers. "He would have blackmailed you into it. At least he'd have tried."

When he finished the story of the confrontation in the mine office, Julia was trembling with anger and fear. Gib managed to soothe her with reassuring words and a few lighthearted jokes; but after he fell asleep, she wept, thinking how close she'd come to losing him—this man she didn't dare love.

* * *

Gib sat in the Pickax drinking coffee and reading the latest issue of the *Sentinel*. Thank God the café had almost emptied out. He'd been interrupted so many times, it had taken him an hour to get through Julia's article on the growth and development of babies.

Two days after the Fourth, Stiles was still in an uproar over the scandal at the Continental and Hughes's arrest. The marshal had wired the company in St. Louis, and a representative was on his way to investigate. As for Gib, he was regarded as some sort of hero. Strangers came up to shake his hand at the Pickax, and at the Bon Ton, Dellwood gave him more respect—although his good mood could be attributed to the town council allowing him to keep his faro layout. Most astounding of all was Harriet Tabor, who'd given Gib a brisk nod right on Main Street.

Gib folded the *Sentinel* and opened a recent issue of the *Engineering and Mining Journal*. As he skimmed an article on gold and silver stocks, he decided it was time he rode up to the Rattling Rock to see Otis, though he was in no hurry to leave Julia. One day soon he would talk to her about their future. Right now he was afraid to raise the subject; he still wasn't sure if she'd ever forgive him for scheming and running off.

"Booth!"

Gib looked up to see Marshal McQuigg stomping through the café. "Wire came for you." He tossed it on the table and signaled the waitress for a cup of coffee. "Happened to be over at the telegraph office when it came in."

"That's mighty kind of you, Marshal." McQuigg was another one who'd changed his tune. The past few days he'd been as friendly as a flea on a dog.

Gib tore open the wire. He read the message and his insides froze: "Drill contests news. Friends heading Stiles. Take care. Will Crutchfield."

Holy Christ! Gib thought. The results of the contest had been printed in the newspaper. Wylie and Trask were on their way.

"Trouble?" McQuigg asked.

Gib got to his feet and tossed some coins on the table. Crutchfield had sent the wire from Butte; those two rawhiders could show up anytime.

"Looks that way. I'll be stopping by your office to pick up my Colt."

McQuigg started twirling his curls. "Anything I can do?"

Gib had a choice—he could stay or he could go. Face his past and risk dying, or move on and lose his future. It took him half a second to make up his mind.

"It's a private matter. If a buzzard in a long duster coat and another with half an ear come looking for me, tell them I'm up at the Rattling Rock. We'll settle things there, away from town." He headed for the door. He had to find Julia.

"Say, Gib." The marshal was on his heels. "I've got a Winchester Repeater and a double twelve Greener in the rifle case, cleaned, brushed, and oiled. You're welcome to them. And Williver's just got in a fresh supply of double-ought buck. You might want to stop by and pick up a box."

"I'm obliged." McQuigg wouldn't have to offer twice.

Julia had her hands full at the Blums', trying to keep everyone under control. Dottie and Louise had all but taken up permanent residence, wanting to gossip about Harlan and Gib, coo over little Susannah, and tiptoe in to see Ruth. Things got worse when Harriet showed up with the same plans. Renate was no help at all; she seemed to love the commotion.

Ruth had just finished nursing, and Julia had put the baby in her basket when Renate came into the bedroom. "I. Z. says Gib's downstairs, Julia. He wants to see you."

Julia washed her hands, took off her apron, and hurried downstairs. Gib was pacing the back room of the shop where Renate did her cooking. One look at his face told Julia something was wrong. "Gib, what is it?"

As soon as he saw her, his expression changed. He slid his hands into his hip pockets and grinned. "I just wanted to find out how things were with Ruth."

"She's uncomfortable, but she's happy." Julia looked at him closely. The bruise on his cheekbone was turning green at the edges, and his eye was darkly ringed. "You should be in bed with ice packs on your back."

"I'm heading up to the Rattling Rock."

"Gib!" Every time she left the house he disregarded her orders to stay in bed. "You're the worst patient I've ever had. You're not supposed to be riding."

"I've got to go up there, princess."

"But you need time to heal."

He took her face in both his hands and bent down, bringing his eyes level with hers. "I love you, Julia. I want you to remember that."

He drew her close and kissed her in a sweet, lingering way, taking her so by surprise that she didn't have a chance to stop him. As the kiss deepened, she forgot even to try.

When he pulled back, his eyes were misty. "That sure was nice."

Julia felt a moment of bewilderment, then a swift clutch of fear. "Are you leaving Stiles again?"

He smiled a little and shook his head. "I'm not running, Julia. Not anymore." He clucked her chin, picked up his hat, and strolled on out.

When Otis heard there'd be trouble, he wanted to stay at the Rattling Rock—till Gib reminded him of Gilbert and persuaded him to go home. Gib tried to get Rawlie to go with Otis, but the old man refused. "Take more'n a couple of jaspers from Butte to run me out. They might be aiming to jump my claim."

"They don't want your claim," Gib said. "They want me. Now, stay in your cabin and lie low."

He went into Digger's cabin and loaded the shotgun. He checked the action on the Winchester and racked in fresh shells. After he'd cleaned and reloaded the Colt, he strapped on his gun belt, tied the holster's leather thong to his thigh, and went down the slope to practice his quick draw.

He propped his heavy artillery against a tree and spent half an hour firing the Colt. He wasn't as rusty as he'd expected, but drawing a gun on pinecones was pretty dull work when there weren't any pretty ladies around to impress.

When he'd had enough, Gib reloaded the pistol, then lay down in the grass to rest his aching back. He listened to the birds chirp and smelled the sweet summer air. He was glad he'd drawn up a will, but he sure as hell didn't want to die—not now, when he had something to live for. He thought about Julia and all he would miss, and his heart felt as heavy as a bucket of lead.

He'd just decided it was time to head back up the hill and get ready for company, when from up the slope he heard the whinny of a horse and then a shout. "Come on out, Booth! We know you're in there."

The blast of a shotgun thundered down the slope.

Renate said the marshal was in the living room. Julia left Ruth and went in to see him.

McQuigg got to his feet, hat in hand. "A couple of fellers've gone up to the Rattling Rock looking for Gib. They got word at the Bon Ton that's where they'd find him." The marshal looked a little sheepish. "I'd have locked them up first thing, except I was at the Continental when they come in."

Julia stared at him in shock. Wylie and Trask, she thought. Dear Lord.

"The description fits the fellers Gib was expecting—long duster coat, queer-looking ear. Seems they mean business. I stopped by Doc Beacham's, but he's out on calls." McQuigg curled his hat brim. "I figure when it ends, somebody up there'll need a doc."

Julia's heart thudded with horror. Gib had known the men were on their way. He'd come to her to say good-bye.

"Lee's brought around a wagon"—the marshal cleared his throat—"for the wounded."

Julia pulled off her apron. "I'll get my bag."

Gib stoop-ran out of the clearing and into the cover of trees. He heard someone screaming, a whole lot of swearing, and more shotgun blasts.

Rawlie! he thought. Holy Christ!

He grabbed the Winchester and ran up the slope, screened by trees, his Colt in hand. Wylie was on the ground, his long duster coat soaked with blood, yelling at the top of his lungs. Trask, mounted, emptied his stubby-barreled shotgun into Rawlie's cabin, two deafening roars.

Rawlie was in there. Alone, half blind, maybe dead.

Gib took cover behind a tree not twenty feet from Trask. While Trask reloaded, Gib aimed the Colt at his hat. He thumbed back the hammer. Sweat crawled down his ribs. Jesus, he couldn't do it. He lowered his aim and pulled the trigger. Dust puffed off Trask's shirt. He yelled and hunched forward, grabbing his arm. Gib got off another shot, winging his shoulder. Trask dropped his shotgun and came out of the saddle in a sideways tumble.

Gib holstered the Colt and stepped into the clearing. "Rawlie! Hold your fire!"

Wylie was howling, his leg riddled with buckshot. Trask started for his revolver, or maybe he just thought about it. Gib levered the Winchester.

"Think again, Trask."

"God damn you, Booth."

Gib collected their shotguns and pistols. "I guess you gents are looking for me. Now that I've got your attention, maybe we can have a peaceful talk about what's on your mind. Rawlie!" he hollered. "You alive?"

The cabin door creaked open. Rawlie emerged, cradling his twelve-gauge.

"What the hell was all that firing?" Gib demanded.

Rawlie sank a paw into his beard. "Sumbitch wanted to steal my claim."

Doc used to say that coffee was good for wound shock, so after Gib stanched the bleeding, he made Wylie and Trask drink a pot of Rawlie's mud. He was trying to figure out how to get them down to Stiles when he heard the rattle of a wagon. He stepped outside the cabin and saw McQuigg mounted on his big bay. Behind him, Lee was driving a flatbed wagon with Julia seated beside him.

"Hey, Gib," Lee said, a big grin on his face. "We thought you might have gotten into a shooting scrap up here."

"We did at that," Gib said. "Me and Rawlie had to waste a few shells."

He ambled over to Julia's side of the wagon, feeling mighty pleased with himself. "There's a couple of rawhiders in the cabin who need your attention, ma'am," he said. "Don't mind their bad language."

Julia didn't return his smile; she didn't even look at him. She passed him her bag and let him help her down. Then without a word, she headed for the cabin, McQuigg trailing behind her.

Gib thumbed up the brim of his hat and stared after her. What the hell? He looked at Lee. "Did I do something wrong?"

Lee tugged at his mustache. "Yeah, Gib. I think you did."

They brought Wylie and Trask back to Stiles in the wagon and left them to recuperate at Mrs. Kitchen's. Julia declined Gib's offer to drive her back to the house. She stopped at the Blums' to check on Ruth, then drove her buggy home. She felt worn to a shoestring. After all that had happened, she wanted to be alone.

After cleaning the instruments she'd used on Wylie and Trask, she went upstairs to tidy herself. Later, just as she sat down at the piano, she heard footsteps on the porch, and Gib halloed.

He stood at the screen door, dressed up in his suit and silver brocade vest. He took off his hat and held it to his chest. "Afternoon, ma'am. I'm Gilbert Booth, a friend of Doc's."

Julia didn't smile. She leaned against the doorframe and looked at him through the screen. "I thought you'd be at the Bon Ton, enjoying all the attention."

"A man can only tell a shoot-out story so many times, especially when he's about talked dry from telling a freeze-out story. I figured it'd be better to come out here and tell you what's happened with the money." He glanced around the porch. "It sure is lonely out here."

Julia's heart felt too weary for anything, even Gib's easy charm. Nevertheless, she opened the screen door and stepped outside.

Gib leaned back on the porch railing, tossing his hat in his hand, and gave her one of his soft-eyed smiles. "Barnet and the marshal and I went down to Mrs. Kitchen's. Had a little talk with Wylie and Trask. Barnet confused them with his legal lingo, and McQuigg threatened to put them behind bars until he checked for their wanted posters. It didn't take much for them to agree to a three-way split of the money and to get out of town. Coolidge'll hand over their share when they leave."

Julia sat down in the rocker. "I'm glad that's settled."

"I thought you would be." Gib scaled his hat onto the porch table and folded his arms. "I thought you'd be glad to see me in one piece up at the mine, too. Those two jackals could have fed me a lead breakfast."

Julia's eyes filled with tears. All the nerve-shattering terror she'd felt driving to the mine came rolling back. "Of course I was glad," she said. "I thanked God from the bottom of my heart that you were safe. If I hadn't had those men to tend to, I would have fallen to my knees. But you should have told me you were in danger when you saw me at the Blums'."

Gib seemed taken aback. "I didn't want you to worry."

"I had a right to worry!" She was furious at him for withholding the truth of his predicament, even as she trembled from head to foot at the thought of what might have happened. "I had the right to know that you might have been killed! Maybe I could have done something— prevented it from happening. At least I could have prepared myself. I could have said good-bye."

She looked at his fine, handsome face with its rainbow of bruises. She thought how close he'd come to dying, and tears spilled from her eyes. "I want you to tell me things beforehand, not afterward—the money that was yours, Wylie and Trask coming to kill you, even Harlan's swindle at the Continental. Don't shut me out, Gib. Don't trick me."

She'd expected a grimace of defiance or even a flash of temper, but he just stared at her, looking surprised.

Julia wiped at her cheeks. "Do you understand what I'm saying?"

He took a few steps across the porch and leaned over her, bracing his hands on the arms of her rocker. "Sure, I understand." He smiled a little. "You don't want me to bluff you."

She nodded and blew her nose. He leaned closer and pressed his lips to her forehead, which made her cry harder.

"I guess I'd better clear the table of a couple of other things I've been keeping to myself," he said. "First off, when I was in Butte, I found Mary Hurley and talked her into coming back to Stiles. She says Butte's too rough. The second thing, I've decided to stick around these parts. I'd sure like us to get married—if you'll have me, that is."

Julia leaned back in the chair and looked at him, trying to stop her hiccuping sobs. "Gib—"

"And since you want to know about things ahead of time, I'll tell you what else I have in mind. I'd like to develop the Rattling Rock with Otis, raise some babies with you, and when I get old, I plan to sit out here on the porch with my princess on my lap and rock myself to death." He raised his eyebrows. "How does that sound?"

Julia shook her head, helpless before his onslaught of candor. She searched her heart for doubt and mistrust, but they had withered and scattered. In their place she found only a blooming happiness and the strong roots of love.

"It sounds like heaven," she said, managing no more than a whisper.

Gib smiled. "I'll make you happy, Julia. And I'll never let you down."

She saw tenderness in his eyes and something else, something new and wonderful—a fierce sort of pride. She reached up to circle his neck. "I love you, Gib."

He leaned closer and kissed her, promising her his heart for a lifetime. Somewhere in the distance, Julia heard a faint cry. Then she felt a thump on her lap, and Bee made a few turns before settling down to purr.

EPILOGUE

"PA?"

"Yeah, Sam?"

"Mary's cross with me."

"That's because you're always up to mischief," Jessie said with an elder sister's lofty impatience.

"But I wanted to make her laugh."

Gib rumpled his son's fair hair. Normally, Mary Hurley put up with Sam's antics—she even encouraged him in her good-natured way. But not these days. "Spring cleaning's serious business, Sam; it's no time for tricks."

The three of them, along with the cat, had been banished to the front porch, where they sat on the top step. Inside the house, Mary carried on in a bad-tempered whirlwind of cleaning.

"Ma said when you did her cleaning, you were as nice as pie," Sam said.

"That's because Pa was in love with Mama," Jessie said,

smoothing Rusty's thick orange fur. "He did her cleaning to make her love him back."

Gib exchanged smiles with his daughter. Jessie was the spitting image of him, though she was lucky enough to possess her mother's clever mind and easy disposition.

"Not only that," Gib said. "I had Mossy to help—that was before he went back east—and he didn't play tricks while I was scouring the walls." He clapped his hands on his knees and started to rise. "I guess I'd better go in and see if I can lend a hand."

"Mama!"

Sam had spotted Julia's buggy coming down the road. He was up and running, down the steps and across the yard, his too-big overalls billowing out behind him. "Mama!" he yelled as the buggy drove in. "I put a toad in Mary's bucket, and she chased me with a broom!"

Julia pulled Biscuit to a halt and set the brake. "Oh, Sam. You mustn't tease Mary when she's doing spring cleaning."

"It was a trick!" He jumped up and down, unable to contain his glee. "I wanted to make her laugh!"

Julia looked at her son's freckled face, bright as butter. Sam was a cheerful, good-tempered boy, but his enthusiasm for mischief sometimes worried her. Her concern amused Gib. "He's got a good heart," he'd say. "I'll make sure he doesn't turn out bad."

"Did Sarabeth have a baby girl, Mama?" Jessie reached up to take Julia's bag.

"A lovely little girl, Jess, with lots of black hair." Julia watched Gib ambling toward her, a smile on his face. One night away, and she missed him as if she'd been gone a week. "Lee's pleased as punch," she said as he swung her to the ground. "He says three boys are enough. Harriet's pleased, too, although she tries not to show it." With Sarabeth driving ore for the Rattling Rock, Harriet kept busy looking after the grandchildren.

"I hid a spider in the drawer!" Sam cried. "Mary's going to scream!"

"Sam Booth!" Julia exclaimed. She looked at Gib, who tried not to grin.

"I think I'll take you out to Whiskey Creek tomorrow when I go to the mine," he said. "How about you staying there till spring cleaning's done?"

"Whoo-ee!" Sam began jumping again. There was nothing he liked better than chasing through the hills after Gilbert, and Mrs. Chapman always fed him full of tarts.

"What about you, Jess?" Gib asked.

Jessie looked at Julia, her gray eyes shining. "May I go too, Mama?"

"Of course," Julia said. "I'll give you some things to take to Gilbert's mother—oh, heavens! You'd better rescue Rusty."

Sam had managed to get the cat and himself up into the old apple tree, where Gib had built a little tree house.

As Jessie raced to the rescue, Gib slipped an arm around Julia's waist. "Jess fixed up Mossy's old room real nice," he said. "She needs a hideaway for herself."

Julia saw the pride in his eyes. From the moment of Jessie's birth, Gib had adored his daughter. They were opposites in nature—Jessie being quiet and fond of books—but they shared a special bond.

"I was thinking," Julia said. "Sam is five already and Jessie's nearly eight. They'll be grown before we know it. I miss having a baby in the house."

Gib looked at her. "I've missed having a baby around the house since Sam started walking."

They'd been careful to plan their family, deciding two was enough, given how busy they were. But Julia had long suspected that Gib wanted more, and children were clearly good for him. Each child made him prouder, more responsible, more certain of his worth. After Jessie, he'd run for town council, and after Sam, he'd agreed to succeed Ab Ames as president of the mining association. Heaven knew what another baby might lead to, Julia thought.

"You're sure about this?" he asked, his eyes searching her face.

"I am, if you are."

He smiled, looking happier and more handsome than any husband she knew. "I'd sure like that, princess. I'd like it a whole lot." He pulled her close and whispered against her lips, "We'll get right to it tonight."

The sound of a shout and a dull thump interrupted their kiss. They turned their heads to see Sam sprawled on the ground beneath the tree house, his mouth open in pained surprise, while Rusty leaped from Jessie's arms and ran for the porch.

"Sam!" they cried together. But before they could untangle their embrace, he was on his feet and running toward them, arms outstretched, howling at the top of his lungs. He collided with their legs, clinging and sobbing, still feeling the sting where the ground had smacked him hard.

Then his ma and his pa and his big sister, too, swooped down and gathered him close, telling him everything would be all right.

National Bestselling Author

JILL MARIE LANDIS

Jill Marie Landis makes the rugged
life of the frontier come alive.
Experience a world where danger
and romance are as vast as the prairies
and where love survives even the
most trying hardships...

___Past Promises   0-515-11207-0/$4.99
___Come Spring   0-515-10861-8/$5.50
___Jade   0-515-10591-0/$4.95
___Rose   0-515-10346-2/$5.50
___Sunflower   0-515-10659-3/$5.50
___Wildflower   0-515-10102-8/$5.50

Coming in July... UNTIL TOMORROW

Cara James passes her days on her Kansas homestead
making dolls and dreaming of California. When
returning Civil War soldier Dake Reed turns up on her
doorstep with an abandoned baby, they begin a
journey through the war torn South to fulfill the heart's
greatest promises: a place to call home—and a love
that lasts forever and a day....

___0-515-11403-0/$4.99